When The Clouds Go
Rolling By

*When The Clouds Go
Rolling By*

JUNE FRANCIS

Allison & Busby Limited
13 Charlotte Mews
London W1T 4EJ
www.allisonandbusby.com

Hardcover published in Great Britain in 2007.
This paperback edition published in 2008.

A CIP catalogue record for this book is available from
the British Library.

10 9 8 7 6 5 4 3 2 1

ISBN 978-0-7490-7947-5

Typeset in 10.5/14 pt Sabon by
Terry Shannon

Printed and bound in the UK by
CPI Bookmarque, Croydon, CR0 4TD

JUNE FRANCIS was born in Blackpool and moved to Liverpool at an early age. She started writing in her forties producing articles for *My Weekly* and has since gone on to have over twenty novels published. Married with three grown-up sons, she enjoys fell-walking, local history and swimming.

Dedicated to the memory of my parents,
Stan and May Nelson, and all my aunts and uncles
who made me welcome in their homes and
showed me what the real meaning of
'family' was all about.

CHAPTER ONE

Liverpool. Spring, 1918.

'Clara, get down here, girl. Yer haven't ate yer tea and I want to get going soon,' called Bernie O'Toole.

'I'll be with you in a minute!' shouted her granddaughter.

Nineteen-year-old Clara gazed at her reflection in the mirror and frowned. Her thin face appeared yellowish in the dim light from the gas mantle. Surely she had not worked long enough in munitions to have earned the nickname *Canary* but if the war went on much longer, she possibly would.

She would have much preferred a job at the Palladium, as she loved watching films. Situated in a prime position on West Derby Road, it was advertised as the most palatial and comfortable picture house in Liverpool. It had opened in 1913 and her father had treated her to a best seat for a shilling in the stalls that first week. The film showing was *The Penalty*, exclusive to Liverpool, and the picture house had also featured a full musical programme by the Palladium Orchestra. But she had been too young at the time to get a job there and now, being the sole wage earner in the house after her father had been called up, had meant she and her gran had desperately been in need of a decent income. She loathed the munitions work but had no choice but to stick at it. She tried not to think how she would cope once the war was over, so was trying to put away as much money as she could. Never an easy task because her grandmother, Bernie, had a tendency to spend money as if it grew on trees. Last year, when the news came that her only son, Clara's father, had been killed, she had started drinking again.

'Clara, what are you doing up there, girl?'

'I'm coming,' she called, picking up her handbag and hurrying down the stairs that led to the lobby.

Bernie O'Toole, her greying hair fastened loosely in a bun, paused in the act of dowsing the bowl of bread and milk in front of her with whisky and peered over wire-framed spectacles at her granddaughter. 'What are yer titivating yerself up for? There's not going to be any young fellas there.'

'I like to look neat and tidy and I don't often get the chance to dolly myself up, Gran. Those blinking garments we have to wear for work don't do anything for me.' She sat down at the table, thinking how different her life would have been if her mother hadn't died when she was thirteen. 'Do you really need to pour whisky on your bread and milk? I don't know how you can afford it or where you manage to get it from with so many shortages.'

'Ask no questions and I'll tell yer no lies. Just believe me when I tell yer it's not coming out of your money,' muttered Bernie, glowering at her. 'Anyhow, it's medicinal. If yer remember I gave up the gin years ago when my Denny asked me to. I only started on the whisky after he was killed.' Her chin wobbled and she gulped down a mouthful of the bread and milk. 'Your father was a saint, always looked after me,' she mumbled.

Clara felt a lump rise in her throat, remembering that terrible day when the telegram had arrived. She had thought her grandmother would go off her head and had needed to suppress her own grief in order to cope with her. The months that had followed had been difficult, but somehow they had both survived. Even so, there had been countless times when she wished that, like so many of her neighbours, she'd had family to turn to. Her father had been the only boy in a family of girls but none of her aunts had survived into adulthood.

She took her tea out of the oven in the blackleaded grate. The food was burnt and didn't look in the least appetising. In fact, she could not tell what it was, but guessed it was Bernie's lunch leftovers from yesterday. She knew complaining was a waste of time; her gran would only say it was her own fault for being upstairs so long. The fact that she had only been up there a quarter of an hour would be neither here nor there.

'Hurry up and eat, girl. I've front row seats and I'm in a mad hurry to see this Mrs Black perform her party tricks.'

'Party tricks! Are you saying you believe this Mrs Black to be a charlatan?' asked Clara. 'Because if so, what's the point of us going? It's not going to bring Dad back.'

'I'm not expecting him to be brought back but she has a reputation and it makes me wonder if there is something in spiritualism,' said Bernie.

Clara said mildly, 'You do surprise me, Gran. I thought you having your feet set so firmly in this world, you didn't really think much of the next.'

'Well, yer wrong there. I mightn't have long to live and I'd like to know if our Denny will be there waiting for me when I kick the bucket.'

Clara forced a mouthful of food down before saying, 'I must admit I'm curious to see whether this medium is as good as rumoured. Imagine if Dad could get a message to us.'

'That's what I'm hoping. There was a special bond between me and my Denny.'

Clara did not believe that for a moment. Her

gran and father had been forever arguing over something or other, but she made no comment and got on with eating the mess on her plate. Fortunately, she was used to her meals at home being done to a crisp and was extremely hungry. But one thing her gran was right about was that Dennis O'Toole had truly been saintly when he had taken his mother in after his wife died. But Clara was of the opinion that he had only done so because he believed she was at an age when a girl needed an older woman on the scene. A lot of use Bernie had been! Clara had found out more about periods and how babies grew from keeping her ears open and listening to neighbouring mothers talk. She really resented her gran always referring to Clara's father as *my Denny*. He had been her mother's Denny and the old woman knew it, and it was the reason she had never set foot in the house while Clara's mother was alive.

It was also not true that she had completely given up the drink. There had been Saturday nights when she had come home rolling drunk. Clara would be upstairs in bed and would hear Dennis giving his mother down the banks for coming home in such a state. Bernie's response had caused Clara to pull the bedcovers over her head and stick her fingers in her ears. She was of the opinion that she and her father would have fared much better on their own, but it was too late now.

She finished her meal and went to wash her plate and cutlery. She lifted the net curtain and gazed outside at the yard. 'At least the rain's stopped. How much is this *show* costing us, Gran?'

Bernie smiled with false sweetness. 'I paid so it's none of yer business, ducky.'

'I sometimes wonder if you won a pile gambling years ago and have it stashed away where I can't find it,' said Clara.

Bernie laughed and then broke into a spasm of coughing, almost choking on a lump of bread. Clara banged her on the back. 'Enough, enough,' gasped her grandmother. 'Do yer want to bloody kill me?'

'Some days it's tempting,' said Clara beneath her breath.

Bernie glared at her granddaughter. 'I heard that. If yer want to get yer hands on what I've got, then just you watch it. You might think yerself somebody because yer talk nice thanks to that Scots mother of yours sending yer to elocution lessons but it takes more than that to attract the men. You mightn't believe it now but once I was young and far more attractive than you. I had an hour-glass figure and luv'ly long, fair hair. The fellas buzzed round me like wasps round a jam pot at Nelson's jam factory. Yous haven't got the same hope because, although you take after yer dad with his black curly hair and brown eyes, you haven't got that *it*.'

Clara stiffened. It wasn't the first time her grandmother had spoken derogatorily about her appearance, and if she hadn't had such a strong sense of duty she would have walked out there and then. Sadly, she might never get the opportunity to prove whether Bernie was right or not about her having *it* because so many men of Clara's generation had sacrificed their lives at the Front. Those who survived were going to have their pick of the women when they were demobbed, and what with the way the chemicals were starting to affect her skin, Clara could see herself being at the back of the queue.

'Nothing to say?' snapped Bernie. 'I wish yer had some fight in yer, girl.'

'I have plenty of fight. I just can't see the point of arguing about it. Why do you say it, I wonder? I can only think you're jealous of me.' Clara poured herself some milk, hoping that what some of the women said at the factory was true – that it helped combat the effects of cordite on the skin.

Bernie snorted. 'If I had yer youth, girl, I'd...' Her voice trailed off and then she added, 'I want to get going.'

'I'm ready when you are.' Clara drained the cup, washed it and shrugged on her black coat before picking up a narrow-brimmed black felt hat trimmed with a broad purple ribbon. She turned to her grandmother. 'Well, get a move on or we're going to miss the start.'

Bernie muttered beneath her breath as she donned her coat and hat. She placed a silver and ivory hip flask and her spectacles inside a capacious handbag.

Clara stared but said nothing.

Bernie muttered, 'I saw that look. Just you think on that the whisky helps keep me blood going around me veins. Now get that door open and give me yer arm and let's be out of here.'

Clara crooked her arm. Bernie clutched her granddaughter's black sleeve with a claw-like hand, leaning heavily against her as they made their way outside. A gust of wind billowed their ankle length skirts, pushing them along the street of red-brick terraced houses.

Bernie gasped, 'I bloody hope this medium is worth all this effort.'

Clara glanced up at the scurrying clouds. 'I hope the wind doesn't bring off any slates. A leaking roof is the last thing we need.'

'Is that all yer care about? Yer not really bothered if I get to speak to yer dad or not, are yer? I did love yer dad, more than I loved yer bloody granddad, who got me up the spout every time he came home from sea. No wonder I had no strength in me and me babies were weak.'

Clara was amazed to hear the word *love* pass her

grandmother's lips but thought it wiser to make no comment. Besides, there were times when she did feel sorry for Bernie. It really must have been terrible to lose her daughters, one after the other, to childhood complaints.

They managed to reach Breck Road without being hit by any flying debris and hurried past the pub on the corner, which was next door to the Theatre Royal. There was no sign of a queue and Bernie's breathing was laboured. Yet she managed to gasp, 'I hope nobody's pinched our bloody seats. It's your fault for taking so long getting ready.'

Clara did not waste her breath arguing. She eased shoulders that ached due to her grandmother's dragging weight and said, 'I'm sure if they have, Gran, you'll kick up enough fuss to get them moved.'

'Don't be pert with me, girl,' Bernie snapped. 'You got the tickets?'

'No. You have them in your handbag, along with the kitchen sink.'

Bernie nipped Clara's arm with her fingers. 'Any more cheek from you and yous won't be going in.'

'Then I'll go home and leave you to it,' snapped Clara.

'No need to get on yer high horse,' said Bernie, beginning to search inside her handbag.

'Can you see what you're doing? You haven't got your glasses on,' said Clara, worrying that Mrs Black would have started before they managed to get inside the auditorium and into their seats.

'I can feel around,' said Bernie. She gave a cry of satisfaction and produced the tickets.

They went inside and it was as Clara had thought – a woman on the stage was already speaking as they made embarrassingly slow progress down a side aisle to the front row seats. Only after she had seated her grandmother and then sat down herself did Clara realise that a hush had fallen over the auditorium. With a heavily beating heart she glanced at the woman on the stage.

She was standing behind a chair, with her hands resting on its wheeled-back, gazing directly at Clara and Bernie. 'Are you comfortable, dears?' she asked, her voice soft.

Clara wished she could sink through the floor. This must be Mrs Black, although she did not look a bit like Clara had imagined a medium to be. Strangely, she had pictured a figure with long straggly hair, dressed in black robes with silver stars and moons sewn onto the material. Stupid, really: that image was more witchlike and very different from the person on the stage. Here was a middle-aged woman with silver hair pinned up in a neat bun on the top of her head, wearing a tweed suit of which the prominent colours were black, red and green.

'I-I'm sorry,' said Clara in a low voice.

'Apology accepted, dear. Welcome, I am Eudora Black.' She laced her hands together and fixed Clara with her dark eyes.

Clara felt a peculiar sensation and surprised herself by saying, 'I'm here about my dad.'

'It saddens me to hear you say those words,' said Eudora, coming closer to the edge of the stage.

She sounds like she really means it, thought Clara, aware of the murmur that rippled through the audience.

Then someone shouted, 'It's not fair, she's only just arrived.'

Another voice said, 'I can't see. Who's speaking?'

Eudora held up a hand and gazed out over the auditorium. 'In answer to the gentleman who spoke first, may I say it is not I who has decided who will go first on this occasion but the spirits. As for the lady who spoke, I will ask this young woman to come up onto the stage and then you will all be able to see her.'

'Hey, hey, I didn't plan on this,' said Bernie, gripping her granddaughter's arm and staring up at Mrs Black. 'I want to see how yer perform before I make my move.'

Eudora's eyes shifted to the old woman and her gaze rested on her face for several moments before she said firmly, 'You are not in control here.' The medium crooked a finger in Clara's direction. 'Come, dear. Do not be afraid.'

Clara freed herself from her grandmother's hold and hurried over to a short flight of steps at the side of the stage. She remembered how, as a girl, she had run down the aisle during a pantomime because the dame had asked for child volunteers to sing. She felt as excited now as she had done then. Her senses were heightened and whispers reached her ears from the wings.

'I wonder why she's chosen her first. I was hoping she'd have you up front, so you could ask her about Seb,' said a woman's voice.

'No thanks,' responded a young male voice. 'You should have asked her yourself.'

'I can't. Alice asked Hanny to get me to promise I wouldn't do it.'

'I won't mention it to Alice if you don't.'

Clara inconsequently thought of *Alice in Wonderland* and wondered who these people were, wishing they would be quiet as they were distracting her.

Eudora came forward and took Clara's hand. 'Over here, dear. Sit down. We don't want your legs collapsing beneath you during this session, do we?'

Clara shook her dark head and sat in the chair, watching as the medium signalled to someone off stage. A young man came forward with another chair and placed it on the stage so that it faced Clara. She glanced at him and gained an impression of wiry strength. He retreated almost noiselessly to the wings and her attention was now on the medium as she sat down.

A minute must have ticked by and still Mrs Black did not do any of those things Clara expected of her; such as close her eyes and go into a trance or start speaking in a voice that didn't belong to her. Then suddenly the medium reached out, causing Clara to start back. Eudora shushed her and, taking the girl's hands, turned them over and looked at the palms before lifting her gaze and smiling at her reassuringly. Then she let go of her hands and closed her eyes. Clara held her breath and it seemed to her as if the audience was holding its collective breath as well.

Then Mrs Black said, 'Horses! Your father loved horses even as a boy, and he would rather die than leave one suffering. His name is Dennis. He tells me that he was driving an ambulance with shells exploding all about him when he and his horse were hit and they passed over.'

Bernie gasped from the front row. 'Here – where is he? I didn't hear my Denny's voice telling yer that?'

Her words were ignored and to Clara, the silence now seemed charged with something heavy and menacing. It scared her but she could not move and her eyes were fixed on Mrs Black's face.

'Dennis O' Toole, you have ten seconds and then you must go,' ordered the medium in a stern voice.

'There is someone with you and I can't permit their presence here.'

Clara felt a peculiar leap of the heart that almost suffocated her, and then an odd mixture of fear and joy. 'Is it true? Is Dad really here?' she cried. 'What about Mam? Is she with him?'

An excited ripple of sound raced through the auditorium. A man shouted, 'It's a fix. That's why that girl has gone up first.'

No one took any notice of him. The audience was caught up in the drama on the stage. Clara could see Mrs Black's eyelids flickering and the muscles of her face twitched as if an insect was scurrying over her skin and she was trying to get rid of it.

Then the medium cried, 'Go away! You're overstepping the mark. There is a distance that has to be kept between your world and this. Dennis, you must watch the spirit company you keep.'

Clara heard whispering from the wings. 'You don't think it's Bert, do you? You know he had it in for her.' Who was Bert? Clara wondered. She reached out to Mrs Black. 'What is it? What is he asking?'

Before she could touch her, someone seized her hand and said, 'You must keep your distance when she's in this trance.'

Clara looked up into the plump face of a woman with light brown hair, gazing down at her with concern. 'Why?' asked Clara.

'Because it's dangerous for her to lose concentration and leave herself open. There are bad spirits as well as good that can sneak beneath her guard.'

'But – but my father isn't a bad man,' said Clara indignantly.

'No. But there is a spirit that would use him to harm her. Please, you must leave the stage now.'

'But…' began Clara.

She did not get any further with her protestations because the young man suddenly reappeared at her side. 'Please, come quietly. Maybe when the show is over my sister will have a few words with you and explain. You might even get the chance to speak to Mrs Black again,' he said in a low voice.

Clara did not move. What was really going on here? Had her father's spirit really spoken to Mrs Black? If that was so, then why hadn't he passed a message on to her? Perhaps he had wanted to but Mrs Black had refused to comply with his request. But what could he have asked her that was so unacceptable? And who was Bert? What had the medium meant when she had spoken of overstepping the mark? Suddenly she remembered the ominous heaviness in the atmosphere earlier and stood up. She wanted out of here.

The young man murmured, 'Thanks. I didn't want to have to drag you off the stage.'

'I presume you are joking,' she muttered, as he

accompanied her to her seat. She noticed he had
blue eyes and curling black lashes that any girl
might envy. Why wasn't he in uniform? Unless he
had a job that was essential to the war effort. He
gave her a nod as she sat down, before heading
back towards the stage.

'Well, that was a right turn-up for the books,'
said Bernie crossly. 'What were you thinking of,
whispering yer dad's name to her, girl?'

'I didn't, Gran!' insisted Clara, watching the
young man vanish into the wings. She wondered if
he was Mrs Black's son.

Bernie dug her fingernails into her granddaughter's arm. 'Look! She's come out of her
trance, that's if she was ever in one. It's a load of
codswallop! What did she mean my Denny
overstepped the mark and needed to watch what
company he kept?' she asked wrathfully. 'He was a
good lad. I'm out of here.' She dug her elbow into
Clara's ribs. 'Come on, girl. I'm going to ask for me
money back. Give me a hand up!'

Clara felt even more embarrassed helping her
grandmother out of the auditorium than she had
when they had made their entrance. Part of her
badly wanted to stay to find out if her father really
had tried to get in touch with her; she could not see
how else Mrs Black could have known his name.
No one had arranged for Clara and her
grandmother to arrive late or for her to go up onto

the stage. She still felt slightly odd but was no longer scared.

Clara was to feel even more embarrassed when the manageress refused to refund her grandmother's money. Bernie raged, threatening her with the police, but the woman, who looked surprising like Queen Mary, even to the toque she wore on her head, was adamant.

'You don't have to leave, madam,' she said haughtily, clasping her hands against her bosom. 'I'm sure if you were to stay then you would see that Mrs Black has an amazing gift.'

'So yer say,' wheezed Bernie. 'But I think she's a charlatan.'

The manageress's eyes narrowed. 'That is slander. Mrs Black gives of her time freely. She is a widow and was left comfortably off. She does not need to exhaust herself the way she does in the service of others.'

'What about the price of the tickets?'

'It pays for the hire of the theatre and the refreshments afterwards. During which time those wishing to consult Mrs Black privately are given the opportunity to make an appointment with her assistant, Miss Kirk. Any money over goes to the Seamen's Orphanage near Newsham Park.'

'I suppose...that's where...she-she lives? In one of them...posh, big houses.' Bernie's breathing had become more laboured and she glanced wildly about her as she clutched Clara's arm.

'No. Although, I believe that Mrs Black originally came from Liverpool before moving to Chester. She now lives in the village of Eastham on the other side of the Mersey.'

'There, Gran, now you know all you need to know about Mrs Black,' said Clara, alarmed by her grandmother's high colour. 'Let's get you home, so you can put your feet up.'

Bernie shook her head. 'I'll never make it, girl,' she gasped. 'I have to sit down now before I collapse.'

'She does look a dreadful colour,' said the manageress, frowning. 'I'll get her a chair and see if there's anyone who can help you take her home.' She bustled away but was back in moments with a chair.

Between them, she and Clara lowered Bernie onto the seat. Clara knelt in front of her grandmother and took her hand. The manageress excused herself and said she would be back soon.

'Feeling better now, Gran?' asked Clara, wondering if she was imagining the old woman's colour was improving.

Bernie moaned, 'I think I'm on me last legs, Clara luv. It's time to make me peace with those I've wronged.'

'Then we could be all night,' joked Clara, trying

to infuse some fighting spirit into her.

'Very funny,' gasped Bernie. 'What I want is to see Gertie before I go.'

'Gertie. Who's Gertie?'

'Me eldest daughter,' she quavered.

Clara stared at her in disbelief and was about to say *But you told me all your daughters were dead* when the manageress reappeared with the young man who had escorted her from the stage.

'This is Mr Kirk,' she said.

'You need help?' he asked, frowning down at them.

'Yes. But I didn't mean for the manageress to fetch you,' said Clara, feeling the colour rush to her cheeks.

'Well, she did. She knows we came in a hired motor.' He added abruptly, 'Do you live far?'

'Within walking distance,' said Clara, getting to her feet. 'But we don't want to be a bother.'

He shook his dark head. 'If you live that near then it's not going to be much of a bother, Miss O'Toole. Your grandmother will have you on the ground if she collapses, and that won't do either of you any good.'

Clara looked at him suspiciously, 'How d'you know my name?'

'Easy. No trickery involved.' He smiled faintly. 'Mrs Black said your father's name was Dennis O'Toole and you didn't deny it.'

'I see. Do you believe in what she does?' she asked impulsively.

He did not seem annoyed by her question but shrugged navy-blue clad shoulders and said, 'There's lots of strange things that go on in the world. I'm in the merchant navy and sailors can be a superstitious lot. Who am I to argue against there being some merit in what she does? My sisters swear that Mrs Black has helped lots of people.'

'You mean by getting in touch with their loved ones who've passed over?'

'Yes, but she's also a healer. So are you going to accept my assistance to get your grandmother home?' he asked impatiently. 'Or do you want her to breathe her last here and now and we do an on the spot séance?'

Clara's dark brows snapped together. 'How can you speak like that in front of my gran? You'll make her believe she's about to drop dead.'

He had the grace to apologise but added, 'She seems a tough old bird to me.'

'Maybe so but she's still human.'

'Will you two stop it. I don't intend dying right now,' wheezed Bernie, 'but I'm game for a ride in yer motor, lad.'

He grinned. 'That's the ticket, missus.'

'Then help me up. I'm ready for me bed but not me bleedin' grave just yet,' said Bernie, scrabbling for his sleeve.

He put an arm round her and hoisted her upright. For a moment she swayed but Clara got the other side of her and they balanced her between them. They managed to get Bernie outside surprisingly quickly but had some difficulty getting her into the motor, which was parked at the kerb. At last she was seated in the back and Clara joined her. She thought her gran was definitely looking exhausted and hoped the evening's outing wouldn't prove too much for her. She saw him bend over in front of the car and fit in the handle to start the engine. As he turned it the vehicle began to shudder and shake. She felt a stirring of excitement as she watched Mr Kirk seat himself in front of the steering wheel.

He glanced over his shoulder. 'So where are we going?'

Clara gave him the simplest of directions.

'Hold tight,' he said.

They were off, past the back entrance to the theatre, a school and eventually the laundry, then zooming past another pub on a corner and a cluster of shops before reaching their street.

Mr Kirk helped Clara out of the motor first, and she was aware of the warmth and strength in his fingers. As she walked up the step towards the house, she noticed the lace curtains being lifted in the neighbouring houses. A slight smile lifted the corners of her mouth and she thought it would be all over the street in no time that the O'Tooles had arrived home in a motor car.

She pulled the key on the string through the letterbox and opened the door before turning towards Mr Kirk, who was hoisting Bernie out of her seat. Clara hurried over to offer her assistance, although he was handling her grandmother in a competent and solicitous manner. Between them they helped her into the house and lowered her onto the sofa in the kitchen.

He straightened up and gazed at Clara. 'You'll manage now?'

She nodded and felt suddenly embarrassed that he should see her in such shabby surroundings, and yet she was also annoyed with herself for feeling such emotions. 'Thanks for your help,' she said stiffly. 'You'll want to be on your way.'

He nodded. 'Goodnight.'

Clara saw him out and watched him climb into the motorcar. She wondered what his home was like and whether he was related to Mrs Black in any way. If he drove a motor, even a hired one, then he most likely lived in a big, posh house with a large garden. A sigh escaped her. Then Bernie called to her from inside. Clara watched him drive off and closed the door, doubting that she would ever see him again.

CHAPTER TWO

Summer, 1918.

'Be careful, Miss O'Toole. What do you think you're doing, girl? Good job you're not in the AMATOL factory. You would blow up the lot of us.'

Clara blinked at the forewoman. 'Sorry!'

She told herself that she must stop daydreaming about Mr Kirk because it would not get her anywhere. She concentrated, making sure her hands were steady, as she dealt with another breech-loading charge of NCT and cordite. The amounts were so small, being weighed out in ounces and parts of an ounce, that she couldn't afford to let her mind drift. She was earning almost three pounds a week on this job and didn't want to be demoted to sweeping up waste from the floor to be recycled. Those girls earned only one pound and seventeen shillings a week. More money could be earned working with trinitrotoluene, known as TNT, which was mixed with ammonium nitrate to produce the highly explosive AMATOL, but that was really dangerous work and not for the clumsy or faint-hearted.

Mr Kirk popped into her mind yet again. She told herself this was stupid. It was several months since her grandmother's funny turn at the theatre and she had not heard anything from him since. Bernie had made a quick recovery and said no more about getting in touch with Clara's father. She had asked her gran about Gertie but the old woman had clammed up and refused to talk about her. Clara found it extremely irritating that she might have an aunt alive somewhere yet could not get in touch with her. She thought it would be marvellous to have family to be friends with and to share the load of looking after her grandmother.

She sighed.

Jean, the girl a few feet away from her, said, 'What's with the sigh?'

'Just fed up, that's all.'

'Me, too. Perhaps we should go the flickers together?'

Clara smiled. 'That's not a bad idea. I'll have to see how Gran goes but maybe we can arrange to go sometime. Since this new strain of flu has made an appearance, she's worrying about herself. For the past week she's refused to step foot outside the house, which is making life more difficult for me.'

Jean's yellowish features were strained. 'It is worrying.'

Clara nodded, then, noticing the forewoman looking their way, got on with her work. She swallowed a yawn, glad that the night shift would soon finish. It was her free Saturday, having worked the last three in the factory, and she was looking forward to having the weekend off. On Monday she would begin a six to two o'clock shift.

An hour later, she made her way with the other women and girls to the cloakroom, where she stripped off her overalls and removed the turban from her head. She took her outdoor clothes from a cloth bag and her shoes out of another and changed into them. The shoes she put on were down at heel and the soles were coming away from the uppers. It was experience that had taught her that some of those on other shifts would steal anything decent, so she always came to work in her scruff.

Once outside she breathed deeply of the early morning air before catching the tram home. The shop on the corner of Boundary Lane was open so she bought a loaf and a packet of Rinso washing powder, which was said to give good results with cold water. At this time of year one lit a fire as seldom as possible, so as to build up a store of coal for the winter. She broke off a piece of crust and munched it as she walked up the street of terraced houses and let herself into her home. She lit one of the two gas rings in the back kitchen and put the kettle on. There was still milk in a jug in a bowl of cold water, covered with a beaded cloth, so she poured some into a cup and drank most of it before using the rest to dab on her face, noticing that a rash had appeared on her chin. It itched and she wondered whether it was scurvy or another side affect of the chemicals used in the factory. She patted her face dry before going upstairs, but not to sleep. Maybe she would have a doze later but she was not going to waste a summer day off in bed. She had tasks to do.

As she reached the landing Bernie called, 'Is that you, Clara?'

'Yes, Gran. I didn't mean to wake you.'

'I was already awake. Come in here. I want to talk to yer.'

'Can it wait a few minutes? I want to get changed.'

'OK. If yer making tea, I'll have a cup, and yer can do me a slice of bread and jam, too.'

'Fine. You been OK through the night?' shouted Clara, stripping off all her clothes, intending to put them in to soak with the Rinso later. Gone were the days when Monday was the only washday in this house.

'No, I bloody didn't,' called Bernie. 'I didn't dare lay flat in case I stopped breathing. You'll have to get me another bottle of Black Magic.'

Clara had paid out for umpteen bottles of cough mixture from the chemist's, without recompense from Bernie, and was starting to believe her grandmother was addicted to the stuff. 'I'm not buying it if it isn't doing you any good. Perhaps you should spend out and see a doctor.'

'I never thought yer'd begrudge yer old gran some medicine,' said Bernie indignantly.

Clara ignored that comment and took clean underwear from a drawer before fishing around in the tallboy for a clean blouse and black skirt. She dressed and then tidied her hair, thinking she must unpin it and comb some Icilma dry shampoo through it later. She pulled a face at her reflection before reaching for a jar of lemon and glycerine and rubbing the ointment into her face and hands. After that she felt heaps better and, picking up her discarded clothing, she carried it downstairs.

She half-filled the deep white sink with water and then dunked her clothing in it before sprinkling some Rinso on top of it. She left it to soak, made breakfast for two and carried the tray up to her grandmother's bedroom.

Bernie was sitting up against the pillows. 'If yer going to catch that flu then yer going to have to find our Gertie for me before yer get it.'

Clara was accustomed to her grandmother's peculiar, selfish logic, so all she said was, 'I mightn't catch the flu, and why the sudden mention of Gertie after all this time? Thought you didn't want to talk about her.' She placed the tray on a chair beside the bed and opened the curtains to let in the sunlight.

'But yer might. I heard it strikes down those of yer age. I'll need someone to look after me if you pop off. I don't want to end up in the workhouse.'

'You really do try and cheer me up, don't you, Gran? It's more likely that with your chest you'd be the one to die.'

'Now who's being cheerful?' said Bernie, reaching for her cup of tea. 'While I've been staying in, I've been giving that evening at the Theatre Royal in April a lot of thought. I reckon that Mrs Black knew our family from old. I think she was a mate of our Gertie's and must have recognised me, although it's more than forty years since last I saw our Gertie and Edith Rogers.'

'Who's Edith Rogers?' asked Clara, sipping her tea. 'And why haven't you seen anything of your daughter?'

'I think that so-called medium, Eudora Black, is Edie. I reckon she must have changed her name.'

Clara was flabbergasted. 'Are you sure about this? I thought she was sincere and knew what she was about.'

'I can't be absolutely sure,' said Bernie, slurping her tea. 'But if I'm right, then her mother used to read the tea leaves and tell fortunes. I still reckon she could be a charlatan. It was rubbish what she said about my Denny. Still, she might know where Gertie is, so all yer've got to do is get in touch with her.'

Clara was exasperated by her grandmother's presumption that she could get in touch with Mrs Black just like that. 'You tell me how I'm supposed to do it. Anyway, I'd like to know more about Gertie before I go on what could be a wild goose chase. You told me all your daughters were dead and Dad believed that, too.'

'He believed it because he was only a little boy when she waltzed off to try and make a living on the stage. She was the eldest and he was the youngest.' Bernie frowned.

'Why lie about her being dead?'

'She could be dead by now for all I know.' She sighed and her chest wheezed. 'I hope not. It could be she's changed her name, too. She hated the name Gertrude and said it was the kind of name yer'd give to a goat.'

Clara was starting to like the sound of her Aunt Gertie. 'Knew many goats, did she?'

Her grandmother gave her one of her darkling looks. 'Yer grandfather chose her name. He used to tell her stories about his travels. He went to sea, as yer might remember me telling yer. He probably saw plenty of goats abroad.' Bernie bit into her jam butty.

A giggle bubbled in Clara's throat. 'So why has she never been in touch?'

Bernie spoke with her mouth full. 'We had a terrible row. She went and that's the last I saw of her. We were too alike, both hot-tempered. The difference between us, if I'm honest, is that she was blessed with the singing voice of an angel. Even so, I didn't want her going on the stage. I said to her, "Why can't yer be content with singing in church and get yerself a proper job, bringing money into the house?"'

'What did she say to that?'

'Told me she'd do what she bloody wanted. I gave her a right clout for that cheek.'

'So she ran away,' murmured Clara, thinking *good for Aunt Gertie*.

Bernie nodded. 'Yer wouldn't believe the arguments we used to have. Stand up to me, she would, again and again. She started singing in the pubs for pennies when she was just a kid but kept quiet about it for ages, and then I discovered what she was up to. When I found out and told her to hand over her earnings she refused, saying she almost bust her guts singing her heart out and I wouldn't see a penny of it.' The old woman looked injured. 'I beat her for that. I couldn't have her defying me and being a bad example to the youngest two.'

'I think she was brave,' said Clara, draining her teacup.

'Aye, she had guts, all right,' complained Bernie. 'She had the bloody nerve to give me down the banks about me drinking. I went for her.' She pursed her lips. 'I shouldn't have used the belt on her. I remember me mam saying to a neighbour, "Always use just yer hand when yer hit them, because if it hurts you then yer've hit them hard enough. They are yer children after all and yer love them."'

Her words almost took Clara's breath away. 'How could you beat someone with a belt if you love them? Mam and Dad never laid a finger on me.'

Bernie shifted her legs and muttered, 'And look how yer turned out. Yer never stop giving me cheek. Still, there comes a time when yer can't hide from the truth. I wasn't a good mother.'

Clara was too stunned by that remark to speak but thought *too right you weren't, you monster*. She wondered what her father would have made of his mother's confession and felt certain he would have wanted to find his sister.

'I started reading the deaths in the *Echo* just before the war, searching for her name,' said Bernie, rousing her granddaughter from her reverie. 'Then I stopped when they started filling columns with pictures and names of our poor dead boys after war broke out.' She shuddered. 'I'll never forget that day the telegram came telling us of my Denny's death. We're not alone, though, even the Proddy Bishop of Liverpool lost two of his sons.'

'One was awarded two Victoria Crosses,' said Clara, remembering that Captain Noel Chavasse had been a medical officer. Her father had so admired him. She returned to the subject of her aunt. 'But Gertie could still be alive.'

'Yeah, girl, she could.' Bernie brightened up. 'Could be alive and with kids and grandchildren of her own, maybe.'

Clara stretched her arms and yawned. 'I shouldn't imagine she'd be able to make a living on the stage if she had kids. Did she act and dance, as well as sing?'

'She could act all bloody right. Was forever pretending to be somebody she wasn't – wanted to be a cut above, if yer ask me.'

'Well, if that's so and she's alive and done well for herself, then she won't want anything to do with you,' said Clara with a sigh.

'Yer don't have to be so bloody honest,' growled Bernie. 'Even if yer right, I still want to know if our Gertie is alive or not. Surely to God, a daughter would take pity on her sick old mother and come home to see her before she dies.'

'Who said you're dying? It's me whom you think is going to die,' said Clara. 'But I'm all in favour of finding Aunt Gertie. If by some miracle she might want to make up your quarrel, then it's possible she might be prepared to help look after you. But how are we going to find her? Any ideas?'

Bernie's rheumy eyes gleamed. 'What about starting with that Mrs Black, and the nice lad who brought me home in the motor?'

Clara's heart seemed to give a funny little jump. 'What about them?'

'They might know where Gertie is and ask her to come and see me.'

Her grandmother's reasoning gave Clara cause for thought. 'You're so sure that Gertie and Edie would still be in touch? You're talking about forty years since you last heard of them being friends.'

Bernie toyed with a piece of bread. 'It's possible. If Mrs Black isn't Edie, then I'll accept that she does have a gift. How else would she know my son's name if she wasn't genuine? I'd also like to know what was it he wanted her to do.'

'It wasn't Dad, it was the spirit with him that wanted something from Mrs Black,' said Clara patiently. 'I remember those people in the wings mentioned the possibility of it being someone called Bert and that he had it in for Mrs Black.'

'You're sounding like you believe in spirits getting in touch now,' said Bernie, chortling.

Clara smiled. 'I don't know what to believe.' She paused before adding, 'So you're expecting me to find Mrs Black and ask her about Aunt Gertie?'

'Shouldn't be too difficult for a clever girl like

you,' said Bernie, giving her a sly look.

'You don't have to bother with the soft soap, Gran. I suppose I could ask the manageress at the theatre for her address.'

'There yer are! I said yer were clever. I have a feeling, too, you fancied that lad,' said Bernie, smirking. 'Not that you'd have a chance with him, girl...'

Clara felt her temper rising and interrupted her grandmother before she could finish. 'You can push me too far, you know. If you want my help then keep your thoughts to yourself. I will write to Mrs Black if I can get her address. I'll ask point blank if she knows Gertie O'Toole and where we might find her. If my aunt's dead, then perhaps she'll arrange a séance for you.'

'I don't know how the spirit world works but I don't see why not,' said Bernie, sounding almost happy as she threw back the bedcovers. 'Now yer can give me a hand up. I need to dress and go down the yard to the lav.'

Later that afternoon, Clara put on her best coat and hat and went along to the theatre, only to find it closed. She read the notice of events for that evening and the coming week on the board outside and decided to return later, when there would be a concert to raise funds for treats for the wounded men home from the Front.

She thought of Mr Kirk saying he was in the

merchant navy and wondered if he had returned to sea. She hoped he had not been killed. And what of his sister? She remembered they had mentioned another woman and, not for the first time, thought back again to that evening. The name Alice popped into her head and she thought again of *Alice in Wonderland*, thinking it was interesting how, subconsciously, one made connections with this and that. The sister had wanted her brother to ask Mrs Black to get in touch with someone for this Alice. Perhaps he was a missing sailor or soldier. She imagined with all the thousands of men killed in the war so far, that would be quite a job.

'A telegram's come for you,' said Tilly Moran, hurrying into the drawing room where her older sister was sewing.

Alice Bennett's face, with its well-defined cheekbones, was drawn; now all the colour seemed to drain from her cheeks. 'What does it say?' she croaked.

'I haven't opened it.' Tilly held out the envelope with a trembling hand.

Reluctantly, her older sister took it from her and, taking a deep breath, tore open the envelope. It seemed ages to Tilly before her sister lifted her eyes from the paper and she saw that they were full of tears.

'Oh, I'm so sorry,' she whispered.

'No, no. It's good news.' Alice put a hand to her mouth and closed her eyes and then opened them again. 'At least it's not the worst news I could have. Seb's alive! I knew it would be wrong to ask Mrs Black to try and get in touch with him. God speaks out against it in the Bible and you know I've always disapproved of that woman. At least she's a subject that both Seb's mother and I can agree on, even if we don't agree on anything else.'

'Thank God,' said Tilly, sounding relieved. 'But is he all right? Or is he injured?'

'Wounded, but I don't know how badly,' said Alice, pressing the telegram against her chest. 'All this time waiting to hear and they've given me so little news. It says he's in a hospital in Oxfordshire and that's all it says.'

'You'll want to go and see him,' said Tilly, getting to her feet.

'Of course. If I can.' Alice stared at her sister and thought how grateful she had been for her company in the last few months, helping out with the children and in the house and garden. She considered how much prettier her younger sister was, even though they shared the same red-gold hair and heart-shaped faces. Right now, Tilly's delicate features were flushed with exertion and damp tendrils of hair hung about her face, for she had been working in the garden in the sun. She was wearing a cream cotton blouse with a mandarin collar and a floral patterned green and red skirt with a flounce at its hem, and looked much more mature than her fifteen years. She felt a rush of love for Tilly, knowing she would not have coped without her support or that of their older half-brother Kenny and his wife Hanny. Not once had either of them told her she was a fool to carry on hoping that her missing husband was alive. She must tell them the wonderful news.

Alice rose to her feet. 'Will you keep your eye on Georgie?'

'Of course.' Tilly smiled. 'You'll want to tell Kenny and Hanny the good news. I wonder where Seb's been all this time.'

'Only God knows! But I don't care. He's alive! That's all that matters.' Alice's voice broke on a sob and she rushed from the drawing room.

She had been so down in the dumps that to be lifted out of them so suddenly made her head whirl and she had to pause on the front doorstep to collect herself. She closed her eyes, picturing her husband. She imagined Seb breezing into the house in that confident, smiling way of his, lifting her off her feet and kissing her, before asking how her day had been. Then he would shout for the children and the two older ones, James and Flora, would come running. Seb had never seen Georgie, the youngest. He was the result of their passionate lovemaking the last night they had spent together before he had left for France. She remembered how it had torn her apart to see him leaving, knowing they might never see each other again.

Her eyes filled with tears and she wiped them away with her sleeve. She must not give way to her emotions but pull herself together before facing Hanny and Kenny. There had been a brief, shaming moment, after Seb had left for France, when she had resented them for not having to suffer the anguish of parting. Yet both of them had suffered their share of grief in the past, and a lot of it had been due to Hannah's swine of a brother, Bert. Whoever he came into contact with, he harmed, and Kenny's crippled foot was a permanent reminder of his evil.

Alice hurried down the drive between beds of radishes, spring onions and herbs, only to hesitate at the gate, uncertain as to where she might find Kenny and Hanny at this time of day. They could both be at the motor repair yard, situated near the Shropshire Union Canal, the other side of Chester. But it was just as possible that they would still be at home, just a few doors away, in the house that belonged to Mrs Black and had been her previous residence. Alice gnawed on her lower lip, still surprisingly reluctant to set foot in that woman's house, despite her no longer being in residence there. It seemed stupid to feel the way she did when she had such stupendous news to tell the two people who had been closest to her since childhood.

Alice decided to try the house first. She found the door ajar and, after a moment's hesitation, stepped inside the hall and gazed about her. When Hanny and Kenny had first moved here she had been delighted to have them living so close by, but she wished they could have chosen another house in the crescent as their home. This one held too many painful memories for her. It was here that her father, Mal Moran, had come to receive healing and spiritual counsel from the woman of whom she so disapproved. And her father had caused her nothing but anguish since she was little. He was another who had brought pain and suffering into the lives of those about him.

Still, she was here now and could hear piano music coming from the front room of the ground floor, which was rented by two elderly spinster sisters who taught music.

She placed a foot on the first step of the stairs and then called up, 'Hanny, it's me, Alice. OK, if I come up? I've some good news about Seb.'

There was no answer but she heard a noise coming from the first floor, so she hurried on up the rest of the stairs and headed for the back of the house, overlooking the River Dee. She pushed open the door but stopped short when she saw a dowdy, squat woman sitting on the sofa. She appeared to be basket weaving. It was Hannah's mother, Susannah

Kirk, who had once believed she had good reason to hate Alice, but now the expression of the woman staring back at her was blank. 'Who are you?' she asked.

Relief flooded Alice. It seemed that whatever treatment she had received in the lunatic asylum before Hanny removed her it had helped her to forget past resentments. Perhaps she and the old woman could start again with a clean slate.

'Is Hanny around?' asked Alice.

'I was to tell callers that she's gone to the yard,' said Susannah.

'Thank you.'

Susannah smiled and, lowering her head, carried on with what she was doing.

Alice lingered a moment, thinking that, except for the colour of her hair, which was now completely grey, Mrs Kirk's appearance had scarcely altered over the past years. She experienced a moment of deep sadness. Mrs Kirk had once been a sensible, neighbourly woman and a good friend to Alice's mother before her death, but between them, Alice's father and Bert had changed all that.

Seb, Seb! Her heart lifted as if it had taken wing. Her husband was alive and, God willing, she would see him again soon. She must find out the extent of his injuries. She felt certain Tilly and Hanny would take care of the children between them while she visited him. A cold shiver trickled down her spine. What if his injuries were life threatening? But they had not hinted at that in the telegram. She prayed fervently that they were not serious, but bad enough for him never to have to return to the Front again. But then she felt guilty at the thought of wishing any injury on her husband. She must continue to be optimistic; the last few weeks, hoping he would be found alive whilst struggling against fearing the worst had been dreadful and she pitied those who had to face up to loss.

She made for the Queen's Park footbridge, singing 'The Boy I Love' in an undertone, then hurried across the Dee and up through Grosvenor Park and along the busy city streets, rejoicing that the weather matched her mood. She found Kenny and Hanny in the office at the repair yard. He was eating a sandwich, whilst Hanny's flaxen head was bent over a rebuilt Remington No. 7 typewriter. Alice remembered her sister-in-law ordering it from Gamage's catalogue for Kenny's thirtieth birthday; a fitting gift to celebrate his growing success at writing articles and short stories for the local press. It had cost a whole ten pounds! If they had known that war was about to break out and the automobile business would suffer, then perhaps they would have been more careful with their money. As it was, the machine had well earned back that initial outlay.

'Alice, are you OK?' asked Kenny, his hazel eyes filled with concern as he limped towards her.

'Yes.' She smiled and for a moment could not continue, as emotion clogged her throat. Then she threw her arms round him and hugged him. 'Seb's wounded but he's alive,' she cried.

'That's wonderful!' Hanny's attractive, fair-skinned face shone with delight.

'It's more than wonderful,' said Kenny, kissing his half-sister on both cheeks. 'It's marvellous news.'

The pair of them drew apart and smiled at each other. 'It's wonderful, marvellous and unbelievable that I feel I can look to the future again. That the children will have their father back,' said Alice.

'Do you know how badly hurt he is?' asked Hanny.

'No. Only that he's in hospital in Oxfordshire. I presume they'll get in touch with me again with more news.'

'Let's hope so...and that his wounds aren't too serious,' said Kenny, brushing back a hank of light brown hair from his forehead with an unsteady, slender hand.

Both women nodded.

'I know so little,' said Alice, taking a handkerchief from a pocket and dabbing her eyes.

'You know the most important thing,' said Kenny firmly. 'He's alive. You'll have to write to his mother and let her know. She must be worried sick. Seb is her only son.'

Alice glanced at Hanny, for she often talked to her about her mother-in-law's shortcomings. 'I will do. But I must admit to feeling angry and hurt that she never bothered to come and see me and the children after I wrote to tell her that Seb was missing.'

'I understand how you feel,' said Hanny. 'But she mightn't be able to get away from the farm.'

'The trains aren't running as they should due to fuel shortages and insufficient manpower,' said Kenny. 'I spoke to Davy and he was telling me about it. I know how you feel about her but you must write. Not only does she need to know he's been found but surely his uncle will want to know he's alive, too.'

Alice slanted Hanny another look. They had discussed Seb's Uncle Martin, his father's brother, in the past, and now she spoke her thoughts aloud to Kenny. 'He hates Seb because he inherited his grandmother's house instead of him. Uncle Martin expected to get the house, the money; the whole lot.'

Kenny frowned. 'He has no right to resent Seb because of that. After all, it was you two who looked after her when she went senile.'

'Whatever he felt, it didn't stop him from marrying Seb's mother,' said Hanny with a grimace.

'Mind you, she was a good catch. Excellent cook and housekeeper, and with her own little nest egg.'

'You're forgetting her temper and her lack of morality,' said Alice, and, getting into her stride, added, 'She likes to rule the roost, too, and hates the fact that I'm the lady of the house where she wanted to be mistress. The truth is that Gabrielle married the wrong brother because the right one wouldn't tie the knot with the hired help.'

'But she couldn't have married the other Mr Waters, anyway, could she?' replied Hanny reasonably. 'Back then, wasn't she still married to that musician, Mr Bennett? The one who left her stranded in America and who Seb grew up believing he was his father.'

Alice nodded. 'That's true, but she was quick enough to divorce him for desertion so she could marry Martin Waters, which surprised me, I can tell you. She makes out she's oh so religious and yet she was Thomas Waters' mistress for years and then goes through a divorce and marries his brother!'

'Perhaps the first time she was married wasn't in the Catholic church,' said Kenny, taking the weight off his gammy foot by resting against the desk. 'So it wouldn't be regarded as a true marriage in her church's eyes, surely?'

'When Seb and I married she said that we weren't legally married because we didn't marry in a Catholic church.' Alice's green eyes glinted. 'She had a nerve. Anyway, if she is unhappy in the country it's her own fault.'

'I must admit I've always thought of her as a townie,' said Hanny, getting up. 'By the way, we've got some good news for you, Alice,' she added almost casually.

'What is it?'

Hanny looked at Kenny. 'Should we tell her? I know we've been worried to say anything in case it jinxed us.'

'Is it the business?' asked Alice, looking anxious. 'You've been generous, giving me what you can from the little that's coming in. I don't know what I'd have done…well, I know what I still have to do,' she said frankly, 'hock a few more things. But don't mention it to Seb. I'm hoping he won't notice I've taken stuff from the attic.'

'It's not that,' said Kenny firmly. 'It's—'

'I'm having a baby!' burst out Hanny, her eyes shining. 'After more than ten years of trying, we're having a baby at last.'

Alice could scarcely believe it. 'It's another miracle,' she said excitedly.

'That's how we feel. I'm frightened to believe it's true,' said Kenny.

'Oh, I can't wait to tell Seb,' said Alice joyously. 'It's incredible. Two lots of good news in one day after such a hard time.'

Kenny smiled. 'Well, while you're in this mood,

write to Seb's mother. I'm sure she'll feel a lot happier if you let her know that Seb's been found, and you'll feel better knowing you've done the right thing.'

Alice did not argue. She would write to her mother-in-law so she could honestly tell Seb that she had kept in touch with her.

CHAPTER THREE

Gabrielle Waters gazed at the Chester postmark on the envelope and her heart began to beat heavily. She recognised Alice's handwriting and guessed the letter must contain news of her son. They had not always seen eye to eye, but she loved him in her way. What if the letter confirmed her fear that she would never see him again? She remembered her husband's reaction when she had told him Sebastian was missing. He had not said anything, but she had seen the glee in his eyes. In that moment, her loathing of Martin had intensified. How she could ever have imagined that he could fill his brother's shoes was a mystery to her these days.

She fingered the bruising on her arm from Martin's latest assault. Before they had married, she would never have believed he could be so vicious and vindictive. She was strong herself but was no match for his brute strength. The thought of his latest drunken attack brought to mind her childhood, when she had stood up to her mam. The fear she had felt as a young girl made her feel sick for a moment, but then she remembered the letter in her hand and wondered how she could have allowed her thoughts to run on so. Taking a deep breath, she slit open the envelope.

Dear Mother-in-law,

I'm sure you will be pleased to know that Seb has been found. Unfortunately he is wounded, but I don't know how badly at the moment. As soon as I hear more about his condition I will be in touch. If you would like to come and visit us you will be made welcome. The children often ask after their grandmother.

Yours sincerely,
Alice.

Gabrielle's fine dark eyes filled with tears. Her son was not dead. Praise be to God and all the saints! She would walk the several miles to church right now and light a candle and give thanks. She fetched her handbag, donned her hat and coat and was in the act of putting on her gloves when the door opened and her husband entered.

He stopped in the doorway. 'Where the hell do you think you're going?' he demanded.

'To church,' she replied, tilting her chin. 'My son's been found and he's alive. I'm going to get down on my knees and thank my Lord and Saviour for his return.'

Martin's bluff, raw-skinned face turned ugly. 'You're not ruddy going anywhere,' he said, slamming the door behind him.

'Get out of my way,' she said defiantly. 'You're not stopping me from doing this. I know you wanted him dead, but he has a wife and three children. If you can't be glad for me that he's alive, then be glad for them.'

'Like hell I will. They have what should have been mine. You're not going to that pagan place with its incense and bloody statues. Heathen, it is. You'll stay here and get my dinner.'

Her dark eyes flashed magnificently. 'Your lunch is in the oven. Now get out of my way.'

'I told you that you're not going to that heathen place.' He removed his cap to reveal a balding pate and flung his headgear onto the table. 'Now take your coat off and put my meal on the table.'

'I will not. It's you that's the heathen!' She threw the words at him. 'I should never have married you in my church.'

'On that we can agree,' he snapped. 'But seeing as how you did, we'll just have to put up with each other. Now, I'm only asking you one more time, get my food on the table.'

'Get it yerself,' she said, her accent slipping as her temper rose.

She made to walk past him but he seized her by the arm and within seconds they were locked in a struggle. He knocked her hat off and grabbed her by the hair. She hit him with her handbag across the face. He swore and forced her down on to the table. There was a knock on the door. Instantly he released her, growling, 'Who's there?'

Gabrielle bent and picked up her hat. As the door opened to allow the farm labourer entry, she covered her messed up hair with her hat and hurried out. She knew that Martin would be even more furious with her when she returned, but she was prepared to face his wrath once she had performed the rituals she felt necessary. Her church had always been a comfort to her, even if she did not always follow its commands.

She had tried to be a good wife to Martin, grateful for the status he had given her as a married woman, bearing the name of Mrs Waters at last. But she had soon realised he had married her only because he wanted to possess that which had been his brother's. Being *Mrs Waters* had paled into insignificance once she realised that, and she had treated his demands with scorn. That was when he had started to hit her. She coped with it as best she could, but, having no easy escape where she could, for a short while, forget her miserable life, living with him on the farm grew more irksome each day. She missed the hustle and bustle of city life. During the winter the countryside was especially grim, and Martin was such a stick-in-the-mud that he refused to leave the farm even for a couple of days in Wales or Liverpool. As for her visiting the house in Chester to see her son and grandchildren, he absolutely forbade her to do so. She had disobeyed once a few years ago and had lived to regret it. She had long realised that he would never forgive her son for inheriting what he saw as his, and as he could not punish Sebastian, he was determined she would pay for it.

If only she could be free of her marriage she would be off like a shot, fulfilling her dream of visiting America again. Perhaps she might even meet up with her first love, Robbie Bennett. My, he had been a fine figure of a man and tinkled the ivories a fair treat as well as making the clarinet sing. If she had been younger instead of on the wrong side of fifty, she would have taken a chance and gone to sing her way to her goal, as she had when she had run away from her mam. But she was no longer the attractive, bold-eyed seductress she had been on that first voyage to America. She needed money if she was to have a last throw of the dice so, for the moment, she had to accept that she had made her bed by marrying Martin and had to lie on it. She could only pray that one day her chance would come to do what she wanted, and when it did, she would seize it with both hands.

CHAPTER FOUR

August, 1918.

'I've got a letter at last, Gran,' called Clara, hurrying into the kitchen. It had been over a month since she had obtained Mrs Black's address and written to her, asking if she knew of Gertie O'Toole's whereabouts. Each day she had waited and waited for a reply to her enquiry, and now it had come.

Bernie appeared not to have heard her and continued to read the newspaper. 'It says here that the Allies have taken loads of German prisoners. They used tanks and there were these new fangled flying machines bombing behind their lines. There's a picture of a tank here. Come and have a look.'

Clara said impatiently, 'Didn't you hear what I said? I've a letter and I'm sure it's from Mrs Black. It's postmarked Eastham.'

'In a minute, girl. It looks like the war's going the

Allies' way, at last, with the help of the Americans. Look at that gun.'

Exasperated, Clara glanced at the picture of a tank with a gun. 'Bit like being in a tin box,' she said, interested despite her impatience. 'I bet there was a lot of shrapnel flying about during the fighting. Did you know that soldiers get paid for any shrapnel they can collect and hand in? It gets sent back here to be melted down and reused.'

'I didn't know that. I bet it's dangerous collecting it,' said Bernie, folding the newspaper.

Clara agreed and moved away to sit in the shabby armchair opposite her grandmother. She was on a two-to-ten shift, so could relax for a moment as she had a few hours before she needed to leave for work. She slit open the envelope.

Bernie watched her. 'About time it came. How long have we been waiting to hear?'

'Never mind that now, Gran. Let me read it.'

Her chest wheezed as Bernie watched her granddaughter for a moment and then she cried, 'Hey, hey. Read it aloud, girl, so I know what it says.' She leaned forward and tapped her on the knee.

'Hold your rush,' said Clara, reading on a bit further before lifting bright eyes to Bernie. 'You were right. She does know Gertie. She is still alive. Isn't that good news?'

'Does it say where she's living? I won't believe

that woman's being honest with me unless I see our Gertie with me own eyes.'

Clara read on a bit further and gasped. 'You've a grandson but he was wounded in France and has recently been sent back to Blighty.'

Differing emotions flittered across Bernie's face. 'A grandson! That's the gear! But oh, the poor boy! How badly wounded is he? He's still got his legs, hasn't he?'

Clara read on a bit further. 'It doesn't say he's lost them. In fact, it doesn't say what his wounds are. Perhaps she doesn't know.'

'Does she say where our Gertie's living?'

Clara shook her head in disappointment. 'She only says that she lives on a farm in the country. Neither does she say where my cousin lives, but she does tell us his name is Sebastian Bennett.'

Bernie sniffed. 'Sebastian! What kind of name is that? Our Gertie really must fancy herself as somebody.'

'It's a saint's name. You should know that.' Clara lifted her gaze from the letter. 'He's got three children, so you've great-grandchildren, too.'

'Well, that's bloody great that is,' said Bernie, her breathing laboured. She hit the arm of her chair with a clenched fist. 'I've got great-grandchildren and the bloody woman doesn't give the addresses. She's bloody playing games with us. Yer should never have bloody bothered writing to her.'

Clara glowered at her grandmother as she folded the letter and replaced it in its envelope. 'You've no right to swear at me. You were the one who wanted me to write to her, so it's your own fault if you're not happy with what she has to say. I must admit I'm made up I've an aunt and a cousin with a family. I'd like to meet them.'

'Well, I'm bloody far from made up,' muttered Bernie, her expression sour. 'What's the use of telling me about me daughter, grandson and his kids if I don't know where to get in touch with them?'

'At least you know about them,' said Clara. 'You should be dancing round the kitchen.'

'I bloody wish...' whispered Bernie, her breathing sounding worse than before.

Clara glanced at her and noticed that she had changed colour. 'Are you OK?'

'No, I feel peculiar. It must be the shock of knowing Gertie's alive and that she's never got in touch.' She rested her head against the back of the chair and closed her eyes.

Clara rose and went over to her. 'Just you take it easy, Gran. I'll write to Mrs Black again. Everything will work out, you'll see.'

'I wish I had yer confidence. Get me some whisky,' urged Bernie. 'I feel as if I'm on me last legs an-and I was hoping...to get...to see our Gertie before I go.'

'Buck up, Gran, you've felt like this before and been OK. Just don't get yourself worked up. I'll sort things out. A nice cup of tea, that'll make you feel better.' Clara left her gran a moment to make tea, reusing the tea leaves in the pot to eke out the rationing.

Bernie made a noise in her throat. 'What about me whisky? Whisky for me poor old heart.'

'You tell me,' said Clara dryly. 'I haven't bought any and I thought you hadn't been going out because you were scared of catching the flu.'

'I took a chance.' Bernie opened one eye and whispered. 'Fetch me handbag from upstairs, but don't you go nosing inside it.'

Irritated by that remark but still concerned by her grandmother's pale colour, Clara bit back the words she'd like to say and took the stairs two at a time. She found the handbag on the bed and hurried downstairs with it. She placed it on Bernie's lap and would have undone the clasps if her grandmother had not knocked her hand away. Clara swallowed an angry rebuke and moved away. As she watched Bernie swig out of the bottle of Black and White whisky, it struck her that it was more likely to be the spirit that would eventually kill her grandmother, rather than any flu epidemic.

Bernie screwed the top back on the bottle and looked up at Clara. 'So when are yer going to get in touch with Mrs Black?'

'Probably today. It took weeks for her to answer my last letter but she does mention having been away.' Clara poured the tea.

'Yer've her address – why don't yer just go and call on her?' asked Bernie. 'It'll save time.'

Clara was unsure of the etiquette of just dropping by on a medium but longed for a day out. It would be a real treat. 'I presume you won't be coming with me?' she asked.

'With my legs? Yer have to be jokin', girl. They won't get me to the Pierhead, never mind the Wirral.'

Clara was relieved. It would be no fun having her grandmother hanging on to her arm, but she had thought she had best ask. She decided that she would write to Mrs Black, informing her that she intended to visit. The more Clara thought of getting away from her humdrum existence for a day, the better she liked it.

'Go this Sunday while the weather's nice. Yer can take a ferry to Eastham. Nice woods there. I remember them from when I was a girl and did some courting there.' Laughter rumbled in Bernie's chest and then she started coughing.

'Here, have a drink,' said Clara. 'I hope you'll be OK without me.'

'Don't I fend for meself when yer at work? said Bernie, with a virtuous expression. 'I'll manage. Yous deserve a day out.'

Clara gave her a droll look and thought it made a change for her gran to be nice to her. For once they were in agreement; she did deserve a day out, away from work and her grandmother. So far, she had not even managed that trip to the cinema with Jean. And she desperately wanted to be united with the family she had never known. They were tied to her by blood. She thought about how she had managed single-handedly to cope with her grandmother, with only occasional offerings of help from the neighbours. She missed her parents. Her mother, Eileen, had been strict but good-natured and fair. She had come from the west coast of Scotland and her family had been connected with shipping, but they had not been in touch since Eileen's death. Clara sometimes thought it would be interesting to know more about the Scottish branch of the family, but it was too late for that now. Instead, all her hopes were pinned on being united with her Aunt Gertie and her family.

'Wait until you read this,' said Alice, her eyes sparkling with annoyance as she tossed a sheet of paper onto her sister's lap.

Tilly yawned. She had only just returned from a day out in New Brighton with Alice's two older children and was feeling worn out. 'I presume it's from Seb's mother. Does she say that she's glad he's alive – but sorry she can't come and visit?'

'That's it in a nutshell. Isn't she the most selfish woman you've ever come across?' fumed Alice. 'I wish Seb had never talked to the children about her, telling them what a good storyteller she was and how she had been in pantomime when she was young, about those gorgeous macaroons she used to make.'

'Hanny told me about the macaroons,' said Tilly, suddenly aware she was hungry. 'Are you going to write back and tell her what you know of Seb's injury and give her the address of the hospital? It's possible she'll say more to him about why she doesn't come and visit you and the children than she does to you.'

'You really think so?' asked Alice in doubtful tones. 'She's only been here once in the last four years.' She fiddled with a reddish gold curl and sighed. 'I will write, but there's not that much I can tell her. I wish Seb hadn't insisted on my not attempting the journey to see him. All the things he says about it being difficult are true, but I keep thinking there's something he hasn't told me. His last letter sounded so cold and distant.'

'But he's not writing them himself, is he? He might be embarrassed, asking someone else to write about his deep feelings for you,' said Tilly sensibly.

'I suppose you're right.' Alice flopped onto the sofa and gazed moodily at the garden through the open french windows. She was still worried, knowing only that an American photojournalist had found her husband half-buried during the German's spring offensive and that Seb had nerve damage to his right arm, which affected movement. He'd already had some kind of operation. 'Perhaps I should ignore what he says and make the effort to go and see him.' She would have to go up to the attic and find something else to pawn to pay for a train ticket, but as long as he didn't ask her where she had found the money, what did it matter? 'I'm going to go. He might be cross because I've disobeyed him but I'm desperate to see him.'

'Like you say, everything he said about the children and the difficulty of rail travel, and the scarcity of petrol if you thought of going south by car, really does make sense. But I understand why you feel the way you do,' said Tilly.

'I'm hurt because I thought he'd be mad to see me.' Alice toyed with her fingernails. 'That's why I feel there's something he's not telling me.'

'He's been through a terrible time. Would you like me to make you a cup of tea?'

'No.' Alice could feel the beginning of a headache and rubbed her forehead. 'I will write to his mother again, although it's possible he might have sent a letter to her, himself. He did ask after her.' She rested her head on the back of the sofa and, closing her eyes, wished she could afford the luxury of a bottle of sherry. Her mother had signed the Pledge as a girl but Alice never had. 'Maybe he's told his mother more than he's told me about the state he's in.'

'Did you tell him about Hanny having the baby?'

'Mmm! He was really pleased. Have you heard from Freddie lately?'

'Yes. He believes the tide of war has turned now the Americans have joined the fight in greater numbers.' Tilly frowned. 'This war always seems to be about large numbers.'

They were silent, thinking of the millions dead or wounded on both sides of the conflict.

'Do you miss Freddie?' asked Alice. 'I mean, from the moment you were born you were in and out of the Kirks' household until it broke up. He was like a big brother to you.'

Tilly chuckled. 'Of course I miss him. I miss the way he makes me laugh. He's bossy at times but I can forgive him that because he's good-looking and takes me seriously when I say I want to follow in Kenny's footsteps and be a writer. He knows I want to get myself a career, enjoy myself and see a bit of the world once the war's over.'

Alice thought of all of the young men who had been killed and decided that, sadly, it could be just as well her sister did want a career. 'What'll you do for money? The business hasn't been doing well, as you know, and we don't have the kind of money in the bank that'll run to trips abroad.'

'I'll work, of course,' said Tilly promptly. 'Then when I've earned enough I'll travel, writing about my experiences here, there and everywhere.' Her eyes sparkled. 'I might even write novels to rival Conan Doyle or H Rider Haggard.'

Alice was amused. 'You're a dreamer. Anyway, who's H Rider Haggard?'

'You've never heard of him?' Tilly looked amazed. 'You must have. He wrote *She* and *King Solomon's Mines*.'

'I don't have time to read books, although I have read a few.'

'But not H Rider Haggard,' teased Tilly.

'I know who Conan Doyle is. He wrote Sherlock Holmes,' said Alice, smiling.

'That's right. He's good. I borrowed him and HRH from the library. The book I've just read is *She*.'

'What a funny name for a book written by a man,' said Alice, wondering with half a mind what she could hock from the attic.

'Not really. It's set in unexplored East Africa and is a really good adventure story,' enthused Tilly. '*She* who must be obeyed. Her name is Ayesha and she's a queen, who's discovered the secret of everlasting life.'

Alice said, 'I thought Jesus did that.'

'This is fantasy. I decided to read the book after seeing the film. Are you listening to me, Alice?'

Alice gave her full attention to her sister. 'Tell me a bit more. I like films. Who did you go with to the picture house?'

'I went with Hanny. Ayesha's a really strong woman, who orders the men around. If they do things she doesn't like they get the chop. She could teach Mrs Pankhurst and her daughter Christabel a thing or two about equality of the sexes and women having power.'

Alice's face showed dismay. 'She doesn't sound a nice person. I'm sure you shouldn't be reading books like that.'

'Hanny and Kenny have read it and it's more fun than reading Elinor Glyn,' retorted Tilly. 'Although, now she's a war correspondent in France—'

She was cut short by a gasp from Alice. 'You've not read Elinor Glyn? That woman's immoral.'

'Have you read *Three Weeks*?' asked Tilly, with a great show of interest.

'I certainly have not,' said Alice indignantly, 'and you shouldn't have either, especially at your age.'

'Well, I have,' said Tilly boldly. 'You do make a lot of fuss, Alice. I do need to learn about *It* so that I'll know what *not to do* if faced with a handsome British lord on a tiger skin. Although I'm not looking to marry a lord but I might marry Freddie if he'll wait for me.'

'Now stop that,' scolded Alice, thinking her younger sister was far too knowing for her years.

Probably that was due to Kenny and Hanny giving her so much attention when she was growing up, educating her from books that she would not have read at school. She put it down to them having been childless for so long.

Tilly shook her head. 'Please, don't. I enjoy reading and we all have to find a way to escape the horrors of the war, sister dear.'

Alice's expression was austere. 'You could find a more useful way of doing so. If you care about what I think at all, *don't* be reading any more of that woman's books.'

'I won't,' she said meekly.

Alice was not deceived but decided to drop the subject. 'I must write to Seb and tell him I'm going to visit him. I need to know what he's hiding from me.'

The teasing light in Tilly's eyes died. 'You're wise. It doesn't always do to turn up somewhere unannounced.'

Alice couldn't agree more.

Clara's thoughts were running along similar lines to those of the two sisters. She had written to Mrs Black but not had a reply, so could only hope the medium had received her letter and was expecting her. She had taken the ferry and it was a relief to be away from the hustle and bustle of the city. She walked jauntily, swinging the bag containing a picnic of brawn butties and bottle of dandelion and burdock. She left the Mersey behind and passed an inn called The Eastham Ferry. She noticed a signpost, one arm pointing to Eastham Village and another to Eastham Woods. She remembered her grandmother's mention of courting and found it difficult to imagine the raddled-faced, overweight Bernie as a young, pretty girl. Clara's grandfather had died at sea before she was born so she had never known him. Idly, she wondered how the pair had met, but soon her thoughts drifted back to the present and finding Mrs Black's house.

It took her twenty minutes or so to reach the village. An attractive place with a number of sandstone houses, it was dominated by a church that looked very old. Women gossiped to their neighbours in their front gardens and children dressed in their Sunday best appeared to be making for the church. She passed a couple of old men with fishing rods. It was a peaceful scene and a wave of unexpected happiness swept over her. It was such a different world from the one she normally inhabited and she remembered her mother was fond of saying that a change was as good as a rest. But none of the houses appeared to be as large as the one she imagined belonging to Mrs Black. The last time Clara had spoken to the manageress at the Theatre Royal, she had distinctly described the house as very large and standing in its own grounds. It even had a name: Fair Haven.

Her grandmother had thought it a fancy name for a house and Clara had not argued with her, carrying an imaginary picture in her head of its likely appearance. She decided to ask for directions to Fair Haven. Noticing an elderly man, carrying a pair of shears, come out of a gate, she walked over to him. 'Excuse me, sir, could you tell me the way to a house called Fair Haven?'

He stared at her from faded blue eyes and let out a cackle. 'You another fool?'

She was taken aback. 'I don't know what you mean. I'm looking for my aunt and I believe the owner will help me find her.'

'Going into detecting work now, is she? Well, if you're so bent on wasting your money – see that bloke a few yards ahead?'

Clara looked in the direction he was pointing and spotted a man with carroty hair straggling from beneath a cap. He was wearing brown corduroy trousers and a grey jacket and his head drooped as he shambled along a few yards ahead of them. He seemed to be heading for a footpath slightly to the right.

'What about him?'

'He lives in the gatehouse. One of my neighbours reckons he's a loony but he hasn't done anyone any harm yet so you should be safe following him.' He chortled to himself and snipped the air with his shears within inches of her nose before turning towards the hedge.

Clara stepped back, thinking he seemed a bit of a loony himself. She hurried away in the direction of the other man, intent on keeping her distance. She had come this far and it would be stupid not to carry on.

The footpath was just a track, hemmed in by flowering willow herb, bindweed and brambles thick with blackberries. She decided that on the return journey she would pick some berries, thinking they would make a nice pie. She remembered blackberry-ing with her parents as a child on the country lanes leading to Lord Derby's Knowsley estate. They had taken along a couple of neighbouring kids who would have eaten more berries than they put in the basket if her parents had not been strict with them.

She avoided a pothole in the path and thought again of that evening in April, wondering whether her father had really been trying to get through to her. She had no idea what his thoughts had been on the supernatural. Perhaps she should avoid mentioning him to the medium. After all, her object in coming here was to discover her aunt's whereabouts so that she could get in touch with her.

Suddenly a voice roused her from her reverie and Clara realised that the man in front had stopped and was staring at her. 'What is it ye wants with me? I wouldn't hurt the bairns even though they threw stones at me as if I were a rabid dog,' he said.

Clara stared at him with a certain amount of pity because his expression was one of abject misery. 'I don't know what you're talking about, mister,' she said, thinking she could use her bag as a weapon if necessary as she walked cautiously towards him. 'It's just that I'm going the same way as you.'

'Are ye sure about that? Ye no' trying to trick me?' He had a Scottish accent.

'Why should I? I don't know you from Adam. I just want to speak to Mrs Black.'

He stared at her. 'Yer skin's a strange colour, lass. How did it get like that?'

Clara had not thought it was that bad, but what with there being a milk shortage she had given up washing her face in the liquid. 'It's the chemicals in the munitions factory.'

Understanding showed in his eyes. 'Dangerous places, factories. The doctors said that the lead in the shot factory affected ma brain. But I'm no' so bad now and Eudora Black has provided me with a roof over ma head.'

'You live in the gatehouse?' said Clara, her sympathy deepening.

'Aye. There's a wee place at the bottom of the drive and I have that to meself. I've started doing odd jobs for her, mending things, scything the grass and the like. With the young men away at the war,

I can be useful to her.' He smiled hesitantly. 'It makes a change having a job to do, and she trusts me.'

'You sound as if you're content there,' said Clara.

He nodded. 'I am. Although I'd like to see ma children, but Eudora says I have to keep ma distance.'

'Are they in Scotland? My mother came from Scotland.'

He shook his head. 'No-oo! It's a long time since I left there. They live in Chester. One lad and two lasses. I'd best be getting on ma way.' He turned away and carried on walking.

Clara walked with him and in a few minutes the path came to an end. There was a grassy opening that led to two gateposts but there was no gate. She presumed the metal had gone towards the war effort. A sandstone lodge stood nearby and the man turned to her and said, 'This is ma place. If ye carry on up the drive, ye'll come to Eudora's house.'

She thanked him and was aware of his gaze following her as she strolled past him and up a sloping drive banked by laurel bushes. She came to a sandstone house with mullioned windows that gleamed in the sun. She gazed about her at the sweep of lawn and flowerbeds. 'Goodness,' she murmured, wondering if Mrs Black would consider her good enough to invite inside her house or whether she would be kept standing on the step before being told she was not welcome.

She walked up to the front door, which appeared to be made of solid oak and had iron studs on its surface. The wood showed signs of there once having been a knocker, but now there was only a letterbox. Feeling nervous, she took a deep breath before lifting the flap and letting it drop several times. The noise echoed inside the house and, after a minute or two, there was the sound of approaching footsteps. The door opened to reveal a young woman enveloped in a white apron. She had curling brown hair, a plump face and brown eyes that surveyed Clara with interest. 'You must be Clara O'Toole,' she said.

Clara sighed with relief. 'Mrs Black received my letter, then.'

The woman's cheeks dimpled in a smile. 'Yes. She's expecting you. I'm Joy Kirk. Come inside and I'll tell her you're here.'

'I remember you speaking to me at the meeting in April, and you have a brother who's a sailor.'

'That's right,' said Joy. 'Freddie. He's back at sea.' Clara stepped inside and Joy closed the door behind her. 'You'll be wanting to know about your dad and for her to do something about your rash, no doubt?' she added.

'Actually, I didn't come for those reasons but I'm willing to listen to her advice.' Clara touched the rash on her chin. 'I'm not sure what's causing this.'

'It could be scurvy if you're not eating enough citrus fruit and vegetables. We all know there's a shortage of oranges, lemons and grapefruit but blackcurrant juice or rosehip syrup are just as good for it. Mrs Black will be able to help you there. She's read up about nutrition and knows a lot about herbal medicine. She's no quack.'

'I didn't think about her being a healer.'

'Oh yes. We get as many people wanting healing as we do needing some assurance about their loved ones who've passed over.' She led Clara into a room situated to the left of the hall and told her to make herself comfortable while she let Mrs Black know she had arrived.

Clara perched on the edge of a rich plum-coloured velveteen sofa and gazed about her. She noticed a framed poster on the wall and rose to her feet and went over to have a closer look at it. She saw that it was dated 1885 and advertised a show at the Rotunda Theatre, Liverpool. A baritone had top billing but further down it said *Eudora Rogers, the Girl in Touch with the Spirit World,* and just below that was written *Gabrielle O'Toole, the Liverpool Songbird with the Voice of an Angel.*

She remembered what her grandmother had said about her Aunt Gertie possibly changing her name and was thrilled. Was it possible that Gabrielle was her Aunt Gertie? Then she remembered what Bernie had said about her daughter wanting to be a cut above her. She did hope that she had not come here on a wild goose chase and that Gertie would want to mend the quarrel. At that moment, she heard a noise behind her and turned to see a woman standing in the doorway. She was smartly dressed in a pale pink blouse and a damson calf-length skirt; her silver hair was knotted into a chignon and from her small ears dangled gold earrings in the shape of stars. Clara recognised her immediately and experienced a buzz of excitement.

'I'm sorry to disturb you, Mrs Black. I hope you don't mind my coming.'

'My dear, I was glad you wrote to me and I'm pleased to see you here in my home.' She smiled warmly. 'I lost touch with Gertie's family a long time ago and was so glad to see you and your grandmother at the hall in Liverpool. She has changed out of all recognition, but you are so like Gertie and her son Sebastian that I guessed you were related to them almost immediately.'

'So there was nothing supernatural about what happened?' said Clara, slightly disappointed.

Eudora gave her a penetrating stare. 'It depends on what you mean by supernatural. It's quite natural for me to talk to those who are no longer with us in the flesh. I did speak to Dennis. Of course, he was only a little boy when I knew him so our conversation was not what you might think.'

Clara was slightly unnerved by Mrs Black's

mention of speaking to the dead as something that was quite natural. 'I didn't really come about Dad. It's Gran wanting to get in touch with Aunt Gertie.'

'I know. You mentioned it. But first things first. Perhaps we should go along to my healing room.' Eudora's smile was gentle. 'I think there are things you need to get off your chest. I remember your grandmother wasn't the easiest person to get along with.'

'She drinks and often flies off the handle. I work hard and sometimes I could do with a bit of peace.' She stopped abruptly, realising she had told Mrs Black more than she had intended.

'What about Gertie's sisters? Can't they help you?'

Clara saw no harm in telling her the truth about them. 'All dead. Gran's outlived all her children except for Gertie, who managed to escape their fate. Sometimes I think she'll outlive me,' she added wryly.

'And what of your own mother? What was she like?'

The question surprised Clara. 'Strict but fair and a hard worker. She was from Scotland.'

Eudora stiffened. 'Scotland, you say?'

'Yes. The west coast. Her father worked in a shipyard.'

'Was it Greenock?'

'Probably. I know it began with a G.'

'Where did your parents meet?'

'The Isle of Man during Scots Week.'

'Interesting.' Eudora looked extremely thoughtful. 'Was your mother religious at all?'

'Not really,' said Clara, surprised by the question. 'She told me that she was brought up Presbyterian but changed to Catholicism to marry Dad. She never went to church but even so, she acted more like a Christian than some that do.'

'Well, well, this is fascinating.' Eudora's dark eyes gleamed. 'But do let's go to my healing room.'

'What is this healing room?' asked Clara cautiously.

Eudora smiled. 'Come with me and you'll find out.'

Clara hesitated. 'Honestly, I only came to find out more about Auntie Gertie and my cousin Sebastian.'

Eudora smiled. 'We will come to them, don't you worry. Although, no doubt Joy can tell you more about Sebastian's family than I can. Now come this way.'

CHAPTER FIVE

'You don't hear of many Sebastians,' said Clara, following Mrs Black out of the room.

'No. I believe the saint was a Roman soldier who helped Christians during the persecution of the Emperor Diocletian. He was shot with arrows but survived, only to be beaten to death. Also, there is a character in one of Shakespeare's plays. No doubt Gertie named him after that Sebastian. One could never call her saintly,' she said waspishly.

It was on the tip of Clara's tongue to ask whether Mrs Black had fallen out with Gertie but decided it was wiser not to. Instead, she said, 'You know a lot, don't you?'

Eudora glanced over her shoulder. 'You find that odd, knowing that I came from a poor background the same as your aunt? Dear Clara, I think of life being like a game of snakes and ladders. You can climb to the heights or slide back into the gutter, depending on luck and the way you play the game.'

She opened a door and held out a smooth white hand. 'Come, you will not regret taking this step.'

The moment Clara entered the healing room, her eyes fixed on a fresco painted on the wall opposite the door. She thought the landscape looked foreign and could imagine walking along the narrow street between the whitewashed walls. She found pleasure in their unfamiliarity.

'Do rest on the chaise longue while I put a record on the gramophone,' said Eudora. 'You do like music?'

'Yes.'

Clara sat on the seat Mrs Black indicated and watched her take a record from a cabinet and place it on the turntable at the top. She inserted a needle in the head and, gripping the handle at the side of the cabinet, began to turn it. The turntable began to spin faster and faster. Clara watched fascinated, having seen pictures in newspapers of such cabinets, the price of which were far beyond her means. She wondered why Mrs Black wanted to play music as she, herself, was far more interested in knowing more about Gertie and what she had done that was far from saintly.

A few minutes later, Clara found the question irrelevant as Mrs Black stared into her eyes and said, 'Relax, dear.'

She did relax, so much so that she stretched herself out on the chaise longue and let the music wash over her. The sensation was like nothing she had felt before. It was as if her body floated.

'So tell me, what do you fear?' asked Eudora, gathering ingredients together. She placed them in a mortar and, picking up a pestle, began to pound common herbs from her garden with some dried ingredients brought from the Orient, which she had visited before the war.

'Catching the flu and dying before Gran, although that would mean I wouldn't have to worry about getting a job earning enough money to keep us both. She thinks I'll never get a husband but I did rather fancy Mr Kirk.'

'Did you indeed? A handsome, thoughtful but sceptical young man,' she smiled to herself and changed the subject. 'I have heard that the new strain of that scourge started in Spain and is really spreading... Something to do with birds, I believe. It's very worrying. Although, dear, I don't think you need to worry about dying just yet if you're sensible. As for your grandmother, I'm surprised she's lasted this long. She must have a heart like a horse.'

'Mam used to say Gran was still here because she thought only of herself. They'd get really angry with each other and argue. Of course, she wouldn't have her living with us and would go mad if she knew Gran had moved in with us. She always said that with Gran in the house there would never be any peace. I know what she meant.'

'I can understand how she felt,' said Mrs Black. 'Gertie has a temper and anger has such power to destroy.' She changed the subject again. 'Can you tell me something of your mother's upbringing?'

'Not much. She seldom talked about her family in Scotland but I occasionally overheard her talking to Dad. She mentioned this old woman who attended the same kirk as their family. Apparently she was to blame for Mam's father casting her off for marrying a *furriner, who was a Catholic.* She was terrible to her own son, I believe. He disappeared after his wife died, taking his toddler son with him. She said that the woman was an interfering bigot and cruel but had once been a close friend of her dead mother.'

'Thank you, dear. That says something to me,' said Eudora, her eyes bright. 'I knew that if I delved deeper we would find out more about your mother's background than you thought you knew. Do you believe in fate?' She finished her pounding and, as the music had wound down, left the table and went over to replace the previous record with one by Mozart before winding up the turntable again. The music was low, not intrusive.

She returned to the table and reached for a jar of honey and spooned some into the mixture and then added some almond milk. She whipped the ingredients together. 'You haven't answered me,' she said softly.

'I don't really think about it,' responded Clara, almost apologetically.

'Do you believe some things are meant?'

'Mam always believed that she was meant to meet Dad.'

Eudora smiled. 'There you are then. I certainly believe we were meant to meet. I tell you now, do not fret yourself worrying that Mrs O'Toole will outlive you. I'm certain she won't.'

Clara sighed. 'That's a relief. I was hoping Aunt Gertie might help look after her but if she's no saint, I can't see it happening. I'd still like to meet her and Sebastian and his family, though.'

Eudora placed the concoction into a sterilised jar and screwed on the top. 'It is true that families can be a support but they can also cause one a lot of grief. Are you prepared for that if you become acquainted with Gertie and her family? You're obviously a caring person, Clara O'Toole, and could end up having to cope with more troubles than you realise right now.'

Clara was silent.

'Do you hear me, Clara?'

'Yes. I'm wondering if you can see into the future.'

Eudora laughed. 'No, dear. But if one uses one's common sense and takes all the facts about a situation into consideration, then one has a fair idea what the future might hold. Your cousin, Sebastian, having fought in this terrible war, has not returned unscathed. There are also people who are attached to him by friendship and marriage. Young Mr Kirk, for instance. You could find yourself becoming involved in the troubles of his family, too.'

Clara considered Mrs Black's words and decided that if she had coped with her parents' deaths, as well as handling her gran, then she should have no difficulties with her yet-to-be-met relatives. 'If they need my help, I'd do my best to give it,' she said sincerely.

'So be it,' said Eudora. 'I thought I'd best prepare you.' She clicked her fingers and her expression was thoughtful as she removed the record from the turntable and put it away. 'I've made up some lotion for your skin. It should help your complexion. I also have a mixture that might deal with the problem of your grandmother.'

Clara blinked and yawned. 'What kind of mixture? She's been dosing herself with Black Magic cough mixture but I stopped buying it because it didn't appear to be doing her any good.'

'Mmm. A popular remedy, made up of morphine, treacle and water, if I'm not mistaken.' Eudora went over to a cupboard painted eggshell blue, as was all the wooden furniture in the room. She took out a bottle and brought it over to Clara.

She sat up. 'What is it?'

Eudora smiled. 'It's freshly made. You make

certain Mrs O'Toole has a spoonful twice daily, it'll do wonders for both of you.'

Clara slowly reached for the bottle. 'What's in it?'

'It's not poison, if that's what you're worried about. I make sure Malcolm, who works for me, has some every day. You could say it's a kind of tonic.'

'Perhaps I should try it.'

'No!' Eudora reached out a hand as if to withdraw the bottle, then allowed her arm to drop. 'It might make you sleepy and you need your wits about you in your job. You give it to your grandmother. I have something different for you. Cordials I make up to my own recipe.' She returned to the cupboard and took out two bottles. One contained a reddish mixture and the other one was purplish. 'A spoonful of whichever takes your fancy each day will help your rash.' She beamed down at Clara. 'You can add water and make it into a drink. You'll soon feel better.'

'How much do I owe you for these?' asked Clara, hoping they were not expensive.

Eudora patted her shoulder. 'A gift, dear. You've provided me with an answer to a question that's been puzzling me ever since that night we met in Liverpool.'

'You mean in connection with my dad?'

'Yes.' Her brow puckered. 'I have an enemy. In

fact, I most likely have more than one but the one I speak of is a spirit. A wicked woman who ruined her son's life because of her narrow-mindedness and cold heart. She killed his wife but I rescued him from her clutches and dealt with her in such a way that she could never hurt him again. She has not forgotten and is trying to find a way in to punish me. I can hazard a guess now why she was able to connect with Dennis's spirit.' Eudora's dark eyes glinted. 'Anyway, I managed to close the portal in time.'

Clara felt goose bumps rising all over her body and there was a tingling in the back of her neck and her scalp. Mrs Black made the other world sound so real. 'So you cut off Dad before he could send me a message?' she asked.

Eudora said briskly, 'What is it you would have liked him to say? You know he loves you and wants you not grieve too much for him and to have a happy life. You can't have a better message than that, can you?'

'You mean he actually said it?'

'What do you think?' asked Eudora gently.

Clara's eyes filled with tears and she rose to her feet, clutching the bottles and jar, and hurried from the room. She had to get out of this place before she broke down.

She reached the front door before remembering the purpose of her visit. Wiping her eyes with the back of her hand, she recalled what Mrs Black had said about Joy knowing more about Sebastian than she did. Where had the other woman gone? She stood a moment and then became aware of someone singing. Could it be another record on Mrs Black's gramophone or was it Joy? She followed the sound and came to the kitchen. The door was open and the delicious smell of baking wafted out into the passage.

She took a tentative step inside the room and gazed about her. The kitchen was large and immediately she felt at home, wishing she had one like it. There were cupboards and lots of shelves. Copper-bottomed pans hung on a wall and bunches of herbs and onions dangled from the darkened beams that crossed the ceiling. A kettle was steaming on the stove and a large table stood in the middle of a red tiled floor. The table held crockery, a tray of scones, a dish of butter and a bowl of blackberries. Joy was standing over by the sink, her head bobbing in time to the song she was singing: 'Life is Just a Bowl of Cherries'.

'Hello,' called Clara.

Joy spun round and smiled. 'She sent you to find me, did she? I guess she wants me to tell you about Sebastian. He's married to my brother-in-law's half-sister, Alice. Family relationships can be so complicated, can't they?'

'I suppose they can,' agreed Clara, remembering what Mrs Black had said about Seb being connected to the Kirks by marriage. 'How is my cousin? I believe he's wounded.'

Joy drew out a chair. 'Take a seat. Would you like a scone and a cup of tea?'

Clara remembered the picnic in her bag but accepted anyway. 'Sebastian's not going to die, is he?'

'Heavens, I hope not. Shrapnel from a hand grenade ripped through his right arm, so he can't use it at the moment. Whether he'll be able to in the future, we don't know.'

'I'm glad it's not his legs,' said Clara, thinking of the ex-soldier she had seen propelling himself along on a low trolley and begging in Lime Street. This was shortly after the news had come of her father's death. The sight still haunted her and she'd had nightmares of her father's limbs being blown away.

'You've gone pale,' said Joy, placing a hand on Clara's shoulder. 'Sorry. I forgot you'd lost your father in the war.' Her voice trembled. 'I lost someone too. At least, I don't know if he's dead or alive. He's been missing for ages. Chris and I weren't married. He was once a professional soldier, so was one of the first mobilised. Unfortunately, my dah took ill and I had to nurse him, so Chris and I didn't even get as far as being engaged, but I was very fond of him.'

'How sad for you.'

'Worse for his mam and sisters because they

also lost twin brothers.' Joy turned away.

'I feel awful bothering you,' said Clara in a low voice.

Joy swung round and faced her, dabbing her eyes with the corner of her apron. 'It's no bother. I've accepted my loss. Mrs Black has been a marvel. She offered me a job and a home when I needed them most after Dah died. Mother was in the asylum and Freddie was at sea. We got rid of the house and I moved in here. Freddie stays with my sister, Hanny, and her husband, Kenny, when he's home. They live just up the road from Alice.'

'That's handy.'

Joy nodded. 'You won't realise until you see him just how like Seb you are. You've the same dark curly hair and brown eyes and his nose and cheekbones. It'll be interesting to see what he thinks of you when you come face to face.'

Clara's eyes lit up. 'You think he'll want to meet me?'

Joy's smile faded. 'I hope so, but it won't be just yet. He's still in a hospital down south.'

Clara was disappointed. 'I hope he gets well soon. I can scarcely believe I've got a cousin.'

Joy smiled. 'Not only a cousin. We're distantly related by marriage, and there'll be another member of the family in a few months. My sister and her husband are having their first baby after more than ten years of marriage.'

'That's wonderful,' said Clara, trying to work out the relationship of the expected baby to herself and finding it almost impossible.

'What else would you like me to tell you?' asked Joy, starting to butter scones.

'Tell me about my Aunt Gertie. Does she know about me?'

'Not yet. We don't have Gertie's address. I only know that she lives on a farm near Delamere. Alice will know where she lives, so you'll have to get in touch with her.'

'You can give me her address?'

Joy barely hesitated. 'She lives in Victoria Crescent, in Chester.' Joy told her the number. 'Gabrielle's a bit of a snob, by the way, and for years she didn't own up to her past.'

Clara's expression was intent. 'So my aunt goes by her stage name?'

Joy nodded. 'It only came out that she was called Gertie and had family in Liverpool when she and Mrs Black had a row in the crescent a few years ago.'

'Who's Seb's father?'

'Mr Waters. He was married and Gabrielle was his fancy woman.' Joy placed the scones on a plate and slid it across the table towards Clara.

Clara could not conceal her shock. 'Did she marry him?'

'No. She married his brother. Apparently she was

married before but divorced the first one on the grounds of desertion. He was in America and they hadn't seen each other for years.' A smile lurked in Joy's brown eyes. 'I told you family relationships were complicated. But it should be simple enough for you to get Seb's hospital address if you write to Alice.'

Clara was truly grateful and thanked her, writing the address in pencil on a piece of paper. She reached for a scone and bit into it. The pastry was light and melted in the mouth. 'This is lovely. Tell me, do you have any more family?'

Joy sat down. 'I did have another brother and sister but they're both dead. You were fortunate in that you met Freddie, who's a love. But my elder brother, Bert, was quite mad and wicked, but a charmer. He caused a great deal of trouble over the years.'

Clara wondered if the words *mad* and *wicked* were to be taken literally. 'How is Freddie?'

Joy's expression was sombre. 'He was wounded earlier this year and that's why he was on leave and able to drive us to Liverpool in April. It wasn't the first time he's had a ship torpedoed under him. His scars might be invisible to the eye but they're there, nonetheless. He doesn't talk much about what happened. He's only just nineteen and, like so many young men, has seen sights that no one his age should have to see.'

'We're the same age,' murmured Clara. 'War stinks, doesn't it?'

'Yes. Fortunately Kenny did not have to go. He was left crippled after a fight with Bert. It was terrible at the time but now Hanny believes it was meant because it saved him from the trenches.'

Clara thought about what Mrs Black had said about some things being meant, and she began to believe that perhaps there was something in it. She and Joy talked a bit longer about Seb and his family and then Clara said that she had best be going.

'It's been nice talking to you,' said Joy, getting up. 'Most likely we'll see each other again.'

'I'd like that,' said Clara, and thanked her for the scone and tea.

'It was a pleasure. Can you see yourself out? I need to get on.'

'Of course,' said Clara. 'Tarrah!'

She left the kitchen and made her way to the front door, but before she could leave the house she was stopped by Mrs Black's voice. 'Wait a moment, dear.'

Clara turned and said hastily, 'Oh, I'm sorry. I forgot to thank you for everything.'

'That's all right. You were upset.' Eudora placed a hand on her arm. 'You must keep in touch, Clara. If you need more ointment or tonic, just let me know. It won't cost you anything.'

'That's really kind of you,' she said, touched by her generosity. 'But next time you really must let me pay.'

Eudora smiled. 'We'll see. Goodbye.'

Clara thanked her again and left, thinking she had a lot to tell her grandmother, but perhaps some information about Gertie might be best left unmentioned.

'Well! What did you find out?' asked Bernie, pouncing on Clara almost as soon as she came through the door.

'Let me get my jacket off,' said Clara, glancing about the kitchen and noticing that the dishes from that morning were still in the sink. Her gran really was getting to be a lazy so-and-so. She might have a bad chest but surely washing a few crocks wasn't beyond her capabilities?

'Where's our Gertie? Did Mrs Black give you her address?'

'No, she didn't. But she did tell me that Dad gave her a message for me…that he loves me and doesn't want me to grieve too much and to have a happy life,' said Clara with a tremor in her voice.

Her grandmother's wrinkled face sagged. 'Is that all? Didn't he mention me?'

'No,' said Clara, knowing it was wrong of her to relish that fact. 'She asked me about Mam and I got the impression that she was pleased with what I told her. She said it answered a question that had been bothering her.'

'He didn't mention me,' said Bernie in a hollow voice, seeming not to have heard the rest of what Clara had said.

'No! And why should he?' Clara's voice was firm. 'He has Mam with him and that thought makes me happy.'

Bernie's expression turned ugly. 'It's a load of rubbish! I don't believe any of it! She's making it up.'

'That's just sour grapes,' said Clara, determined not to harbour any doubts. 'I believe her.'

Bernie punched her on the arm. 'Then more bloody fool yous. It was a waste of bloody time yer going there.'

'Don't hit me!' cried Clara, enraged, rubbing her arm. 'You've got no right...and it wasn't a waste of time.' She turned from her grandmother and opened her bag and took out a bottle of cordial. She poured a measure into a cup and added water and drank it off in several gulps.

'What's that yer drinking?' asked her grandmother suspiciously, hobbling over to her.

'Cordial. Rosehip. It's full of goodness and is going to cure my rash.'

'Did you get it from her?'

'Yes. She's a healer as well as a medium. I've a tonic for you, as well.'

Bernie looked gratified. 'How much did you have to pay for this stuff?'

Clara hesitated, knowing that if she told her grandmother it had come free, she wouldn't think twice of drinking the tonic down in no time at all and asking for more. 'Never you mind.' She produced a bottle from her bag. 'Go easy with this; it doesn't come cheap.'

Bernie took it and squinted at the label before taking out the cork and sniffing it. 'Smells OK.'

'Good. But only have two spoonfuls a day. By the way, I did learn something about Auntie Gertie, who likes to be called Gabrielle now, from Joy, who is kind of related to us,' said Clara. 'She works for Mrs Black and was there that night.'

'So what did *she* have to say about our Gertie?'

'That I should be able to get her address from Sebastian's wife. He's in hospital down south.'

'Poor lad. What's wrong with him?'

Clara did not answer immediately but sat down and kicked off her shoes; her feet were killing her. She would have a rest before washing the blackberries she had picked on the return journey to Eastham ferry. 'He was wounded in the arm and can't use it.'

'I'm glad it's nothing worse.' Bernie took a swig of the tonic from the bottle.

Clara rolled her eyes. 'Be sparing with that. I told you, it's special.'

Bernie put the cork back and placed the bottle on the mantelshelf. 'So we're a bit closer to getting in touch with Gertie.'

'Yes. I'm going to write to Sebastian's wife and introduce myself and hopefully she'll be pleased to hear from me. I'll tell her how ill you've been, lay it on with a trowel, and maybe she'll take pity on you.'

'Glad I'm getting a mention.'

'That was my reason for going. I know Dad expected me to look after you, but I'm telling you now, Gran, if you raise a finger to me again, then I'm out of this place. It's time you realised which side your bread's buttered on. Now I've discovered I've other relatives, I might just up sticks and go and live near them if you don't start being a bit nicer to me.' Clara got to her feet. 'Cup of tea?'

Bernie glowered at her and, reaching for the tonic, took another swig.

Later that evening Clara spread some of Mrs Black's concoction on her face. The ointment had an earthy, spicy smell and the feel of it on her skin was not unpleasant. She could only hope it would do the job. She thought back on the day and told herself that she would write to Alice as soon as possible. In getting in touch with her, perhaps there was a possibility that she would get to meet Freddie again one day.

CHAPTER SIX

Chester. September, 1918.

'I've had a letter,' said Alice, waving an envelope in the air as she walked into the office at the motor repair yard. 'You'll never guess who it's from in a million years.'

'Tell us then,' said Tilly, lifting her gaze from the typewriter and winking at Hanny, who was sprawled in a chair, knitting a matinée jacket. Tilly was learning the job, so she could take over from Hanny now her pregnancy was more advanced. She was practising by typing out the article she had written.

Hanny stared at Alice with a faint smile. 'Go on, put us out of our suspense.'

'It's from Seb's cousin.' Alice perched on the edge of the desk and crossed her black lisle clad ankles.

Hannah's fair brows furrowed. 'I thought Martin Waters was childless.'

'He is. This cousin is on his mother's side of the family. Joy gave her my address.' Alice frowned, she had never approved of Hanny's sister going to work for Mrs Black.

'What's this cousin's name?' asked Hanny.

'Clara O'Toole. Her father was Gabrielle's brother, but he was killed at the Front last year.'

'What a shame he and Seb never got to know each other,' said Hanny, her hands stilling on her knitting. 'But where does our Joy come into this? How did she make contact with her?'

'Mrs Black had a hand in it, of course,' said Alice, her green eyes glinting with annoyance. 'This Clara O'Toole went with her grandmother to see if Mrs Black could make contact with her father. I ask you, what kind of person consorts with mediums?'

'Be careful what you say, Alice,' murmured Hanny. 'You're forgetting that my family has much to thank Mrs Black for and many others have benefited from the comfort her readings have brought. They're desperate to know that their loved ones live on. You're lucky that you still have Seb!'

Alice's cheeks reddened. 'I know I'm fortunate but you know my feelings about trying to get in touch with the dead.'

'And did she manage it?' asked Tilly, lifting her head and gazing at her sister.

'She doesn't say. The main point of her letter is that the grandmother wants to make up her quarrel with Seb's mother, so she wants her address. From what this Clara says, there's only her and the grandmother still alive and the old woman could be on her last legs.'

'So what are you going to do?' asked Tilly.

'I'm thinking about it. Perhaps I need to ask Seb what he wants me to do before I send an answer.' Alice tapped the letter against her teeth. 'She's also asked for his hospital address so she can write to him.'

Hannah resumed her knitting. 'Have you heard from Seb since you last wrote about going to see him?'

'No.' Alice's expression was suddenly bleak. 'If I don't hear in the next couple of days, I'm going whether he likes it or not. I feel awful about not visiting him.'

'Kenny thinks you should have gone straight away despite what Seb said,' murmured Hanny.

'I know, but it's too late now to worry about it.' Alice sighed. 'I'm going to go now, so better late than never.' She changed the subject, asking Hannah whether she had felt the baby quicken yet. The two women started to discuss pregnancy and babies in hushed voices.

Tilly finished her typing and placed the sheets of paper into an envelope before slipping out of the office. Alice's youngest child, Georgie, was outside in his pram, playing with some wooden bricks. She chucked him under the chin and he gave her a smile, revealing six teeth. She kissed him on the top of his head. As she strolled towards the open gates she waved to Kenny, who was talking to a youth standing beside a car.

She came out onto Canal Side, planning to drop the written article through the letterbox of the branch office of the *Manchester Evening Chronicle* on City Road. It was a long thoroughfare that ran from Foregate Street in the city centre to Station Road, where Chester's main railway station was situated. On the way she passed the Wesleyan Methodist Chapel that Alice had attended with the mother Tilly had never known. There were times when she felt something akin to guilt because her mother had died giving birth to her. She wished Alice would be more open with her about her parents. She was positively secretive, and so Tilly had almost given up asking her about them. Kenny was also reticent on the subject, as were Hanny and Joy. She had mentioned the matter to Freddie but, although he knew the two families had been close neighbours, he had been very young when her mother died. It had upset her that she had never even seen a likeness of her parents. When she had mentioned this to Alice, she had shown her a photograph of their mother but said she did not have one of their father. It was extremely annoying.

Tilly disposed of her article through the letterbox

and prayed that the editor might see some merit in what she had written about the need for decently paid jobs for young women due to the lack of young men for them to marry. That done, she headed towards the city centre and the river, passing the Royalty Theatre on the way. She liked visiting the theatre but knew Alice was short of money and Tilly had yet to be paid her first week's wages.

To her surprise, on reaching the house on Victoria Crescent, she saw a motorcycle and sidecar parked at the kerb. She wondered who it belonged to. With a shrug of slender shoulders, she pushed open the gate and walked up the drive and round the side of the house to the kitchen. There was no one in the garden, so she decided that perhaps the owner was visiting a neighbour and had parked in front of the wrong house.

She opened the kitchen door and stepped inside, only to freeze when she saw two men sitting at the table. The one facing her was a stranger. He had tawny hair and a drooping moustache. He stared at her as if seeing an apparition before struggling to his feet. There was something familiar about the other man despite his having his back to her. Then slowly he turned his head and she had to bite back a cry. It was Seb, and where his right eye should have been, there was just scar tissue, the cheek below it pitted with several ugly lesions. Yet the left side of his face was not damaged at all.

'Hello, Tilly,' he said.

Her throat felt raw with emotion and for a moment she could not speak. Then she blurted out, 'Alice said you were keeping something from her.'

'There, I told you, mate, you should have been honest with your family,' said the stranger.

Tilly estimated his age to be in the mid-twenties and he was a good six foot. He was wearing a white shirt and tie beneath a leather jacket and dark brown corduroy trousers, one leg tucked into a high leather boot, whilst the other was strapped up. 'Who are you?' she asked.

His grey eyes met hers and he inclined his head. 'I'm Donald Pierce.'

'The name doesn't mean anything to me,' she said, her eyes sliding towards Seb, but he had turned his head away so she could not read his expression.

'I was the one who found him. He'd been left for dead, covered in earth and torn vegetation. He was completely off his head for a while, so I was determined to keep in touch. I reckoned I had a stake in his survival.'

'But that was months ago,' said Tilly in amazement. 'What are you? A medical officer?'

'Nope. A photojournalist. I arrived back in Blighty, last week having dropped a tripod on my left foot, broke it, so decided to see if Sebby boy was still at the same hospital. It was just as well because when I turned up, he was packing to leave without their permission and making a pig's ear of it.'

Tilly glanced at Seb and pity filled her heart, not only for him but her sister, too. How was Alice going to react when she saw him? He had been such a handsome man, so confident and kind, with an inner strength and determination to succeed in whatever he did. Now...

She squared her shoulders. 'I'm glad you brought him home.'

'Best place for him to be, with his family. You must be Tilly, Alice's sister. He spoke a lot about his family, so I thought I'd like to meet them.'

She glanced at his strapped foot. 'You managed to ride that motorcycle all the way up here?'

His teeth gleamed beneath his moustache. 'Sure was a crazy thing to do. Miracle we got here but we managed somehow, me with my two good arms and Seb with his two good feet.'

She marvelled at their madness and courage and knew she had to say something more to Seb. Do something. Hug him. So she went and placed an arm about his shoulders and gave him a wordless hug. He reached up his left hand and covered her hand with his. The gesture was enough to cause tears to fill her eyes and spill over. She lowered her head and rested her cheek on his hair for a moment.

'I'll go and fetch Alice,' she whispered.

Freeing her hand she hurried from the kitchen, dabbing her face with her sleeve as she walked round to the front of the house. Halfway down the path she saw Alice and the children with the perambulator outside the gate.

'What's wrong with you?' asked Alice, gazing at her blotchy face.

Tilly cleared her throat. 'It's Seb. No! Don't look like that,' she added hastily as the colour drained from her sister's face. 'He's here, in the kitchen. An American brought him home on that-that motorcycle.'

Alice's face quivered. She made to speak but no words came. Then she brushed past Tilly and ran up the path towards the house.

'Alice, I've something to tell you,' called Tilly.

But it was too late. Her sister disappeared round the side of the house.

James and Flora made to go after her but Tilly seized hold of the pair of them and drew them against her. 'Not just yet. Give your mother a chance to greet your father on her own.'

'But why?' asked eight-year-old James, gazing up at her from beneath a bang of curling black hair.

'Yes, why?' His sister, who was two years younger, also looked up at their aunt from anxious green-brown eyes.

Tilly hesitated, not knowing whether to tell them

the truth straight out. But before she could make the decision, her nephew wrenched himself out of her grasp and tore after his mother; Flora was only a few seconds after him. Tilly followed in their wake.

Alice burst through the door into the kitchen, her breath coming fast. She saw a strange man out of the corner of her eye but most of her attention was for her husband, sitting at the table. 'Seb, love, sweetheart!' she gasped.

He did not look up and, bewildered, she hurried around the table so that she could see his face. As he lifted his head, shock splintered through her, shooting along her nerves into her brain and every part of her body. She went hot and cold, and then slipped into unconsciousness.

The children were just in time to see their father's attempt to prevent their mother from falling to the floor. But it was a stranger who caught her and lifted her into his arms. He looked at Seb as if for instruction but his face was stricken and he turned away, bending over the table.

'Dad!' James's voice was hesitant. Why had his mother fainted? And why didn't his father look at him? He wanted to see his face properly, noticing that his shoulders were shaking as if he was either laughing or crying; both seemed impossible.

'Daddy, Daddy!' screamed Flora as she flung her arms about Seb's legs.

Tilly had hurried after the children with the pram and now appeared in the doorway. Her gaze swiftly took in the situation. 'Carry her into the drawing room, Mr Pierce. I'll show you the way.'

'Wait! I'll...come...with you,' said Seb, sounding as if he was being strangled. He reached down a hand and ruffled the red-gold hair of his daughter.

'Dad!' James had moved round the table, so when Seb lifted his head, the boy was able to gaze straight at his father's disfigurement. For a moment neither moved; their eyes glued to the other's face. Then Flora tugged at Seb's jacket and, almost reluctantly, he gazed down at his daughter. This time her scream seemed to shatter his eardrums. Then she went stumbling backwards. He reached out a hand but she evaded it, turned and scurried from the kitchen. James looked one more time at his father from unbelieving wide-eyes, and then went after her.

Donald Pierce swore. But Tilly hurried over to Seb and put a hand on his arm. 'They'll come round,' she said. 'Alice...'

He nodded as if in a dream and croaked, 'The drawing room, Don.'

'Alice, wake up!'

At the feel of cold water on her face, Alice took a shuddering breath and opened her eyes to see Tilly gazing down at her. Alice lifted her head and looked about her, and realised she was lying on the sofa in the drawing room. She remembered seeing Seb and everything spun round her.

'Where's Seb? I didn't dream he was in the kitchen, did I?' she asked.

'No,' said Tilly, putting a hand on her arm.

Alice sat up. 'Where is he?'

'In the garden with Mr Pierce. He carried you in here despite his bad foot.'

Alice clutched her sister's sleeve with a shaking hand. 'What about Seb? Why isn't he here with me?'

'He was but he left through the french windows as soon as you started coming round.'

Alice could not make sense of why he had left her alone. 'You're sure he's in the garden?' she asked.

'Yes. I heard their voices only a few moments ago. Fortunately, Seb prevented you from hitting the floor, but he couldn't lift you up because he has hardly any strength in his right arm.'

'So it was true what he wrote about his arm, but he kept quiet about...about...' She paused and put a hand against her mouth. 'What must he think of me?' she asked in a muffled voice.

Tilly hesitated. 'He looked devastated.'

'Don't!' whispered Alice. 'I can't bear it.'

'You have to bear it,' said Tilly, her voice trembling. 'James and Flora followed you in and they had a terrible shock, too. They ran out of the room and are upstairs. I'll go up to them later.'

'His-his face…it's not so bad. It-he cou-could have…' Alice's voice trailed off and she took several deep breaths before saying, 'Help me up. I must see him. I have to speak to him, I can't let him think…'

'No, you can't let him think he looks like a freak in a fairground show,' said Tilly, her voice cracking on the words.

'Oh my God, is that what he thinks?' The tears ran unheeded down Alice's face.

Tilly helped her sister to her feet. 'I'll come with you. Get Mr Pierce away…ask if he's staying for tea. Then I'll go up and speak to Flora and James.'

Alice laughed on a slightly hysterical note. 'It sounds so normal asking someone if they're staying for tea. Yet everything feels so peculiar.'

Tilly hoisted her sister to her feet. 'Perhaps I should ask him if he would like to stay the night. He's come a long way to get Seb home and he's got a damaged foot.'

'How did they manage it?' Alice rested a hand on her sister's shoulder and steadied herself.

'By a miracle. He found Seb, you know, said he felt responsible for him.'

'Then we must feed him and he has to stay the night. We owe him that. Perhaps I should bake a cake,' she said, still feeling on the edge of hysteria.

'I'll bake the cake,' said Tilly.

'OK. You bake the cake. Oh, Tilly, why did I

have to faint? I never faint!' she wailed.

Tilly hugged her sister. 'Stop worrying. A few big kisses will convince Seb just how much you still love him,' she said bracingly.

If only that could be true, thought Alice, not convinced. She freed herself from her sister's embrace and walked over to the french windows. Her knees were shaking as she stepped outside. What was she going to say to her husband? Accusing him of keeping the truth from her would certainly not help. Yet he should have been honest with her. Had he believed her not strong enough to cope, thought that she would turn from him in disgust? Had her fainting proved him right? But if he had told her then she would have been prepared and most likely not have fainted. If she could have visited him and seen him alone she could have prepared the children. Instead she was unsure how she was going to cope with him and the children and continue doing all her duties now Tilly was working at the yard. She was aware of her sister just behind her and was glad to have her nearby. She realised that she vaguely resented her wanting a career like a man, instead of being set on marriage and having children. Was that because, at the moment, she felt unable to cope with those things herself? One thing was for sure, she held the suffragette movement responsible.

Alice now saw the two men and her heart seemed

to jump into her throat. They were standing near the rose arbour and had their backs towards the house. For a moment she was reluctant to interrupt them, guessing they were discussing her. She wished that she did not feel so sick with apprehension. Seb's homecoming should have filled her with joy, but now she was nervous about facing him and worrying too much about what she should say to speak naturally. Her feet made no sound as she trod across the grass and she realised that they were still unaware of her approach. It was not until she was a yard or so away that their heads turned in her direction. At the sight of Seb's face she felt that shock again like a blow.

'I shouldn't have fainted,' she burst out. 'Stupidly, I was expecting you to be just the same, but neither of us are that.'

'No. Nothing can ever be the same again,' said Seb harshly, and looked away, presenting her with what she was to come to call his old or good side.

Donald Pierce touched his arm. 'Listen, mate. You two are better talking in private. I'll leave you alone.'

Alice turned and flashed him a genuine smile. 'You'll stay to tea, Mr Pierce?'

'Of course, he'll stay to bloody tea,' snapped Seb, whirling round. 'We've travelled hundreds of miles today. He must stay the night, too.'

'Hey, take it easy, mate,' said Donald. He

dropped his voice to add, 'I'd appreciate a bed for the night but remember what we decided. Your wife's not to blame for what happened.'

Seb's lips tightened and without a word he seized Alice's arm and pulled her into the shelter of the rose arbour.

Tilly turned away then, aware that Donald Pierce was watching her. 'I find it hard to believe you're only fifteen. Seb said you were an old soul.'

Tilly was taken aback. 'What does he mean by that? Alice has called me mature but...'

'I'm sure it was meant as a compliment. Now, shall we give them some time alone,' he said, taking her arm.

Tilly shrugged off his hand. 'I didn't plan on staying and listening to their conversation,' she said, her colour high. She had never met anyone quite like this American. 'I'm going to make a cake. Would you like another cup of tea?'

He shook his head. 'What I'd like is a walk but that's a dumb idea with this damned foot. Pardon my French.' He cocked a comical eyebrow. 'Perhaps I could watch you make your cake.'

An idea suddenly occurred to Tilly. 'I tell you what you could do. You could talk to James and Flora about how you found Seb and about what happened to him. I know they're only children, but I think they need to understand he's still their father and is going to need their support. Trouble is, they're upstairs. You can manage stairs?'

'Will do, if you think that will help.' He smiled down at her. 'There's just the little question about my motorbike and sidecar. Are they an honest lot round here?'

Tilly smiled. 'As honest as most but perhaps you're best bringing it onto the drive. You don't want to put temptation in people's way.'

'Will do,' he said, giving her a mock salute before limping round the side of the house.

She felt a pang of sympathy, thinking of Kenny and his difficulty with walking. Then she headed for the kitchen, noticing that Georgie was asleep in his perambulator outside. She wondered what Seb thought of his younger son – that was if he had noticed him, of course.

The air was heavy with the scent of the second flowering roses as Alice and Seb sat on the rustic seat in the arbour. There was a space between them and they were looking straight ahead.

'The children have grown,' said Seb, gripping his damaged arm.

'Yes. Although, it would be odd if they hadn't. What do you think of Georgie?'

'I can't say that I noticed him.'

Alice half-turned to her husband. 'You must have seen him. He was asleep in the perambulator outside the kitchen door.'

He frowned. 'I didn't come out that way. I came through the french windows.'

'Of course. I forgot. Tilly told me.'

A muscle in Seb's throat constricted and for a moment he felt as if he could not breathe, and then he managed to ease the tightness by swallowing. 'How are James and Flora getting on at school?'

'Fine. I did write and tell you.'

'Of course, you did. It slipped my mind. James is enjoying his football and Flora's doing well with her reading.'

Alice smiled. 'He likes drawing, too. Kenny encourages him.'

Seb felt an ache inside him, thinking that it should have been him encouraging his son. 'Good old Kenny. He's taken care of the business. Where would we be without him?' Barely pausing for thought Seb added, 'But then he didn't have to go and fight, did he?' He could not conceal the note of bitterness in his voice.

Alice was shocked. 'It wasn't his fault. You know what Bert did to him. He could never have marched or stood in the trenches.'

'Or gone over the top.' An odd little laugh escaped Seb, which trailed off into a sob.

Alice felt a terrible ache inside her and steeled herself to look at him. 'Are you all right?'

'What a daft question,' he said, turning the damaged side of his face away from her.

'I'm sorry. It's just that you sounded…'

He interrupted her. 'I can imagine how I sound but then if you'd been living in my head for months you might sound a bit peculiar too.'

'I understand.'

'No, you don't. You can't,' he muttered, fumbling for a packet of cigarettes and taking one out. He put it between his lips and lit it with a match.

'You didn't used to smoke,' she said.

Seb inhaled a soothing lungful of smoke. 'I do now.' They had been given free smokes in France. At first he had resisted smoking but then, what with the din of the big guns and the slaughter and mud, he had needed the nicotine to calm his nerves. He thought of the German advance and them having to retreat. So many dead. He remembered the hole he had dug himself into and then the Hun had come and a grenade had exploded near by. He had been told that was what must have happened later when the doctor had dug shrapnel out of his arm and face. He had come round not knowing what had happened. It had felt as if everything inside his head had shifted and there were holes where bits of his memory had fallen through.

'You should have told me the truth and I'd have come to the hospital,' blurted out Alice.

'I hoped you'd come in spite of what I said,' rasped Seb.

Alice frowned and pleated her skirt with unsteady fingers. 'But why did you tell me to stay away if you wanted me to come?'

He faced her, staring at her from his undamaged eye. 'I was bloody scared of your reaction, that's why, and I was right to be, wasn't I? You bloody fainted when you saw me.'

'Don't swear at me, please,' she whispered, placing a hand on his knee and staring into his face. His eyes had been what first attracted her to him. They were the colour of treacle toffee and she remembered the devilment glowing in their depths when he had tried to help her escape from her father. Now the left one was completely ravaged, the socket empty and the eyelid dragged down. She burst into tears.

Hastily he stubbed out his cigarette. 'Don't cry! For God's sake, don't cry! Do you want me to feel worse? I'm ugly. Marred. My looks aren't something you can cry over and then kiss better. Take it on the chin and accept this face as it is or else I don't know what I'll do.'

Her tears shuddered to a halt and she scrubbed at her damp cheeks with both hands. She gulped and took several deep breaths. 'You're not ugly. It was just so unexpected, and…and I felt your pain.'

'Did you really?' He laughed long and hard.

She felt a dart of fear. When he laughed like that he did not sound like himself. The memory of her father's inappropriate wild laughter came into her mind. Unable to bear the thought that her husband's brain might have been damaged and that he would go mad just like Mal, she stood and turned away. Never in a thousand years could she imagine herself showing the same courage as her mother had done when she had faced her husband and taken a beating. Alice fled.

Seb watched her go, cursing himself for not saying what he had planned to say on the way here. For a moment, when she had placed her hand on his knee, he had wanted to bury his head against her and weep. What a bloody fool he was; that's what he should have done. He rose to his feet and hurried up the garden, but Alice was nowhere in sight.

Outside the door, he noticed a rocking perambulator. Georgie! Seb stopped in his tracks and remembered the last night he had spent with Alice before going reluctantly to war. This son was the result of that frantic lovemaking. He was now curious to see how this one had turned out. His approach was cautious because the image of his older children's faces when they had seen his scars was still vivid in his mind.

He stood at the back of the perambulator and peeped over the hood. He caught sight of a mop of curling, dark hair and the tip of a nose and heard noises that sounded suspiciously like 'Da-da-da!'

Tears threatened to overcome him and he

struggled to empty his mind of fear as he had done in the trenches. 'Georgie,' he said quietly.

The mop of dark hair tilted and a pair of brown eyes flecked with green gazed up at him. Seb waited for a scream but when one was not forthcoming he looked down on his younger son again. Georgie was still gazing upwards. 'Bo-boo,' he said, then chuckled.

Seb felt an odd sensation inside his chest. 'Boo!' he managed to say.

His son seized hold of a blanket that he had kicked to the bottom of the perambulator and covered his face with it and then lowered it. 'Boo!'

Seb smiled. It seemed this son did not care what he looked like and appeared to be a friendly little chap, so he played the game and hid above the hood and then peeked out and said, 'Boo!'

They were still playing when Tilly came to the kitchen door. 'Will you bring him in, Seb? He probably needs his nappy changing,' she said casually, having watched the pair from the kitchen window. She went back inside.

Seb hesitated but, realising Tilly had resumed whatever she was doing, walked to the front of the perambulator and, for the first time, looked straight at his younger son. To his surprise, Georgie reacted by holding his arms up to him. Seb gazed at the straps constraining his son and remembered when this vehicle had held his other two children. He wanted to weep. He loved his older children so much but they had found him repulsive. This son had not.

Somehow he managed to unfasten the straps and lift his son out with one arm, but it wasn't easy, due to the lack of coordination between muscles and nerves and tendons in his right arm. The doc and physio had experimented with stretching nerves and transferring bits of this and that. He had difficulty in understanding the medical jargon.

Almost immediately Georgie wriggled to get down and, thankfully, Seb complied, terrified in case he dropped him. The toddler clutched his father's trouser leg and reached up to him with his other hand. Seb grasped the small, soft mitt and, with Georgie toddling at his side, walked towards the door. His heart was beating fast as they entered the kitchen because he was expecting and hoping to see his wife sitting at the table, but she was not there.

As Alice crossed the bridge she was aware of the sound of laughter coming from those trippers enjoying themselves boating on the river. Before the war, it had been a popular sight, but these days there were few young men dressed in white flannels and blazers, wearing boaters, and rowing their lady-loves. She wondered how many of those young men were alive today. Those who returned would be scarred, physically, mentally or emotionally. She grieved for all those who had lost loved ones and for the young women who would never know the joy of marriage. She had been so blessed, for she and Seb had shared so many joyful moments.

Thinking of how she had felt when he had laughed before, she was now horrified by her reaction. How could she have possibly thought he could be in any way like her father? It was she that was the mad one for even considering it for a moment. Seb had suffered and was still suffering, so it was no wonder if, for a short while, he had appeared a little crazy.

She had reached the far side of the Queen's Park bridge. She paused and considered whether she should return home. What must Seb have felt with her fleeing from him the way she had done? She gazed towards the Groves, where people were strolling beneath the trees, and unexpectedly remembered strolling beside the river with Bert in the days when she had believed, just like Bert's mother, that he was an ideal man. Hannah and Kenny had warned her that he had a nasty side to him but she had refused to listen and had paid for her mistake. He was one young man she was glad would never be returning home from the war.

After her experiences with Bert and her father, she had vowed never to get herself into a position where she was terrified of a man again. Yet here she was, going down that road, fearing her husband just because of the way he had laughed. She must not allow her fears from the past affect her relationship with Seb and spoil her marriage. She had changed so much since they first met. Marriage and motherhood had strengthened her. She had a good husband and fine children, and she knew she must go back and apologise to Seb for behaving so foolishly.

Yet having made that decision, she still lingered on the bridge for a few minutes longer, wishing the war had never been and that life could return to the way it had been in those happy days before the Germans marched into Belgium.

When Alice did return to the house, it was to find Seb in the drawing room, kneeling on the floor, watching Georgie build a tower with his wooden bricks. She stood in the doorway, thinking that already she felt differently about the scars on his face. Studying the damage to his cheek and his ruined eye, she no longer felt shocked, she just wanted to comfort him.

Suddenly he looked up. 'I'm sorry, love,' she said.

His smile was one of relief. 'It should be me apologising. I was wrong; Donald was right. I should have told you. But I looked worse than this a few months ago before they operated. I didn't want you seeing me and I didn't want you worrying.'

'I worried anyway. I knew from your letters that you were hiding something.'

'Women's intuition?' He cocked a dark eyebrow and looked her straight in the face before turning his head, so that he presented his undamaged profile towards her.

'No. The you I knew would have been longing to see me.'

'So you knew I wasn't the you that you knew?'

'That's a bit of a tongue twister.' She knelt beside him and kissed him. It was not a long kiss because Georgie butted his head against Alice, and when she drew back, he wriggled between them.

Seb ruffled his son's hair and said gruffly, 'He's a good boy.'

'He's more easygoing than the other two were at his age.' She hesitated, wanting to say to him that she needed him to look directly at her – that she would do what he said and get used to his face as it was now – but something held her back.

'He's got my curls, though there's a touch of red in his hair,' said Seb. 'James's hair is completely black like mine.' His voice was unsteady.

Alice said, 'I wrote to you about Georgie's hair after he was born and sent you a photograph.'

'I remember.' He sighed deeply and several moments passed before he added, 'Thinking of babies, it's great news about Hanny and Kenny. But I've forgotten when you said the baby is due.'

'December or January.' Alice hugged Georgie, so glad that he and Seb seemed to be getting along. 'It'll be good for them to have one of their own. They've made Tilly a substitute daughter and given her too much attention. She has an old head on her shoulders.'

'She's a bright girl. Hopefully Tilly's generation of women will have more opportunities to make life better for themselves...to be paid decent wages so that widows and single women can support themselves and have a say in how this country is run. We don't want another war.'

Alice agreed, then changed the subject. 'I suppose I'd best get a room ready for your friend, Mr Pierce.'

'Yes, do that,' said Seb, putting his good arm round Georgie as Alice rose to her feet. 'I don't know where I'd be without him.'

She gazed down at her husband. 'Tilly said he saved your life.'

Seb nodded. Alice waited a moment, wondering whether he would tell her more about what had happened to him, but all he said was, 'Ma wrote to me. Said that you'd written to her about my being found.'

A look of annoyance crossed Alice's face. 'I'm still waiting for a visit. The children ask about her and wonder why she doesn't come and see them.' She paused. 'Which reminds me...'

He looked up at her. 'Reminds you of what?'

'I had a letter from your cousin.'

Seb looked bemused. 'I don't have a cousin.'

Alice smiled. 'You do. Her name's Clara O'Toole and her father was your mother's brother. He was killed in the war. She wants to meet your mother. Apparently your grandmother is ailing and wants to make her peace with her daughter, Gertie.'

Seb's expression changed to one of disbelief. 'My Liverpool grandmother is still alive? Ma was convinced she was dead. How did this Clara get our address?'

'Joy gave it to her. Your cousin and grandmother attended one of those meetings Mrs Black held in a hall over in Liverpool.'

'How odd.' Seb got up from the floor and sat on the sofa. He drummed his fingers on one of its arms. 'How come they made the connection with me and Ma?'

'Jiggery-pokery, in my opinion. Your uncle was killed in the war and your grandmother wanted to get *in touch* with him,' said Alice disparagingly.

'And did she?' There was a hopeful expression in his face.

Alice rolled her eyes. 'I doubt it. Anyway, it turns out that Mrs Black saw a likeness to you and your mother in your cousin. Of course, she might have recognised your grandmother, come to that; Mrs

Black and your mother were friends when they were young, after all.'

Seb rubbed his face.

Silence.

'So what do you want to do? Do you want me to write back? Do you want to see your cousin? Should I give her your mother's address?'

He closed his eye. 'I need time to think about it. I've only just come home. As for Ma, she didn't have a good thing to say about her mother so I can't see her wanting to meet up with her again.'

Alice thought he looked exhausted. 'You're tired. Perhaps you should go to bed and rest.'

He nodded and said drowsily, 'I used to dream of being in bed with you. I never thought of it when I was awake, thought it would be unlucky to do so.'

'Well, you're back and everything's going to be fine,' said Alice, touching his damaged cheek.

He pressed her hand against his face a moment and then drew her to her feet. He glanced down at Georgie, who had resumed building a tower with his bricks. 'Will he be OK on his own for a short while?'

'I'll tell Tilly we're just going upstairs for a few minutes and for her to keep her eye on him.'

Seb hesitated. 'What about the other two?'

'Tilly will see to them.'

Seb nodded and the pair of them left the room.

* * *

Don settled himself in a pink-painted wicker chair, his painfully throbbing foot stretched out in front of him. He gazed at James and Flora, who were sitting on the bed. The boy held a protective arm about his sister's shoulders. Tilly had left the room a few minutes ago, after introducing him to the children as the man who had saved their daddy's life. Back home in the States, Don had several nieces and nephews but he'd never had to dredge up the right words in a situation like this before. But he believed in giving it to kids straight, so here goes, he thought.

'D'you love your daddy, kids?' he asked. It was a relief that they barely hesitated before nodding. 'Then you'd rather have him alive than dead?'

They nodded again. But this time Flora accompanied her nod with the words, 'Mummy worried about him being dead when he was missing but she said, "We mustn't give up hope."'

'And you didn't,' he said.

Her pretty little face looked pensive. 'I tried not to, but he seemed to be gone a long, long time. And there was a girl in school whose daddy has been missing for ages and he's still not been found.' Flora heaved a sigh and plucked at her navy blue skirt. 'Mummy cried when Daddy was found. I did, too.' Tears welled up in her eyes.

James cleared his throat. 'That's because they were happy, Mr Pierce,' he explained in a strained voice. 'I didn't cry. I just wanted him to come home. I wanted to see for myself that he was really alive and...' He stopped abruptly, a muscle in his throat constricting.

Don was tempted to reach out a hand and pat the boy and tell him to take it easy, but instead he said, 'If you'd seen your daddy then, his face would have been swathed in bandages and you wouldn't have recognised him at all. Your daddy's a hero, you know. When I found him he was in an even worse mess from his fighting with the enemy. He was half buried and covered in dirt and...' Don shook his head. 'You don't really want to hear about that but let me tell you, kids, that your daddy is gonna need your help now he is home.'

'We want to help him,' put in Flora hastily, leaning towards Don.

'Good.' He smiled. 'I know the way he looks might have frightened you...'

'I wasn't frightened exactly,' said James hesitantly, 'But...' He bit down on his lip.

'Excellent! Good man!' said Don bracingly, patting the boy's shoulder. 'He might get bad-tempered at times, you know, but that'll be due to his being in pain – and, besides, he has lots to sort out now he's back home. At the moment he can't use his damaged arm, so you'll have to help him with little jobs about the house, James, until it improves.'

The boy nodded and squared his shoulders.

'What about Daddy's face, will that get better?' asked Flora, heaving a sigh. 'He was so handsome, my daddy.'

Don's heart sank and he said gravely, 'He'll always bear the scars, Flora, and he'll never get his sight back in that eye – but what you mustn't forget is that he's still your daddy and it's what we're like inside that's important. He's still a kind, thoughtful, brave and generous man. When he was away from you, he never stopped talking about you. He really missed you. Now he's back, you've got to behave yourselves and be good.' He gave them a rueful smile. 'Now I want you to promise that you'll do your darndest to do that.'

'We promise,' said James, his youthful face serious.

Flora nodded. Then she reached for her teddy bear and hugged it against her.

Don pushed himself out of the chair and limped from the room, knowing that the coming months were not going to be easy for the family. He really wished he could help them more, but knew it was out of his hands now.

CHAPTER SEVEN

November, 1918.

'Still no news of that daughter of mine. It was summer when you sent that letter,' wheezed Bernie, glancing up from the newspaper.

'So you said earlier, Gran,' said Clara, putting on her coat. She was disappointed that Seb's wife had not replied to her letter, but life had dealt her enough blows to know that things did not always go the way you wanted them to. 'I'm off to the picture house. I won't be late.'

'You be careful about breathing in any germs,' warned her grandmother. 'I don't want you dead yet. Neither do I want you bringing them home here.'

'I love you, too, Gran,' said Clara sarcastically. 'I've my scarf so I'll cover my nose and mouth with it.'

'What about my tonic? When are you going to get some more?'

'I'll get some when I have the chance. It gets dark early these evenings and the weather hasn't been good enough on Sundays for me to go traipsing off to Wirral.'

'Well, that tonic did me good. I might even give you sixpence towards the cost of it if yer feeling short.'

'Now there's an offer I can't resist,' said Clara dryly. 'I'll keep you to that.'

She left the house, thinking she would write to Mrs Black during the week. Keeping healthy was vital at the moment. She thought about Liverpool's medical officer, Dr Hope, recommending that places of entertainment be emptied between performances so that auditoriums could be ventilated. The idea was to get rid of any influenza germs that might linger in the air. Protecting children under fourteen was considered so important that they were not allowed in picture houses, theatres or music halls at all. She knew that if she was utterly sensible she would not risk going to the pictures, but she was in need of cheering up, so was meeting Jean outside the picture house on Daulby Street, near the city centre. Charlie Chaplin was starring and he was well worth watching, so most likely they would have to queue up. There was also an orchestra providing music and they would probably play several numbers before the film began.

Clara was annoyed for letting herself get miserable over Alice not getting in touch with her. It looked like the war was coming to an end. Just over a week ago, Turkey had surrendered and the armistice had been signed in Dardanelle and Bosporus. The news from France was also good. During the last few weeks, Britain and its Allies had advanced over a huge front and, only yesterday, America's President Wilson had told the German Armistice Party to apply to Marshall Foch of France, the Allied Supreme Commander, for peace terms. Today's news was that the Kaiser had abdicated because revolution had broken out in Berlin and in the German fleet. She hoped Freddie Kirk was still surviving.

Of course, when the guns fell silent at the Front, it meant that the demand for armaments would drop drastically. The munitions factories would close, and that would mean an end to a decent wage. How was she going to manage? She did have a few savings but her little nest egg would soon go if she had to keep delving into it. There would be other jobs, of course, but they wouldn't pay what she had become accustomed to and most likely she would need to find two jobs to manage. It wasn't going to be easy because there would be women who had lost their men folk needing work, as well as the men returned from the war and wanting their jobs back.

Realising that she was getting in a tizzy over the future, she pulled herself up short. She had come out to forget her worries, not to wallow in them. There were thousands worse off than her.

She arrived at the cinema to find Jean, already in the queue, saving a place for her. A one-legged man was playing an accordion and singing 'Keep the Home Fires Burning'. Clara dropped a penny in his cap, wondering how many more like him were trying to scrape a living throughout the length and breadth of the country. If only attitudes and laws could be changed to make provision for those suffering so badly. She thought of her cousin and wondered if he had left the hospital in the south yet. She hoped he was all right. She so wanted to meet him and her Aunt Gertie. Perhaps her letter had gone missing in the post and that was why she had not received a reply. Perhaps she should write again, but she did not want to appear a nuisance to them.

Clara enjoyed the film and the music, and she and Jean came out of the cinema singing. They were greeted by fog but it was not so dense that they could not see where they were going and it did not dampen their spirits. 'That was marvellous,' said Clara, linking arms with Jean. 'He really does make me laugh does Charlie...and he's one of our own.'

'That girl in the film, I wish I had her looks,' said Jean with a sigh. 'At least once we finish with

munitions our skin should improve. Although...'
She glanced at Clara. 'I think you must have a
magic potion because yours isn't as bad as mine.'

'I do have one actually,' said Clara, smiling. 'And
I've no idea what's in it. I've just about used it all
but I'll try and get some more and let you have
some.'

'Thanks,' said Jean, looking pleased.

'So, what job will you try for once we get the
push?' asked Clara.

'I'm not sure. I have heard a rumour that the
Government might give us some kind of severance
pay to tide us over until we find other jobs.'

Clara's brown eyes shone. 'Where d'you hear
these rumours? I hope it's true.'

'I keep me ears open. I wouldn't mind working in
another factory. The pay will probably beat that in
a shop or in service. Trouble is, it'll take some time
before the factories adapt to peace-time work.'

'I know what I'm going to do,' said Clara firmly.
'I'd like to work in a picture house. In the
Palladium, if I can.' She paused as they reached the
stop where Jean needed to catch the tram home.

'Good luck to yer,' said Jean. 'I'll see yer in work
on Monday.'

'Bye. Enjoy your Sunday.' Clara raised a hand in
farewell and then hurried in the direction of her
own tram, praying that the rumour Jean had heard
about severance pay was true. Hopefully it would

be enough to tide them over Christmas and she would not have to delve into her savings. But she was not going to say a word to her gran about it just yet.

It was after lunch on Sunday afternoon that Clara decided that, instead of writing to Alice, she would write to Joy. She would kill two birds with one stone by asking her whether she thought Mrs Black would let her have some more skin salve, a bottle of tonic and some cordial. She would pay for them, of course. Also, she would ask her whether Alice had received her letter and whether Freddie was safe. She posted the letter and prayed for a speedy reply.

But all thought of letters and tonics was forgotten the next morning when it became known that the Prime Minister had announced that the armistice had been signed. The workers were told they could have the day off and there was a rush to leave the factory.

The news spread like wildfire and flags were hoisted on buildings. As she hurried home, Clara could hear cheer after cheer breaking out and hundreds of people appeared on the streets carrying Union flags. In the shop windows in Breck Road, the flags of all the Allies were displayed. Ships' sirens on the Mersey cock-a-doodle-dooed and there was a part of Clara that wanted to dance and sing, but another part wanted to weep because her father was not there to celebrate the peace with her.

When Clara arrived home, Bernie was standing in the doorway, wearing a coat and hat and with a scarf about her neck. 'I wondered if yer'd be home early. I thought we might go down to the pub,' she said.

'The pub,' echoed Clara.

'Yeah,' said Bernie, her eyes bright. 'I thought yer might like to treat me to a celebratory drink.'

'Now, if you were paying, Gran, I might agree,' said Clara with a faint smile. 'Right now, I'd like a cup of hot tea.'

Bernie's face fell. 'Tea?'

'You heard me. And later maybe there'll be some dancing in the street.' She pushed past her grandmother, aware of her cursing her under her breath, and questioned why, if her gran cared so much about *her Denny*, the old woman felt in a mood to celebrate.

The celebrations in their street were subdued. Too many people had lost loved ones for them to go wild with joy and excitement. Besides, November was not the best of months to spend hours outside in gay abandon and many were wondering what the future would hold for them after four years of war. Clara could not prevent her thoughts straying to those related to her on the other side of the Mersey.

* * *

'Have you heard the news? The headlines are up on the newspaper stands,' said Kenny, limping into Alice's sitting room. 'The armistice has been signed. The fighting's over and the Allies are victorious.' He put his arms round his half-sister and held her tight.

Seb stared at them both as if in a daze and sat down heavily on the sofa. He clutched his damaged arm and thought of his dead comrades. He still could not get the screams of the wounded and dying, the roar of the guns and the *thud, thud* of the shells, the smell of death and cordite all around him, out of his head.

He blundered to his feet, knowing he had to get out of the room. As he hurried towards the front door he heard Alice calling him but he ignored her and ran until he reached Queen's Park bridge. He stopped in the middle and gazed down at the grey waters, aware of a tightness about his skull. The headaches were not as bad as they were in the beginning, but lately they had grown worse. He guessed it was due to his continuous worry about his useless arm. Seb thought about the orthopaedic surgeon he had seen recently. His prognosis had not been good; he had said that, without the full use of nerve and muscle, the arm would be nothing more than a dead weight in the end. Perhaps if there was no improvement in the months that followed, he should consider amputation.

Seb had been horrified and refused point blank to

consider the idea. The doctor had looked at him with a weary, sympathetic expression and asked him to give it some thought. Seb had not mentioned the conversation to Alice. He considered it was difficult enough for her having to look at his ugly mug all the time without having to accept his having only one arm. He slammed his fist against the metal ledge of the bridge and swore long and hard. Then suddenly he became aware of cheers and someone calling his name.

'Sebby-boy!' A hand clapped him on the shoulder.

He looked up in amazement into the moustachioed face of Donald Pierce. 'What are you doing here? I thought you were back in France,' said Seb.

'I was. But the old foot has been giving me gyp, so I was sent over to London. I saw some quack there who suggested maybe it's time I went home.'

Seb noticed he was using a walking stick. 'I saw a doc last week and he thinks I should have my arm off,' said Seb. He had not meant to tell anyone that just yet and could have bitten off his tongue.

Donald's expression altered, became angry. He put his arm about Seb. 'I hope you told him to go to hell. I did to my quack. Never told you several little bones were crushed in my foot, did I? Bugger to fix and hellishly painful. The quack said I'd be better off without the foot.'

Seb swore. 'I suppose you told him you'd soldier on.'

Donald's eyes lit up. 'I wish I'd thought of those exact words. Anyhow, I thought I'd come and see how you were doing before I set sail for New York. I'm leaving from Liverpool in a couple of days.'

Seb noticed he was carrying a suitcase. 'That's good of you. You'll stay with us tonight?'

'I was hoping you'd ask.' He hugged Seb against him and together they made their way across the bridge, discussing the news of the armistice as they went.

On reaching the end of the bridge, they were met by a pale-faced Alice. After a swift, intense look at Seb, she turned her attention to the American. 'Mr Pierce. What a surprise!'

'It's great to see you, Mrs Bennett, and looking so lovely,' he said gallantly.

She fought down a blush. 'It's nice of you to say so. Will you be staying with us?'

'Of course he's staying with us,' said Seb, reaching out a hand and clasping hers. 'Is Kenny still at the house? I'd like him to meet Don.'

She nodded. 'He's talking to Tilly. The children have been sent home. They want to put up a Union flag in the window.'

'Why not? Between us we should manage it.'

Alice looked relieved. 'Let's celebrate. I've managed to get my hands on some whisky and sherry.'

He glanced at Donald. 'I bet you're ready for a wee dram?'

The American grinned. 'Surprised you needed to ask.' Arm in arm, they hurried up the crescent.

Tilly and Alice decided to serve a buffet meal in the drawing room. James, aided by his father, managed to hang the Union flag up in the dining room window, while Flora fussed around, telling them to move it when it was crooked and at last when it hung straight. Seb patted his son on the back and thanked them both. They wandered into the kitchen, pleased with themselves.

Meanwhile, Kenny and Donald appeared to have found a common interest in journalism. Tilly wished she could have listened in on their conversation instead of helping Alice. After what her brother had told her about Seb rushing out of the house, it was a relief to see him and Alice seemingly on good terms with each other again. The atmosphere in the house had been strained since Seb's return two months ago, and she worried about the pair of them. Now, with the armistice signed, she had high hopes of life getting back to some semblance of normality and resuming her writing.

She was in the process of carrying in a tray of sausage rolls, meat pies, cake, sandwiches and scones when Donald came out of the sitting room.

'Can I help you with that?' he asked.

'No thanks. But perhaps you can help Seb with the drinks. He's still having trouble with his arm. Alice is making a pot of tea for those of us who aren't allowed alcohol.'

'Your brother was telling me about your writing.'

She laughed. 'I'm only a beginner.' She couldn't think what else to say, unable to boast of having even one letter to the editor published. She wondered if he was famous in America for his work in photojournalism.

'If you stick at it, kid, one day you'll get there,' he said. 'What is it you're wanting to write?'

'Books, eventually, but I need more experience of life. I'd like to travel.'

He smiled. 'Where to?'

'London, Paris, Venice.' Her eyes sparkled. 'Of course, I'll need to make some money first.'

'What about the United States?'

She pursed her lips. 'Never thought of going that far.'

'I'll be going back home in a couple of days. I'll send you some pictures.'

She was surprised by how dismayed she felt at the news. 'Will you ever come back here again?'

'Maybe, but I've things to sort out at home before I can think of going travelling again.'

'But what about your work?'

'I'm sure I'll find something to photograph at home.' His eyes twinkled down at her. 'I'd like to take a shot of you before I go. Show my mom and sisters what pretty girls they grow in England.'

'There's prettier girls than me,' said Tilly, flattered none the less.

'You're the one I reckon is photogenic. I might even get your picture in a magazine.'

She shook her head at him, not knowing whether he was serious or teasing her. He appeared to her to be so sophisticated that suddenly she longed for the plain-speaking familiarity of Freddie. 'I don't know why you should bother,' she said. 'We hardly know each other and you're so much older than me.'

He winced. 'Ouch! Only by nine years. By the time you're twenty-one the difference in our ages won't matter.'

She thought, he can't be serious. 'This is a daft conversation,' she muttered. 'I've loads to do before I settle down.'

His smile deepened. 'Sure you have, but just to make sure you don't forget me, I'll write a long letter and send you some pictures of my home town.'

Tilly did not know how to answer that so she just nodded and hurried to place the contents of her tray on a large occasional table set between two chintz covered sofas near the fireplace. How could she possibly take the American seriously? Words were cheap and he would soon forget her once he arrived back in his own country. If she was to marry in a few years' time, Freddie really was a much safer bet.

Her heart lifted at the thought that now the war was over it shouldn't be too long before he was home. Perhaps in the new year, before Hanny's baby was born. Births, marriages, deaths, all were important life experiences, she mused.

'You look like you've gone off into a dream,' said a voice nearby.

Tilly turned and saw Hanny. 'I was just thinking of you.'

'Something nice, I hope.' Hanny glanced round the room and her blue eyes rested on her brother-in-law, 'So how do you think Seb is doing now?'

'Hopefully now the armistice has been signed we'll start getting back to normal, but I wouldn't count on it. Things still aren't right with them. I think he's really worried about his arm. Sometimes I hear them arguing during the night,' she whispered.

Hanny nodded. 'I know, it must be terribly difficult for them both. By the way, do you know if Alice has answered Clara O'Toole's letter yet? I wrote to Freddie about her wanting to get in touch with Seb. They met, you know.'

'Did they?' Why did that knowledge irritate her?

'Alice should have answered that letter by now, even if Seb doesn't want to meet her. It's not fair to leave her on pins. After all, the poor girl is related to Seb and has lost her father. I know Alice has a lot on her plate but she's not the only one with troubles.'

Tilly said, 'Perhaps I will mention it to Alice, but not today.'

At that moment a tiny bell drew their attention. They looked in the direction of the sound and saw Seb standing in the middle of the room. 'A toast and then we can eat.' He raised his glass. 'To the valiant dead and to peace.'

All echoed his words.

After that they ate and the conversation became more general, but Tilly did not forget what Donald Pierce had said, or Hanny's words about Seb's cousin. She supposed Joy was the proper person to speak to about the girl. She wondered how old she was and what she did for a living. Perhaps she would ask Joy the next time she visited Hanny.

CHAPTER EIGHT

Clara stood in the queue at the Women's Employment Exchange in Upper Newington Street, her shoulders hunched up against the cold. A light drizzle was falling and she wished herself anywhere other than where she was right then. She had gone in search of a job at the Palladium picture house, but it was closed due to the influenza epidemic. Thankfully, Jean had been right about the rumours of severance pay, and Clara had a sum of money tucked away in a box under the floorboards with the rest of her tiny savings. If she had difficulty getting the right job, then at least she and her gran were not going to lose the roof over their heads or starve for a while.

Feeling flush for a change, Clara had just over a pound or so burning a hole in her pocket, which she planned on spending later. At the moment she was waiting to fill in forms to register with the Women's Employment Exchange as available for work. The trouble was that a lack of stationery was causing frustration to all involved. Half an hour ago word had gone round that this building was just not big enough to cope with the number of women now unemployed, so the Liverpool Scottish Drill Hall in Fraser Street was being turned into a new centre, but that didn't help those waiting as it wasn't ready yet.

Perhaps she should have told her gran that she had a lump sum put by then she would not have insisted on her getting out of the house and finding herself another job almost immediately she was out of work. Having said that, her gran was being so difficult at the moment that Clara preferred facing the miserable weather to remaining in the house with her. She just wished that Joy would reply to her letter soon. At least then she would know whether or not to give up hope where her relatives across the Mersey were concerned.

Clara stamped her feet in an attempt to warm them, thinking of all that had happened since the armistice had been signed. Within days of that longed-for event, the King's Fund for the Disabled Officers and Men of Navy, Army and Air Forces had launched Gratitude Week. At least something was being done for all those poor men whose lives had been ruined by the war. She thought of her cousin and hoped he would benefit. Trouble was, it wasn't the Government who were being asked to fork over money but the ordinary people who were being urged *to give as they gave for you*. As if they hadn't already given enough for the war effort. She had given something but she could not keep doing that. She hoped that now the coalition government had been disbanded, the party that would be voted in would be one that would help the poor and needy. If she had the vote, she knew which party she would vote for: The Labour Party.

Clara was roused from her reverie by a woman behind her saying, 'This is a bloody mug's game, this. What's the bloody point of queuing up in the rain when there's hardly any jobs available?'

'But we'll only have to queue up again if we leave the queue now,' said another next to Clara, who was wearing an old-fashioned, huge brimmed hat with a bedraggled feather in it. 'We need to get our name down if we want the out-of-work donation from the Government.'

'Well, I don't mind coming back tomorrow,' said the first woman. 'It mightn't be raining then, and today TJ Hughes are selling ladies woven combinations for three shillings and eleven pence, halfpenny. I could do with some of them.'

Clara had seen the advertisement and decided she needed some new underwear for the winter, too. That's why she had a pound on her. She made a decision. 'I'll come with you, if you like. I'm freezing in my summer underwear and they could all be sold out by tomorrow.'

'That's the ticket,' said the first woman, grinning at her. 'We could walk along together.'

With their heads lowered against the rain, they hurried in the direction of Lime Street, discussing what else they would like to buy if only they could spare the money. When they reached TJ Hughes, they had to queue up again and, once inside, there was a bit a scrum. Fortunately, Clara managed to get her hands on a set of combinations and also had enough money over to buy herself a pair of winter gloves. Pleased with her purchases, she also treated herself to a cup of cocoa and a bun in a Lyon's café to kill time, knowing that if she arrived home too early, her gran would have something to say to her about quitting her search for a job too easily.

The rain had stopped by the time Clara arrived home to be greeted by a smiling Bernie, toasting her toes in front of the fire. 'There yer are, duck,' she said, turning her head as her granddaughter came through the door. 'A parcel's come for yer. I opened it. I didn't think yer'd mind.'

'You opened something addressed to me!' said Clara indignantly. 'You had no right.'

Bernie's expression altered. 'Don't you give me cheek, girl. I had every right. It contained my tonic.' She produced a bottle from the other side of her chair. 'I didn't open the letter, though. That's on the mantelpiece.' Her eyes narrowed. 'I've discovered something while yous were out, girl. Yer've been keeping something from me.' She tapped the newspaper on her knee. 'It says here, those working in munitions received severance pay. Been spending it, have yer?' She nodded her head in the direction of the bag Clara carried. 'Treated yerself, have yer?'

Clara's annoyance spiralled. 'If I have, it's none of your business. I bought badly needed underwear. I more than pay my wack in this house. Now I'm going to read my letter.' She placed her shopping on the table and snatched up the envelope from the mantelshelf.

'There's no need to get in a twist. I'd just like yer to be honest with me. I wouldn't have been worrying about Christmas if I'd known about yer severance pay,' said Bernie in milder tones. 'By the way, there was a couple of bottles of your cordial and a jar of ointment in the box, as well.'

That news pleased Clara but right then she was desperate to know whether it was Joy or Mrs Black who had written to her.

Dear Clara,

I was so glad to receive your letter. Mrs Black was pleased to hear that your grandmother is benefiting from her tonic and also that your complexion is much improved. She is pleased to send you – just this once – replacements for the medicines you have used. She requires no payment for these as she feels certain that now the war is over, you will soon have no need for the ointment. As for Mrs O' Toole, if she gets through the winter then it will prove that she is much stronger than we all thought and won't need another tonic.

Now on to the next matter of importance. I am assured that Alice did receive your letter. Seb is now home but life is not easy for him at the moment due to the injuries he received. I would suggest that you write to him and Alice once he's had time to adjust to his new circumstances. Perhaps in the new year?

With my very best wishes,

Joy Kirk.

P.S. Freddie is fine but still not home.

Clara had trouble concealing her disappointment that her cousin did not wish to get in touch with her just yet. She felt deeply sorry for him with his injuries, whatever they were. She wished she could help but what could she do? She noticed there was no mention of Gertie, so could only assume they had not been in touch with her.

'Well, what does the letter say?' demanded Bernie. 'Any news of Gertie?'

Clara shook her head. 'It looks like we'll have to carry on playing a waiting game, Gran, and get on with life as we know it for now.'

Bernie's face fell. 'But how long do I wait, girl? At

my age and with my chest, I don't know how long I've got. I'd like to see me daughter again, and what about me grandson and his kids?'

'He's home, but life's not easy for him because of his injuries. I'll write again in the new year, don't you worry. Perhaps then we'll get a positive reply.'

Bernie removed the cork from the bottle of tonic and took a large swig. 'Pigs might fly, girl. You can carry on hoping but I have to accept that my daughter and grandson don't want to know me, or you. They think themselves too good for us. Yer a dreamer if yer think things will change. Snobby, that's what they are.'

Perhaps they were, thought Clara. She had no way of knowing without meeting them. Even so, she wished them well and hoped that one day they would change their minds and she could get to know them. She believed it was what her dad would have wanted.

CHAPTER NINE

Alice clenched her fists and curled her toes as Seb ground his teeth in his sleep again. She found it intensely disturbing, but at least it was better than his crying out men's names and then starting awake and seeming not to know where he was. In those first weeks, he had allowed her to put her arms round him and comfort him, but more recently, he had told her to leave him alone and left their bed and went downstairs when he woke in the night. She guessed he had a lot on his mind and wished that he would share his thoughts with her. She believed only then would she be able to be honest with him about her fears for their future.

He sat up suddenly, causing her to almost jump out of her skin. 'What is it?' she asked.

'You're bloody doing it again,' he rasped.

'Doing what?' Alice turned over and could just about make out his face in the dim light coming through a gap in the curtains.

His features twisted into a snarl. 'Lying there listening to me. Are you waiting for me to draw my last breath? Wishing I was bloody dead.'

'Of course not,' she said, aghast. 'If you want to know the truth, you grind your teeth in your sleep.'

'I what?'

'Grind your teeth. It keeps me awake.'

'Well, excuse me if I should keep your bloody ladyship awake. I'll remove myself from your presence. You can have the bed to yourself.' He threw back the bedcovers and slid out of bed.

Alice was horrified by his tone. 'Don't talk to me like that. You know I didn't mean it like that.' There was a tremor in her voice because suddenly she was reminded of her father speaking in that harsh way to her mother. In her mind's eye, she could see his hand coming up and she could even hear the smack.

'Are you sure?' He lowered his head and pressed the scarred side of his face against her smooth cheek. She did not answer, scared of saying the wrong words. He straightened up. 'Enough bloody said,' he muttered and left the bedroom.

She felt cold with the fear of what Seb was becoming. Her father had once been kind and loving, speaking in a caring way to her mother and herself. He had taken them out on Sundays, and they had had happy times as a family. Yet she had always been aware that Kenny was never relaxed in his presence. Life had changed as her father gradually became more violent. Of course, there were times when he was almost normal, but then had come those dreadful days just before her mother died, giving premature birth to Tilly after a beating.

Suddenly, her ears caught the sound of the squeaking of a bolt downstairs and she sat up. What was that? She left the bed and padded across the cold linoleum in her bare feet. Drawing back a curtain, she gazed down onto the crescent and her heart seemed to leap into her mouth when she saw Seb, still dressed in his pyjamas, opening the front gate. Where was he going? He would catch his death of cold. Only for a second did she hesitate. Then she realised, with mounting horror, that he was heading in the direction of the river.

Quickly, she found her slippers and put them on and went downstairs. Taking her coat from the hall stand, she put it on over her nightgown and, leaving the front door on the latch, hurried out into the night. He was already out of sight and Alice did not want to put a name to the different fear she felt now. What could he be thinking of, leaving the house in his pyjamas? Now she ran, slipping and sliding on the icy path that led to the footbridge.

She found him standing in the middle of the bridge, shivering and clutching his right arm as he gazed down at the black silky water. 'You're mad,' she said.

He clenched his teeth. 'I'm perfectly sane. Go back home, Alice.'

'No. I'm not going anywhere without you. Let's go home.' She went to put an arm round him but he shook her off.

'I'm no bloody use to you or the children,' he said savagely. 'It would have been better if I'd died in the trenches with the rest of them.'

'That's a stupid thing to say.' Her voice was shrill with anger and fear. 'What would the children think? That their daddy was a coward who couldn't cope with being alive? Who didn't care about them?'

He flinched. 'Go on. Stick the knife in. Say what you're bloody really thinking! Well, you're wrong. There'll be no dramatic exit with me jumping off the middle of the bridge. You tell me how I can do it when I can't get the leverage with my bloody arm.'

She was silent, relieved that he did sound sane.

'There you are, that proves I'm thinking straight,' he said.

'OK. It does. Now let's go home before the pair of us catch our deaths of cold.' She reached out a hand and, for a moment she thought he was going to ignore it, but then he gripped it tight. She knew that for now they were both safe, but for how long? she wondered.

* * *

'Have you read this?'

'What?' asked Alice, lifting her eyes from her sewing and gazing at Hanny, who had dropped by to ask what she was planning for Christmas and Boxing Day. Having decided that they would gather at Alice's for the big day, Hanny was reading the newspaper.

'"Changes in the aims of the suffragette movement have caused a widening gap in its membership as well as the Pankhurst family,"' read out Hanny. '"The WSPU has become the Women's Party, with Mrs Pankhurst and her daughter Christabel standing for opposition to Home Rule for Ireland and the abolition of the Trade Unions."' She frowned. 'It's all right for them now that they've got the vote. What about working-class women and those under thirty?'

'I don't know how you can take an interest in that now you're so close to your confinement,' said Alice, with a yawn. She recalled the happy days after the birth of her first two children, when she and Seb had looked towards the future, confident that all would go well for them.

'Because it interests me and should be of interest to you, too, Alice,' said Hanny firmly. 'This country wouldn't have won the war without women taking over so many of the men's jobs on the home front.' She lowered her eyes to the newspaper again. 'At least her other daughters, Sylvia and Adela, considered that suffrage is a class struggle. And it's partly thanks to them and others like them that Lloyd George gave the vote to working-class men.' She stared at Alice with a concerned expression. 'You used to care about these things when we were younger. If I had the vote I'd be voting for the Labour Party on the 14th. We've both been poor and know what it's like to struggle to make ends meet.'

'Still do,' murmured Alice, not looking at her.

'I know it's not easy even now. We'd both like more money. Especially with the baby coming and mother to care for. But we're fortunate to have decent roofs over our heads and food in our stomachs. Labour says that the housing of the people is a task for the nation to solve and that there should be no going back to low wages for the working classes.'

Alice put down her sewing and placed a log on the fire. It was one from a tree that Kenny had cut down due to the warning that there would be a shortage of coal that winter. 'They're not the only party who believe that. Lloyd George's Liberal Party feels the same. He said in his opening speech that it was the Government's task to make Britain a country fit for heroes.'

'I read that,' said Hanny, smiling because she had got Alice interested in something outside herself.

'He also said that, where jobs are concerned, he

thinks that a return to the land is called for and that agriculture is important as a basis for industrial policy.'

Hanny's blue eyes brightened. 'I suppose you remembered that because of Seb's mother being down on the farm?'

Alice shrugged. 'I pointed it out to Seb because I thought he might be interested. It roused him enough to agree that we should be producing more of our own food instead of depending on the colonies and the United States. He said that the U-boats wouldn't have had such a devastating effect during the war if we had done so.'

'So what's Seb going to do about work?' asked Hanny, dropping the newspaper on the occasional table and placing a hand on her swollen belly. 'Kenny hoped he would have taken an interest in the company by now. Business is bound to improve when the country gears itself up for peace work.'

Alice resumed her darning. 'Seb says he's not ready yet. That he's too tired and has too much on his mind.' She hesitated. 'It's true that he doesn't sleep well, and neither do I. He grinds his teeth when he does manage to doze off. When he first came home, he would shout out men's names in his sleep and then start awake. Sometimes he didn't seem to know where he was, even when I spoke to him. Eventually, when he did realise he was in our bedroom, he'd get up and go downstairs. I'd fall asleep and wake when he came back to bed just before dawn. He's resting upstairs now.'

'No wonder you both look worn out,' said Hanny sympathetically.

Alice dropped her needle and said in a rush, 'It's got worse lately. We had a disagreement and he got up and then I heard the door opening downstairs. I followed him out and found him on the bridge in his pyjamas.'

Hanny stared at her in dismay. 'You don't mean...'

Alice nodded. 'I was that scared I didn't even bother getting dressed. I told him to come home. Put my arms around him but he-he pushed me away and swore at me. He thinks me and the kids would be better off without him, that he should have died in the trenches.'

'Poor Seb and poor you,' said Hanny, distressed. She reached out and covered her friend's hand. 'But I'm sure he's not alone amongst the survivors in feeling guilty because he's alive when so many were killed.'

'I think it's more than that but he won't talk to me. I don't know what to do to make things better for him,' murmured Alice. 'I only know that I can't go on like this much longer. I hate to say it, but he scares me sometimes. I keep thinking of Dad. You know what he was like.'

Hanny shook her head in disbelief. 'You can't really believe that Seb would beat you? Let's look at this practically, he can hardly use his right arm.'

'I know. I'm not being logical,' she admitted, getting up and going over to the drinks' cupboard. 'Sherry?'

'No. It's too early in the day for me.' Hanny looked at her with concern. 'I wish I could help you.'

Alice came back over to the fireplace empty-handed. 'You do help me,' she said, smiling faintly. 'Just knowing you're a couple of doors away is a comfort. If things get really desperate, I know I can run to you and Kenny.'

'That's what family and friends are for, love,' said Hanny, her voice uneven. 'You mustn't think twice about dropping in at ours. Don't wait until you're desperate. That goes for Seb, too.'

Alice was near to tears and could only nod wordlessly. 'I just wish he'd talk to me more about how he's feeling.'

'Perhaps he could talk to Kenny.' As soon as the words were out Hanny contradicted herself. 'No. I've come to realise lately that he's not the right person. He wasn't there at the Front. If Freddie was here…'

'Freddie!' exclaimed Alice. 'How could he help? He's too young and he wasn't there either.'

Immediately Hanny sprang to her brother's defence. 'His ship was torpedoed and he's seen men die. He almost lost his life! I think Freddie can be of help to him.'

Alice was not convinced. 'He's a good lad, I'm not disputing it, but all things considered, he's not here, is he?'

'But it shouldn't be too long before he is home,' said Hanny brightly. 'In the meantime, Alice, keep your chin up. I'm sure things will come right in the end.' She stood up and kissed her sister-in-law on the cheek. 'I'd best be going. Mother will be wondering what's happened to me. I only meant to be out for half an hour.'

Alice followed Hanny into the hall and helped her on with her coat. 'I'll see you soon.'

Hanny nodded, and was almost out of the door when she stopped. 'By the way, did you ever get round to answering that letter you had from Seb's cousin?'

Alice shook her head. 'I can't even remember where I put it now.'

'Pity. Joy said she's a nice sort.' Hanny smiled. 'I suppose if she's really keen to meet up with Seb and his mother then she'll be in touch again. Trouble is, his grandmother is not getting any younger. That's if she's still alive.'

Alice could only agree. She watched Hanny walk carefully down the drive and then closed the door.

If she could have remembered where she had put the letter then perhaps she might have answered it. She knew from experience that it was extremely frustrating waiting for someone to tell you what you long to know.

CHAPTER TEN

Clara was thinking about Seb and Gertie as she passed the Olympia theatre on West Derby Road. The billboards were advertising *Jack and the Beanstalk,* due to open on the 2nd of January. She thought of Gertie having had a career on the stage and knew she would have enjoyed listening to her talk about it. She was determined not to give up her attempt to reunite her aunt and grandmother but in the meantime, it was more important that she found a job. She was on her way now to see whether the Palladium picture house had reopened.

When she reached the building, she was pleased to see a notice declaring that the picture house would be reopening soon and that there was a vacancy for a cashier. She felt certain that she was capable of such a job. She had always received top marks in arithmetic and she had her references in her handbag. She tried the door and to her delight it opened beneath her hand. A woman was washing the floor, so Clara hurried over and asked where could she find the manager.

The woman paused to wring out a floor cloth. 'Mr Walsh is standing in for Mr Eaton at the moment. You'll find him in the office. D'yer want me to show yer where it is?'

Clara thanked her and was pointed in the right direction. On the office door there was a notice saying 'Samuel Eaton, manager'. She remembered the name and that the managing director was Don Ellis, famous for producing variety acts. She wondered if there were to be more of them now that the war was over and the troops would be coming home.

She knocked on the door and a voice called, 'Come in.'

She went inside.

Behind a desk sat a jolly looking middle-aged man with rosy cheeks and pale blue eyes. He was wearing a pinstriped suit. 'Hello, love. What can I do for you?' he asked.

'I've come about the job,' blurted out Clara. 'I've always wanted to work here since it opened, but first I was too young and then I went into munitions for the war effort.'

He smiled. 'I like enthusiasm. Sadly, the last cashier died of the flu. How's your arithmetic and have you any references with you?'

'I can add up and make columns balance if that's what you need,' said Clara, thinking modesty would get her nowhere. She produced a brown envelope from her handbag and placed it on his desk. He stretched out a hand for it but at that moment the telephone rang.

'Excuse me,' he said, picking up the earpiece.

As a conversation ensued, she stepped back, not wanting to appear as if she was listening. He looked up at her and said, 'Leave your references, love, and come back later.'

She thanked him and walked out, wondering how long she should wait before returning. Perhaps she should walk home, have a bit of lunch and see how her gran was doing. It should only take her an hour or so. Having made the decision, she left the picture house and crossed the road. Passing St Michael's church, she eventually turned into Boundary Lane and decided to buy a portion of chips from the wet fish shop to save her cooking lunch. When she arrived home, it was to find Bernie dozing in front of the fire. Sometimes it seemed to Clara that her grandmother had become even more lazy recently and, like a cat, spent most of her time in front of the fire, half asleep.

She shook her shoulder and Bernie woke up. Almost immediately she sniffed and said, 'Something smells good.'

'It's only chips. I thought we could have some on butties before I have to go back.'

'Back where?' wheezed Bernie, chomping on her gums. One of her few remaining rotting teeth had recently dropped out.

'To the Palladium. It's reopening and they're advertising for a cashier.' Clara could not conceal her excitement. 'I went in and left my references with the temporary manager. I've to go back soon and see whether he'll take me on.'

Bernie's face brightened. 'That's good news. But yer won't be earning the money you did in munitions,' she added, watching Clara take a loaf from the bread crock.

'Tell me something I don't know, Gran,' said Clara with an edge to her voice. She put on the kettle then sliced the loaf and spread margarine on it before dividing the chips.

'Yer'll have to get another job or we won't be able to pay the rent.'

'I've enough money if we're sensible,' said Clara, who had stopped giving her gran money and had started to do most of the paying out herself. 'A roof over our head, burial insurance, and then food and warmth. You won't be able to have the fire on all day in the new year. You'll have to let it go out and put on extra clothes.'

'Bloody hell, girl. D'yer want me to freeze to death?'

'Wrap up and get your legs going. Walk to the nearest library. Don't buy a newspaper. It will be warm inside the library and you can read theirs for free.'

Bernie glared at her. 'I see that it's me that's got to give up me comforts. Yous'll be nice and warm in the picture house.'

'Not in the cash box I won't,' said Clara promptly. She handed her gran a chip butty and took a bite out of her own.

Bernie was silent for a while then suddenly she said, 'If I'm going to die of the cold, you'd best try and get in touch with that grandson of mine again. With it being Christmas soon he might take pity on me and send me greetings and a couple of bob if yer tell him how hard up we are.'

Clara was scandalised. 'I'm not telling him any such thing. He has a family. I'm not having him think that I only want to get to know him for a handout. Besides, we can manage if we're careful.'

Bernie looked sulky. 'More fool you. What are families for if not to help each other?'

'You can say what you like, Gran. I'd rather have three jobs than go begging to them for money. I want to hear no more about it.' Clara picked up her handbag and marched out of the house.

When she reached the Palladium, she saw Mr Walsh in the foyer, talking to another man. She knew better than to interrupt their conversation, so went over to study the posters of forthcoming attractions. She read the descriptions of the exciting adventures and passionate love stories in store for the dedicated flicker-goers wishing to escape their humdrum lives for a short while. Such was the hold that film was having on folk that the Church had begun to speak out against it.

At last the two men's conversation came to an end and the other man left the premises. She hurried over to Mr Walsh. 'You told me to come back. I left my references with you,' she said.

'Ah, Miss O'Toole.' He beamed at her. 'I see you live quite locally and your schoolmistress and former employers both stress your honesty and ability to learn from instruction. We've decided to give you a trial period. We have our grand reopening on New Year's Day. I expect to see you here at ten o'clock on the twenty-ninth of this month, when my wife Miranda will show you the ropes. Your wages will be eighteen shillings and sixpence a week. Free cinema tickets for close family members and one Saturday off a month. So, see you on the twenty-ninth. Happy Christmas.'

'It will be now,' she replied with a smile. The wages were far below those she had earned in munitions but she had not expected any different. She strolled outside and did some shopping in West Derby Road before heading for home.

'So did you get the job?' asked Bernie as soon as Clara entered the house.

'I did. Although, it's nowhere near the same wages I earned in munitions, but the work will be more interesting and easier.' She began to unpack the shopping. 'I thought we could have a rabbit for Christmas, a bun loaf and a decent fire.'

'What about my whisky?'

Clara gave her a look. 'If you want whisky you're going to have to fork out for it yourself.'

Bernie sighed. 'I thought yer might have softened now yer've got the job. I've no tonic left, yer know.'

Clara knew it and that it's lack was making Bernie grumpy. But the old woman was crafty and would nag if she thought Clara would weaken. She had to steel herself against her gran's self-pitying words or her insults. 'I'm sorry about that but you should have made it last. Mrs Black said there would be no more.'

'What about a bar of chocolate for Christmas?'

Clara smiled to herself at her grandmother's refusal to give up. 'OK. Chocolate and a bottle of port.'

'Oh happy day!' said Bernie sourly. 'Yer'll have me dead before I get a chance to ask for Gertie's forgiveness and go cleansed to me grave.'

'I tell you what, Gran, I'll send a Christmas card to wish my cousin and his family all the best for the festive season and the new year. Perhaps I should tell them that you're at death's door. Who knows, they might just show it to Gertie and she'll come running so she can dance on your grave.'

'You do that,' said Bernie. 'It just might do the trick.'

CHAPTER ELEVEN

On her way out of the house, Alice almost trod on the post that had just been pushed through the letterbox. It was Christmas Eve and ten minutes ago Tilly had come flying into the kitchen with the news that Hanny had gone into labour. She picked up the envelopes and placed them on a chair in the hall before rushing out of the house. Tilly had told her that Kenny was in a flap, waiting for the doctor and midwife to arrive. He wanted his half-sister to keep Hanny calm. Alice hadn't had time to go up into the attic to let Seb know what she was doing, but had left the children in Tilly's care.

Still wearing her apron, Alice hurried down the drive, praying that all would be well with Hanny. Her mind went back to the time the pair of them had sat on the Kirks' outside lavatory roof in Francis Street, listening to the screams of her mother in labour in the house across the entry when Tilly had been born and her mother had died. It was a day that Alice and Hanny would never forget, and she suspected that her sister-in-law and closest friend would be thinking of it now.

As she opened the gate to Hanny and Kenny's home, she saw her half-brother standing in the doorway, obviously watching out for her. His lean face was drawn and his eyes were dark with anxiety because he, too, must remember the day his stepmother had died. 'Thank God you've come!' He reached out a hand and drew her inside the house.

'What's wrong? I know the baby's not due for another eight days or so but it's not so early that you have to worry,' said Alice, feeling a need to reassure him.

Kenny's fingers tightened on hers. 'I know. But her pains are coming regularly and her mother's started to take an interest. I wanted her to stay out of the bedroom but she forced her way past me and shut the door in my face...said that it was no place for a man.'

'Good God!' gasped Alice, squeezing his hand as she felt a chill go through her. Surely Mrs Kirk didn't remember the day she had delivered Tilly? 'How can she remember what to do when she's forgotten so much else?'

'That's what I thought. You've got to get up those stairs quick and keep an eye on her whilst I go after Freddie. I sent him to fetch the doctor and the midwife, I only hope they're in.'

'Freddie! Freddie's home?' cried Alice, remembering what Hanny had said about his being able to help Seb.

'Yes. He walked through the door only a couple of hours ago. I couldn't believe it when I saw him but by God was I glad to see him. You go up! I'll be as quick as I can.' He shoved Alice in the direction of the stairs and hurried out of the house.

Alice took a deep breath and climbed the stairs. She knew their bedroom was on the second floor and, as she reached the first landing, she half expected to hear screams. But all was quiet. She hurried on up the next flight of stairs and knocked on the bedroom door before pushing it open. The sight that met her eyes took her by surprise. Hanny was bent over the bottom of the bed, clinging to the bars of the brass bedstead, taking slow, deep breaths. Her mother had her hand on her back and was patting it. 'That's a good girl,' she was saying.

Alice knew when the contraction had passed because Hanny straightened up and looked in her direction. 'I'm glad to see you,' she said, trying to smile bravely, but her eyes were scared in her flushed face and her flaxen hair hung in damp wisps either side of it. 'Not much fun this,' she added.

'No,' said Alice, going over to her and kissing her cheek. 'But it'll be worth it in the end.'

'I hope so,' said Hanny, accepting a glass of water from her mother. She took a sip and tried to make light of matters. 'But what if I get a screamer who keeps us awake nights?' she said, trying to make a joke of things.

Alice laughed. 'He or she will stop screaming eventually. Just keep that in mind. Everything's going to be fine.'

'Say it often enough and I'll believe you.' Hanny handed the glass back to her mother. 'Will you stay with me, Alice?'

Despite knowing it was not going to be easy watching her friend suffer the agony of childbirth, Alice nodded. 'As long as I can,' she promised.

And Alice did so, encouraging Hanny to breathe slowly and not tense up when the contractions came. 'Let the pain wash over you,' she advised, and was aware of Mrs Kirk nodding in agreement. She seemed to have decided to take a back seat since Alice's arrival.

Hanny's waters broke just before the midwife arrived and immediately Alice and Mrs Kirk were ordered out of the bedroom. They both protested but when the doctor came he insisted that there was not enough space in the room for two extra people. Alice realised then they had no choice but to do as they were told and, after whispering to Hanny that she would be downstairs praying for her, she escorted Mrs Kirk out of the bedroom, saying that they must go downstairs and boil some water.

Susannah shook her head. 'You boil the water.

I'm staying here.' There was a chair on the landing and she sat on it, obviously determined to stay close to her daughter.

Alice wondered just how much she really understood but, knowing she could not force her to accompany her downstairs, she left her there.

'How are things going?' asked Kenny, pouncing on his half-sister as soon as she entered the kitchen.

'She's coming on.' Alice smiled in a way that she hoped was reassuring. Then she noticed Freddie over by the window. 'Hello. Fancy you arriving home in time for Christmas.'

He turned and presented a strained face to her. 'I was determined to be home but I didn't expect to have to rush off for the doctor. Do you think the baby will be born today? Are you sure Hanny's going to be OK?'

She hesitated to give him a straight answer, knowing that no delivery was ever exactly the same as another. 'They do say that first babies generally take some time to arrive. I know James did, but Hanny's seems to be getting along quite quickly.' Alice shrugged. 'So who knows, it could be that she'll be delivered before Christmas Day.' She smiled. 'How about a cup of tea?'

Both men nodded so she put the kettle on.

It was mid-evening when they heard a baby's cry. Kenny immediately stopped pacing the floor and rushed upstairs. He found a trembling Susannah standing outside the door. 'There's a baby crying. D'you think it's a boy? My Bert was a boy but he's all grown up now.'

'Yes, Mrs Kirk, I know,' said Kenny, wondering if she would ever forget her swine of a son. He knocked on the door. 'Is my wife all right? Is the baby?'

The door opened and the midwife stood there, holding an infant in her arms. 'You've a son, Mr Moran. But we've not finished here yet,' she said with a severe expression, 'so you'll have to be patient.'

Kenny paled. 'Wh-what d'you mean?' he stammered. 'My wife's all right, isn't she?'

'I mean that her job's not done yet. The doctor's felt another baby. It's been hiding behind this one. Perhaps you'd like to hold him whilst we get on with our work?'

Gingerly, Kenny took his son in his arms and gazed down at the tiny face smeared with mucus and a trace of blood. He marvelled that this was his child, but a sudden scream from inside the bedroom sent a chill slithering down his spine. 'Hanny!' he yelled, and would have forced his way into the room if at that moment Alice had not arrived on the scene.

'What's happening?' she demanded.

Hurriedly, the midwife closed the door.

Kenny turned and looked at his sister. 'She said

there's another baby and then Hanny screamed.' Tears filled his eyes and his face crumpled.

'Oh, my goodness,' said Alice, flabbergasted, thinking *Poor Hanny, she must be exhausted*. She prayed that she would be all right and forced herself to focus on her brother and the baby in his arms. 'What is it?' she asked.

'A boy.' He stared at her from frightened eyes. 'But how will I cope with him if anything happens to Hanny? I'd rather not have children than lose her.'

Alice understood how he felt but knew that she had to stop him from panicking. 'Hanny's going to be fine. She's strong, not like Mam. You must have faith and look after this little man here.'

Kenny gulped and nodded. 'Sorry. You're right.' He gazed down at his son, and suddenly such love welled up inside him that he felt as if he might explode with it. This was his son, the child he and Hanny had waited for all their married life. He must not think the worst. Hanny had the best midwife and doctor in Chester attending her.

Thirty nail-biting minutes later the door opened to reveal the smiling doctor. 'You can come in now, Mr Moran. You have a daughter. Isn't that just perfect? A daughter and a son at one fell swoop. Congratulations.'

Alice let out a joyous cry and flung her arms around the doctor. 'Thank you, thank you. My sister-in-law is all right?'

Laughing, he untangled himself. 'My dear, she has behaved exceptionally well during a difficult birth. The girl's presentation...no, I'll not go into that.' He patted Alice on the shoulder. 'A pot of tea and some biscuits would not go amiss. Then I must be on my way.'

Alice thanked him yet again. Kenny was not there to do so as he had brushed past the doctor and entered the bedroom. He saw a white-faced and exhausted Hanny resting against the pillows. Her lower body was raised so that her legs were about a foot above the mattress.

'Are you all right, love?' he whispered.

'Aye. I can't believe it's over and I'm still alive.'

'Oh, love!' he exclaimed. 'My dear brave girl. Never again!' he added, hurrying over to her, still carrying his son, and burying his head against her neck.

The next few minutes were so wrought with emotion that they could not speak. But later, when Alice entered carrying a tray containing a teapot, cups and saucers and a plate of biscuits, the new mother and father had control of themselves and were admiring their offspring. Susannah, also stood a few feet away, gazing down at her first grandchildren, lying top to tail in a crib.

'What are you going to call them?' asked Alice, placing the tray on a bedside table.

'Allan Kenneth for our son, after Allan

Quatermain from *King Solomon's Mines*, he was the bravest hunter in Africa,' said Hanny.

Alice could not understand them naming their firstborn after a character in a book but accepted each to their own. 'And your daughter?'

'Janet,' said Kenny firmly, 'after my Scottish mammy who died far too young, and Susannah after Hanny's mother.'

Alice gazed at the twins' grandmother and saw Mrs Kirk smile, and then she began to sing a lullaby. Alice felt a sudden ache inside her, wishing her children had a grandmother to sing lullabies to them. Her own mother would have done so but Seb's mother... She felt angry that they had not even received a Christmas card from her. Seb had made no comment but surely it must hurt him that his mother had sent only one paltry letter to him since his return.

It was almost ten o'clock by the time Alice made her way home. She wondered what Seb was thinking about her being out so long. How would he greet the news of the birth of Hanny's and Kenny's twins this Christmas Eve? She realised that she had neglected her family all that day and hoped Tilly had everything in order for the children's stockings and Christmas dinner tomorrow. One thing was for sure, Hanny and Kenny would not be spending Christmas Day with them now.

When Alice entered the house all was silent, but

she found Seb alone in the drawing room, smoking a cigarette in front of the fire. 'Where's Tilly?' she asked.

'Upstairs. I sent her to bed. I told her that it was not her job to fill the children's stockings or tell them a bedtime story,' he rasped.

Alice felt a prickle of fear. 'So have you filled their stockings?'

'Don't be daft! How can I do that with my useless arm?' he snapped.

She flushed. 'Sorry. I didn't think. You could have told them a story, though.'

'I was in no mood for storytelling, so James said he would tell Flora the story of *The Three Billy Goats Gruff*.'

'I see. Tilly did tell you where I'd gone?'

'Yes. But I thought you would have been home by now. You didn't actually help deliver the baby, did you?' he asked sarcastically.

'Of course I didn't, but I did keep Hanny company for a while until the midwife came.' She could feel herself trembling and went over to the drinks' cabinet and poured herself a sherry with a shaking hand. Then she thought that perhaps Seb might want a drink and turned to ask him.

'I've had one...or two, maybe three.' He drew in a deep breath. 'What were you doing there so long? Are Hanny and the baby OK?'

Alice gave a delighted smile. 'She's fine and

there's not just one baby but two. One was hidden behind the other, so they've a boy and a girl. Isn't it wonderful?' She took a sip of sherry. 'Hanny's going to have her hands full but at least Bert's mother will be able to help her.'

Seb stared at her with a fixed expression. 'You said *Bert's* mother.'

Alice was taken aback. 'Did I? I didn't realise.'

Seb stood up and thrust his face within inches of Alice's. 'I remember him being a handsome devil when I saw him in court. You still have feelings for him, don't you?'

Alice denied the accusation. 'I hate him. How can you believe otherwise after the way he behaved towards me? Mrs Kirk mentioned him, so that's likely the reason his name slipped out.'

Seb seized her by the chin, causing her to spill her drink. His undamaged eye glinted with an angry light. 'It seems to me that you haven't forgotten that smarmy devil.'

Alice wrenched herself free. 'For goodness' sake, Seb. I told you I hate him. He's dead, thank God. Don't let his memory cast a shadow over our lives now. It's you I love. Let's see to the children's stockings and go to bed.'

'How can you still love me looking like this?' He dug his fingers into his scarred cheek. 'Even Ma doesn't want to see her ugly son at Christmas.'

'She's written?'

'Yes. Martin says they can't leave the animals and he doesn't believe in Christmas, anyway.'

'What was the other post?' She gulped a mouthful of sherry.

He walked unsteadily over to the occasional table and took a card from it. 'My long-lost Liverpool cousin and granny have sent us Christmas greetings. What do you think I should do about it?'

Relieved that he appeared to have calmed down, Alice remembered what Hanny had said about Joy saying something along the lines that Clara was a decent sort. Perhaps meeting her might turn his attention away from himself. 'You could write back thanking them and asking after your grandmother's health. I thought she was on her last legs but if the card's from both of them, she must still be alive. Perhaps they look to you because you're the only man in the family now.'

Seb's mouth tightened. 'Some man! How can I help them if I can't even help myself with this damned arm?'

She said rashly, 'You probably can do something. Just make a decision and give it a try instead of…of…' Her voice trailed off.

'Instead of moaning, were you going to say? I've thought of doing something about it.' He threw the card in her direction. 'If you want to write to her, do so. But I don't want the old woman in my house.

According to Ma she was a cruel demanding bully.'
He walked out of the room.

Alice sank onto the sofa, wishing the day could
have ended on a lighter, happier note. At least
Hanny had been safely delivered and she and Kenny
now had the children they had always longed for.
Also Freddie was home safely. She had forgotten to
mention him to Seb. Perhaps Freddie did hold the
key to unlocking the secrets that troubled her
husband. Assuming he would allow him to get
close. Alice was feeling desperate: if Seb was going
to be moody over Christmas it was going to take all
her willpower to keep a smile on her face for the
children's sake. Once the season to be jolly was
over, she would write to Clara O'Toole and suggest
a Sunday in January for her to come to lunch.
Perhaps she should also invite Freddie to tea that
day.

CHAPTER TWELVE

Clara was humming 'Life is Just a Bowl of Cherries' as she left the house for work. She was feeling slightly nervous but was looking forward to getting started at the Palladium. Christmas had come and gone and she was relieved it was over. Her grandmother had been as miserable as sin with no whisky or tonic to imbibe, and she had laid the blame firmly on her granddaughter's shoulders, saying that she was a tight-fisted young Scrooge. On Boxing Day, Clara had met up with her friend Jean and been invited back to her aunt's home. Unfortunately, the family had lost a son, so although they had made her welcome, the atmosphere was sadder than it was at home. She had been relieved when it was time to leave.

When she arrived at the Palladium, it was to find a number of people in the foyer with Mr Walsh. He was talking to a tall, well-built, blonde-haired woman.

He spotted Clara almost immediately and said, 'Ah, there you are, Miss O'Toole, come and join the team.' He beamed down at her. 'Now, I like to think of those in my charge as a family who will support each other, so come along, come along.' Clara blushed as the others stared at her. 'Let me introduce you,' he said, beckoning her over.

She walked over to where they were gathered in the vicinity of a couchette and a low table, on which there were several cups and saucers and an ashtray. First he introduced the tall blonde as his wife, Miranda Walsh. Then he waved a hand in the direction of a man who looked to be in his late forties. 'This is Alan Cormick, our doorman. He fought in the Boer War.'

Clara recognised the grey-haired man with a large moustache from her visits to the cinema and smiled. He winked at her. 'Welcome to the team,' he said.

She thanked him.

'Next to him is Peter Grant, our projectionist,' said Mr Walsh.

Mr Grant was also an older man but he was sallow-faced with bags under his eyes and only nodded briefly in her direction. She responded with a shy hallo.

'Our four usherettes, Amy, Iris, Joan and Dorothy.' One had reddish-brown hair with a round face and pouty lips, another was fair with freckled skin, then there was one who was mousy-haired, and the last was a brunette. 'Pleased to meet yer,' they chorused.

'And this young man…' Mr Walsh clapped a hand on the shoulder of a carroty-haired youth with a spotty face, 'is my brother's boy, Teddy. He's learning the trade and he'll be starting in the projection room as Peter's assistant.'

Despite Teddy being a couple of years younger than Clara, he looked her up and down with bold yellowish-brown eyes. 'Nice to meet you, Miss O'Toole. I presume you have a Christian name?'

'Clara,' she answered stiffly.

Mr Walsh rubbed his hands together. 'Now, I want to do a run through of our grand reopening. You, Miss O'Toole, will be in the cash box and will have to be nimble-fingered and have your wits about you. There'll be quite a crowd and the auditorium can hold nine hundred people. We've some important folk coming. Mrs Walsh will be overseeing the refreshments, but first she'll show you the ropes, so you shouldn't have any trouble. But she will keep her eye on you and come to your assistance if need be. Amy and Iris, you'll be downstairs. Naturally, take folk's tickets and show them to their seats as politely and speedily as possible. Joan and Dorothy, you'll be upstairs. Alan, Peter, you know what to do. Teddy, you'll do as Peter tells you.'

'Will the Palladium Orchestra be playing and will there be any turns?' asked Clara.

'Turns, Miss O'Toole!' exclaimed Mr Walsh with a chuckle. 'Surely you mean variety acts by top stars.'

'We've a new musician in the orchestra, haven't we, Mr Walsh?' said Iris, the pouty-lipped usherette. 'Lost a clarinet player to the flu.'

'Sadly, that is true,' said Mr Walsh with a sigh. 'But on the other hand, Mr Bennett is an even better musician and can also play the piano. He worked in America for years and did extremely well there. But now he's returned to Liverpool to help support his widowed sister, who has several children.'

'What a nice man,' said Amy.

'Well, yes, thoughtful,' said Mr Walsh, nodding vigorously. 'Anyway, folks. Our special guests will be arriving at five-thirty on the dot on New Year's Day. The performance will start at six-fifteen and there'll be an interval at eight.'

'Are we having one of Charlie's films?' asked Amy eagerly.

'Of course, that goes without saying,' said Mrs Walsh, her face alight with enthusiasm. 'He's one of England's own, isn't he? Even if his films are being made in Hollywood.' She stared at Clara. 'Don't you just love make-believe, Miss O'Toole?'

'I do,' replied Clara swiftly, warmed by Mrs Walsh's friendliness. Up until then she had considered Mrs Walsh a little austere and possibly stuck-up, but her smile had changed her face completely and now to her relief, the older woman appeared approachable.

'Will it be a two-reeler?' asked Teddy. 'And what about the experiment?'

'Patience, my boy. I was coming to that. But it won't be tonight.'

'What won't be tonight?' asked Amy.

'We're going to try showing two films,' said Mrs Walsh excitedly.

Mr Walsh threw up his hands. 'I was going to tell them.'

'Will it be Mary Pickford; America's sweetheart?' asked Dorothy, her eyes shining. 'I love her. Is there going to be a dog in it, as well?'

'No, it's a Lillian Gish and it's a drama,' said Mr Walsh, turning to his wife. 'They'll love it, won't they, Mrs Walsh? It's a real tear-jerker.'

'They certainly will.'

'So who are these special guests?' asked Peter, the projectionist.

'Our backers and the press for a start. We want them to give us a good write-up to bring in the audience,' replied Mr Walsh, adopting a serious manner.

'Shouldn't you have given them a pre-showing then?' asked Clara. 'So they could have told their readers in advance about the films?'

Mr Walsh's expression told her that was an idea that had occurred to him, but he only said, 'Good thinking. We did send them the distributors' flyers and also information about our very special guests, so it should be in the *Liverpool Echo* this evening. The reporters should be here on the opening night. Most local people know what a wonderful place this is to spend an evening. An excellent film programme, comfortable seats, a marvellous orchestra.'

Mrs Walsh turned her bright eyes on her husband and clasped her hands against her bosom. 'Now, dear, will you tell them who the main guests are...I can still hardly believe they agreed to come.'

'I will, I will.' He raised himself up on his toes and then lowered himself down again. 'Dorothy Ward and Shaun Glenville,' he said in a rapt voice.

'Gosh,' said Clara at the mention of the husband and wife team who were famous throughout the country for their appearances in plays, musicals and pantomime. 'Aren't they appearing in *Jack and the Beanstalk* at the Olympia in the New Year?'

'Correct, Clara,' said Mr Walsh, rising up on his tiptoes again and clasping his hands behind his back. 'As it happens, one of Shaun Glenville's drinking pals is a friend of mine and he had a word with him about our reopening.'

'I can scarcely believe it,' said Iris, her eyes

glowing. 'Will Dorothy Ward sing for us, d'you think?'

'Of course. I thought we could decorate the place a bit before the opening night. Put up some garlands and a banner and get some balloons.'

Dorothy wriggled her shoulders with excitement. 'It sounds like it's really going to be a grand occasion,' she said.

Clara could not agree more.

Shortly afterwards, Mrs Walsh instructed Clara in what was expected of her as a cashier. She ushered her into the cash box and told her the cost of the various seats; three pence, sixpence and a shilling, and showed her the rolls of tickets. Also, she brought out the cash bags in which she would need to place the takings. 'You'll be given a float before each performance and you must keep a note of that and take it out of the amount of cash you finish up with at the end of the evening. You will need to balance the price of the tickets sold with the takings. You'll bring the bags to the office to do that and either I or Mr Walsh will assist you until Mr Eaton's return.' She produced a keyring containing two keys and fingered the largest. 'This one is for the door of the cash box, because you'll need to lock yourself in.' She adopted a more serious note. 'We don't want anyone getting away with the takings. This way you and the cash will be safe. One must be so careful. There are lots of desperate people around since the war. Hopefully the films we show will help to alleviate some of their misery.'

Clara could see the sense in what Mrs Walsh said and looked forward to being part of the exciting media of cinematography. She could not wait to get home and tell her grandmother about it.

But Clara had barely set foot in the house when Bernie called out, 'There's a letter for you from Chester.'

Clara almost ran into the kitchen. 'Have you opened it?'

'It's on the mantelpiece, propped up against the cat.' Bernie took a swig from her hip flask.

Clara stared at her and then reached for the envelope resting against a cat painted bilious green, orange and purple, and wasted no time in opening it.

Dear Clara O'Toole,

I hope you'll forgive us for not answering your last letter but life here since my husband has come home has been hectic. Sad to say he doesn't feel up to meeting your grandmother and is of the opinion that his mother won't wish to see her either. I'm sure you'll understand if you know anything of the background to their falling out.

Putting that aside, I would be happy to see you and hopefully you will be able to meet Seb, as well.

I'd best warn you that he's been very badly injured: one side of his face is scarred and he's blind in one eye. He also has a weak arm. I'm hoping that meeting you will be good for him. He never had any real family life until we were married.

I'll say no more but please come and take us as you find us. A Sunday will be best. I suggest the second one in January. Come for lunch at 2 p.m. Please let me know if this suits you.

Yours sincerely,
Alice Bennett.

'Well?' demanded Bernie. 'Is it from him? What does it say?'

'It's from his wife, ' said Clara, lifting her smiling face from the letter. 'She's asked me to lunch the second Sunday in January.'

'Hasn't asked me, though,' mumbled Bernie. 'And you don't look too pleased about it.'

'I am pleased, but I feel sad for them both because of his injuries.' Clara sighed. 'Anyway, as far as your going is concerned, it's not as though you'd manage to get there, with the way your legs are.'

'I could in a motor. If that young man who brought me home would fetch me.'

'He doesn't live with them.'

'No mention of Gertie?'

Clara hesitated. 'She hasn't given me her address if that's what you mean.'

'I want to see her again before I die.'

Clara's lips twitched. 'Better than when you're dead. I'll see what I can do to persuade them to give me her address.'

'So you're definitely going?' said Bernie. 'Despite it's going to cost you.'

Clara nodded and felt a soaring excitement at the thought of visiting Seb and Alice and their children. But first there was the grand reopening at the Palladium to enjoy.

'Look, look, look,' stammered Amy, her nose pressed against a glass pane. 'D'you think her stole is real silver fox? And what d'yer think of her gown?'

'It's lovely,' said Clara, watching Dorothy Ward smiling at Mr Walsh as he shook hands with her husband, Shaun Glenville, outside the front entrance. She could hear the *ooh*s and *ahh*s of the crowd outside and saw the actress wave her hand in the direction of those gathered there. 'I love that ice-blue satin frock she's wearing.'

Iris giggled. 'It's generally him that wears the gown but he's got a penguin suit on this evening.'

'It's their motor I'm interested in,' said Teddy, stubbing out his cigarette. 'I'm going to have one like that when I'm rich.'

'*When* being the operative word,' said Dorothy, with a wink at Clara.

Mrs Walsh suddenly appeared. 'Come on, come on, get in line if you want to be introduced.'

Clara ran her hands down the skirt of her maroon uniform and did as she was told. A thrill raced through her at the thought that, in a few minutes, she might get to shake the hand of a celebrated actress whom she had admired from newspaper articles and the billboards. She wondered what her Aunt Gertie would think of it.

They were coming!

There was the tap-tap-tap of high heels and the famous couple were inside the foyer. The electric light sparkled on the necklace at Dorothy Ward's throat as she allowed her fur stole to slip off her shoulders to reveal her bare shoulders and neck. Clara wondered if the gems were real diamonds or just paste. She gazed admiringly at the actress as Mr Walsh introduced his wife to the stars before passing on to one of the musicians. He was the new one from America and was wearing a dinner jacket and bow tie. He must have said something funny because both husband and wife laughed.

Clara smiled, thinking back to their first meeting yesterday. She had thought he must have been a heartbreaker when he was young because he was still a handsome man with a thick head of silver hair and there were scarcely any wrinkles on his face except for a few laughter lines. He had asked her opinion about the piece of music he had played earlier and she had told him that it had filled her head with pictures of hustle and bustle and then of horses galloping. His brown eyes had twinkled at her. 'That means I'm doing my job properly.' He had spoken with a slight drawl.

The other musicians came next and then it was the projectionist's turn to be introduced. Clara was next in line to Teddy and she was aware of his impatience, but they passed him over swiftly and then she was face to face with them.

'How nice to meet you, Miss O'Toole. And what is your opinion of the silent screen?' asked Shaun Glenville in his lovely Irish accent. He was a well built man with a fighter's nose, which might have given him a pugnacious expression if it hadn't been for his smiling eyes. 'Do you think it will ever replace live theatre?'

She had not expected to be asked such a question but answered easily and from the heart. 'Oh no! I do enjoy a good film but it's not alive the same, is it? It's so different hearing actors and actresses speak the words, as well as sing and perform on the stage.'

'Now, isn't that the kind of answer we like to hear,' said Shaun Glenville, turning to his wife.

Clara blushed and murmured, 'Thank you. My-my aunt used to be on the stage.'

'What was her name?' he asked with interest.

'Gabrielle O'Toole, the Liverpool Songbird.'

His face lit up with recognition. 'Now there's a name to remember,' he said. 'I saw her perform in Dublin when I was just a small boyo.'

Clara was thrilled to have confirmation that Gertie had trodden the boards in a city other than Liverpool and thanked him.

He nodded and passed on.

The moment was over and it seemed no time at all before Clara was locked in the kiosk and was preparing to face her first excited customers. Fortunately for Clara, most tendered the right amount of money for their tickets, so she was able to deal with the queue quickly and efficiently. Soon a notice was placed outside saying, Full House. The doors were closed and Alan Cormick mounted guard in the almost deserted foyer.

As Clara began to count the money, she was hoping to be able to slip into the auditorium. Once she had totalled the cash, she wrote the amount in the ledger and then placed the money in the cash bags. They were terribly heavy because most of the takings were in coin, but she managed to lift them and lock them in the cupboard beneath the ledge – no use taking them to the manager's office where the safe was because he would not be there but with their special guests. She worked out how many tickets had been sold and at what cost and balanced the totals. Pleased that they had balanced, she let herself out of the cash box, locked it and made her way to the auditorium.

To her delight, she was in time to catch the end of the two-reeler before the interval. Then Dorothy Ward and Shaun Glenville got up onto the stage and sang a number from their forthcoming pantomime for the audience. Clara wished she could see *Jack and the Beanstalk* but knew it would not be possible as she was working, so she gave up the idea and concentrated her attention on the stage. There was another song by the husband and wife and then it was time for refreshments.

A room had been set aside for special guests and it was decked out with garlands and balloons. Clara managed to sneak a few sandwiches, a sausage roll and a cake into a paper bag for Bernie and concealed it in her shopping bag. She was hoping to listen to the stars sing again but Mr Walsh called her away and she had no choice but to go with him.

'Well, Clara, how do you think this evening has gone?' he asked as they went downstairs.

'It's been wonderful,' she said, her eyes shining. 'If we have a full house like this every evening, Mr Walsh, you and your backers will soon be laughing all the way to the bank.'

His plump face split into a smile. 'I'm a great believer in laughter being good for the soul, Clara. You have your keys?'

She nodded and produced them.

The cash bags were collected and she went along with him to his office. There he checked the ledger and counted the money again.

'Just to make certain,' he said.

When the sum balanced with her original amount, he beamed at her. 'Oh, what it is to have young eyes and nimble fingers.' He lifted the cash bags one at a time and placed them in the safe. After locking it, he told her to run along and watch the end of the show.

Clara did so but managed to leave before there was a mad rush from the audience when it came to an end. She went outside into the foyer and wandered over to where Mr Cormick was standing, ready to open the doors to let the public out.

'So did you enjoy your first night, Clara?' he asked.

Yawning, she nodded. 'I'm tired, though.'

He smiled. 'Yer'll sleep all the sweeter, queen.'

Clara did not dispute it. She caught the sound of hurrying footsteps and the doors to the auditorium were flung open. She could have been knocked down as swarms of people came flooding out if she had not left swiftly. She wasted no time hurrying home as it was freezing cold outside.

She entered the house to find her grandmother dozing in front of the kitchen fire. 'Do you want a cup of cocoa, Gran?' she asked loudly.

Bernie knuckled her eyes. 'I don't mind if I do.'

She yawned. 'Did yer bring me anything, girl?'

Clara nodded and, after putting the kettle on, produced the food from her shopping bag and placed it on a plate. 'It was a good evening, Gran. A pity you couldn't have been there.'

'Doesn't matter. My legs couldn't have coped with the walk and any standing. You tell me about it.' Bernie bit into a sandwich.

So Clara told her grandmother about her evening and how Shaun Glenville had said that he had seen Gertie on the stage in Dublin years ago.

'She was performing as Gabrielle O'Toole and styled herself as the Liverpool Songbird.'

Bernie was silent for a few moments and then said, 'She must have made some money and I never saw a penny of it.'

Clara felt like saying that if her grandmother had behaved less selfishly then she might have done so. She made the cocoa and then put a bit more coal on the fire, because she was still cold and, besides, she wanted to relive the moment when Dorothy Ward and her husband had got up on the stage and sung. At a word from Bernie, she took a hot shelf out of the oven of the blackleaded range and wrapped it in newspaper, then took it up to the old woman's bed to warm it up. She then helped her down the yard to the lav before seeing her to bed.

'I wonder what our Gertie would say if she knew that you'd spoken to a couple of the top stage stars,' wheezed Bernie, as she heaved her bulk into the middle of the bed.

'I'll ask her what she thinks when I see her,' said Clara, feeling so optimistic about everything that evening.

She went downstairs to lock up and then curled up in front of the fire for a few moments. Gazing into the glowing coals, she allowed her mind to drift, thinking of Alice's invitation to Sunday lunch. She really hoped that 1919 would turn out to be a very good year.

CHAPTER THIRTEEN

'It's odd that you should mention Clara sending a Christmas card,' said Joy, cuddling her brand new niece and stretching her legs out towards the fire. It was freezing cold outside but Hanny had a lovely fire going and it was cosy in the drawing room overlooking the River Dee.

'Why is it odd?' asked Tilly, who was sitting on the sofa next to Hanny, who was feeding her son. Kenny had gone out with Freddie for a pint.

'She wrote asking me whether Alice had received her letter. I told her that she had and what I knew of the situation in your household. I suggested that she write to Seb and Alice again in the New Year.' Joy smiled. 'But she had the sense to send a friendly Christmas card instead.'

'Which resulted in Alice inviting her to Sunday lunch next week,' said Tilly, looking put out. 'So tell me, what do you know about her and Freddie?'

Joy looked surprised. 'What about them?'

'Well, they've met already, haven't they?' said Tilly, her colour high. 'Even Hanny and Alice know they've met.'

'Only briefly,' said Joy. 'Freddie ran Clara and her grandmother home that evening in Liverpool, but that's all. No need to get worked up about it.'

'Not quite all,' said Hanny, brushing her lips against her son's downy head. 'Freddie mentioned her and the grandmother in one of his letters.'

'Well, she mentioned him to me,' said Joy. 'Clara's a caring person so wanted to know if he'd survived the war.'

Tilly's eyes narrowed. 'There you are then, she's interested in him. A girl from Liverpool.'

'What's wrong with Liverpool? Seb was brought up in Liverpool,' said Hanny, frowning at her.

'Probably not from the same area,' she muttered, toying with her fingernails.

'No. But he did work for the Waters and wasn't brought up to live the lifestyle he does now,' said Hanny. 'Seb's no snob and I wouldn't want you to be one either,' she added firmly. 'Our brother is a presentable young man. I can see him having more than one young woman chasing after him before he makes his choice, if that's what you're worried about.'

'Probably has them chasing after him, already,' said Joy dryly. 'But he needs to get some money behind him before he can think of marriage.'

Tilly looked relieved. 'I suppose you're right. He

won't be in a rush to tie the knot with anyone yet. Although, if I get the chance, I'm going to tell him I've someone interested in me, too,' she added casually.

The sisters stared at her. 'I can guess who that is,' said Hanny, taking her son from the breast and putting him against her shoulder. 'I noticed the way he was looking at you in November. I was relieved he was returning to America. You've some growing up to do yet.'

Joy's gaze went from one to the other. 'So who's this we're talking about?'

'Donald Pierce, the bloke who found Seb,' said Hanny, patting the baby's back. 'So you haven't mentioned him yet to Freddie?' she murmured.

'Not yet. I've hardly seen Freddie,' protested Tilly. 'He seems to be out here, there and everywhere since he's been home. Once I hear from Donald, I'll tell him,' said Tilly, her cheeks even redder now. Swiftly, she changed the subject. 'Christmas wasn't the least bit like I thought it would be in our house.'

'How did you think it would be?' asked Hanny, feeling a niggle of concern.

'I thought it would be a lot happier than last year. Instead, Alice and Seb were pretending to be happy for the sake of the children.' Tilly toyed with her fingernails. 'I'd swear on Christmas Eve I heard him and Alice arguing. And not so long ago, he got up out of bed in the middle of the night and went downstairs. He didn't come back to bed until dawn. I know because I was awake, thinking up a story I'd like to write. I really am worried about the pair of them.'

'Alice has mentioned a few things to me,' said Hanny. 'I'm sure given time and patience everything will work out.'

'I just hope if Clara does come she won't make things worse,' said Tilly.

'Enough said,' murmured Hanny. 'Put the kettle on and make some cocoa, there's a good girl.'

Tilly did as she asked but still could not help worrying about the possibility of Clara becoming a regular visitor to Victoria Crescent.

Seb frowned down at the postmark on the envelope and then took out the letter. He began to read:

Dear Alice and Sebastian,

Thank you for your kind invitation to lunch on Sunday, January 12th. I am pleased to accept. Hopefully there will be no delays on the trains and I'll arrive on time. I really am looking forward to meeting you both and your children. Gran would love to meet you, too, but her health means that she can't walk far, but she does sends her best wishes.

Yours,
Clara.

He dropped the letter on the occasional table and clenched his fist. So his grandmother could not walk far due to bad health. Why should he care? Yet he could not get out of his head what Alice had said about his being the man of the family. Perhaps they were expecting him to give them a helping hand. His grandmother would probably only have her five shillings old age pension to live on and so his cousin would have to work to support herself and the old woman, too. Work very hard, most likely, if she was to do so.

It was possible that they thought his living in Chester meant he was comfortably off and so he could afford to help them. Little did they know it was unlikely that he would ever be able to work again if he had his arm off. A chill of horror gripped him at the thought but he fought against it. Lots of soldiers had arms and legs amputated and just had to get on with it. But what could he do to earn money with a missing arm? He might get some kind of disability payment, but how far would that go? He wouldn't be able to drive or do any repairs, and when it came to selling the motors, which he used to enjoy, he was convinced that any prospective buyers would be put off by his scarred face. Yet he had to earn a wage somehow. The money that had come to him after his paternal grandmother's death was on deposit, but was going steadily down as there was so little coming in. Perhaps he should consider mortgaging the house. If anything went wrong with the amputation and he died, then at least Alice would have a lump sum. She could buy a smaller house and have something to live on. She was bound to get some kind of widow's pension... He stopped, aghast, as he realised the direction his thoughts were taking. He would have himself dead and buried in a minute.

'Who's the letter from?'

He jumped at the sound of Alice's voice. 'My cousin,' he said tersely.

'Clara's answered mine already!' His wife brushed past him and picked up the letter from the table. Georgie toddled after her.

'I thought I told you not to write to her,' he said harshly.

Alice did not look at him. 'You said on Christmas Eve that I could invite her here, but stressed that I was not to ask your grandmother to come, so that's what I did.'

'I must have been drunk. You should ignore what I say when I'm in that state.' He flopped down on the sofa.

She glanced at him. 'It's true you'd been drinking but you were in control of yourself.'

'You think so?'

'Yes. I-I don't know why we're having this-this argument.' The hand that clasped the letter shook.

He noticed it and felt bad that she should be

getting into a nervous state and tried to speak more calmly. 'We wouldn't be arguing if you didn't constantly go against my wishes. I don't know what she thinks to gain by coming here.'

Alice looked at him directly. 'Your mother's address, most likely.'

'Well, she won't get it from me.' His tone was brusque. 'Why d'you think Ma kept her early life in Liverpool secret for years? She didn't want to have anything to do with that family.'

'I can understand her not wanting to see her mother,' said Alice quietly, 'but she doesn't even know Clara exists, so how can you be so sure that she wouldn't want to meet her? Joy said that Clara's a good sort.'

'So what Joy says is more important than what I say? You think that I don't know my own mother?' he said forcefully.

'I-I didn't say that. I-I just know that it helps when you're in trouble to have family and friends who care about you. I know when my father...' She stopped abruptly and reached down to pick up Georgie, cuddling him against her.

There was a long silence.

Seb felt that familiar stab of guilt and irritation whenever Alice mentioned her father. 'Go on. What about your father?'

She remained silent.

His face darkened. 'You're thinking back to

when you wanted me to quit my job and leave Chester, all because you didn't trust me to keep you safe from him. You wanted us to run away and I refused to do so.'

'I was scared!' she burst out. 'And I had every right to be. He came looking for me and you weren't there to save me.'

'Good God, that still rankles with you, doesn't it?' he snapped. 'Yet it was your fault for not trusting me. If you had done so, I would have been around to save you. Instead you said you didn't want to see me anymore and walked away. I tried to see you several times but you refused to have anything to do with me.'

'You didn't have a father who beat your mother or had fits of madness. I was terrified of him, like I am now…of you…' Her words trailed off and she placed a hand to her mouth, gazing at him with frightened eyes.

Seb's head felt like it was exploding. 'You're comparing me with your father? You've no idea what I've been through and what I'm still going through,' he yelled, starting up.

Alice backed away and managed to wrench open the door. It caught her on the nose but, ignoring the pain, she slammed the door behind her. She had made Seb mad and had to hide. For a moment she did not know where to go, and then, still clutching Georgie to her, she headed for the kitchen. There she stood a moment, gazing about her. Then she made for the larder and, with Georgie balanced on her hip, closed the door behind them. Tears rolled down her cheeks, thinking that she should have watched what she said to Seb and not made him angry.

Her son's chubby hand touched her wet face in the dim light. 'Don't c'y, Mama, don't c'y! Georgie make it better.' He pressed his lips against her nose, which throbbed. 'Is dat better?' he asked.

'Yes, sweetheart, it's better,' she assured her son, and marvelled that her voice could sound so normal.

'Alice! Alice! Where are you? Why d'you have to rush out like that? Why can't you bloody understand I'm going mad with worry? I wasn't going to hurt you,' shouted Seb.

She put a hand lightly over Georgie's mouth and hushed him.

'Hide an' deek?' he whispered.

She nodded, thinking that her being able to hear Seb's voice so clearly meant he was close. Never would she have believed in all the years of their marriage that she would be hiding in a cupboard for fear of the man she had fallen in love with the moment she had set eyes on him. She knew that he was suffering, too, but fear was driving them apart.

She put her eye to a crack in the door and could see Seb standing in the middle of the kitchen. Her heart ached for him as he gazed wildly about him with his one eye. 'I won't hurt you,' he shouted. 'I can understand why you think I'm going mad. Perhaps I am. I was even thinking of wearing a mask when my cousin comes. An iron mask.' Seb's voice had an edge to it. 'Remember Tilly telling us once about the story of the man in the iron mask?'

Alice remembered. Something about a man having his head locked in an iron mask and hidden in a dungeon because he was the rightful king of France and his brother or cousin, who looked like him, wanted his throne. 'Remember Tilly saying, "How can people be so cruel?" as if the book was real life instead of fiction?' he added.

Alice was so upset that Seb should consider wearing a mask that she could remain silent no longer. 'I remember. But there's no need for a mask where you're concerned. You're thinking your cousin will be shocked when she sees you. Perhaps you're remembering my fainting. You think I was repulsed but I wasn't. I was in shock.'

'I wouldn't deny it did come as a shock to you, and the children, but why can't you be honest with me and say you hate my face like this?'

Alice heard a sound as if he had punched the wall and she winced. 'You're wrong, Seb. I've become accustomed to your face as it is now. I believe James and Flora have as well.'

'You're saying that one can get used to anything.

Even if that were true, my cousin's going to be put off by the sight of me.'

'For God's sake, Seb! She knows you're scarred. The worst happened to her. She lost her father in the war. Why can't you be grateful that you're alive and she wants to meet you? Have some pity on her and the old woman.'

'Pity!' He laughed. 'I've had a bellyful of that. At least Ma has the sense to stay away and save me her pity. Every time I look in Kenny and Hanny's eyes I see pity.'

'Compassion, Seb! That's what you see…compassion,' cried Alice. 'Wasn't that what you felt for Kenny when Bert crippled him?'

Sebastian was silent. Then she heard his footsteps approaching and the next moment he said in a singsong voice, 'I can see you.'

She started back as an eye appeared at the crack in the door. Georgie giggled. The door was wrenched open and Alice's heart seemed to bounce against her ribs as she confronted her husband. They stared at each other and suddenly she was weeping.

'Don't!' He grabbed her shoulder and drew her and Georgie out of the larder.

She placed a protective hand round Georgie's head as he wobbled in her arms. 'You've got nothing to hide. There's no need for a mask,' she sobbed.

Sebastian's eye glistened. 'I disagree. With a mask I just might be prepared to see this cousin you're so determined for me to meet. You can go to the yard now and tell Kenny he can make me one. He's talented with his hands.'

She was tempted to tell him to go to the yard himself and ask for this preposterous thing but did not dare. He freed her abruptly. 'Well? What are you waiting for? Go! Take Georgie with you. The fresh air will do him good. I'll fetch his perambulator.'

Relieved that he had not hit out at her or Georgie, she agreed to do what he said, although she had no intention of going to the yard. But she needed to get out of the house. She put her son down and he toddled after his father into the hall. She marvelled at the sunny, accepting nature of their youngest child, so different from the awkwardness that was still there between their eldest son and Seb. Of course, James was nearly nine and remembered Seb taking him fishing along the Dee. With Seb finding difficulty casting a line, it seemed unlikely they would ever go fishing together again. Most likely their elder son was grieving for that easygoing comradeship with his father.

She went and fetched her outdoor clothes and returned to find her husband leaning against the hall wall, watching Georgie attempt to climb into his perambulator unaided. She knew that Seb's damaged arm was a constant frustration to him and wished desperately that its strength would return. Perhaps he should get in touch with the specialist surgeon who had first operated on it. She had seen the scars snaking down his arm but Seb had spoken little about what the operation had involved.

She scooped up her son and fastened him into his perambulator. Seb had moved away from the wall and was now holding the pram handle, steadying the vehicle as it rocked with their son's movements as she dressed him in his outdoor clothes. Once she had completed that task, Seb held the door open for her, watching her lower the perambulator down the step and onto the path with a fixed expression.

She felt a need to say, 'Georgie will want you to play ball with him in the garden when we get back.'

He hesitated. 'I'll be here. I'll have a look for the ball.'

She heard the door close behind her and part of her wanted to rush back and say, *Please, Seb, don't do anything stupid,* but she had to trust he would keep his word and be there waiting for their return. She would have so preferred Tilly to be at home instead of at the repair yard office. Her sister could have kept Seb company then. But what kind of life was that for either of them? She must stop worrying about him. So often she was torn in two between wanting to get away and being scared to leave him alone.

Alice hurried along Victoria Crescent towards the bridge across the Dee. The trees were bare on the far bank and the water was so still that their image was reflected on its surface. She felt her heart lift at such beauty. Perhaps when spring came, Seb would be glad to be alive. She thought of what he had said about wearing a mask to face his cousin. There would be no mask, she though fiercely. Perhaps she had done the wrong thing by inviting Clara to Sunday lunch, but it was too late now for regrets. She wanted to believe that she could become part of their family and be a blessing in disguise.

CHAPTER FOURTEEN

'Clara should be here soon,' said Alice, watching her sister put the finishing touches to the table.

'Do you think the snowdrops look all right in this little vase?' asked Tilly, twisting round to face Alice.

'They're fine. Stop fussing.' Alice's hands twisted nervously. It was not only Clara's imminent arrival that was causing her to feel on edge but that Seb was up in the attic, supposedly tidying it up. She was scared that he would notice items missing and ask her about them. Then she would have to tell him that she had been taking stuff to the pawnshop that really belonged to him. 'At least I can be thankful that James and Flora are at a birthday party this afternoon so I don't have to worry about how they'll behave, although, on the whole, they've both coped well when Seb's been short with them,' she murmured. 'And Georgie's having his nap so he's out of the way for the moment.'

'Perhaps you should have written to Seb's mother

and asked her to come for lunch,' suggested Tilly, tongue in cheek. 'At least if she was here it would have made it worthwhile Clara coming if she doesn't get to see Seb. I'm sure you're thinking he's hiding up there so he doesn't have to meet her.' Tilly moved away from the table and went to look out of the window.

'I'm surprised at you saying that,' said Alice tersely. 'I thought my mother-in-law was your least favourite person. To suggest something that means you'd be spending time in her company goes beyond the call of family duty. Yours and mine.'

Tilly laughed. 'It was easy for me to say. If she hasn't responded to your invitations to see her grandchildren and then her own son, then why should she make the effort for her niece? But you're right about how I feel towards her. I remember her being horrible to me when I was little and living here with you.'

Alice followed her sister over to the window and put an arm about her waist. 'It's because you were pretty, clever and young – still are. She also hated that Seb was prepared to pay for piano lessons for you. It wasn't until later that we discovered what a tough life she'd had as a girl. She'd been acting a part for years. Even Seb didn't know the truth about her upbringing until Mrs Black spilt the beans. But I'm not going to go on about the past.'

Tilly pushed back a hank of long red-gold hair.

'So what will you talk about to Clara? It's strange to think that she's related to Seb but it's Joy and Freddie who have met her first.'

'I don't want to think about how they met. You know my thoughts about séances. Have you spoken to Freddie about her?'

'No. He always seems to be out when I call there. Yesterday he was driving Kenny somewhere.'

'Kenny's too easygoing. I can't understand why he encouraged Freddie to learn to drive during his sick leave last year. What good will it do him if he's in the merchant navy?'

Tilly said easily, 'Freddie could already drive. Seb gave him his first lessons a couple of years ago when he had shore leave after that collision in the fog on the Mersey.'

'Even so...' began Alice, only to break off as she noticed a dark-haired young woman opening the front gate. 'This must be her!'

Tilly pressed her face against the window. 'Shall I answer the door or will you?'

'I'd best do it. You go and check if the roasties are done and then light the gas under the rest of the veggies.'

The sisters left the dining room together, parting in the hall. Alice hurried to the front door and opened it. Instantly, she was struck by the young woman's likeness to her husband. 'Heavens! You have to be Clara! You and Seb could be twins!'

Clara chuckled and held out her hand. 'Hello. You must be Alice. I'm so pleased to meet you, and I'm really looking forward to meeting Seb.'

Alice's heart sank but she shook Clara's hand and said, 'Do come in. Seb's upstairs in the attic. You'll have to forgive him if he doesn't come hurrying down.'

Clara stepped over the threshold. 'How is he?'

'So-so. Up and down.' Alice sighed. 'I asked him to leave things until he could have some help but I can only think that he likes mooching around up there on his own. It's full of stuff that's been dumped: unwanted furniture, pictures, dolls with broken heads…'

'He might find something he can fix,' said Clara.

'Not with an almost useless arm.'

Clara's smile faded. 'I'm sorry. I forgot about his arm. It was…his other injuries that played on my mind. I tried to imagine what it must feel like for that to happen to you.'

Alice was touched by her words. 'I know. Awful, isn't it? He feels it. Thinks people are looking at that side of his face all the time.' She stretched out a hand. 'Here, let me help you off with your coat.'

Clara removed her coat and hat and handed both to her. Then she fluffed out her long black curls. Alice smiled. 'You've got Seb's hair – and much as I regret to admit it, you really do have a look of his mother.'

Clara looked surprised and uncomfortable. 'Is that a bad thing?'

Alice grimaced. 'We aren't the best of friends, but I suppose that's not so unusual between daughter-in-laws and mother-in-laws.' Absent-mindedly, she turned Clara's hat between her hands and gazed down at it before hanging it on the hall stand with her coat. 'She hasn't even been to see him since his return.'

Clara could not hide her astonishment. 'Why? Isn't she well?'

'Her excuse is that she can't get away from the farm. Seb thinks it's because she doesn't want to see him the way he is now.'

'But that's...terrible. If he was my son, I'd be desperate to see him to assure him that, if there was anything in my power I could do to help him, then I would do it.'

Alice stared at her. 'Joy was right. You really are nice. I wonder if it's worth risking his anger.'

Clara blushed. 'It's good of her to say that but...what d'you mean...risk his anger?'

'Can I be honest with you?' asked Alice.

'I'd prefer it,' said Clara. 'Although, if you're going to tell me Seb doesn't want to see me, then I'll be honest in return and say I'll be disappointed.'

'In that case, perhaps we need to force his hand.' Alice seized Clara's arm. 'Come upstairs with me.'

Clara did not argue but went with her. When

they reached the first landing, Alice said, 'I did mean it when I said he might be angry. You need to be prepared for that. He's not going to be pleased by us disturbing him.'

'I just want to be friends with the family.'

'I understand that and normally Seb would be prepared to welcome you, but at the moment he's feeling pretty useless and is worried that you'll want something from him that he can't give.'

Clara groaned. 'He isn't telepathic, is he?'

Alice stopped and stared at her. 'You mean – does he read minds from a distance?'

'Yes. I don't want to be disloyal to Gran, but your husband is really as much family to me as she is. I've done what I can for her but she always wants more. She thinks family are there to get what she can from them.' She paused and bit her lip. 'I'll add to that it must have been difficult for her when she was young with my grandfather at sea and a new baby started nearly every time he came home. Most of them died in infancy. You said you were going to be honest, well, that's what I'm being. But I'd never ask for money or take any from Sebastian if that's what he's worried about. I haven't come here on the scrounge,' she said firmly.

Alice was relieved. 'That's good because we haven't any cash to spare. You might think we're comfortable when you look at this house but we haven't much money coming in.'

'I understand,' said Clara, glad that Alice felt that she could be honest with her and was so easy to talk to. As they went up the next flight of stairs, she added, 'The war's changed everything, but even before it, my life took a change for the worse. I had a pretty carefree life until my mother died when I was thirteen. That was when Gran came to live with us, and then Dad volunteered in his late thirties. I knew why he did it. It was because he saw a film of the Somme and wanted to help. Then he was killed and I wanted the clock to go back, but one can't go back.'

Alice said, 'There must be millions of us that wished that, but we just have to go on.'

Clara nodded. 'Dad would want me to look to the future and that's what I'm doing.'

'I told Seb that I couldn't have managed my difficult times in the past without help from family and friends, so I reckon it's the same with the present and the future; we all need ongoing help.' Alice dropped her voice because they had reached the top floor of the house. 'I hope he won't be too annoyed. I find it difficult when he gets angry with me. I start thinking of my father, who went mad. He used to hit my mother. I hated him for it and I still do.'

Clara was silent. She could feel her heart beating rapidly. Part of her wanted to go back because Alice's mention of madness made her think of wild-eyed monsters, and then, unexpectedly, the memory of the man she had met on the way to Mrs Black's last year popped into her mind. He'd mentioned that his madness had been the cause of a rift with his family. Ahead of them, along a short landing, was a closed door. 'Is he in there?' she asked.

Alice nodded, listening intently. 'Can you hear anything?' she whispered.

Clara shook her head. 'Are you going to knock?'

Alice's green eyes were apprehensive and she clutched Clara's arm. 'Wait,' she whispered.

Clara did not move for several minutes and she could feel the tension rising within her. Suddenly, she could stand it no longer. 'If you're so worried about his losing his temper,' whispered Clara, 'we don't have to go in.'

'But it's so cowardly of me to feel like this.'

'Would you like me to knock?'

Alice did not answer and Clara could see clearly that she could not make up her mind what to do. Taking a deep breath, she removed Alice's hand from her arm and walked over to the door and knocked.

'Is that you, Alice?' demanded a harsh voice. 'I told you I didn't want to be disturbed.'

Neither woman spoke.

When the voice did not come again, Clara tried the door. It opened and, after a brief hesitation, she stepped inside. A dark-haired man was standing over by the window, holding a picture frame in one hand. At the sound of the door opening, he glanced her way. She saw him give a start and felt a similar sensation because, from her viewpoint, she could have been looking at a younger version of her father. She waited for her cousin to speak first, but when the silence stretched into what felt like an age, she decided it was up to her to say something.

'You are my cousin Sebastian?'

He did not answer and for a moment she was at a loss how to proceed. Then he said in an abrupt tone, 'Did Alice tell you I wanted to meet you?'

'No. In fact she said that you didn't want to be disturbed. I said I'd be disappointed if I didn't see you.'

He frowned. 'Why do you want to see me? I can't do anything for you or your grandmother. I'm having enough difficulty caring for my wife and children.'

'I'm not here on the scrounge. I'm perfectly capable of supporting myself! I've got a job in a picture house as a cashier.' A slight smile curved her lips. 'I love films and music, so although it doesn't pay as much as when I worked in munitions, I enjoy it so much more.'

'Good for you,' he said. His voice sounded raw. 'At least the war did some women a favour. Probably did more to free them than all the window smashing and hunger strikes of the suffragettes.'

His words amazed her and she took several steps towards him. 'I suppose that's true in a way. But what about those who've lost their fathers, sons and brothers?'

'Damn! Of course you're bloody right. I was looking at it from a different angle. I forgot you lost your father.' Seb's hands fumbled with the back of the picture frame.

'That's OK. You didn't know him. I wish we had known about you. He would have liked to have met you. I'm sure he would have liked a son, just as much as I'd have liked a brother…or a sister.' He did not speak so Clara continued, attempting to make him understand why meeting him was so important to her. 'I grew up amongst children who, more often than not, were from big families. I often envied them because I felt the odd one out. On the other hand, I had most of Mam and Dad's attention.'

'I could echo what you say so far but you were luckier than me. I grew up fatherless, believing he was dead,' Seb's voice was strained.

She remembered what Joy had told her about Seb's parents. 'Did you want brothers and sisters?'

Seb shrugged. 'The company might have been fun.'

'Did you feel the odd one out? Is that what you feel now?' she dared to add. He did not answer but turned away from her. Was this the end of their conversation? wondered Clara, and hesitated before taking a few more steps towards him. 'I've been told I look like your mother. You remind me of my father, so the family likeness is there.'

'Don't come any closer,' he said, glancing over his shoulder before facing the window again. 'You seem a sensible girl but, despite the family likeness, Ma is not going to want a grand reunion with her mother. So you're wasting your time coming here.'

'She's ailing,' burst out Clara. 'Gran probably doesn't have much longer to live and I know she's no angel but she needs your mother to forgive her. She's your grandmother, too, so it's your duty to help that come about.'

He rounded on her and she saw the scar on his face and the ugly dragged-down eyelid. 'I have no sense of duty towards her. Why should I? She's nothing to me.'

'Then get to know her. You mightn't like her but you'd be doing her a favour, as well as me.'

Seb glared at her from his single eye. 'Why should I want to do you a favour? I don't know *you* either.' He jammed the picture frame against his chest and tugged on the cord.

Clara watched him, wondering what he was doing. 'That's not my fault,' she murmured.

He pulled the cord free. 'I knew you wanted something from me.'

'Yes. But it won't cost you anything. All I want is your mother's address.'

A sharp laugh escaped him. 'That's all? It's a lot. She hates her mother, so much so that I thought I came from a completely different background.'

'I don't blame Aunt Gertie for hating her. It was only recently that Gran told me about her. She was honest and said that she was a lousy mother. Admitted beating her and knows she only has herself to blame for her running away from home.'

'I suppose that's something at least.' Seb put down the picture and the cord swung from his hand. 'Ma goes by the name of Gabrielle these days.'

Clara smiled, thinking that at least he was still talking to her. 'I know. I saw a poster in Mrs Black's house. It was advertising a variety show in Liverpool. Your mother's name was on it and so was Mrs Black's, except her surname was Rogers then. I'd really love to meet Aunt Ger-Gabrielle and listen to her talk about her life on the stage.'

A low laugh escaped him. 'They were Ma's golden days...although she had tough times, too. She told me some lies. Gave herself a whole different background set in America. She married a musician. Perhaps Ma will be willing to see you but you'd have to go to the farm because she never leaves there these days. I haven't seen her for ages.'

'You'll give me her address?' There was a lilt in Clara's voice.

He nodded. 'I'll do that for you but don't expect too much. I doubt she'll do what you want. I suggest you write to her first. It's not a place that you can reach easily.'

She took a deep satisfying breath. 'I really appreciate this.'

'Right. You've got what you want. You can go now.'

Clara moved towards the door. 'I have been invited to lunch. I will be seeing you later. I can tell you more about Dad.'

'I know as much as I need to know about him. He was killed at the Front like thousands and thousands of other poor sods.' Seb smashed the picture against the wall.

Clara jumped violently and stared at the broken picture with its splashes of reds, yellows and purples that depicted flowers against the walls of white-painted houses and thoughts ran crazily through her mind.

Alice burst into the room. 'Are you all right, Clara?' she cried.

Seb glared at her. 'Of course she's all right. What did you think I'd do to her?'

'Nothing. I...' Alice stared at the broken picture. 'How did that happen?'

'My fault. I felt like smashing something.'

'No. It was mine,' said Clara in a low voice. 'I reminded him of how terrible it was out there.'

Seb stared at her in surprise and then nodded. 'If the pair of you will get out of here now, I'll tidy up this mess.'

'Leave it to me,' said Alice. 'It'll be easier for me.'

His face twisted in an ugly grimace. 'Get out of here! Get out!' he roared.

Alice backed away, grabbed Clara's hand and dragged her out of the room, only to pause in the doorway and stare back at her husband. 'There's no reasoning with him in this mood,' she said in a low voice, before ushering her over to the stairs.

Seb was mortified by his behaviour in front of his cousin and thought what he needed was putting out of his misery. He looked at the cord in his hand and then up at the skylight in the ceiling. Suddenly, everything began to spin around him. He put out a hand to save himself from falling but it was the wrong arm and he toppled forward, banging his head on the wall. He did not lose consciousness but slid slowly to the floor so that the crown of his head ended up resting against the skirting board. His body arched in such a way that the toe of his shoe almost touched his nose.

He was stuck and felt too weak to move. What a ridiculous position to be in! Then he felt a peculiar quivering in his stomach. Slowly, the sensation spread until his whole body was shaking with what must surely be insane laughter. It was bubbling in his chest despite his telling himself that he had nothing to laugh about, but the feeling grew, rising into his throat until it burst out of his mouth. He felt he was going to choke. He managed to lift his head, scraping it up the wall, and, stretching and straining, he managed to unlock his body. Now the laughter was pouring from him, and then the tears came.

Seb had no idea how long he cried but eventually he stopped and wiped his wet face with the back of his sleeve and shifted so that he faced the room. He had to make a decision about his arm and he had to talk to Alice about it first. Glancing about the attic, he thought she had been right, it would have been more sensible to let her tidy up the mess. He looked at the picture in the broken frame and thought that, if it could be fixed then it was a decent enough view for someone to want to buy it. Now there was an idea.

He managed to get to his feet and left the attic. He was halfway downstairs when he heard Georgie talking to himself in the small ante room that led off the master bedroom. He went inside and found his younger son trying to climb out of his cot. Noticing Seb, his feet slid down the bars and he held out his arms. 'Dadee!'

Seb felt a warmth in his heart and wondered how he could have considered leaving his family to fend for itself. Somehow, they would come through this. After a struggle, he managed to lift Georgie up against him. Instantly, he realised there had been a leakage from the legs of the rubber pants that his son wore.

'You'll need changing, my lad. I suppose we'd best go down and tell your mother.' He was not looking forward to facing his wife or cousin, but he had to prove to them both that he was sane again and regretted his momentary madness. He set Georgie on his feet and, with his son's small hand in his larger one, went downstairs.

CHAPTER FIFTEEN

'Are you sure you want me to stay?' asked Clara, standing near the table.

'Of course! You've come all this way and you're not going away without being fed,' said Alice, placing a tureen of carrot and turnip on the table. 'Sit down.'

Clara did as she was told. 'Did you hear any of our conversation?'

'Some of it, but not all.'

'He said he'd give me Aunt Ger-Gabrielle's address. I'm going to write to her.'

At that moment Tilly entered the room carrying a plate with a shoulder of mutton on it. She had been introduced to Clara a few minutes ago. 'What about Seb? Will he be eating with us?'

Alice shrugged. 'We won't wait for him if he's not here in five minutes.'

'He's probably wishing me to Timbuktu,' said Clara, aware of Tilly's eyes on her.

'I wouldn't say that,' said Alice, sitting down and beginning to carve the meat. A task that Seb had done before he went to war. 'He wouldn't have said what he did about his mother if he wished you far away.' The words were no sooner out of her mouth than Seb's voice was heard on the stairs. 'He's coming,' she whispered.

The three of them stared at the door that was slightly ajar and watched Seb enter the room with Georgie. 'His nappy needs changing, love,' he said to Alice. 'He was trying to climb out of his cot. In future it would be a good idea to leave one side of it down so he's nearer to the floor. He's less likely to fall and hurt himself then.'

'You're right,' agreed Alice, sounding relieved. 'I remember we did that for the other two.' She signalled to Tilly to take over the carving and stood up. 'Sit down, Seb. Talk to Clara.'

He handed their son over to Alice. 'Sorry about earlier,' he whispered.

She was surprised into a smile. 'Apology accepted. Don't wait for me to eat.' Swinging her son up into her arms, she hurried from the dining room.

Seb took a deep breath before sitting at the head of the table and facing Clara. 'I'm sorry about losing my temper before. It won't happen again.'

Clara was pleased to get an apology, she was aware that there were a lot of men who would never admit to being in the wrong. She smiled at him with warmth in her eyes. 'We all have bad moments and some can be worse than others.'

'Thanks.' He toyed with his fork. 'I'm sorry, too, about…about your father. I believe Mrs Black tried to get in touch with him.'

'She did.' Clara's eyes gleamed. 'It was very interesting.'

'In what way?' asked Tilly, glancing up from slicing the mutton.

'Well, what happened was enough to send a shiver down my spine. And later when I saw her at her house in Eastham, she talked about portals and the evil spirit of a wicked woman whom she had dealt with for someone, trying to get back at her.'

'She said that?' asked Seb, looking amused.

Clara nodded. 'But she also told me that Dad loved me and wanted me to get on with my life. I know it could all be baloney but I made up my mind then that I was going to believe that he was still himself and was with Mam. I determined to get on with life as best I could without them.' She glanced at Tilly, then Seb. 'Don't get me wrong. I wish they were both still alive and I'll never forget them, but wishing won't change things.'

'You were lucky to have them so long,' said Tilly, placing mutton on plates. 'I never knew my parents. Mam died when I was born and I've never known my dad. A veil of mystery hangs over him because nobody in the family will talk to me about him.' She fixed Seb with a questioning stare.

'Why's that?' asked Clara.

Tilly shrugged slender shoulders. 'I wish I knew. But one day I'm going to unwrap the mystery.'

'That's enough, Tilly,' admonished Seb firmly. 'Kenny and Alice have a good reason why they don't want you to have anything to do with your father. Sometimes it's wiser to leave the past alone. Now hurry up with that meat. I'm sure Clara's hungry after her journey.'

Tilly said softly, 'Keeping secrets from me isn't the right way to get me to drop the matter. It just makes me more curious. But I'll say no more on the subject right now. Perhaps Clara would like to dish out the vegetables for us.'

'Happy to,' said Clara, pleased to be asked. She did wonder, though, what the mystery about Tilly's father could be. She picked up a tablespoon and began to dish out the vegetables. 'So where does Aunt Ge-Gabrielle live, Seb?' she asked, tagging on hastily, 'I can call you Seb?'

'Of course. We're cousins, aren't we?' he said easily. 'Besides, I've just called you Clara.'

'Of course, so you did.'

'Ma lives on a farm near Delamere Forest. Have you heard of Delamere?' he asked.

'Yes. I did know she lived on a farm but not the name of it. Is it far away?' She glanced at him and felt that slight sense of shock because on his good side it was like looking at her father.

'It's a good few miles from here; further from Liverpool, of course. There is a railway station but you'd still have a bit of a walk to get to the farm. That's why it's best to write first, so that you can be picked up at the station. It's Pine Farm, Delamere, Cheshire, and her married name is Waters. Mrs Martin Waters. I hope she writes back to you, but Ma's not the best of correspondents, so don't build up your hopes too high.'

'I'll try not to but it won't be easy,' said Clara, putting down a tureen. 'I'm hoping she'll remember Dad, so will write back to me for his sake if for no other reason.'

Seb looked thoughtful. 'It's possible. So tell me…what did your dad do before the war?'

'He was a carter. He loved his horses. In fact, according to Mrs Black, he died whilst driving a horse-driven ambulance.'

Seb gave her a sharp look. 'She was able to tell you that?'

Clara nodded and picked up her knife and fork. 'Amazing, isn't it? I don't know how she could have known.'

Tilly said, 'So there could be something in this getting in touch with spirits? I find the thought quite exciting.'

Seb shook his head at her. 'Don't let Alice hear

you say that. You know how she feels about Mrs Black.'

Tilly raised her eyebrows. 'Stop worrying, Seb. My lips are sealed.'

Clara smiled. She was finding Tilly quite fun. 'I believe Mrs Black and Aunt Ge-Gabrielle...' She closed her eyes briefly. 'I'll get the hang of her new name sooner or later. I believe they were childhood friends? I'll admit I did have my doubts about Mrs Black when I discovered she knew the family from old, but then, as I said earlier, she's convinced me since that she definitely has some kind of gift. She's a healer, too. And has really been of help to me. If you could have seen my face a few months ago! My skin was turning yellow and I had a rash.'

Seb leant across the table towards her. 'It looks all right to me now.'

She blinked as their noses were only a few inches away, so she had a real close view of the damage to his face. It occurred to her that if it was as Alice had said and he hated people looking at him, then he must have got over that worry where she was concerned.

Clara said, 'That's because she's a marvel.'

'Pity she couldn't help Seb then,' murmured Tilly, frowning at the pair of them.

The cousins drew apart.

Seb ignored that remark. 'I have to admit that I do wonder what Mrs Black's motives are in trying to reunite Ma with you and your grandmother. You'll have to forgive me if I say I'm a mite suspicious, knowing that they fell out years ago.'

'You're remembering the confrontation between Mrs Black and your mam outside this house,' said Tilly promptly. 'I heard Hanny discussing it with Alice. It wouldn't surprise me if she was out to cause mischief. I bet she hasn't forgotten your ma calling her a murderess. And knowing Gabrielle always acted like she was a cut above some, Mrs Black would be delighted if your grandmother proved to be an embarrassment to her.'

Clara wondered if she had misheard something that Tilly said and instantly asked, 'Why did Gabrielle call Mrs Black a murderess?'

'Take no notice of Tilly. Ma's got a quick temper and she can fly off the handle and say things that aren't true,' said Seb. 'I've always believed there was nothing more in what she said than Ma wanting to get back at Mrs Black because she was jealous.'

Clara said, 'She sounds just like Gran. But your mother won't have to worry about Gran embarrassing her. As I said in my letter, Gran's not fit to travel that far. If your mother does decide to see her then she'll have to come over to Liverpool.'

'Unless Freddie could take your gran in one of the firm's motors to the farm,' murmured Tilly.

'Why should Freddie do that?' asked Seb.

Tilly shrugged.

There was a silence.

Alice chose that moment to enter the dining room with Georgie. 'Haven't you started eating yet?' she said in surprise.

'No. We've been talking,' said Tilly smoothly.

'What about?' asked Alice.

'Family, amongst other things,' replied Tilly.

'I suppose that's natural with Clara coming to visit us,' said Alice, sitting Georgie in his feeding chair and seeing to him before she sat down beside Seb and began cutting up his meat.

It made Clara realise just how serious the damage to his right arm was, way beyond Mrs Black's abilities to fix. She wished that she could do something to help him but could not see what. But when they had finished their first course, at least she felt able to offer help to Tilly in clearing the dishes away.

The younger girl shrugged and said, 'Why not? Bring the tureens and follow me.'

Clara did so and discovered that she liked the size of the kitchen as much as she had liked Mrs Black's larger one. She placed the tureens down on the table and asked if there anything else she could do to help.

'Would you mind washing the crocks whilst I see to the pudding?' asked Tilly, looking surprised. 'It's apple pie and custard.'

'I wouldn't have offered if I minded,' said Clara, taking Tilly's place at the sink, where she had placed the dishes and started to run hot water on them. She gazed out of the window and said, 'I wish we had a garden. It would be lovely to sit in and watch the flowers grow.'

Tilly chuckled. 'Gardens are hard work! There's digging, sowing, planting feeding, watering, and there's always weeding. I know because I help.'

Clara turned off the hot tap, felt the water and ran some cold. 'Surely Seb and Alice have a gardener? Mrs Black has a man to help her.'

Tilly shook her head. 'They're not rich, you know. This house belongs to Seb but he hasn't worked since he came home. He and Kenny, my half-brother, own a motor business, but it hasn't done much during the war. Hopefully things will improve this year, although Kenny seems to think it'll be some time before the motor factories are all geared up for peace-time work. Then he will need Seb's help. He used to be good in the showroom because he knew better than Kenny how to speak to the customers, he was a natural salesman.'

'You think Seb's lost his confidence?'

Tilly said, 'Can you blame him?'

Clara shook her head. 'But he needs to get out there if he wants to get it back.'

Tilly frowned. 'You don't have to say that. All of us who know Seb are aware of it. It's all right for you to come here and start thinking you can give advice just because he's your cousin. It's easier to say things than do them. At the moment, he prefers hanging round the house.'

Clara was taken aback by the girl's rebuke. 'I didn't think that at all,' she said, placing another plate on the draining board. 'But I am entitled to my opinion. This is a lovely house but I wouldn't want to stay in it all day.'

Tilly's cheeks reddened. 'Sorry. I know what you mean about this house. Alice believed it was haunted when she and Seb took over here after they returned from their honeymoon.'

Clara stared at her. 'Honestly?'

Tilly's pretty heart-shaped face was solemn. 'I was only about six at the time and was not supposed to know about it, but I've always had big ears and the grown-ups forgot I was there sometimes. Miss Victoria, who was the daughter of Mr Waters, Seb's father, was murdered in the living room.' She paused. 'At least, Alice always believed it was murder, although Bert didn't get hanged for the crime because they couldn't prove he meant her to die. He wasn't arrested immediately, but when he was it was for grievous bodily harm and theft.'

Clara was stunned at her casual mention of murder. 'I've a feeling I've heard the name Bert before. You're not joking about his being a murderer?'

'No. If you've heard his name then you'll know he's Freddie's older brother. You've met Freddie Kirk, haven't you?' There was an odd note in her voice again that caused Clara to wonder whether Tilly resented her being there.

'Yes. I met him briefly. He was kind enough to give Gran and me a lift in his motor.'

'It wasn't his motor, it belongs to the company,' said Tilly, pouring milk into a saucepan. 'We hire them out sometimes. Freddie's just a common sailor, in case you thought he had money,' she added, just as casually as she had mentioned the murder. 'Anyway, where were we?'

'You were talking about his brother,' said Clara, deciding to ignore the slight and placing one of the tureens in the water. 'Did he look like Freddie at all?'

'I scarcely remember Bert now. I was only a tot when he went away. But I have seen a likeness of him. He's fair-haired and good-looking. Anyway, Alice was in such a bad way about the whole thing that an exorcist from the Church of England was summoned. If Miss Victoria's ghost really was here, then he got rid of her.'

Clara was fascinated by this further example of the supernatural. 'Why did Freddie's brother murder her? Was it a lovers' tiff?'

'I'm pretty sure it wasn't. She was a lady.' Tilly stirred an egg and sugar into the milk. 'He's another one that the family generally avoid talking about in front of me. Secrets! This family is full of them.' She stilled as if a thought had suddenly occurred to her. 'Of course, they're your family now. I wonder what Freddie will think of that. We're only related by marriage, so we're not blood relatives.'

Clara nodded, remembering Mrs Black asking if she was certain that she wanted to get involved with Sebastian's family because it could mean her getting caught up in his extended family's problems, as well. 'Bert is dead now, though, isn't he?'

Tilly nodded. 'So I've heard. It was a relief to one and all, I can tell you. Except for Mrs Kirk, who's unaware of it. She's not quite right in the head but harmless. Bert was her blue-eye and for some reason she's convinced he's in Australia.'

'Why?' asked Clara.

Tilly shrugged. 'Something to do with his having written to her years ago that he was emigrating to that country. Now I'll have to shut up, so I can concentrate on this custard.'

Clara washed the other tureen and the pans and had just finished and was drying her hands when a knock came at the door. 'Come in,' called Tilly, who was pouring custard into a jug.

The door opened and Freddie entered. Both girls stared at him. 'Oh, you've decided to visit us at last. I wonder why,' said Tilly, sounding irritated. 'We're just having pudding.'

'I like pudding,' said Freddie, smiling. 'Will there be enough for me?'

'I'm not sure. We have a guest, as you can see.'

Freddie's gaze slid away from Tilly to Clara. 'Miss O'Toole,' he said, inclining his dark head.

'Mr Kirk. I didn't realise you were home.' Clara felt flattered that he should have remembered her. It did not immediately occur to her that someone in the family might have mentioned to him that she was visiting her cousin. She was aware of his bold, blue eyes upon her face and was glad to be rid of her rash and that the colour of her skin was almost normal. He was as handsome as she remembered, his weather-beaten appearance adding to his attractiveness. He was wearing a navy blue jumper and dark trousers and seemed taller than she remembered.

'I got back on Christmas Eve. I never thought I'd see you here, that night in April,' he said, smiling. 'How are you?'

'I'm fine, thanks. How's yourself?' she asked, wishing her heart would not jump around like a leaping frog inside her breast.

'Glad to be home. How's your gran?'

'Still alive.'

'I knew she was a tough old bird.'

There was a brief silence. Clara tried to think of what to say next but she was feeling quite breathless and could not understand why he should have such an effect on her.

Freddie drew closer and gazed even more intently into her face. 'I can see the likeness to Seb better in this light,' he said. 'What did he say when he saw you?'

Clara had no intention of telling him. That was private. 'Not what you might think. It was Alice who said I looked like his mother. I'll add that he could have easily been mistaken for my father.'

Freddie looked surprised. 'They're that alike?'

'Were. Dad passed over, if you remember.'

Freddie nodded. 'It was quite a night, that. Mrs Black was all shook up. She almost convinced me that there was an evil spirit present. So will you be seeing Seb's mother? If you want company, I'd be happy to go with you.'

'You are forward, Freddie,' said Tilly, breaking into their conversation. 'How can Clara say no without being rude?'

Freddie turned and stared at her. 'Mind your own business, Tilly. I'm sure if Miss O'Toole doesn't want my company, she's got the guts to say so. I just thought that Delamere isn't an easy place to get to – and as I've just bought a second-hand motorbike, I could pick her up in Liverpool and we could make a day of it.' He returned his attention to Clara. 'What d'you say?'

Clara was about to tell him that she would need to write to her aunt first when Tilly said crossly, 'She'd be better off on the train than riding pillion on a smelly machine. Now, out of the kitchen and let us get on with our work.' She made shooing motions towards him. 'You'll find Seb and Alice in the dining room.'

Freddie took two strides and reached her and ruffled her hair. 'You've too much to say for yourself, *child*. I can see I'll have to get Miss O'Toole alone to speak to about this. I'll leave you to it for now. Give her time to consider my invitation.' He winked at Clara and strolled out of the kitchen.

Clara felt really annoyed with Tilly for interrupting their conversation. Earlier she had felt friendly towards the younger girl, but now she had a strong feeling that Tilly did not want her to be part of this family. She wondered if she was jealous because Freddie had given her most of his attention. Yet surely Tilly was too young to have romantic feelings towards him? Deciding that now was not the time to discuss the matter, she forced a smile onto her face and offered to carry the jug of custard into the dining room whilst she brought the apple pie and bowls.

Tilly accepted, but it appeared that she had not quite finished putting her oar in yet where Clara and Freddie were concerned. 'I hope you realise that Freddie flirts with all the girls? You know what sailors are.'

Clara wondered how Tilly could possibly know

that Freddie was a flirt when he had been away at sea for most of the war, but all she said was, 'I come from Liverpool, so of course I know what sailors are. Lots of them gave their lives for their country.' She walked out of the kitchen.

Freddie was singing softly to himself as he knocked on the dining room door. 'It's me, Freddie, may I come in?' he called.

Silence.

Then he heard Seb say, 'Of course, come in, Freddie.'

Freddie entered the room and immediately had the feeling that he had interrupted something important. His sisters had told him something of the testing time that the Bennetts were going through and he wanted to help. From his own experience of having a ship torpedoed and sunk beneath him, Freddie could imagine something of what Seb had been through.

'It's good to see you home again, Freddie,' Seb said.

'Good to see you, too,' responded Freddie, approaching the table and having a proper glimpse of Seb's face. He was not repulsed because he had seen far worse facial injuries from burns. 'Have you thought of getting a black patch for that eye?' he said.

Alice gasped. 'Freddie, how could you? You

don't say such things when a man has...'

'Sorry,' said Freddie, 'but it just came out. I knew a bloke who lost an eye and that's what he did. It made him look really rakish. The girls swooned over him.'

'Do you mind?' she cried. 'We don't need to hear that kind of thing.'

'Hush, Alice,' said Seb, frowning. 'Strange as it might seem, Freddie, a black patch is something that never occurred to me. A mask did, but that idea didn't go down well.'

With that opening, Freddie decided to further state the case for eye patches. 'You never thought of Lord Horatio Nelson of Trafalgar fame? One of the greatest sailors England's ever known? He was never what I'd call a handsome man, not like you, Seb.' He brought his face closer to the older man's. 'With those scars and a patch you'll knock the girls dead. You're still an attractive bloke, which I'm sure Alice has told you.'

Seb's mouth twitched. 'Go on. Say more that'll make me feel better about this ugly mug.'

'Not ugly,' protested Freddie. 'You should wear those scars like trophies. It was Shakespeare who wrote something about that.'

'What's this about Shakespeare?' asked Tilly, entering the dining room in Clara's wake. 'I wouldn't have thought you knew much about him, Freddie.'

He turned and gave her a severe look. 'You've a bad habit of interfering in other people's conversations, Tilly. I know plenty about Shakespeare. Our Hanny used to read his plays aloud and I asked questions.'

'So what battle is it this time you're talking about, Freddie?' asked Seb.

'Agincourt. Henry V,' he replied. 'The king said it to build up his troops before they faced the French.'

'Did we win?' asked Clara.

Freddie turned and grinned at her. 'Of course we won. You don't think Shakespeare would be writing plays in which England got beaten by the French?'

'I suppose not.' She smiled.

Clara was not the only one smiling. 'You really are a head case, Freddie,' said Seb, running a hand through his black curls. 'I'd look like a pirate.'

'Only if you wore a frock coat and a tri-cornered hat and went round singing *Yo-ho-ho and a bottle of rum*,' said Freddie.

Seb laughed, stood up and clapped him on the shoulder. 'I don't know about you, but I feel like a pint.'

Alice stared at him. 'I can't remember when you last went out for a pint.'

'Well, I'm going now, if you and Clara have no objections?'

'Who am I to come between a man and his pint?' said Clara.

Freddie caught her eye. 'Perhaps I can catch up with you later?'

She flushed. 'If you want.'

Alice glanced from one to the other and then at her sister. She looked stricken. As the two men walked out of the dining room, those remaining caught Freddie's words: 'You could have two eye patches, Seb. One of black buckram and another painted gold for parties.'

'That's not a bad idea,' was Seb's response.

'Well,' said Alice brightly, staring at Clara and Tilly. 'What do you think of eye patches?'

'Trust Freddie to come up with such an idea,' said Tilly, not meeting her sister's eyes. 'Are you ready for your apple pie and custard now?'

'Please.' Alice added, 'Hanny was right after all when she said Freddie would be good for Seb. I just hope he'll carry on keeping his spirits up, because he's going to need it in the weeks to come.'

'What d'you mean?' asked Tilly, darting her a concerned glance.

'He's got to make a decision about his arm. It could turn out that Seb will have more in common with Lord Admiral Nelson than a missing eye.' Her voice was strained.

Clara stared at her. 'You don't mean…?'

Alice said, 'That's what Seb's been worrying about.'

'Oh God,' whispered Clara, 'as if you didn't have

enough on your plate to worry about.'

Tilly was pale but did not speak, just dished out the pudding into three plates. It was not until she was sitting down and had picked up her spoon that she said, 'At least Freddie made him laugh, and I hope he carries on making him see there's still fun to be had in life.'

Alice reached out across the table and pressed her sister's hand. 'Whatever happens, at least it's out in the open now.'

Tilly nodded. 'If he's been worrying about that then it makes sense of all that's been going on. I'm a selfish so-and-so and will stop acting childish.' She glanced at Clara. 'I'm glad you came. I want the people about me to be happy. I think Seb's changed his mind about you and I hope you'll come again.'

Clara was touched by her words. 'Thanks. I'll come when I can if I'm invited.'

'Oh, you'll be invited again,' said Alice, spooning up some pudding and placing it in Georgie's mouth. 'You know Joy and Freddie, so you have to meet their sister, Hanny. She's been my best friend since I was Georgie's age. She's just had twins and they're gorgeous.'

'I'd like that,' said Clara.

She listened as Alice told her about not only the twins but also of her own children and the funny things they did. She was aware that Tilly was taking no part in the conversation and wondered if, despite her kind words, she was upset because Freddie had given her so much attention. She hoped he'd return before she had to leave to catch her train. But as it was, Freddie and Seb had still not arrived back when she had to take her leave. She comforted herself with the thought that at least her journey had not been wasted. Alice and Seb had made her feel wanted and, despite what they had both said about believing Gabrielle wanted nothing to do with her mother, she did have her aunt's address and intended writing to her in the not too distant future.

CHAPTER SIXTEEN

Dear Mrs Bennett. No! Clara crossed out the name and replaced it with *Mrs Waters*, having remembered that her aunt had remarried. She rubbed her fingers, which itched because she had a couple of chilblains, and took up another sheet of notepaper and started again. It had taken her a couple of weeks to get down to this because her gran had not been too well. Also, there was so much more to do now she was working longer hours, because there were days when they had a matinée.

Dear Mrs Waters,

I would like to address you as Aunt Gabrielle but you might consider that presumptuous of me, although you are my aunt. My father was your brother Dennis. I am sad to tell you that he was killed in France in 1917. Gran and I feel his loss greatly. He was such a lovely man and a good father to me and son to your mother.

You are probably wondering why I am writing to you now and how I came by your address, as I didn't know of your existence until nine months ago. It's Gran, her health is failing and she would like to make her peace with you. I managed to trace your son Sebastian and he gave me your address. If you could see your way to visiting Gran at our home here in Liverpool, it would be much appreciated. You're the only one of her children left.

Yours very sincerely,

Clara O' Toole.

She huddled inside her coat and read through what she had written, wondering if there was anything further she could say that might persuade her aunt to be reunited with her mother, but she could not think of anything. She glanced at her grandmother.

'Is there anything you'd like me to put in the letter?'

'Have yer mentioned how bad I am?' wheezed Bernie.

'Yes. I think I've said all that needs to be said where your health's concerned,' murmured Clara, folding the letter and placing it in an envelope. 'I'll post it on the way to work.'

'You make sure yer do,' admonished Bernie. 'Who's to say how long I've got on this earth. It's bloody freezing in here.'

Clara said, 'There's a coal shortage, Gran, and

we have to conserve what we've got. At least we seem to have escaped the flu.'

'Let's hope it stays that way. The sooner spring arrives the better my chest and old bones will feel,' said Bernie, her breathing laboured. 'If Gertie doesn't come soon, d'yer think me grandson will visit?'

'I told you that he has a lot on his plate.' Clara had not told her that there was a possibility of his losing his arm.

'What about that young man, that Freddie, yer told me he asked after me.'

'I don't know.' Clara stuck a stamp on the envelope and thought about Freddie. What had been in his mind when he discovered she had gone home? Had he cared enough to want to get in touch with her? 'I'd best be on my way,' she said, wrapping a scarf round her neck and putting on her gloves, determined not to get obsessed with him. What would it gain her, thinking of him all the time? He would probably be off to sea again before she knew it. 'See you later, Gran.'

Bernie nodded and stared gloomily into the fireplace where a miserable fire burnt. She wore several skirts and a couple of jumpers, and a jacket with a shawl on top of that. Another shawl covered her head. 'I just hope I'm not dead when yer get back,' she said.

'Then get out and go to the library, as I

suggested,' said Clara, not knowing what more she could do for her grandmother. 'You can read the newspaper in there. It's nice out, even if it is cold, and you can take your time. You might even meet someone you can talk to.'

Bernie did not respond so Clara left her, hoping she might just make an effort to get out. She popped the letter through the pillar box on her way to work and hoped that her aunt would do her the courtesy of giving her an answer.

Gabrielle took the mail from the postman and thanked him. She tucked the envelopes under her armpit and finished feeding the hens before hurrying indoors, out of the icy wind. She dropped the post on the kitchen table and removed her coat before going over to the sink and washing her hands. She put the kettle on and then riffled through the post. There were a couple of catalogues and what appeared to be bills, and two envelopes addressed to her.

She reached for her reading glasses on the mantelpiece and put them on, and was able to recognise Alice's handwriting. She felt a vague sense of guilt, knowing that she should have made the effort to visit her son. What kind of mother was she for being so negligent of him? Making the excuse that she was marooned here on the farm because it was some distance from the railway station was not a good defence. Yet if she asked for a lift to the station it would result in another row with Martin. She hesitated to open the letter, fearing what it might say, and instead turned to the other one. The handwriting was unfamiliar and she was just about to open the envelope when she heard running feet outside in the yard. She looked up as the door burst open.

One of the farm labourers stood there, red-faced and panting. 'Missus, you've got to come quick. The master's had an accident and is real bad. Frank's gone for the doctor.'

Gabrielle's heart began to thud. Swiftly, she shoved the envelopes in a drawer and followed him out of the house. 'What happened?' she asked.

He gulped. 'Daisy went crazy and the rest of the herd panicked. The master had no time to get out of the way and was trampled on.'

Gabrielle did not need him to say anymore. She had always had a vivid imagination. When she reached Martin's bloodied and battered body she saw for herself just how serious her husband's condition was. For a moment she gazed down at him in disbelief and fought back the bile that rose in her throat. She must be strong.

He was barely conscious when she bent over him and took one of his hands in hers. He tried to speak but she told him to save his breath. 'The doctor will be here soon,' she said in an attempt to reassure him.

'We didn't dare move him, missus,' said the farm labourer in a trembling voice.

'Of course not. You behaved rightly. I'll stay with him,' she said calmly, kneeling down in the filth and mud left after the cattle's passing. 'You go back to the house and fetch a couple of blankets from the chest on the landing upstairs. We need to keep him warm.'

The man hesitated. 'You'll be all right with him by yourself?'

Gabrielle nodded and shooed him away. She gazed down at her husband and considered the possibility that she might soon be a widow. Her mind turned over the advantages such freedom would bring her. But then a little voice in her head said, *But what if Martin were to survive his terrible injuries and was crippled for life?* He would need constant care and it would be her task to look after him. She could not see him paying out for a nurse to take care of him. She thought about what her life would be like in those circumstances and rebelled. She had worked hellishly hard all her life and wanted to get away from this farm and have some fun before she was old and decrepit.

She focused on one of her favourite dreams, that of sailing to New York, buying a whole new wardrobe, and appearing on Broadway to become the toast of the town. How far-fetched was that? And yet dreams did occasionally come true. Maybe she might even meet up with Robbie Bennett again. With Martin's insurance money and what he must have in the bank, which included the money his mother had left her after having worked for her for years, she could do some of the things she had always wanted to do.

She gazed down at her husband, knowing he would hate being a cripple. Besides, why should he live when so many young men had given their lives for their country? Yet still she hesitated, partly horrified by the thought of what she was considering. Yet was it really so wicked? If an animal was in his condition it would be put down. Slowly, she reached out a hand and placed it over his nose and mouth. She watched his face slowly change colour and thought it shouldn't be so difficult to act the part of a grieving widow.

Alice looked up from her darning at Seb as he entered the drawing room. His skin looked pale against the black eye patch and her heart sank. 'What's wrong? Have you heard from the surgeon?'

'No, it's not that.' Seb sat beside her on the sofa. 'I've just received a letter from Ma. Uncle Martin's dead! The funeral's on Friday. She says if I want to go not to bother answering her letter but just to turn up at the farm in time to travel with the cortege.' The paper shook in his hand as he held it out to his wife.

Alice was furious. 'She's got a cheek expecting you to go when she hasn't bothered coming to see you. Does she mention our letter?'

He shook his head.

Alice pressed her lips together on a rude word. 'I bet she hasn't even read it. She pretty well ignores every letter I send, but now she wants something from you we hear from her.'

'Read the letter,' he said. 'She doesn't insist on my going.'

Alice dug the needle into the woollen sock she was darning and set it aside before taking Gabrielle's letter from him. She read it swiftly while he paced the floor. It was short and to the point, and she did not get a mention. Perhaps Gabrielle took it for granted that if Seb went to the funeral she would not accompany him. 'Will you go?'

'Why don't you come straight out with it? You mean, can I cope with facing all those people who knew me before the war, when I worked for my father?' His tone was bitter.

'I wasn't thinking that at all,' she protested. 'You've coped so much better since that day Freddie came round and you went out for a drink.'

Alice remembered him coming in late that evening. After Clara had gone, and Tilly had left the house without saying where she was going. Alice had felt so alone, even when the children had come home and told her about the party. They were in bed before Seb had come rolling home. She had been watching for him and had the door open before he reached it. 'S-Sorry if I'm late fo-for supper,' he'd said. 'Cele-bration, 'cos both Freddie and I survived the war. I-I've decided I'm going to wear a black patch. Yo-ho-ho and a bottle of rum and all that.' Laughing, he had leant against her and planted a sloppy kiss on her cheek. She had returned his kiss, glad to have him safe and so happy, despite the decision he had made about his arm.

After that day, their life had definitely improved in the weeks that followed. Not only had Seb taken to wearing an eye patch, but they had discussed spending some of their precious savings. She had suggested his writing to the surgeon down south who had operated on his arm to ask whether he would see him. This he had done and they were now waiting for a reply.

Seb sighed and rested his head against the mantelshelf. 'I suppose I'll have to go.'

'I thought you would,' she murmured. 'Why don't you get Freddie to drive you there? It'll be easier for you than going by train.'

Seb felt a rush of relief. 'That's a good idea. I'm sure Kenny won't mind my borrowing one of the motors and Freddie always enjoys driving. If he takes me, then you don't have to come with me, which means Tilly won't have to take time off to look after Georgie.'

Alice said, 'I didn't intend going unless you insisted. I'd prefer to stay at home. I'd probably lose my temper with your mother if I went with you. Will I drop by at Hanny's and see if Freddie's in...or will you go while I make some scones for tea?'

'You make the scones.' He kissed her lightly and left the house.

Despite venturing outside more and more during daylight hours, it was still something of an ordeal for Seb to face people. But on that cold but crisp February day, there was only a middle-aged man with a thatch of rusty hair sticking out from beneath a cap in the crescent. He seemed vaguely familiar, so Seb gave him a nod, thinking he must be one of the neighbours he didn't know that well. Then he covered the short distance to Hanny's and hurried up the path and knocked on the door. It was several minutes before he heard approaching footsteps and the door opened to reveal Hanny.

'Seb!' she cried, her face lighting up. 'Come in!'

There was no doubting her pleasure at seeing him and that made him feel better about himself. 'How are you today, Hanny?' he asked, stepping over the threshold. 'How are the twins?'

She groaned and dropped her head onto his shoulder. 'I love them to bits, but they're such hard work.'

He patted her back. 'I can imagine. I wish I could comfort you by saying it'll get easier, but wait until they're crawling and then walking. In your case, they'll be double trouble.'

She lifted her head and smiled at him. 'Go on, cheer me up! Happily Joy's got time off today and has taken Mother and the twins into town. Come up and have a cup of tea and you can tell me why you're here.'

He wiped his feet on the mat and removed his cap. 'I want you to give Freddie a message that I'd like to see him when he comes in.'

She glanced over her shoulder as they climbed the stairs. 'Can you tell me what it's about?'

'Uncle Martin's dead.'

Hanny's fine blue eyes widened. 'Goodness. That's unexpected. He wasn't ill, was he?'

'Not that I know of. Ma doesn't mention what killed him. Just told me the date of the funeral and said if I wanted to go, just to turn up.'

Hanny shook her head but kept her thoughts to herself as they climbed the stairs. She led the way into the beautifully proportioned drawing room with french windows that led onto a wrought-iron balcony. She waved him to an armchair near the fire. 'Sit down while I make tea.' She left the room.

Instead of doing what she said, Seb walked over to the french windows and let himself out onto the balcony. He gazed towards the River Dee. At this time of year there were few day trippers walking along the Groves or using the boats, but he could see the pedestrian bridge and people crossing towards the old city. He stood a while watching them, enjoying his bird's-eye view, trying to ignore the heaviness in his heart, wondering when he would hear from the surgeon. Could be that he would never be able to row Alice or the children in a boat again. He remembered how carefree he and Alice had been in the early days of their courtship. They could not afford to take a boat along the river so they had walked along the path. One particular day stood out in his mind. It was a beautiful sunny late spring day and they had walked some distance, leaving the town far behind. They had lain in a field of buttercups, kissing and loving, their eyes only for each other.

Hanny called him and he turned and went inside.

'You'll catch your death of cold out there,' she said, placing a tray on an occasional table close to the fire.

Seb sat down and watched her pour tea into delicate white china cups with gold rims. 'I meant to ask Alice if she would help me out by doing some baking when we have the twins christened,' said Hanny. 'We want to have a bit of a celebration. It won't be for a while. Eastertide in April, when the weather should be warmer.'

'I'll mention it to her. I'm sure she'll do anything she can to help.' He thought how he had always found it easy to talk to Hanny but it was ages since they had been alone together like this. He stirred the tea and gulped down a mouthful. 'You mentioned Joy. How is she? It was terrible Chris Griffiths going missing. He wasn't even with the Cheshires but with his old Liverpool regiment.'

Hanny agreed. 'Emma and his sisters and her mother felt his loss even worse than Joy, I think. She seems quite content working for Mrs Black, though.'

He smiled. 'I still find it incredible that my cousin Clara traced me through Mrs Black. What a woman!'

Hanny smiled. 'Joy said that she's gone to Liverpool for the day. As you know, Mrs Black has lots of property over there and so most likely she's gone on business.'

There was a note in her voice that caused Seb to give her a second look. 'You say that as if you think she might have had another reason for going.'

She shrugged. 'Alice and Joy have both mentioned Clara and her grandmother to me. Mrs Black knew the family when she was a girl, so I just wondered...'

Seb was taken aback. 'You think she's gone to look up the old woman?'

Hanny's eyes twinkled. 'You know how she takes an interest in people.'

'Too much interest, sometimes,' he said dryly.

'You mean Alice still blames her for caring what happened to her father, even when he was no longer one of her clients?'

Seb nodded. 'D'you think Mrs Black knows where he is?'

'I'm sure she does. After all, she visited him in the asylum for years. I can't imagine her just ignoring him once he was released.'

'Perhaps your Joy knows where he is.'

'If she does then she's not cracking on to me.' Hanny leant back against the cushions. 'Are you going to tell me why you want to speak to Freddie?'

He drained his cup and placed it on the saucer. 'I'm hoping he'll drive me to the funeral. I'll pay him.'

'Don't be daft. He'll be happy to do it as a favour. Is Alice going, too?'

He shook his head. 'You know what the pair of them are like when they meet. Right now, Alice is madder with her than ever.'

Hanny did not blame Alice for the way she felt towards Gabrielle. 'What do you think your mother will do now she's a widow? Can you see her running the farm on her own?'

He shook his head. 'She's never liked the country.'

'So you think she'll come back here?'

'I haven't thought about it.'

'Then it's a case of just waiting and seeing,' said Hanny.

He agreed.

'What about you? When are you going to reopen the showroom, advertise and persuade people to buy new cars?'

He shifted restlessly on the sofa and then rose. 'I don't know. Alice has written on my behalf to the surgeon who operated on my arm. We're just waiting for a reply.'

'You think he might be able to do something more for you?'

'I'm hoping so. Otherwise...' Seb did not finish what he was going to say because at that moment there was the sound of the front door below opening. 'That could be Joy and Mother with the twins,' said Hanny, getting to her feet.

But it was Freddie. 'Aye, aye, Captain!' he said, saluting Seb. 'What are you doing here?' He tossed his cap on the table. 'Any tea in the pot?'

'I'll boil some more water,' said Hanny, smiling lovingly at her younger brother. 'You talk to Seb. He needs you to drive him to his mother's place in Delamere.'

'Oh! Why's that then?' asked Freddie, sitting down.

Seb told him about his uncle's funeral.

'Doesn't sound like much fun,' said Freddie cheerfully, 'but I'll certainly drive you.'

'Good,' said Seb, relieved. 'It's on Friday. When do you go back to sea?'

'I'm not going,' said Freddie. 'I've decided the seafaring life is not for me.'

Seb was taken aback. 'I thought it was what you always wanted to do.'

'I've changed my mind.' He rubbed his hands together and blew on them. 'It's cold out. It gets even colder at sea. I thought I might work for the company, if you'll have me?'

Seb laughed. 'It's not making enough money at the moment to pay a decent wage to Kenny and myself, and we have to pay the bloke who does the repairs.'

Freddie did not look the least put out. 'Let's talk about it downstairs.'

Seb said, 'OK.' He wondered what else Freddie had to say to him and asked whether he had spoken to Kenny about working for the company.

Freddie nodded. 'I thought of maybe going across to the yard and learning motor mechanics from the repair bloke. I don't expect to get paid. I'm sure business will improve but it may take a bit of time. So in the meantime, I'll also see what odd jobs I can do to keep body and soul together. I do have some money. Great-aunt Joan left me some and I was paid a lump sum when I left the ship. I might have spent out buying the motorbike but I don't plan on sponging off my sisters.'

Seb smiled. 'I'm glad to hear it. Who was this Great-aunt Joan? I don't remember hearing about her.'

Freddie jingled the change in his pocket. 'She was Mother's spinster aunt. She had a house at Moreton-by-the-sea. I vaguely remember staying there when I was young. We used to go cockling. In fact, she left the house to Mother, but what with the way she is now, we haven't done anything about it. Perhaps in the summer when the weather gets better.' He grinned. 'I still love a seaview but don't want to be on it day after day. Too many memories of being terrified. It was hell knowing the U-boats were lurking not far away, wanting to blow us to bits. We were living on a knife's edge all the time. It must have been similar for you in the trenches.'

Seb nodded in understanding. 'I'll never forget it. No one here knows what it was like. It takes time getting used to that and everything else.'

'It's been more difficult for you than me,' said Freddie, hesitating before adding, 'Have you heard anything from Clara?'

'No. Alice wrote to Ma telling her that Clara had visited and wanted to see her, but we've heard no more from my cousin.'

Freddie frowned. 'I want to get in touch with her. I've visited the house but I don't have the address. I wondered if you could let me have it.'

Seb smiled. 'Sure. She's a nice girl, isn't she?'

Freddie smiled cheerily. 'I like what I know of her so far.'

'Then you'll have to ask Alice for her address. You can do that when you pick me up on Friday. Best make it early if the funeral's at eleven-thirty.'

They said no more and parted at the gate.

CHAPTER SEVENTEEN

March, 1919.

Gabrielle gazed at her reflection in the cheval mirror and twisted the waist of the calf-length black skirt round so that the kick pleat was in the centre. Then she adjusted the black felt hat with its sweep of ostrich feathers so that it slanted over one eye.

'Not bad for a fifty-plus-year-old,' she murmured, smiling and shaking her head, so that the ornate gold and diamond earrings old Mrs Waters had left her brushed her neck.

There was a knock at the bedroom door. 'There's an automobile here, missus. It's your son,' called Mabel, who had worked at the farm since she was a girl.

So he's come, thought Gabrielle, relieved. She had convinced herself that, despite her invitation, he would stay away because she had not visited him. 'Show him into the drawing room and give him a drink. Tell him I'll be down in a few minutes,' she called.

There was the sound of retreating footsteps.

Gabrielle pulled on black suede gloves and picked up her handbag. A last look in the mirror and then she opened the door and left the bedroom. She descended the stairs with extra care because she was wearing new black patent leather high-heeled button boots. Already she was steeling herself for her first sight of Sebastian's scarred face and knew she had to come up with a really good reason for not having visited him. She should have defied her husband and made the journey to Chester.

As she reached the lobby the murmur of voices coming from the drawing room came to her ears. She had expressed a wish for those attending the funeral to go straight to the church and wondered who he was talking to. Could Alice possibly have come with him? The possibility filled her with dismay. Since that fracas in the crescent with Edie Black, she had felt her daughter-in-law could see beyond the posh façade she had adopted to the girl from the Liverpool slums beneath. Well, she was just going to have put on the act of her life. She pulled back her shoulders, tilted her chin and opened the drawing room door.

Seb turned with glass in hand and stared at his mother. She returned his regard, taking in the silver eye patch before noticing the scars disfiguring the right side of his face. She flinched and put out a hand to steady herself.

'Don't tell me you're going to faint, Ma?' he rasped.

For a moment she could not speak, but then she regained control of herself. 'My poor son! What you must have been through. I can't bear to think about it,' she said huskily, hurrying over to him with her arms outstretched.

He put down his glass and warded her off with his left hand. 'If you don't mind, Ma, you've never been one for hugs and kisses, so there's no need to start now.'

Despite the truth of his words she was taken aback.

'Nothing to say?' rasped Seb, the muscles in his face tightening. 'How about complimenting me on my eye patch? It was Freddie's idea.' He nodded in the young man's direction. 'I have one in black, but I thought, as this was a special occasion I'd ring the changes. I'm going to have a gold painted one for celebrations.'

She cleared her throat and said brightly, 'That's a good idea. Quite theatrical.'

'Glad you think so. You're the expert when it comes to putting on a show. By the way, I hope you don't mind my bringing Freddie with me. You might not remember that he's Hanny's younger brother. He drove me here.'

She inclined her head, almost regally, in Freddie's direction, remembering his sister, whom she had considered a sensible girl until she consulted Edie Black.

Freddie said, 'I'm sorry to hear about your husband, Mrs Waters.'

'Thank you,' she said, before giving her attention to her son once more. 'I presume you can't drive yourself because you've no sight in that eye?'

'No, Ma,' he said tersely. 'The nerves in my right arm were damaged, so I have little strength in it. It's possible I might have to have it amputated.'

She felt sick inside. 'I'd forgotten about your arm. You must have been calling me the most heartless mother on earth for not visiting you, but I had my reasons.'

'They'll have to be earth-shattering,' said Seb in an icy tone.

'I'll tell you but first I need a drink.' Somehow she managed to totter over to the enormous oak sideboard, which held bottles and glasses. She unscrewed a bottle of Navy rum and poured a small measure into a tumbler.

Freddie glanced at Seb and said in a undertone, 'Would you like me to wait outside so you can talk to your mother privately?'

Seb shook his head. 'I'd rather you stayed. Alice will want to know all that's said and I might forget some of it.'

Freddie nodded, wondering what Clara O'Toole would make of her aunt if she could see her now.

Gabrielle downed half the rum and then turned to face her son with a bleak expression on her face. 'I'm not one of those who believe in not speaking ill of the dead, so I'll tell you the truth. Martin beat me and kept me a virtual prisoner on this farm. Even though he's been dead for days, I still bear the bruises of the last time he hit me. I'd show you them but they're in places...' She did not finish but drank the rest of the rum.

'Are you telling me the truth?' asked Seb, incredulously.

Gabrielle nodded.

'How long has this been going on?'

'Since old Mrs Waters died.' A note of bitterness crept into her voice. 'He believed he should have inherited everything. He was furious that you got the house and a third of her money, so he took his frustrations out on me. I grew to hate it here but I couldn't escape.' She went and poured herself another tot of rum. Normally she limited herself to two drinks in the evening but during the past week had found herself topping her glass up a third and fourth time. She despised herself for needing alcohol to steady her nerves but she was haunted by what she had done to hasten her husband's death. But other ghosts also hovered on the edge of her consciousness; Navy rum had been Seb's father's favourite drink and she kept imagining him meeting up with his brother in the spirit world and comparing notes about her.

'I knew he begrudged me my inheritance but he had the farm and no children, so what need did he have of the Chester house? Anyway, Victoria would have inherited it, not him, if she had still been alive, so it naturally came to me after she died as Father had acknowledged me in his will as his son.'

Seb's words roused Gabrielle. 'You don't have to tell me that. Martin was a greedy, envious man and only wanted me because he wanted anything that had belonged to your father.' Her voice cracked and she gazed down into her glass.

Seb protested. 'It had to be more than that. You're an attractive woman, Ma, and an excellent housekeeper. If only I'd known what was going on and how unhappy you were, I would have taken you away from here.'

'From my legal husband? To live with you and Alice?' Her dark eyes sparkled with anger and unshed tears. 'He would have come after me. Besides, Alice and I living under the same roof would never work.' She tossed off the rum and placed the glass on a tray before dabbing the corners of her mouth with a lace handkerchief. Squaring her shoulders, she added, 'Confession's over. He's dead now, I'll say no more. You didn't want to see him, did you? I mean, I've had the coffin lid screwed down. He wasn't a pretty sight after being trampled on by the cattle.'

Seb ran an unsteady hand through his hair. 'So that's how he died? You didn't say in your letter. You must be relieved he's dead?'

Her only reply was a shrug of black-clad shoulders.

Seb was silent for a moment and then said, 'This puts a different complexion on things. What'll you do after the funeral? Will you stay on here for a while?'

'Holy Mary, no!' Her voice was vehement. 'A week, two maybe. Then I'm out of here.'

'Will you come back to Chester?'

'I haven't made up my mind yet.' She flashed him a tight smile. 'I have no plans to be a burden to you and Alice.'

'So where will you live?'

Her dark brows snapped together. 'You don't have to worry about me. I've been looking out for myself since I left home at thirteen.'

The silence that followed those words did not last long.

Seb said, 'About your leaving home, did you get my letter? It would be in Alice's handwriting.'

She stared at him uncomprehendingly, and then her brow cleared. 'I remember two letters arriving the morning Martin died. One was in Alice's handwriting and the other I'd never seen before. I didn't have a chance to read either of them so put them away somewhere. I can't remember where. What did yours say?'

Seb glanced at the clock. 'Have we time to talk about this now?'

'Mabel will tell us when the hearse comes,' said his mother.

'We had a visitor a few weeks ago,' said Seb. 'Her name was Clara O'Toole. She's my cousin. If I'd been in any doubt about that, then seeing her proved to me my mistake. She's the spitting image of what I reckon you must have looked like when you were young. She even has a look of me.'

Gabrielle blinked at him in surprise. 'How did she find you?'

'Never mind that right now. I bet the other letter is from Clara, telling you that your mother's health is bad and she wants to make her peace with you.'

'Mam's still alive!' Gabrielle reached blindly for the bottle of rum again. 'I thought the old bitch would be dead by now. That's it. I've made up my mind. I'm definitely going now. I don't want to ever see her again.'

'Go where?' asked Seb.

But before Gabrielle could either answer or pour herself another drink, the door opened and Mabel popped her head inside and said, 'The hearse is here, missus. Let's hope to God you have a good turn out at the church. I bet that carriage and them black horses cost you a pretty penny.'

'Mind your nose,' snapped Gabrielle, banging down the bottle. Holy Mary, why had Sebastian had to tell her about her mam right now? Her emotions were in turmoil and she felt light-headed, yet somehow she had to get through this funeral and play the role of grieving widow to the hilt.

She turned and stared at her son. 'Come on if you're coming. I've more on my mind right now than my bloody mother. Did you bring a wreath? If you have, give it to the undertaker.'

'It's outside in the porch.'

'Good.' She pointed a finger at Freddie. 'He can deal with it. Now give me your arm.'

Seb forced down his irritation and offered her his left arm. She slid her hand through it and then glanced up at the undamaged side of his face. 'Right,' she said on a sob. 'Let's get this show on the road.'

They walked out, followed by Freddie, who picked up the wreath. Seb climbed into the carriage with his mother while Freddie slid behind the steering wheel of the motor and followed after them at a snail's pace.

Seb had to admire his mother's control and the manner in which she carried off the whole affair – in the church, at the graveside and afterwards at the farmhouse. From the way she spoke about Martin, it was difficult to believe that she had not loved him. Seb remembered what a relief it had been to him when his mother had married his father's brother. He had not had to worry about her anymore and enjoyed years of freedom from her histrionics, for which he was grateful. Even so, he was shocked that the marriage had been such a sham and wondered why his mother seemed to specialise in relationships that went wrong. First, the one with the musician, Robbie Bennett, then the highly irregular affair with his natural father, Thomas Waters. Seb would never get over the revelation that he was his employer's illegitimate son. He had walked out of the house after a row with his mother and within the week he and Alice were married and on a ship to Egypt. Thomas Waters had died whilst they were away and his mother disappeared. He wondered who she might have her eye on next.

He watched her talking to an austere-faced priest in black robes. Well, she certainly could not marry him. Seb decided he'd had enough and, when Freddie approached and asked if they could leave soon as the narrow country lanes would be even more difficult to negotiate in the dark, Seb agreed.

'I'm going to have to go, Ma,' he said, strolling over to her.

She looked up at him and he wondered if it was relief or regret he saw in her brown eyes. 'If you must, son.'

'You'll visit us in Chester? There's matters we need to discuss.'

'Don't worry. I'll keep in touch,' said Gabrielle, holding up her face for him to kiss.

His lips scarcely brushed her powdered cheek. Despite what she had told him about his Uncle Martin, he was still finding it difficult to believe that she could not have made the effort to visit him. 'We'll see ourselves out,' he said.

She thanked him for coming and he left, wondering when he would see her again. He supposed he should have set a firm date, but told himself that she knew where to find him if she needed him.

On the journey home Seb was silent, not wishing to distract Freddie from his driving. The surrounding fields and woods were shrouded in mist, and although it was only late afternoon, it felt as if night had already come. Freddie needed all his concentration to get them home safely.

When they arrived back at the house, Seb invited Freddie inside for a hot drink. 'Thanks,' he said, removing his gloves and rubbing his cold hands. 'I can't stay long, though, I have to pick up Kenny from the yard. Besides, are you sure you don't want to be alone with Alice to talk about your mother?'

Seb smiled and shook his head. 'I think I'll need you to back me up in what I say.'

They found Alice in the drawing room with Tilly

and the children. Immediately, Georgie spotted his father and toddled over to him, holding up a wind-up car. Seb was getting adept at managing to lift his son single-handed and did so now. He was aware of James and Flora's eyes on them and wondered what they were thinking as he blew a raspberry kiss against the back of Georgie's neck. His son chuckled, he felt such a rush of love for him that it almost bowled him over. He doubted his parents had ever felt like that towards him and the thought hurt.

'How did it go?' asked Alice, placing the never-ending darning in the basket at the side of her chair.

'Quite an occasion and I'll tell you about it over a hot drink.' He looked at Tilly. 'How about it, love? One for me and Freddie. Perhaps you can take James and Flora with you, as well.'

'Can't we stay?' asked James.

'This isn't for children,' said Seb.

The boy's face hardened and he marched out of the room.

'Why can't we stay?' asked Flora in a trembling voice. 'Georgie's staying and he's younger.'

'He's only a toddler,' said Seb, looking surprised. 'He'll get in the way in the kitchen.'

'But we'd like to hear what the funeral was like and know what Granny said when she saw you.' Her dainty pretty features were earnest. 'Did she mention us, Daddy?'

Seb hesitated. 'Now her husband's dead, I'm sure she'll come and see you. She was kept busy at the farm. Now you go with Tilly and give her a hand.'

Tilly glanced at Freddie. 'You coming to tell me what the funeral was like?'

Before he could answer, Seb said, 'I want him here.'

'Oh!' She looked put out but said no more and left the room with Flora.

Alice looked up at Seb. 'I'd best tell you before we go any further – a letter's come for you from Oxfordshire.'

He stiffened, guessing it was from the surgeon and his heart began to thud. He was desperate to read what he had to say but wanted to do so in private. 'I'll read it later,' he said.

She nodded. 'I just thought you'd like to know. So what was your mother's excuse for not coming to see you?'

Seb told her what Gabrielle had said about Martin beating her.

Alice was flabbergasted. 'I don't believe a word of it.'

Seb glanced at Freddie. 'You were there. Isn't that what Ma told us?'

He nodded. 'I had the impression she was telling the truth.'

A sharp laugh escaped Alice. 'She's a good actress – always has been. We know she doesn't always tell the truth. I can't see her putting up with being beaten. It's not as if she was a slip of a thing like my mother.'

Seb put Georgie down on the floor and frowned. 'I agree with Freddie. There was a ring of truth in what Ma said.'

Alice pursed her lips and after a moment she said, 'All right. So maybe there was some truth in what she said and Martin beat her. But can you honestly see your mother not fighting back and storming out of the house?'

Absent-mindedly, Seb rubbed his chin. 'No,' he said finally. 'But the farm is in the back of beyond, which does make it difficult for her to travel. She's not intending to come and live here, so you don't have to worry about that.'

Alice said, 'What about the letter I sent her? Has she read it?'

He shook his head. 'She said it arrived the day Martin was killed, so she didn't have time to read it. I told her about Clara and her mother being ill and wanting to see her, but I doubt she'll make the effort to visit. She clearly still hates her. Wouldn't you agree, Freddie?'

He nodded.

Before he could say any more, the door opened and Tilly entered. She was accompanied by Flora, carrying a plate of scones. After that little was said about the funeral and conversation became general.

Tilly asked Freddie how Gabrielle had reacted when she had got her first glimpse of Seb.

'She was shocked, as you'd expect,' he said.

'But she didn't faint?'

He shook his head and drained his cup. 'I don't think she's the fainting kind. Look, I'm going to have to return the motor to the yard.'

Tilly almost snatched the cup and saucer from him and said coolly, 'You go. I was going to tell you about the letter I received from America but I can see you're not interested. See you around,' she said with a tilt of her chin. Swooping down on Georgie, she picked him up, and walked out of the room.

Freddie stared after her in astonishment, wondering what had got into her, but he dismissed her from his mind pretty quickly because he remembered he had not asked Alice for Clara's address. Fortunately, Seb had remembered to mention it to her, so she had it to hand and gave it to him. She thanked him for taking Seb to the funeral.

'It was…interesting,' he said with a grin.

'Seb didn't say how his uncle died. Did his mother tell you?' Alice stared at him intently.

'Trampled on by a herd of cattle, apparently.'

'Oh. I never thought of that.' Alice looked almost disappointed. 'Nasty. Anyway, see you soon, Freddie. And if you write to or see Clara, then give her our warmest wishes and tell her I'll be in touch.'

He nodded and hurried out, in a rush now to pick up Kenny from the other side of the city. Despite his crippled foot, Kenny could drive himself, but he found it painful and appreciated Freddie doing so, especially when it was obvious that the younger man enjoyed driving anything on wheels.

As Freddie started up the motor, he noticed a man loitering outside the house opposite and gazing up at the Bennetts' home. He dropped his gaze when Freddie looked his way and began to amble in the direction of the footbridge. At any other time Freddie might have given more thought to what the attraction was, but right now he had other things on his mind. An idea had occurred to him and he decided to mention it to Kenny when he picked him up.

His brother-in-law had on his tweed overcoat and a cloth cap covered his light brown hair, and he was obviously waiting for Freddie.

'How did the funeral go?' asked Kenny, hoisting himself into the passenger seat.

'It was an experience,' said Freddie seriously. 'She's a real character, is Seb's mother. I'll tell you more in a minute.' He drove the motor out of the yard and then, taking the keys from Kenny, closed the large wooden gates and locked them before climbing back into the driving seat and heading for Lower Bridge Street and the Old Dee Bridge. After a few minutes he said, 'You know about Clara, Seb's cousin?'

'Yes. Joy's told us about her. So is Gabrielle going to visit the grandmother? I have doubts about it myself.'

'Is she hell! You can tell she still hates her.'

'A woman of strong passions, is Gabrielle, inclined to give herself airs and graces. I remember the first time I met her she made me feel about two inches high. I was trying to trace Alice, and Seb was going to give me a hand,' said Kenny. 'You were only about three at the time. It seems a long time ago now.'

'Clara's going to be upset. She wrote to Seb's mother but she hasn't even opened her letter. Mind you, it was the day her husband was killed so I guess it's understandable. I'm going to see Clara and tell her the news.'

Kenny glanced at him. 'You like the girl.'

Freddie nodded, his hands steady on the steering wheel as he frowned ahead. 'I feel sorry for her, too. I'd like to bring some fun into her life. I suspect she doesn't have much of that.'

'Hanny would like to meet her. I know it's a good few weeks off but invite her to the twins' christening. Tell her we'd like to see her there.'

Freddie's face lit up. 'I'll do that. It'll mean she can see Alice and Seb at the same time.'

Kenny smiled. 'Great. I'll look forward to it.

Now, tell me more about the funeral. How did Gabrielle behave when she saw Seb?'

'I'll tell you in a minute but first I've something I want to suggest to you. I've been thinking about how the business can make some money while we're waiting for sales to pick up. How about hiring a motor out with me as a driver if necessary? I've driven Mrs Black so far, and now Seb. We could also give driving lessons to those considering buying a car in the near future.' Freddie glanced at Kenny. 'What d'you think?'

Kenny did not answer immediately but after several minutes, said, 'It's not a bad idea. We'll have to price it, thinking of the cost of fuel and wear and tear to the car... I'll need to consult Seb, too.'

Freddie was delighted that Kenny could see merit in his proposal and suggested eagerly, 'We could put an advertisement in the *Chester Chronicle* and the *Daily Post*.'

Kenny nodded. 'Good idea. I've had articles in both newspapers. I could do a couple more so we won't have to pay out cash for the adverts.'

Freddie gave a sigh of relief. 'Thanks. I really do want to pull my weight and really get the business on the road. That's almost the same words Seb's mother said about the funeral: *Let's get this show on the road*. I tell you, she really is some woman, and is glad her husband's dead. I'm going to have a lot to tell Clara when I see her.'

CHAPTER EIGHTEEN

Clara covered her nose and mouth with her scarf and hurried along Boundary Lane. Earlier that day the sun had shone in a clear blue sky but round about four o'clock the fog had descended. In the distance she could hear the foghorns issuing a warning to shipping in the Mersey and pitied those sailors having to navigate in such weather. She thought of Freddie and wondered if he had returned to sea yet. A sigh escaped her because she had not heard from him and she was starting to believe it was as Tilly had said – that he flirted with all the girls.

She felt miserable and lack of contact with Freddie and the weather were only partially to blame. Not only had she still not heard from her aunt but, worse than that, the Palladium had closed down again. She had scarcely been able to believe it when it happened. But several members of the orchestra had gone down with the flu, as had she, herself, two of the usherettes, Mr Walsh and his wife, as well as his nephew, Teddy, and the projectionist. Sadly, the usherette, Iris, had died, and so had Teddy. The projectionist and Mrs Walsh were still very ill. Luckily, Clara was feeling a lot better now, but it had really brought the danger from this unseen enemy very close. The death toll in Liverpool now stood at a hundred and sixty, and twenty schools in the city had closed down. Her grandmother had also suffered a scary bout of bronchial trouble. Clara had called out the doctor, believing she had passed on the flu to her, but he had soon washed his hands of the old woman when she swore at him. He had told Clara bluntly that Bernie would be dead within the week for refusing his advice.

Concerned that her gran might die without seeing her daughter, Clara had written another letter to her aunt. She was still waiting to hear from her. By some miracle, her grandmother was still hanging on to life, and Clara now reckoned that Bernie might not have had the flu at all, but just her old trouble with her chest. Even so, her grandmother had refused to take to her bed, so Clara had brought down blankets and pillows and pulled the sofa close to the fire so she could lie there in the warmth, as they could scarcely afford to keep one fire going, never mind two. Their stock of winter coal was nearly all used up and she could only hope that spring would come early that year.

The Chinese laundry loomed up through the fog and Clara's heart lifted. She was nearly home. A gas lamp glowed yellow and the sound of her boots echoed eerily on the pavement. Besides making familiar sights appear mysteriously alien, the freezing fog penetrated one's clothing. She could not wait to get in and make herself a hot drink. She took a short cut through an entry into their street. She began to count the front doors and did not see the motorcycle parked on their step until she almost fell over it.

Who did that belong to?

She wasted no time dragging out the key on the string, opening the door and hurrying inside. She slammed the door, marched up the lobby and pushed open the kitchen door. She could scarcely believe her eyes when she saw Freddie Kirk sitting in an armchair at the side of the fireplace. For a moment she was lost for words.

Bernie glanced round the side of the sofa at her. 'Yer've got a visitor, girl. Take off yer coat and come and get warm by the fire.'

Clara found her voice. 'As if I couldn't see him sitting there. What are you doing here?' she asked him. 'I thought you'd returned to sea.'

'Hello, Clara. I've given up the sea.' Freddie smiled as he rose to his feet. 'I know I should have written and warned you I was coming but I didn't know exactly when I'd be able to make it and I didn't have your address.'

She removed her scarf and returned his smile. 'You chose the right day to come, didn't you? It's like pea soup out there. I presume you got here on that contraption outside?'

Freddie nodded. 'Came over on the luggage boat but it was still sunny when I reached the Pierhead.'

'Then you've been here a few hours,' said Clara, drawing off her gloves and manoeuvring her way between sofa and table so that she could get to the fire. She held out her cold hands to the pathetic little blaze.

'Not here. I reached Liverpool about two. Had a look at a couple of motor showrooms that Kenny had mentioned and then I rode up here. I wasn't sure I would find you in but I thought if your gran didn't mind, I'd wait for a bit. Then she told me that the picture house where you worked is closed and you've had the flu.' He gazed intently at her face. 'You do look a bit peaky. Could do with a holiday, if you ask me.'

'If only,' she said with a wry smile. 'Right now I need to find myself a temporary job to tide us over until the Palladium opens again. No luck today, though, another girl beat me to it.'

'Bad luck,' he commiserated.

'Has Gran been keeping you amused?' she asked.

He grinned. 'Your gran's got a good sense of humour.'

'Tell me about it,' said Clara dryly.

'She wants me to speak to Joy and ask her to tell Mrs Black she'd like a visit when it's convenient. This side of the grave, not the other, if she doesn't mind.'

Clara gasped and looked at Bernie. 'You've got a cheek, Gran.'

'He hasn't told you all of it,' smirked Bernie. 'I asked him to arrange a cruise for me, but he said no can do.'

'I don't think I want to know any more,' said Clara, covering her eyes.

'Don't be worrying about what your gran says to me,' said Freddie, his eyes twinkling. 'If I could arrange a cruise to a nice warm part of the world for her then I would. I agree with her that it could give her a new lease of life.'

Clara could not help giggling. 'She's awful. What did you reply?'

'I told her the truth – that I had worked on a merchant ship and also that hundreds of ships had been sunk during the war and it's going to take some time before they're replaced. That fact more than anything convinced me that I've made the right decision in giving up the sea. I plan to work in the family business.'

'Yer lucky to have a family business so yer can

choose to do what yer want,' said Bernie. 'Women aren't so fortunate.'

'I wouldn't argue with you,' said Freddie easily. 'Both my sisters were involved with the Women's Socialist Party Union. They felt strongly about improving the lot of working-class women.' He turned to Bernie, 'Your grandson's wife, Alice, who is my sister's best friend, even went to London and marched through the streets to a rally in Hyde Park.'

Clara was impressed. 'London! Chester's the furthest I've ever been. At least you have seen a bit of the world, Freddie.'

'It wasn't much fun,' he said, folding his arms. 'Christmas 1917 I was in the North Atlantic. It was freezing and miserable and there was no Christmas pud.'

'I like Christmas pud but we didn't have any this past Christmas,' wheezed Bernie. She cocked an eye in Clara's direction. 'Talking about food, what have we got to eat?'

Clara hesitated. 'I've some potatoes. I could do us scallops...and there's bread.' She turned to Freddie. 'Are you hungry?'

He nodded. 'And I love scallops. But I did bring some food with me. Hanny knows my appetite and said I mustn't eat you out of house and home if you invited me to tea.'

Relief flooded through Clara and she beamed at

him. 'All we need is to check that we've enough pennies for the gas meter and we're in business.'

'Then put the kettle on, girl,' said her grandmother, 'and peel the tatters.'

'I'm a dab hand at peeling potatoes,' said Freddie, a lazy smile in his blue eyes as he gazed at Clara. 'Peeled hundreds when I was at sea. Lead me to them and I'll peel while you put the kettle on.'

She led him into the back kitchen. 'Remember you volunteered,' she said, taking the potatoes out of her shopping bag and fetching the specially sharp potato knife. 'I want no complaints that I forced you into this,' she said in a teasing voice as she handed the knife to him.

'Aye, aye, Captain.' He proceeded to prove that he was as he had said, a dab hand at ridding the vegetables of their skins.

Clara still had some dripping from the very small joint they'd had at the weekend and spooned it out of a cracked cup into the frying pan and lit the gas ring beneath it. 'We've no butter so you'll have to do without that on your bread,' she said, watching him slice the potatoes as she filled the kettle.

'Don't need butter if we're having nice crispy scallops. But you do have salt?' he asked.

She smiled. 'Yes.'

'Good. I like salt on everything.' He sliced the last potato and tipped the scallops into a handy bowl and brought them over to her. She patted them dry with a clean tea towel and started to place the slices into the frying pan.

He watched her for a moment and then went over to the window and lifted a curtain. Clara glanced at him. 'Are you worrying about the fog? Do you think you'll be able to get home in this?'

He shrugged. 'You mustn't worry about me. If the luggage boat isn't sailing, I'll put up at a lodging house in Mount Pleasant here in Liverpool.'

Clara was stupidly about to offer him the sofa in the kitchen when she remembered her grandmother was sleeping on it. Though, there was a cold, leatherette horse-hair stuffed couch in the parlour, or she could offer him her father's former bedroom. Of course, both rooms were like iceboxes at the moment and most likely damp. Even so, she could take out both oven shelves, one to warm his bed and one hers, and she could air some clean sheets. Trouble was, Gran might not approve of them both sleeping upstairs, unchaperoned. She decided to keep quiet for the moment.

When both returned to the kitchen with plates of hot scallops and slices of bread, Bernie looked up at the pair of them. 'I was just thinking,' she said. 'We can't expect the poor lad to go out into the fog. He'll have to stay here.'

'That's very kind of you,' said Freddie, darting a look at Clara.

She flushed. 'I did think of it, myself, only I was

trying to work out exactly where to put you,' she said, before hurrying out into the back kitchen to fetch the teapot.

'He can go into Denny's bedroom,' said Bernie, as Clara poured the tea. 'I'm sure I can trust yer to behave yerself, can't I, lad?' She winked at Freddie.

Clara felt a deeper blush flood her face and she did not dare look at him.

'Of course you can, Mrs O'Toole,' he said solemnly. 'My sisters brought me up to treat young ladies with respect.'

'I'm glad to hear that,' said Bernie, her breathing laboured as she hoisted herself up into a more comfortable sitting position to eat. 'So what's this food yer've brought?' she asked.

From a black bag he produced a couple of paper bags. He emptied a greaseproof paper bag of boiled ham onto one of the plates and from the other bag he carefully drew out six tarts. Three were lemon cheese tarts and the others raspberry jam.

'Oh, I love lemon cheese,' said Clara, wanting to give him a thank you kiss for this unexpected treat. 'Did your sister Hanny make these?'

He shook his head. 'She told me to get them from the bakery where she used to work. Now she has the twins, she doesn't have time to make things like she used to, but she said Bannister's food was as good as her homemade.'

Clara fetched more plates and, as she handed one

to him, she felt strangely content, despite having plenty to depress her.

They ate in peaceful silence and after every crumb had been consumed, Clara got up and washed the dishes. When she returned to the kitchen it was to find that Bernie had dozed off and Freddie was placing the last of the coal from the bucket in the alcove beside the fireplace on the fire. She knew there was little left in the cellar. A couple of shovelfuls, maybe, but there was no point in telling him that. He was a welcome guest and the hotter the fire, the warmer the shelves in the oven would be. Fortunately, she had brought the potatoes home wrapped in newspaper, which could go round the shelves.

He straightened up and smiled at her as he brushed the coal dust from his fingers. 'You'd best wash them,' she said. 'We can put the kettle on the fire for cocoa later but right now there's still some warm water in it.'

He nodded. 'We used to have a blackleaded range in the house where I grew up. Mother used to take in lodgers.'

'How did you feel about that?' asked Clara, interested to learn something more about his background.

'I didn't mind. Some were interesting, most kept themselves to themselves.' His eyes were thoughtful as his gaze rested on her pale face. He patted the seat of the armchair. 'Come and sit down. I've something to tell you.'

She did so. 'Is it about Seb? How is his arm?'

Freddie sat on the arm of the chair. 'Alice told Hanny that he's had a reply to a letter he sent to a specialist at the hospital where he stayed in the south. He wants to see him. It's just arranging a time when he can go. But that's not the main thing I want to tell you.'

Clara was finding his closeness disturbing but told herself to ignore it. 'What is it you want to tell me?'

'I saw your aunt.'

Clara's eyes widened. 'When? Did she visit Seb and Alice?'

'No. I drove Seb to Delamere to attend your aunt's husband's funeral. He was killed in a farm accident.'

'When did this happen? No wonder she hasn't answered my letters.'

'She received your letter but because it arrived the day of the accident she hadn't opened it. But Seb told her about your visiting him.' Freddie brought his head closer to hers and lowered his voice. 'He said about your gran being ill and wanting to see her.'

'What did she say?'

He hesitated.

'Tell me the truth,' whispered Clara.

'Firstly, she was surprised that her mother was still alive…'

Clara's spirits sank because she guessed what was coming. 'She doesn't want to see Gran, does she?'

'That's the impression I got. Sorry. Of course, she might change her mind.'

'But you don't think so,' said Clara with a sigh. 'What's she going to do? Will she stay on at the farm? I could visit her when it gets warmer, I suppose.'

He grimaced. 'Waste of your time, love. She can't wait to leave.'

Clara's heart leapt at his use of the word *love* but she told herself it didn't mean a thing. 'You think she'll move in with Alice and Seb?'

'Unlikely. She and Alice don't get on.'

'Best not to mention it to Gran until I know more, then,' she muttered, pulling a face.

They were silent for a moment and then he said. 'I didn't only come about your aunt but to ask you to keep a date free so you can come to a party.'

'A party?' Clara felt warmth flood through her at the smile he gave her. 'You want me to go to a party with you?'

'The invitation is actually from Hanny and Kenny. The twins are getting christened at Easter and they'd like you to come. I know it's a few weeks off but I thought you might need advance warning,' said Freddie casually. 'I mean, for all I know, you might have a boyfriend and have other plans.'

'Oh no,' said Clara, slightly disappointed that the invitation and the party wasn't what she had thought, but even so, she was eager to accept. 'I'd love to come. I'll have to give some thought to what to wear, that's all.' She would also have to find the money for the fare to get there.

As if reading her mind he said, 'I'll come and pick you up on my motorbike. You don't have to worry about getting there and back.'

Her smile seemed to start deep inside her and she beamed at him. 'That's so kind of you. Thank you.'

'Who are yer thanking?' asked a slurred voice from the depths of the sofa.

It was Freddie who explained things to Bernie.

'So who's going to be at this party?' she asked.

'Family and friends.' He glanced at Clara. 'Hanny thought of asking Mrs Black but Joy said she's going away for Easter, so she won't be there.'

'I take it yer family's not Catholic, lad, if the babies aren't baptised yet?' said Bernie.

'No. But you won't hold that against us, will you?' he said with a smile.

Bernie blinked across at him. 'None of my business. What about our Gertie? Will she be there?' She did not wait for an answer. 'I remember her being baptised. A lot of good it did her. Sinful place, the stage.'

'I once thought of going on the stage,' said Clara seriously.

Freddie looked amused. 'What would you do? Do you sing, or dance? Or perhaps you play an instrument? Or are you double-jointed? You could be an acrobat or the amazing rubber-armed woman! You could reach up without a ladder and rescue cats from trees.'

There was a rumble of laughter from Bernie. 'That I'd like to see,' she wheezed.

A tiny smile played about Clara's mouth. 'That was then. Now I'd enjoy being in a flicker as Clara the Cowgirl and have adventures in the Wild West.'

'I wouldn't mind dressing up as a cowboy. I remember Hanny telling me that Mother and Dah took me to see Buffalo Bill's Wild West Show when I was a kid. It came to Chester and performed on the Roodee and was lit by electric lights in a big marquee.'

'I'd have liked to have seen that,' said Clara wistfully. 'Instead, I've had to make do with the flickers.'

Freddie's expression altered. 'Will it be long before the Palladium opens again?' he asked. 'What if it's weeks? What if you can't get another job?'

Clara said, 'I'll find something, and it's not as if Gran and I are down to our last penny. I do have some money tucked away against a rainy day. It's just that I didn't expect it to rain so heavily, so soon,' she added with a touch of a smile.

'Have you thought of taking in a lodger?' asked Freddie. 'It would bring in some money.'

Clara hesitated. She glanced at Bernie. 'What d'you think, Gran?'

'I suppose it's a thought. It would have to be someone working. We wouldn't want them in the house all day, and they'd need to pay up front. We wouldn't want any moonlight flits without paying the rent.'

'I might have to ask the rent man,' said Clara. 'I'm not sure of the ins and outs of things when you let out part of the house you're renting.'

'Mrs Black would know,' said Freddie. 'She owns property over here. I could drop by hers on my way home in the morning and speak to Joy if Mrs Black's not in. She could ask her about it and I'll write and let you know what she says.'

'You do that, lad,' said Bernie. 'We've a parlour and a bedroom fully furnished going for let. I'd like a man but I can't see us getting one of them when there's going to be a shortage.'

So it was decided.

Soon after, Clara went upstairs and brought down the bedding to air it. 'Is there anything I can do to help?' asked Freddie.

'You can put the kettle on the fire. Might as well save the gas. I'll make the cocoa in a minute.' She looked up at him. 'Will Hanny and Kenny be worried about you if you don't turn up tonight?'

'I'm sure when they see the fog they'll realise what's happened and expect me back tomorrow,' he answered. 'Don't start worrying about them worrying about me. I was at sea for years and so my not coming home one night isn't on that scale.'

She smiled. 'Sorry if you think I'm fussing.'

'You're not fussing, you're just thoughtful of people,' he said warmly.

'Yer right there,' said Bernie, looking up at the pair of them. 'She thinks I don't appreciate her but I know where I'd be without her.'

'Goodness, Gran. Are you feeling all right?' asked Clara, startled.

Bernie scowled ferociously. 'Learn to take a compliment, girl. I'll be glad when yer both get to bed and leave me in peace. But no shenanigans upstairs.'

Clara felt like sinking through the floor but Freddie said, 'I could sleep in the parlour if you prefer, Mrs O'Toole?'

'No, lad. Yer've got long legs and yer might as well have the bed.'

Clara and Freddie heard little from her after that. He helped her take the shelves from the oven and wrap them in newspaper, and then carried them upstairs for her. He stayed outside on the landing while she went into her bedroom and offered to make his own bed. She shook her head. 'No. You're our guest. But you can put a match to the gaslight.'

He did that while she made the bed, watching her swift, smooth, competent actions and thinking he would like to have tossed her onto the bed and kissed her, but he stayed where he was in the doorway until she came out, and then placed the oven shelf between the sheets.

'I do appreciate this,' he said when they both went downstairs.

She glanced over her shoulder at him in the darkness. 'It's the least I can do after you made the journey over here to tell me about Aunt Ge-Gabrielle. I wonder if she's received my second letter and read that, or whether she's just stuck it in a drawer somewhere. I suppose I might never know if she doesn't want anything to do with us.'

'More fool her,' said Freddie firmly, and he reached for her hand as they came to the bottom of the stairs. He squeezed it gently before releasing it and pushing open the kitchen door.

Shortly after, they drank their cocoa and Clara told him where the lavatory was and helped her grandmother down the yard after he had visited it himself. The foghorns on the Mersey could still be heard and she hugged to herself the thought of Freddie being safe under their roof.

There was no sign of him when she went upstairs to her bedroom but, as she lay in bed, she could picture him lying the other side of the wall and imagined what it would be like to have him around all the time. She thought of her father and was of the opinion that Dennis O'Toole would have liked Freddie Kirk.

CHAPTER NINETEEN

Denny was dead! Her little brother was dead!
Gabrielle crunched the letter in her hand and felt a
need to sit down. A quarter of an hour ago she'd
finished her packing and decided to make herself a
sandwich before the taxi came to take her to the
station. She had dismissed Mabel and so was
looking after herself that morning. Absently, she
had reached into one of the drawers beneath the
table top for a knife and discovered not only the
letters that had arrived the day of Martin's death
but another one that she must have placed there in
a moment of absent-mindedness.

Reading her niece's letter, it came as a terrible
shock to learn that the brother she remembered
being born was dead. She had forgotten the delight
she and her sisters had felt when their mam had
given birth to a boy at last. They had lit candles in
church, praying that he would survive. Well, it
seemed he had grown into a man, only to be killed

in the bloody war. She was amazed at the grief she felt because she had deliberately put him out of her mind, knowing that if she thought of him too much she would never be able to break free of her mother. But now she remembered Dennis toddling around after her while she polished and scrubbed. She recalled giving him a pan and a wooden spoon to amuse himself and the din he had made. Her mother had complained that the noise hurt her head and wrenched the spoon from him.

She felt a familiar anger, thinking of Bernie. What a terrible mother she had been to all of them. So why should she go and see her when in her heart she hoped she'd die and rot in hell? But her niece sounded a different kettle of fish altogether. She would like to meet her but she had to get away; she could not alter her plans. Perhaps she would send her a postcard from New York. Right now, she had little time to waste, as she'd had difficulty getting a berth on a liner and had to be in Liverpool within a few hours. Thank God, the snowfall that had delayed the first Grand National in years had gone. She'd wager a pound to a penny her mother would have had a bet on the favourite, which had won. No! She was not going to think about her anymore but concentrate on the holiday ahead. She had bought nothing in the way of new clothes, planning to purchase them in America instead. Preparing everything in a rush had meant not paying a visit to her son, but she would write to him once she was on the ship. Hopefully she would get the letter on a mail boat when the liner stopped off in Ireland and it would reach him in a few days.

'I don't believe it!' exclaimed Seb, gazing down at the letter in his hand.

'What don't you believe?' asked Alice, placing two pairs of clean pyjamas in a suitcase before looking across the bed at him. The letter he had received the day of the funeral had caused a similar reaction, but at least that letter had given them hope.

'Ma's gone to New York.' He sank onto the bed.

Alice felt a stir of indignation mingled with relief. 'Typical of her to tell you something after she's done it.' She snapped the suitcase shut and placed it on the floor.

His face darkened. 'She doesn't even say when she'll be back.'

Alice sat on the bed and slid her arm around Seb's waist. 'You mustn't let this upset you. We've got by without her for years and we'll carry on doing so.'

'I wouldn't argue but... I'll never understand how her mind works in a thousand years.' He tore up the letter and tossed the pieces up in the air. They both watched as the scraps fluttered to the floor.

'I won't say the obvious,' murmured Alice.

He stared at her. 'You think she's only ever thought of herself.'

'Wouldn't I be right? I'm sure she does have feelings for you, but she's always put herself first. And she's got worse as she's got older.'

'I wonder why she's going to America when she must have unhappy memories of the place. She was abandoned there by Robbie Bennett.' He scowled. 'When I think that for years I believed he was my father... But when I learnt she had lied about him, I realised she had lied to me about a lot of things and came to believe I hardly knew her at all.' He sighed heavily. 'It's obvious she's not going to visit her mother.'

'Poor Clara. After all her efforts to try and unite them.' There was a short silence. 'I wonder what your mother's going to do about the farm?'

'She's put in a manager,' said Seb tersely.

'At least she hasn't left that for you to arrange,' said Alice. 'Which is a good job because you wouldn't have been able to do it with going to Oxfordshire.' She squeezed his waist. 'I still wish I could go with you.'

Seb reached out and touched her soft-skinned cheek with the back of his hand. 'We've discussed this, love. Tilly's working at the office and Hanny's got her hands full with the twins and her mother. We can't expect either of them to look after Georgie during the day. I'd like you with me but...' He got up and went over to the rain-splattered window and gazed out towards the grey waters of the Dee.

Alice followed him over and slipped her hand through his arm, feeling a need to touch him and reassure him all the time at the moment. 'At least the snow has gone and the river isn't flooding here,' she murmured. Parts of low-lying Wirral were flooded.

'What time did I say Freddie was coming to drive me to the station?' he asked.

'Nine o'clock. And I've just remembered something.' Her green eyes brightened. 'Did Freddie tell you that he went over to Liverpool the other week and saw Clara? Hanny has invited her to the twins' christening party.'

'He told me that he saw both Clara and her grandmother. Clara had had the flu and the old woman had a bad bout of bronchial trouble, but it seems she's still holding her own. She must be as tough as old boots. He also said that the cinema where Clara is a cashier had to close down, so she's not working at the moment. Several members of the staff died.'

Alice shuddered. 'I couldn't bear it if I lost any of the children.'

Seb agreed, looking back to the day when Donald had mentioned the Spanish flu to him and of the soldiers going down like nine pins to it. He had recently received a letter from him, and when he had gone into the office yesterday, he had discovered Tilly typing a letter to him, apparently thanking him for some photographs he had sent her and bringing the American up to date with what they were all doing.

'At least some good has come out of Clara's determination to get in touch with your mother. It looks like Freddie's interested in her,' said Alice.

Seb glanced at her. 'It mightn't last. They're both only young.'

'Perhaps it will. Although I don't think Tilly's pleased.'

'Has she said anything to you about them?'

'No. But I know her and I've seen her face when Clara and Freddie have been mentioned in one breath. Anyway, we'd best drop the subject. We've got enough on our minds with your trip to Oxfordshire. I do hope you get the diagnosis you want and that you make it back for the twins' christening. Right now, though, we have to make the most of this time together.' He nodded and kissed her. She wished with all her heart that she could have gone with him, but as they lay on the bed, all she could do at that moment was to show him that she loved him.

The evening of the following day Alice received a telegram from Seb assuring her of his safe arrival. Three days after that she received another one saying that he'd had an operation and that the surgeon had sounded positive. If only they'd had a telephone, at least she could have spoken to him. Being kept in the dark was driving her to distraction, but the next day she received a letter in which he had written:

They use medical jargon but the bit I understood was that they've done a tendon transplant, which should give me more movement in my arm. Trouble is, love, I could be down here longer than I thought because I'll need physiotherapy.

Her heart sank when she read those words and she knew that this time she could not bear waiting to see how he was coping for weeks on end. She presumed that, financially, Seb had scraped the barrel in order for him to have this operation, but she was determined to go and see him. It was a while since she had rooted in the attic for stuff to take to the pawnshop but that was what she was going to have to do if she was to visit him. But, of course, even if she was able to raise the money to make the journey, she would need someone to look after Georgie during the day. Naturally, her thoughts turned to Hanny and Kenny, they'd be able to advise her. So she hurried out with Georgie to their house.

As it happened, Freddie was home and, as soon

as she told Hanny her problem, he suggested that she get in touch with Clara.

Alice and Hanny stared at him. 'Clara!' they chorused. 'But she...'

'She's not working at the moment and if it's only a couple of days, I'm sure she could cope,' said Freddie, 'and she can keep Tilly company in the evenings.'

Hanny looked amused. 'And I presume you'll pop in to see how the two of them are getting on,' she said. 'There's only one thing wrong with the idea, and that's that she doesn't know anything about children.'

'Surely most mothers don't until they have them,' said Freddie.

'I helped look after you,' said Hanny promptly, 'so I had some experience.'

'I had none,' said Alice, keeping her eye on Georgie as he wandered round the room. 'I learnt by trial and error. Georgie is such an easygoing little boy that I can't see her having any real problems with him – and if she did, she could nip here and ask you for advice, couldn't she, Hanny?'

Hanny barely hesitated because she knew how desperate Alice was to make amends for failing to visit Seb the last time he was in hospital. 'Of course Clara can come to me for help. But what about the grandmother? Who'll look after her?'

Freddie had an answer to that question too.

'They have neighbours. I'm sure they'll pop in and see Mrs O'Toole has what she needs. Besides, they might have a lodger by now. It was something they were thinking of doing to make ends meet.'

'Well, if you can persuade her to come then I suggest, Alice, that you have her over here before you go and visit Seb. Give her a day of your time to show her how to look after Georgie.'

'You're right,' agreed Alice, nodding her auburn head. 'So who's going to get in touch with Clara? You or me?' she asked Freddie.

He brushed back a lock of hair. 'I tell you what – you write a note and I'll deliver it by motorbike. If it's convenient, I could bring her back over with me.'

'Tell her she doesn't have to bring clothes with her – we've enough for her to borrow some, and I'm sure you'll never manage her and luggage on that contraption of yours,' said Alice, thinking of practicalities despite having so many thoughts running through her head. Uppermost was that there was a copy of the train times and connections to the hospital in Oxfordshire in a sideboard drawer in the dining room. If Clara returned with Freddie that evening, she could make her travel arrangements tomorrow by going across to Newtown where Chester's general station was situated. There was a pawnshop close to Brook Street nearby and the owner had brought stuff from her before.

* * *

Clara was feeling fed up. She had still not found herself a suitable temporary job, and it was a waste of time looking now because Mr Walsh reckoned that the Palladium would be open for business again on Easter Monday. Those who had been ill were almost fit for work and there had been several interviews to fill the posts of those who had died. She glanced through the newspaper, where she had placed her advertisement for a lodger, and noticed an article about a Yorkshire girl who had won a film competition. Her name was Lavender Lee and she was nineteen, the same age as Clara, although she would be celebrating her twentieth birthday soon. But the main difference between them was that, according to the reporter, *Miss Lee had a remarkable resemblance to Miss Mary Pickford.*

Clara sighed and flung down the newspaper. There was no way she could claim a likeness to any star of the silver screen. She gave a rueful smile and decided there was no point worrying about it. After all, she had other things to think about. If only the days would hurry by so that she could see Freddie again and return to work. He had written to tell them what Mrs Black had advised and it had paid off; they now had a lodger, Mary. She was a nurse, who had served in Flanders, having lost her fiancé on the Somme. She had recently found herself a job at the Royal Infirmary on Pembroke Place, not far from TJ Hughes. She worked shifts and should be home soon.

Whilst Clara was home all day they had arranged that she would cook meals for Mary when she came in at a small extra charge. The spare ribs were roasting in the oven and soon would be ready. Clara glanced across to where Bernie was dozing in the chair on the other side of the fireplace. 'You'll have to be waking up soon, Gran. Mary will be in.'

The old woman started awake and blinked at her granddaughter. 'So what happened to that Mrs Black, then?' she asked.

Coming out of the blue, the question took Clara by surprise. 'I don't know, Gran. What were you expecting to happen to her?'

'I asked for a visit off that young man you have a fancy for and she hasn't been.' She paused. 'Now, what's his name? I thought we'd have had another visit from him by now.'

As if on cue, there was a knock on the door, and Clara sprang to her feet and hurried to answer it. She could scarcely believe it when she saw Freddie standing outside. He was wearing his long waterproof coat, a leather helmet and gauntlets. 'Gran was just asking about you.'

'She's not still expecting me to get her onto a cruise ship, is she?' asked Freddie, grinning.

Clara shook her head. 'Mrs Black. She wants to know what happened to her. She thought you were arranging a visit.'

Freddie said easily, 'I thought she was joking, but I'll have a word in Joy's ear and see what she can do when she comes back from Scotland. She's forever saying that Mrs Black is a very busy woman.'

'That's fine,' said Clara, smiling. 'Come on in. Tell me, to what do we owe the pleasure of your visit?'

'A temporary job for you, if you're willing, during the rest of Holy Week.' He wiped his feet on the doormat. 'Seb's in hospital in Oxfordshire and Alice wants to visit him for a couple of days. She needs someone to look after Georgie.'

Clara was quick on the uptake and, placing a hand on her chest, said in astonishment, 'She wants me to look after him?'

He nodded. 'I've a note from her. She needs a quick response. If you say I do, then I'll take you back with me.'

She thought about how nice it would be staying in Alice and Seb's house, only a few doors away from Freddie, for a couple of days. If it had not been for Mary lodging with them, she could not even have considered it. 'I don't have much experience when it comes to handling kids, but he seemed a pleasant little boy.'

'Alice won't be going until the day after tomorrow and, if you have any problems, Hanny can help you.'

'Then I'll definitely come,' she said, her smile

growing. 'That's if it's OK with Gran and Mary, our new lodger.'

'So you've found a lodger?'

Clara nodded. 'She should be in any moment.'

And so she was, almost on their heels as they entered the kitchen.

Bernie's eyes widened in amazement. 'It's him!' she wheezed. 'Now that's what I call magic. That woman! It was her, wasn't it? Mrs Black.'

'This is Mary, Gran,' said Clara patiently. 'Remember, she's come to lodge with us?'

Bernie nodded in Mary's direction and said truculently, 'I hadn't forgotten. But she doesn't have Mrs Black's magic potion.'

'Sorry about that,' said Mary, removing her coat and smiling at Freddie. 'Who's this?'

Clara introduced them and wondered what he thought of the woman in front of him. Mary was perhaps thirty, with light brown hair secured tidily in a net in the nape of her neck. She was slender but not skinny, and of medium height.

Freddie took off a gauntlet and shook her hand. 'Nice to meet you.'

'Same here.'

'I'm going to ask a favour of you, Mary,' said Clara.

Bernie screwed up her face, causing hundreds of wrinkles to drag at her thin lips. 'What favour's that then?'

Clara told the two women Freddie's reason for coming, 'You'll be OK, won't you, Gran? It's not as if you'll be alone in the house all the time,' she said persuasively. 'And the neighbours will pop in if you can't get out and Mary's at work.'

'I'm sure we'll manage fine together,' said Mary firmly. 'If your cousin's wife needs help, then you must go.'

Bernie opened her mouth and grumbled, 'I haven't said she can go yet. Yer a stranger to me.'

Freddie smiled at her. 'But you will say yes, won't you, Mrs O'Toole. It is your grandson who's in hospital and needs to see his wife.'

'He hasn't been to visit me, though, has he?'

'But he might when he comes home,' said Clara, crossing her fingers.

Bernie stared at them both and then nodded. 'But don't you be away for ages, girl,' she said roughly.

Clara almost hugged her but instead dished out the ribs, potatoes and cabbage. She did ask Freddie whether he wanted some but he refused, saying his sister would be doing supper for him. 'And Alice said you're not to worry about bringing anything to change into as you can borrow from her.'

Clara was unsure about that but, remembering there was nowhere to put baggage on the motorbike, she agreed. Even so, she would have to take a handbag. Within half an hour, she was hoisting up her skirts in order to sit on the cushion tied to a carrier above the back mudguard of Freddie's motorbike. 'Sorry, I haven't a proper pillion seat,' he said.

'It doesn't matter,' she said cheerfully, only to regret her words a few minutes later after landing on her bottom on the road when the motorbike accelerated.

Freddie apologised. 'I should have warned you,' he said, helping her up and onto the cushion again. 'You'll have to put your arms round my waist, link your hands together and hold on tight.'

She thanked him for the instructions and, with a sparkle in her eyes and a heavily beating heart, she climbed onto the cushion again. Off they roared to West Derby Road, then along past the Palladium and the Olympia Theatre. Soon they were travelling along Dale Street amidst the towering buildings of the commercial part of the city, then on the floating bridge that led to the Prince's landing stage and the ferry that would take them across the Mersey. To say that the ride had been exhilarating was a glorious truth. It was a long time since Clara had enjoyed herself so much.

Freddie had bought ferry tickets earlier in the hope that Clara would be able to accompany him, so they didn't have to queue up. He trundled his motorbike straight up the gangplank onto the boat. It seemed ages to Clara since she had crossed the river by ferry and she was looking forward to the trip.

The sun was going down but it was not cold, and when Freddie took her hand and walked with her over to the side of the boat where they could watch the crew casting off, she felt a moment of pure happiness. Their shoulders brushed as they stood watching the huge ropes being wound round the capstan and the boat being pushed away from the landing stage. The dark waters churned up white foam as the screw began to turn and the vessel drew away from the landing stage.

As the line of docks retreated into the distance she caught sight of the Liver Building, which had been opened almost eight years ago by Lord Sheffield. It had been the day of the king's coronation. She remembered coming to the Pierhead with her parents and her father telling her that, from the ground to the top of the Liver birds, the building stood three hundred and twenty-two feet high.

'It's hard to imagine Liverpool now without the Liver Building looming over the waterfront,' said Freddie.

'I was just thinking about the Liver Building, too,' she said. 'Doesn't it look different from out here on the river?'

'It's a sight that many a sailor is happy to see when he sails up the Mersey from the Irish Sea,' said Freddie. 'Seb's mother sailed from here. She'll have reached New York by now.'

Clara's happiness evaporated. 'What are you talking about?' Her voice rose almost to a squeak.

'Damn. I forgot you didn't know,' said Freddie ruefully. 'She wrote to Seb and he didn't get the letter until she'd gone.'

Clara was furious with her aunt. 'How could she do that to her own son, never mind her mother? I can't understand people who bear a member of their own family a grudge for ever and ever.'

Freddie was silent and she wondered if her words had annoyed him. Then he kissed her cheek and said, 'You've a nice nature, Clara O'Toole, but I think you'll find there are plenty of families who find it hard to forgive and forget past sins of their relatives. Our Bert, in the case of me and my sisters, despite his being dead. Now, do you want to stay here or shall we move somewhere else so we can watch the sunset?'

She settled on watching the sunset and, as they gazed across the silver and gold silk shot waters, she decided that it was too lovely an evening to argue about the matter. After all, wasn't she extremely cross with her Aunt Gertie right now? She changed the subject and asked him about some of the places he had visited whilst at sea.

'Nowhere I thought exciting, especially as we were on turnaround more often than not and saw little of the ports except for the docks.' He talked instead of his plans for the business and finished by saying, 'It would all bring in extra money, and I need to save if I'm to have the future I have in mind.'

'Most things boil down to having money, don't they?' said Clara, wondering if she had any part to play in his plans.

He agreed but then changed the subject to the cinema, and for a while they discussed films and music. 'You must come to the Palladium when we open again,' she said. 'They have a wonderful orchestra.'

'I will,' promised Freddie.

They were silent for several minutes after that but it was a companionable silence. It did not occur to Clara to ask what Tilly thought of the idea of her coming to stay, and perhaps that was just as well. For if she had known, she might not have gone.

Tilly stared in dismay at her sister, who had just informed her that, all being well, Clara was coming to take care of Georgie whilst she went to visit Seb.

'I don't believe it. Whose idea was that?'

'Does it matter?' asked Alice, gazing at the mess her youngest son was making as he fed himself. She comforted herself with the thought that at least most of the food was getting into his mouth.

Tilly's green eyes sparkled with annoyance. 'Of course it matters. I bet it was Freddie, who knows nothing at all about looking after children. I hope he doesn't think he's going to carry on his flirtation with her in this house while you're away.'

Alice said, 'Surely you're not jealous? What about you corresponding with Donald Pierce? I think Seb should put a stop to that. He's too old for you.'

Tilly swelled up with indignation. 'We're only writing to each other. It's not as if I'd run off with him to America. He writes an interesting letter and I don't see why I shouldn't say what I think about Freddie and Clara coming here just because of a couple of letters and photographs. I think it's a mistake having her here. She doesn't know anything about taking care of kids. I mean, she's an only child, isn't she? What does she know about little boys?'

Alice was not going to put up with her sister speaking out against the plan. 'At this stage of his development, it doesn't matter whether Georgie is a boy or a girl. She's probably seen enough of children playing in the streets of Liverpool to know something about them. Besides, Clara and I will be spending tomorrow together, if she comes, so she'll have some idea of Georgie's routine and I can explain things to her.'

'Such as changing a nappy?'

'Yes,' said Alice firmly, 'and if she has any problems she can go and see Hanny.'

Tilly said no more and Alice breathed a sigh of

relief. She noticed that all the food on her son's plate had gone and so wiped his hands and mouth with a cloth. Suddenly, she was aware that her older two children were watching her. 'You two will have to be good for Clara,' she said.

James's dark brow furrowed. 'Who is she again?'

'Yes, who is she?' asked Flora, who often echoed what he said.

'Clara is Daddy's cousin,' replied Alice.

'What's a cousin?' asked Flora.

Alice said patiently, 'The twins are your cousins because your Uncle Kenny is my brother. Cousin Clara's daddy was your daddy's mother's brother.'

Flora looked puzzled but James said, 'So what does that make her to me, Mummy?'

Alice had no idea so said shortly, 'Family. And families look after each other. No playing her up. You'll need to behave yourselves or your daddy and I will want to know why when we get back.'

James assumed an angelic expression. 'Of course we'll behave ourselves. We're always as good as gold, not that Daddy notices what we do half the time.' He placed his knife and fork neatly alongside each other on his empty plate and asked to be excused.

Alice frowned. 'What do you mean by that?'

James shrugged and asked to be excused again.

'You just hang on there,' said Alice firmly. 'You spoke as if you thought Daddy didn't care about you. He does, lots, but for months he's been worried that he might lose his bad arm.'

James hesitated before mumbling, 'He gives lots of attention to Georgie.'

Alice stared at her eldest son. 'You're not jealous of your little brother, are you?'

He did not answer but Flora piped up, 'Daddy's always giving Georgie's hugs and kisses – we get none.'

Alice sprang to their father's defence. 'That's because you're so much bigger.'

Her two older children looked at her disbelievingly. 'He kisses you, Mummy,' said Flora. 'And I've heard you say "One's never too old for a kiss."' Her bottom lip quivered. 'Daddy loves Georgie more than he loves us.'

For a moment Alice did not know what to say, then she beckoned them over to her. They got up and came round the table and she placed an arm around each of them. 'You've been so well behaved most of the time that Daddy hasn't realised how you feel,' she said softly. 'Have either of you thought that he might think that you don't want him kissing you? That you mightn't want that *ugly mug,* as he calls his face, close to yours? He doesn't want to upset you any more than you have been already by all that's happened.' She gazed first at James's intent listening expression and then into Flora's screwed up pretty face. 'Perhaps Daddy's waiting for you to hug and kiss him. D'you understand what I'm saying?' James hesitated, then he nodded, and so did Flora. 'He really does love you,' added Alice, kissing both of them. 'Now you can play in the drawing room for half an hour and then it's bath and bed.'

'What about Daddy's cousin?' asked James. 'Will she be coming this evening?'

'I hope so, but I can't say for sure.'

'And will Daddy come back with you when you go, and will his arm be better?' asked Flora.

'He'll probably have to stay in hospital for a bit longer to make his arm work properly,' said Alice quietly. 'I'll find out more when I see him. Now off you go.'

As they left the room, Tilly said, 'Will she be putting those two to bed while you're away?'

Alice was surprised by the question. 'You'll be home in the evening. Surely you can bath them and read them a bedtime story?'

'I suppose.' Tilly leant back in her chair. 'What about meals?'

'You mean, will she cook them?' Tilly nodded.

Alice wrinkled her nose. 'You know, I haven't thought about that. The pair of you are going to have to sort that out between you.'

'Are you paying her?'

'Questions, questions, questions,' groaned Alice,

putting a hand to her head. 'She's not even here yet. I'll decide that if she comes.'

She had given no thought to rewarding Clara and her heart sank. Perhaps she should have. She had found a couple of china figurines, some old curtains and cushions in the attic that she reckoned might raise enough to pay for her trip south, but there would be little left over. But her sister had a point about giving Clara something for her troubles.

'So where will she sleep?' asked Tilly, lifting Georgie out of his feeding chair.

Alice snapped. 'In the spare room. I suppose you've a complaint about that?'

Tilly shrugged. 'It is a nice room but not exactly close to Georgie's if he were to wake in the night.'

'But near enough to you if he does,' said Alice, pushing back her chair and standing up. 'You've been a very fortunate young lady. When Mam died and Dad went off his head, you could have easily been placed in an orphanage. Instead, between the four of us, Hanny, Kenny, Seb and I made sure you had a home and lots of love. You've never gone without. In fact, you've been earning a wage recently and I've not taken a penny from you for your keep.'

Tilly reddened. 'I do help in the house and with the children. It's just that I feel she's not one of us.'

'Perhaps she isn't yet but she's going to be. She's

Seb's cousin and, as I said to James, she's family,' said Alice firmly. 'I think you lied before when you said you weren't jealous. I think you resent Freddie flirting with her.'

'You make me sound selfish,' she protested. 'And I'm not. It's just that...'

'Just what?' Alice raised an eyebrow.

Tilly took a deep breath. 'I suppose I have been used to having his attention in the past. I'm fond of him. He's always been there in my life, teasing me and looking out for me – that is until he went to sea. I've always looked up to him, Kenny and Seb because I've never known my father. Now you've just said he went off his head. Is that why you don't talk about him? Because he's a lunatic? Or when you say "off his head", do you mean he just was very angry at times?'

'I don't want to talk about it,' said Alice brusquely. 'I have bad memories of those days. Just forget about him.' She hugged Georgie tightly.

'I can't,' said Tilly simply. 'And what of my mother? You seldom speak of her either.'

Alice sighed. 'Your mother was a lovely person with a tremendous faith that she lived by. She was brave and forgiving, and Kenny loved her as much as I did. He scarcely remembered his own mother and Mam treated him well.'

'But Dad?'

Alice's face tightened. 'Enough, Tilly. I'll say only

that Mam believed his madness was out of his control. She always forgave him. I can't. Right, I'm going to bath Georgie. Will you listen for the door in case Clara comes? And be nice to her if she does.'

It was dark by the time Clara and Freddie arrived in Chester. He parked his motorbike outside Hanny and Kenny's and helped Clara down from her cushion. She stumbled and he steadied her. 'A bit stiff, are you?'

'Yes. But I enjoyed the ride.'

'Great. When the weather gets better we could go to Wales for a day out.'

She smiled. 'I'd enjoy that.'

He escorted her to Alice's. Both were surprised to hear a voice reaching out to them through the darkened garden. 'Is that you, Freddie?'

'Yes. Is that you, Tilly?' he answered.

'Yes. Of course it's me.'

Suddenly, Clara and Freddie spotted her rising up from a flowerbed like some ghostly figure.

'I've Clara with me,' said Freddie. 'Did Alice tell you about the plan?'

'Of course she did,' replied Tilly easily. 'I've just been picking some daffodils to put in Clara's bedroom.'

Clara had never had flowers in her bedroom and was touched by the younger girl's thoughtfulness. 'That's really nice of you,' she said.

'Well, we want to make you feel welcome, don't we?' said Tilly, her voice light.

'I'm glad to help,' said Clara sincerely. 'But I'm no expert when it comes to kids. Especially little boys.'

'I'm sure you'll be fine. If you get stuck, Hanny will help you, and I'll be here in the evenings when the other two are home. Although, I will be going out on Thursday, but I'm sure you'll manage,' said Tilly.

'I'll come round and keep her company,' said Freddie.

'I expected you to volunteer. Of course, we'll be seeing more of you now that Clara's here.'

Clara wondered if she had imagined the slight edge to Tilly's voice.

'You've no objections, have you?' asked Freddie, sounding surprised.

A tinkle of laughter and a slap on his arm was her response. 'Of course not. Are you coming in?'

Freddie shook his head. 'Alice will have things to discuss with Clara.' He turned to her. 'I'll be out tomorrow evening but I'll call round the next day.'

She smiled. 'Thanks for everything.'

'My pleasure.' He smiled down at her and for a moment she thought he was going to kiss her, but he only touched her chin lightly with his knuckles and then walked away.

Neither girl spoke but both watched him until he

reached his motorbike. He turned and waved before opening the gate and trundling it up the path.

Clara's emotions were all churned up but she was not alone, so were Tilly's. She could sense that Freddie really liked Clara but was that all it was or was it something deeper? It was only when he was out of sight that she blurted out, 'Seen enough of lover boy? We'd best get inside, so Alice can tell you your duties for the next few days.'

'Duties?' The use of that word surprised Clara.

Tilly linked her arm through Clara's. 'Well, you have come to work, haven't you? And I can tell you right now kids can run you right into the ground. I hope you don't regret allowing Freddie to persuade you to come.'

Clara knew for certain now that Tilly did not want her there, but as there was no going back that evening or the next, she was going to stay. Alice needed her and if Tilly intended being awkward the next few days, then she would do her best to take no notice of her. Especially if she tried to treat her like she was a skivvy.

CHAPTER TWENTY

If Clara doubted the warmth of Tilly's welcome, who had disappeared upstairs, she could find no fault with that of Alice. 'I'm so glad you're here,' said the older woman, giving her a hug.

'I was glad to come. It'll make a nice change for me,' said Clara, returning her smile.

Alice laughed. 'If you're not used to children then it'll certainly be that. Do you want a cup of tea or would you like to see your room first?'

'Room, please. I brought a nightie in my handbag and a few odds and ends. Then I'll have a cup of tea and you can tell me what I need to know.'

'You'll need to have patience, for a start,' said Alice, leading the way upstairs. 'For some reason little ones like to do the same thing over and over again.'

'It's probably the way they learn,' said Clara cheerfully, following her. 'Repetition. It's the way we were taught our times table.'

'You're right. But I admit I've never seen telling the same story over and over again in that light. Tell me, is there a children's matinée at the cinema where you work – when it's open?'

'What are you talking about being open?' asked Tilly, appearing at the top of the stairs.

'The Palladium picture palace,' said Clara, wishing she had a dress as pretty as the one Tilly was wearing. She must have rushed to change because it was different from the one she'd had on earlier. 'It'll be opening again next week.'

'I prefer the theatre, myself.'

'I like the theatre, too,' said Clara, smiling. 'Especially musicals.'

'I prefer something more serious,' said Tilly, and turned to her sister. 'The children are asleep, by the way.'

'I know. I checked them earlier.' Alice frowned. 'Why have you changed? Are you going out?'

'I thought I'd go along to Hanny and see how the twins are.'

Alice raised her eyebrows. 'Sudden, isn't it? Don't be late back.'

'I'm only going up the road,' said Tilly, her expression mutinous. 'I don't need being told. I'm not a child. I'll be sixteen in July.'

'So you will, but you won't have a key to the door until you're twenty-one, my girl, so don't take that tone with me.'

Tilly flushed and, brushing past them, hurried down the stairs.

A tight-lipped Alice gazed after her sister for a moment, before turning to Clara and saying, 'This way.'

Clara followed her to a bedroom at the front of the house. 'I hope this'll do you,' said Alice with a smile as she clicked on the light.

Clara gazed about her and felt a lift of the heart. The room was large, its walls decorated in a pink, cream and green floral wallpaper. A dressing table reflected a vase of daffodils through triple mirrors and there was a proper wardrobe of pale wood. A patterned rug lay on the floor next to a double bed covered by a patchwork quilt.

'It's lovely! If you could see my bedroom back home...' Her voice tailed off.

'I haven't always lived like this,' said Alice, understanding in her voice. 'I used to live in a terraced house with a backyard. It took me some time getting used to the idea that I was actually mistress of this house. This room used to be Seb's paternal grandmother's, who owned the house when I first arrived to work for Victoria. Seb had it completely redecorated and refurnished after the old woman died.' Alice smoothed the patchwork quilt. 'I made this myself. I've always enjoyed designing and sewing. I used to make hats for a living.'

Clara showed interest. 'Do you still make hats? For yourself, I mean.'

Alice nodded her red head. 'Yes. And for my daughter and Tilly and Hanny...although, not very often. I just don't have enough time, what with Georgie and the house and shopping.'

'Perhaps when Georgie goes to school you could take it up again, have your own little hat shop,' suggested Clara with a smile.

Alice straightened up from the bed with an arrested expression on her face. 'Now there's a thought,' she murmured. 'Women will always want to wear hats, won't they?'

'Definitely,' said Clara, going over to the dressing table and shifting the vase of daffodils. They reminded her of Tilly. Putting them there had been a thoughtful gesture. She wished they could be friends but the way the younger girl had spoken to her earlier had been irritating. Still, she would not let it get her down. She gazed at her reflection in the mirror and removed her black felt hat.

'We need to settle terms, Clara,' said Alice abruptly. 'I can't pay you much but...'

Clara whirled round. 'I don't expect payment. I'm doing it to help you and Seb.'

Alice looked relieved. 'That's really good of you, but it's not going to be easy looking after Georgie...and you'll have to shop and cook and clear up any mess he makes, as well.'

'It can't be any more difficult than coping with the house and Gran on my own and going out to work,' she said, placing her hat on the dressing table.

Alice frowned. 'It's kind of you to say so, but it doesn't seem right you working so hard for nothing.'

'I'll have my keep and I'm bound to learn from the experience. And I'll be able to see a lot more of Chester.' She placed her handbag on the bed and took out her cotton nightie.

'Well, if the weather is fine then you'll certainly enjoy wandering round Chester. Pushing a pram is a good way of walking miles without noticing it too much.'

'Sounds good to me,' said Clara. 'It's different here from Liverpool.'

'Of course it is,' murmured Alice, picking up Clara's hat and turning it round between her hands before replacing it on the dressing table. 'I'll leave you alone for a few minutes to get your bearings. I'll show you my bedroom later, so you know where to go if you need any clothes to change into while you're here. Come down when you're ready and you can have tea, cocoa, sherry, whichever you feel like.'

Clara thanked her. She placed her nightgown under the pillow and removed a couple of pairs of drawers from her handbag, not liking the idea of wearing someone else's. She put them away and then took a comb from her handbag and tidied her hair. She sang softly as she did so, thinking of Freddie only a few doors away. Then she remembered that Tilly was visiting Hanny, so that meant she could be talking to Freddie right now. She probably hadn't gone to see the twins at all! For a moment she thought how pretty Tilly was and how stylishly she dressed. Then she reminded herself that it was she whom Freddie had almost kissed and wanted to take to Wales come summer. She gave herself a final look in the mirror and went downstairs, determined not to think about Tilly making eyes at him.

Tilly stood in the middle of Hanny's living room looking annoyed. 'How could Freddie have gone out so quickly? It's not half an hour since he dropped off Clara.'

Hanny yawned. 'Sorry, love, you've missed him. Kenny was on his way out to a lecture about the Bolsheviks and Russia, so Freddie volunteered to run Kenny to the hall. As it's something he was interested in, too, he said he would stay and bring Kenny home when it finished.'

Tilly groaned and flopped onto the sofa a foot or so from where Mrs Kirk was sitting. 'I wish Kenny had mentioned the lecture to me. I'd have liked to have gone.'

'Too late now. It'll have started. So what did you want with Freddie? He said that he saw you earlier.'

Tilly shrugged. 'Nothing in particular.'

Hanny put aside the magazine she had been glancing through and gave Tilly her full attention. 'Is this to do with Clara?'

Tilly sighed. 'How did you guess? I thought he was going to kiss her right in front of me there in the crescent. I felt so mixed up I was mean to her. Now I feel ashamed of myself. I lied to Clara last time she was here. I went and told her that Freddie was a flirt.'

A tiny smile lifted the corners of Hanny's mouth. 'I know you and Freddie have been close but he's bound to be interested in other girls. You have to accept that. Obviously he fancies Clara if he's visited her a couple of times and was prepared to pick her up and bring her here.'

Tilly looped her arms around her knees. 'It made me feel all cross and hurt inside.'

'Of course it hurts when someone you've been close to fancies someone else. It doesn't mean he's stopped liking you. But if you still want to be friends with Freddie, I'd make a friend of Clara, because it's possible she might be the one for him.'

'I know you're right but it won't be easy seeing him go off with her,' muttered Tilly, frowning. 'What I find difficult is that Freddie's not interested in travelling anymore. All he wants now is to work for the business.'

'So what's wrong with that? He's seen sights neither you nor I have seen and faced death, so it's not surprising he wants the security of a job and a home.' She smiled. 'And you won't be going anywhere, love, until you've earned enough money to travel. It could take you a good few years.'

'I know,' said Tilly. 'But you do realise that if I'm going to be a rich and famous writer one day then Kenny's going to need to advertise for a new secretary.'

Hanny laughed. 'I doubt we'll have trouble finding someone else with the glut of women in the country.'

'You know what that means – a large market for women's novels.' She stood up. 'Shall I make us a cup of cocoa?'

'Good idea. Make one for Mother as well.'

Tilly did so and the next hour passed in desultory conversation before she decided it was time to go home. She left Hanny's to walk the short distance to her sister's home, breathing in the sweet scents of spring and the damp odour of the river. She thought how evocative smells could be and wondered if she ever did get to some far flung corner of the globe or America, would she wish she was back here? For a moment she felt sad, knowing it was going to be a wrench being parted from those who had stood in place of parents to her, but she was determined to do her utmost to follow her dream.

She pushed open the gate and closed it behind her. As she began to walk up the path, her ears caught the sound of rustling in the bushes. There was no wind and she wondered if it was a cat. She paused and listened but now all was quiet, so she continued on her way. Even so, she kept thinking that there might be someone hiding in the shrubbery, ready to jump out on her. She glanced sideways and thought she saw a shadow move near one of the bushes. Her pulses leapt. Was it her imagination or was there really someone there? She was not going to wait around to find out and ran the remaining few yards and hammered on the front door, looking behind her as she did so. It was then she heard the squeak of the gate and saw a dark figure sprinting away.

Her sister opened it and Tilly almost fell over the threshold. 'Why the racket, Tilly?' asked Alice.

'There was someone lurking in the garden,' gasped Tilly.

'Honestly?' Alice stared over her shoulder into the darkness. 'What did you see exactly?'

'I heard rustling in the bushes and then I actually saw him! By then I was banging on the door so I wasn't going to go after him. Hurry up and let me in and close the door.'

If Seb had been home, Alice would have gone

down the path to see if she could see anyone, but because they had no man in the house she closed the door and shot the bolts top and bottom. 'Are you absolutely sure you saw someone?'

Tilly said, 'I told you what I saw.'

Alice continued to stare at her. 'I suppose I'd have panicked, too,' she said. 'It could have been a youth playing a game.'

Tilly frowned. 'I didn't panic. I just wasn't chancing someone jumping out on me. There are plenty of desperate people around since the war.'

Alice placed an arm around her sister's shoulders. 'Better safe than sorry. Let's not worry about it now we're safely locked inside.'

'Is Clara still up?'

'No. She's gone to bed.' Alice patted her sister's shoulder and released her. 'Did you speak to Freddie?'

'No.' Tilly avoided her gaze. 'He and Kenny had gone to a lecture about the Bolsheviks in Russia, so I had a chat with Hanny, drank a cup of cocoa with her and then came home. She told me that I had to make a friend of Clara.'

'Sounds sensible to me,' said Alice, looking relieved. 'I'd hate to think of the two of you being at daggers drawn while I'm away. Now, let's get to bed. I've a lot to do tomorrow and must be up early.'

'Make sure I'm up early, too,' said Tilly. 'I'll do

breakfast and take it up to Clara so she can have it in bed.'

'Now that's more like the Tilly I know and love,' said Alice, smiling and kissing her on the cheek.

Without more ado they went upstairs to bed.

So that was Tilly, thought Bert, gazing at the house from across the road. He stood, smoking a cigarette. Quite the beauty but not the first target he had in mind. He thought of Alice as she had sat in the court and clenched his fist. He had considered long and hard in that stinking jail how best to punish her, if he ever got the chance. Now he knew exactly what he was going to do.

He tilted back his trilby and gazed up at the house from coldly amused blue eyes and thought about the little girl, playing with a toddler in the garden the other day, who must surely be Alice's daughter. He imagined the silky feel of her red-gold hair between his fingers and the softness of her skin beneath his lips. His mouth went dry and his heart began to thud. That child could have belonged to him if Alice had not so cruelly jilted him. Those others might have angered him but her rejection of him was when everything had really started going wrong. She must be punished first. The girl was his by right and, when the opportunity rose, he would take her and do what was necessary to cause Alice anguish. Then off back to Liverpool, where he planned not only to make some quick money but consider further punishment for those who had put him behind bars. They all believed him dead, so would have no idea who was responsible when they found the little girl's body.

The following morning Clara woke and straightaway knew where she was, not only because the bed was so roomy but because there was no sound of Bernie wheezing and coughing from the next room. For a moment she lay, thinking about Mary coping with Gran and hoping Bernie wasn't playing her up and being a nuisance. She did not want to lose the nurse as a lodger. Then she thought about Freddie and looked forward to seeing him soon. But before that she was going to have to face Tilly and learn how to cope with Georgie. Suddenly, she became aware of the murmur of voices below and the smell of frying bacon.

Had she overslept?

She pushed back the covers and climbed out of the bed, and then went over to the window to see what the weather was like. Pulling aside the curtain, she looked out and saw a cloudless sky. Her spirits lifted and she just knew that she was going to enjoy the day ahead. She gazed down at the garden below and noticed a blackbird tugging at a worm in a flowerbed. As she watched, the worm twanged free of the soil and the bird flew off with it dangling from his yellow beak. She smiled. It was an unfamiliar sight because at home there was no garden, although, occasionally, she heard the cooing of pigeons and the chattering of sparrows from under the eaves.

Clara was about to turn away from the window when she caught sight of a man standing on the other side of the road, gazing up at the house. They stared at each other and then, to her surprise, he doffed his cap revealing reddish-grey hair. She had a vague feeling that she had seen him before and lifted her hand in greeting. A smile broke out on his face and he, too, waved, then called, 'Good morning, lassie!'

Clara smiled and then remembered she was only wearing her nightgown and drew back so she could not be seen.

There came a knock on the bedroom door. 'Who is it?' she asked.

'Tilly. I've brought you some breakfast.'

'Oh. You'd best come in,' said Clara, unable to disguise her surprise.

The door opened and Tilly carried in a tray. 'Alice is seeing to Georgie, so I thought you might like breakfast in bed,' she said.

'Thanks!' Clara was even more surprised when she saw that it was a proper cooked breakfast.

'I won't do it tomorrow so make the most of it,'

said Tilly. 'You'd best get back into bed.'

'I will after I've been to the lav.'

'You'll have to wait. Flora's in there. What were you doing over by the window?' asked Tilly, placing the tray on the dressing table.

'Seeing what the weather was like. I saw a blackbird pulling up a worm and there was a man outside looking up at this house.'

'A man! In the garden?' Tilly hurried over to the window.

'No. On the other side of the road.'

Tilly opened the window and leant out. 'There's a man shuffling in the direction of the path going down to the river. Is that him?'

Clara looked out of the window. 'Yes, I'm sure it is.'

Tilly muttered, 'Then it couldn't have been him last night.'

Clara said, 'Last night?'

Tilly closed the window and turned to face her. 'I saw someone lurking in the garden last night but he'd be younger. I can't imagine the one below managing a sprint, can you?'

Clara shook her head and smiled. 'I'm sure I've seen him before. He wished me good morning in a Scottish accent.'

Tilly chewed on her lip. 'Where d'you think you've seen him?'

'Can't remember,' said Clara, moving away from

the window. 'But it might come back to me. Should we mention him to Alice?'

Tilly hesitated and then shook her head. 'We don't want her worrying about us while she's away.'

That made sense to Clara. After all, the man hadn't looked dangerous. She was about to ask Tilly more about the person she had seen lurking in the garden when she heard the sound of the lavatory being flushed, so excused herself and hurried from the room. She bumped into Flora and wished her a good morning.

'Hello, Daddy's cousin,' said the girl with a grin, before skipping along the landing to her room.

Smiling, Clara gazed after her and felt part of the family. Then she went into the bathroom. Tilly had followed her out and now went downstairs.

Several hours later, after Clara had eaten her bacon and egg and then been initiated into the messy business of changing a nappy and shown a variety of other things to do with taking care of Georgie, Clara was happy to be outdoors and pushing the pram through the bustling streets of Chester, accompanied by Alice. She gazed with interest at the shops surmounted by black and white upper storeys that Alice told her had been fashionable in the Middle Ages.

'They're in good nick for buildings having been around all that time,' marvelled Clara.

'I'm pretty sure some have been renovated,' said

Alice, steadying the cardboard box that rested on the brown gabardine apron of the pram. 'You need to ask Kenny or Hanny if you're interested in history,' she added. 'They know far more than I do about Chester. But I do remember my mother telling me that some buildings in the city centre were in such a bad state when she was a girl that they would have fallen down if something hadn't been done.'

'That sounds sensible to me,' said Clara. 'I'd be hard put to find which ones have been renovated. What about the cathedral?'

'That's pretty old, too. You'll see it closer up because we're taking a shortcut through Abbey Square right next to it. There used to be monks living in an abbey here, you know, in the Middle Ages.'

'It's so different from Liverpool,' said Clara, not for the first time since she had arrived in Chester. She gazed up at the sandstone edifice of the cathedral. 'We don't have anything near this old back in Liverpool. There's a Proddy cathedral going up on St James' Mount. You get a really good view from up there, right down to the Mersey and across the river to Birkenhead and Eastham. Then there's the Liver building.'

'I haven't seen it since it was finished,' said Alice. 'I found the docks quite scary when my father took me there once.'

Clara said, 'It's huge. I love watching the ships coming and going. It gives me a thrill thinking of them travelling to faraway places with odd sounding names...and the smells coming from the dock road make my nose twitch,' she said dreamily. 'There's Bibby's soap factory. You should smell the nut oil after the peanuts have been ground down. Then there's the sugar and tobacco factories, and we've several breweries. I love the smell of yeast fermenting.'

'We have a brewery here in Chester,' said Alice, not to be outdone. 'I notice you haven't mentioned cotton. I remember going with Victoria Waters, when I worked for her, to meet her father and Seb off a liner from America. Mr Waters was a cotton broker.'

'I didn't know Seb had been to America,' said Clara in surprise.

'Oh yes. And when Seb and I were first married, we went to India and Egypt, combining a honeymoon with business. It was a lovely experience. Unpleasant at times because of the insects and the heat, though.' Alice paused before adding, 'You do know that your aunt has gone to America, don't you?'

Clara nodded. 'It seems an odd thing to do when you've only just been widowed.'

'I agree,' said Alice firmly. 'But Gabrielle has always been a law unto herself. I wish I knew why she's gone there. As far as I know that country holds unhappy memories for her because, supposedly, her first husband deserted her and left her to starve.'

'I think someone's told me about this. Wasn't he a musician?'

'That's right,' said Alice. 'Seb grew up believing Robbie Bennett was his father. He's kept the name on. I think he told you about him, didn't he?'

Clara's brow knitted in thought. 'I've a feeling he did. Strange, there's a new musician started at the Palladium. He plays in the orchestra. His name is Robbie Bennett.'

Alice darted an excited glance at Clara. 'Some coincidence, two musicians with the same name.'

Clara said slowly, 'He's been to America, too. I believe he did well for himself and has come back to Liverpool to help his widowed sister.'

'What's he like? It could be the same man.'

'I suppose it could. He's got a shock of white hair and isn't bad looking for his age. A brilliant musician, he plays the piano and the clarinet.'

'Goodness,' said Alice, her green eyes sparkling. 'Wait until I tell Seb about this. He'll be really interested. For years he believed him to be his father, but of course, it turned out Mr Waters was. Even so, this Robbie Bennett could be said to be his stepfather, couldn't he?'

'Possibly,' said Clara, feeling confused. 'I find it

difficult to believe that, if Mr Bennett is the kind of man to return to England to help support his widowed sister and her children, he'd leave a young wife to fend for herself in a strange country.'

'You're saying that Seb's mother might be lying?' said Alice.

'I can't see why he should lie about why he's come back to Liverpool,' said Clara. 'But I've only spoken to him once, so I really don't know much about him.'

'Then speak to him next time you get the chance,' said Alice. 'Find out if he knew your aunt.'

'I will,' said Clara, thinking it would be interesting if he really had been married to her aunt. He would know what she was like and might have some stories to tell about her. It would be really odd if she had gone to America to find him after all these years and all the time he was in Liverpool, performing not far from where the mother she hated lives.

Alice changed the subject. 'I'm hoping to make my travel arrangements at the General Railway Station. But first I've a detour to make,' she added.

Clara wondered where this detour would take them and it came as a surprise when they turned off the main thoroughfare into Trafford Street, where she was told to stop outside a pawnshop.

'I won't be long,' said Alice, lifting the cardboard box off the pram and disappearing inside.

It was the first pawnshop that Clara had noticed in Chester and she reckoned that was because there were few desperately poor people living in the city – unlike Liverpool, where there were numerous premises, nicknamed *Uncle's*. This shop was called Pope's and was situated in a far less salubrious area than that where Alice lived.

Her thoughts were disturbed by Georgie holding up his arms and saying, 'Out! Mamma!'

Clara shook her head, convinced that Alice would prefer her son to stay where he was. 'No,' she said firmly.

'Peas.' He smiled winningly, revealing a number of teeth. 'I be good.'

She felt herself weakening but shook her head. He repeated her action and the word, 'Peas.'

She turned her back on him and gazed at the window display. It was amazing the range of goods that people had hocked but not redeemed and were now on sale; chamber pots, vases, dolls, tablecloths, jewellery. What could have been in the box Alice had carried inside? Alice had told her that they were not rich and Tilly had said almost the same about Freddie but she hadn't realised they needed to hock things for money. The squeak-squeak-squeak of the pram caused her to turn and she saw to her dismay that Georgie had somehow managed to kneel up in the carriage, causing his harness to twist in a way that could possibly strangle him. 'You're naughty,' she said, setting about trying to untangle him from the fix he was in.

He clung to her hand. 'Out,' he gasped.

And out he eventually came because no sooner had she released him from his harness, than he pushed himself upright and clung to her. He placed a starfish-like hand on her face and squeezed her lips. 'Kiss,' he said, puckering up.

She could not help laughing as she removed his hand. He giggled and would have put his hand on her face again if she had not prevented him. 'No, naughty,' she said.

'You two having fun?' asked Alice.

Clara smiled. 'He wanted to get out.'

Alice smiled. 'Of course he did. He wants to walk but he'll slow us down if he does so now. He can walk in the park on the way back.' She took her son from Clara and strapped him back in his pram to a roar of protest. Alice ignored the sound and, releasing the brake, began to push the pram.

'We'll go to the station now and buy my ticket and after that I'll treat you to a bun and cup of tea down by the river.'

Clara was dying to ask her could she afford it but knew that would be overstepping the mark. They were still in the early stages of getting to know each other and, although it was obvious that Alice must trust her to have her as a guest in her house and to look after Georgie, Clara could not expect her to tell her all her troubles. Obviously, Alice had pawned whatever was in that cardboard box and was now in funds to the tune of enough money for her journey south and to buy them a treat.

Once Alice's ticket was purchased, they returned home via Grosvenor Park and a tearoom overlooking the Dee. It had been an enjoyable outing and Clara was a little more confident that she would be able to cope with Georgie, most of all because she had fallen for his childish charms. Nappy changing was going to be an ordeal but having to deal with Bernie when she had been ill and bedridden for a short while had been much worse.

The following morning, Freddie arrived early in the motor to convey Alice and her luggage to the station. He had called in briefly the evening before to tell them that Kenny had suggested his giving her a lift. Clara only had the slightest opportunity to exchange a few words with him as he had been in a rush to get back to the yard, where he was going to help the motor engineer on a big repair job. She was looking forward to seeing him again later that day.

Alice hugged and kissed everyone, including Clara.

'You'll give Seb our love, won't you?' said Tilly.

'That goes without saying,' said Alice gaily, climbing into the passenger seat. She was wearing a homemade costume of green woollen cloth. The collar and sleeves were piped with white and she wore an eau-de-nil crêpe de Chine blouse underneath. Her hat was a frivolous bit of nonsense constructed of yellow buckram, ribbon and veiling.

'You look really lovely,' said Clara, doing her best to prevent Georgie from climbing onto the running board and thinking of some of the lovely clothes in Alice's wardrobe.

'Thanks,' said Alice.

Freddie said, 'Hold on tight.'

Clara swung Georgie up into her arms.

There were tears in Alice's eyes as she gazed at him because she had never been parted from him before. She would not have left him now if Seb had not needed her. She trusted Clara to take care of her baby, knowing Hanny was not far away. Indeed, she and Kenny had come to wave her off. Alice gripped the seat with one hand and waved with the other. 'See you all when I get back,' she said. 'Be good, children.'

'Give Daddy a kiss for me,' shouted Flora, waving madly as the car moved off.

Those left behind stood watching until it was out of sight. Then Tilly called the two older children to her because she was taking them to school.

'Hope all goes well with your day, Clara,' she said, adding in a low voice, 'Don't forget to keep your eyes open for that prowler.'

'Thanks,' she replied, wishing Tilly hadn't tagged on that last bit.

'I'll be at hand if you need advice,' said Hanny.

Clara thanked her, too, feeling suddenly terribly nervous.

They all went their separate ways. Clara going indoors, holding Georgie by the hand.

By twelve o'clock Clara was feeling ready to put her feet up. She had soon discovered that taking care of Georgie without Alice on hand was far more difficult and tiring than she would have believed yesterday. Fortunately, Hanny dropped by with the twins, bringing with her a package of sage and onion stuffed cooked pigs' hearts from the cooked meat shop in Foregate Street. 'I thought this might do for your evening meal,' she said.

Clara accepted them gratefully, thinking that, with potatoes and cabbage, she could make them all a nice supper. She was feeling better now and there had been no sign of a prowler. As she made a cup of tea, she thought of Alice and hoped that she would arrive safely at her destination.

CHAPTER TWENTY-ONE

Alice's high heels rang hollowly on the asphalt as she strode through the open gates into the hospital grounds. She had telephoned ahead from the station so that the matron and Seb would know when to expect her arrival. She had been informed that her husband was not confined to bed and she was likely to find him in the gardens as it was such a fine spring day. Alice was pleased about that, knowing that, if he was up and about, he would be feeling better in himself. She was nervous. He was bound to ask her where she had found the cash to make this journey and she was going to have to tell him the truth. For months she had tried not to make demands on Seb for any extra money beyond her housekeeping. She felt certain it would be a blow to his pride when he was told that she had been rummaging in the attic and pawning stuff. There had always been the hope that she could redeem it within the allotted time but, unfortunately, she had never had the money to enable her to do that. No doubt he was going to be hurt and even angry, but she could no longer delay telling him what she had done. But of course, money was not their only worry.

As she walked up the drive between beds of daffodils and budding tulips and lawns, she was determined to keep calm if there should be bad news. At the moment, it was easy to remain at peace in such pleasant surroundings. Suddenly, she spotted her husband pacing the ground beneath an elm situated on a rise. She noticed that he was wearing his eye patch and was smoking a cigarette; his right arm was in a sling.

'Seb!' she called, putting on a spurt.

His head turned so that his unmarred profile was turned towards her. He dropped the stub of his cigarette and extinguished it with the heel of his shoe. Then he came striding towards her with an eagerness that reminded her of a day long ago when they had arranged to meet in Grosvenor Park. She had been in a bit of a state over her father and had been desperate to persuade Seb to run away with her. He had reminded her of that day not so long ago. It had ended in tears, but she had never forgotten how eagerly he had come to greet her. Now, he reached out a hand and she gripped it tightly.

'I never expected to see you here. How did you manage it?'

She looked him straight in the eye. 'I hocked some of the stuff from out of the attic. I've been doing it for ages.'

He stared at her as if he could not believe what he was hearing. 'You've what!'

Alice felt the blood rush to her cheeks. 'Each time the children needed shoes or a new winter coat, I went up there and rooted through stuff and took them to the pawnshop.'

His face darkened. 'Why didn't you tell me you were short of money?'

'Because I didn't want to worry you. Have you forgotten what you were like when you first came home?'

'I know, I know. I thought there were a few things missing up there.' He squeezed her hand. 'Hell! What you must have been through and I kept insisting that I couldn't work.'

'I'm sorry. I was hoping I wouldn't have to tell you, but I just had to come and see you this time, so I found a few more things and took them to Uncle.'

'You amaze me.' A faint smile lit his face. 'Where is this pawnshop? I can't say I've ever noticed one in Chester.' She told him. 'You walked all the way up there carrying stuff?' he said on a rising note.

'On the pram! Clara came with me last time. She's a gem. Asked no questions, although she must have been wondering.'

'What's Clara got to do with this?'

'She's staying at the house and is looking after Georgie – and she won't accept any payment.'

He frowned. 'That's good of her. But you'll have to give her something. We can't have her losing out.'

'She won't because she doesn't go back to the picture house until next week. I have something in mind to give her but it's not money.' Alice smiled at the thought of what she had planned.

When he saw that smile, Seb drew her against him and kissed her long and deep. It was a very satisfying kiss and they parted reluctantly.

'How are you feeling now?' she asked.

'Happier for seeing you.'

'I've missed you, too.' She rested her head against his chest and breathed in the familiar scent of him, which was overlaid with the antiseptic smell of hospitals. 'I don't want ever to be parted from you again.'

'I feel the same.'

'Has the doctor said how long you'll be here?'

'No. And I can't even start physiotherapy until the wound's healed.'

She touched his arm lightly and felt the splints beneath the sling. 'You're not in pain?'

He did not answer immediately because he was thinking of the agony of some of the wounded and dying men in the clearing station Don had taken him to in France. What were his sufferings compared to those men?

'I'm damn fortunate to be alive, so what's a little bit of pain? The surgeon has told me that I should get back a fair amount of mobility in my arm.'

Alice's face lit up. 'That's marvellous.'

He nodded. 'Seeing you has made me think that there must be decent physiotherapists up north. I mean, there's big cities, Liverpool, Manchester. I'm going to ask the surgeon if there's a man he can recommend nearer home. It's not as if I need to stay in hospital to have the treatment.'

Alice felt a rising excitement and joy. 'I'm all for that.'

'Then I'll certainly ask him.' He grinned. 'I bet they could even take the stitches out up there.'

'And in the meantime, I'll stay at a bed and breakfast in the village,' she said.

He cocked an eyebrow. 'You must have received a fair amount of money for that rubbish in the attic.'

She smiled. 'Watch what you're calling rubbish. Some of it was good stuff. I was hoping to redeem them but...'

'Don't bother,' he said firmly. 'We can live without it. Instead of pawning, why don't you sell the lot? Flora will be needing a new frock for Easter in a few days and you must have one, too.'

She was glad that he felt the way he did. 'I think

Flora will have to wait for Whit for a new frock because it's too close to Easter for me to go shopping.' She paused, before adding, 'And talking about Flora, she told me I was to give you a kiss from her.' Alice promptly kissed him.

'That was nice of my daughter,' murmured Seb against his wife's lips. Alice was uncertain whether to tell him about the talk she'd had with Flora and James. To her surprise, Seb said, 'What is it?'

'You know me so well,' she marvelled. 'It's just that I had a talk with James and Flora the other evening. They're jealous of the attention you've been giving to Georgie. According to Flora, they're missing out on hugs and kisses.'

Seb looked astounded. 'Honestly? But I thought…'

'I can guess what you thought but you're wrong. I did tell them that you probably thought they mightn't want you kissing them because of your scars. They hadn't thought of that,' she said, hugging him tightly. 'Now you know…'

'I can do something about it,' he concluded with a sigh.

She kissed him and then eased away from him to gaze into his eye. 'I'm sorry you'll miss the christening.'

'Who said I will?' There was a determined expression on his face as he drew her close once more. 'I'll ask to speak to the specialist in the morning and, if he's in agreement, we'll head home within a couple of days. After the christening, I'll speak to Kenny about what we can do to build up the business – and after treatment I'll get more involved with the practicalities of selling motors.'

She was so filled with relief and joy by his words that she flung her arms round his neck and kissed him again and again. She could not wait to get home, but in the meantime she was going to make the best of having Seb all to herself.

'Alice should well be there by now,' said Freddie, flicking over the pages of that week's *Chester Chronicle* as he leant against the dresser in the Bennetts' kitchen.

'I wonder if she'll telegraph,' said Tilly, perched on the edge of the table, swinging her legs and watching Clara attempting to strap a wriggling Georgie into his feeding chair. 'Do you want any help there?' she called.

'No. I can manage,' Clara replied without looking up. 'If you want to help, you could mash the potatoes.' Clara managed to hold both of Georgie's hands in one of hers whilst fastening the final buckle of his harness. 'We're having them with cabbage and stuffed hearts.'

'Shop bought or did you cook them yourself?' asked Tilly, opening a drawer and taking out the masher.

'Hanny brought them and I wasn't going to look a gift horse in the mouth.' Clara straightened up. 'There, all done,' she said, smiling down at Georgie.

'I presume you can cook,' said Tilly, draining the potatoes. She took margarine out of the larder.

'Of course I can. Can you?' asked Clara, slicing off a knob of butter and mashing it with chopped boiled egg in a dish.

'Well enough if I have to look after myself.'

Freddie glanced at Tilly. 'Why should you have to do that?' he asked. 'You're comfortable here, aren't you?' Then he groaned. 'You don't still have that daft idea of being a writer and travelling? It's not the right life for a girl.'

Tilly glared at him. 'I wasn't going to do it tomorrow or the next day,' she said jerkily as she began to mash the potatoes. 'But I thought you were in favour of my having a go at writing.'

'Yes. What's wrong with Tilly having a career?' asked Clara, buttering a slice of bread. 'If the war proved anything, it was that women are capable of doing a lot of jobs that men can do.'

'That's right,' said Tilly, smiling at Clara. 'Did you know that Elinor Glyn, the romance writer, was a newspaper correspondent in France during the war? If she can go abroad and write, I don't see why I shouldn't be able to one day.'

'You mean to report on women's fashions from Paris and Rome?' said Freddie with a hint of a smile. 'I suppose that would be OK because you seem to love clothes.'

Tilly's eyes flashed green fire. 'I want to do more than that! At least Don believes I'm capable of becoming a good writer. He encouraged me. Fashion reports! Pah!' she muttered, thumping the potatoes with the masher.

'I think you've probably done them enough,' said Clara, glancing at Tilly as she, herself, cut the bread into fingers.

'Sorry,' muttered Tilly, banging the masher on the side of the pan so that several bits of potato fell back into the mash.

'Who's Don?' asked Freddie, taking up the newspaper again.

Tilly smiled sweetly. 'Wouldn't you like to know.'

'That's why I asked,' he said shortly. 'I hope you haven't got a follower. You're far too young.'

'I'd rather call him an admirer,' said Tilly, licking mashed potato from a finger. 'He's tall and handsome with fair hair.'

'Do Alice and Kenny know about him?' asked Freddie, frowning.

'Yes. It was Don who found Seb and saved his life. He and Alice like him. He writes to me regularly.'

'So he doesn't live in Chester?' said Freddie.

'No. In America.' Tilly smiled. 'He sent me photos of his home. He reckons that when I'm twenty-one the age difference between us won't matter, so he's going to come back to England then.'

'So he's not in a hurry to claim you.'

Tilly frowned. 'You think he's toying with my feelings, don't you?' There was a note in her voice that caused Clara to pause in the act of placing Georgie's food on his feeding tray.

'Did I say that?' protested Freddie. 'I'm stating a fact that absence doesn't always make the heart grow fonder. How old is this American?'

'None of your business. If Kenny and Seb don't object to us writing to each other, then I don't see what it has to do with you,' she said.

'You're getting pert, young lady,' said Freddie, but he said no more on the subject after that.

Clara wondered just how much Freddie did care about Tilly writing to the American, but she must not start reading more into what he had said than there was. They were related by marriage and had known each other from childhood, so it was natural that Freddie spoke to Tilly with an easy familiarity that Clara almost envied. It had not been an easy day and she must not allow herself to get hot under the collar because of their conversation or because they had arrived at the house together. Freddie had explained that he had been helping out at the repair yard and, as Tilly was working in the office, it had made sense to give her a lift home.

Clara was a little on edge, feeling a need to prove

that she could cope with Georgie and do everything else that she set out to do, such as keeping the place tidy and preparing the meals. Georgie was not a naughty boy or terribly demanding, but he did need watching and that wasn't easy when she was doing other things.

'So what are we going to do this evening?' asked Tilly, after they had finished their meal and the children had left the table.

'We?' asked Freddie, glancing at Clara. 'Would you like to get out of the house for a while and go for a walk?'

'But who'd look after the children?' asked Tilly.

He smiled at her. 'Clara's looked after Georgie all day. Surely you can put him to bed and let her have a break?'

For a moment Clara thought Tilly was going to protest, but then she said, 'OK. But be back before dark.'

'Yes, Ma,' teased Freddie.

'I mean it,' said Tilly. 'I spotted a prowler in the garden the other evening.' She glanced at Clara. 'I mentioned it to you, didn't I?'

'You did,' answered Clara, 'after I saw that man looking up at the house yesterday morning – but we didn't think they were one and the same.'

Freddie's eyes sharpened. 'Was the one you saw a tramp? You do get men down on their luck wanting a handout.'

'But he didn't ask for handout,' said Clara. 'He just wished me good morning and moved off towards the bridge.'

'And the one I saw must have been younger because he sprinted out of the gate,' said Tilly promptly. 'Alice thought he might have been just a youth playing a game.'

'Could be,' said Freddie, his expression intent. 'I remember hiding in doorways and even in neighbour's yards when I was a kid. What did Alice say about the other man?'

'Neither Clara nor I mentioned him because we didn't want to worry her any more than she already was,' said Tilly.

'Besides, he looked harmless,' said Clara, stacking the dishes.

'You said you thought you'd seen him before,' said Tilly.

Freddie stared at Clara. 'I suppose you don't remember where?'

'I haven't had time to give it much thought,' she murmured, frowning and staring into the distance. 'I can't remember. I'm taking these dishes out and washing them. After that, if you still want to go for a walk, Freddie, we'll go.'

'Let Tilly wash the dishes,' said Freddie firmly. 'Give me the tray. I'll carry them to the kitchen while you get your coat on.'

'Thanks a lot,' said Tilly. 'It obviously doesn't

matter that the children's lives and mine could be in danger.'

'Don't be melodramatic,' said Freddie. 'D'you think Clara would be suggesting us going out if she believed that?'

Tilly did not answer but as she walked out of the room, her voice floated back to them. 'I'm going to be locking all the doors so when you come back, the two of you are going to have to knock very loudly if you want to be let in.'

Freddie rolled his eyes at Clara and she grimaced. 'I'll go and fetch my coat.'

'Have you thought some more about the bloke you saw?' asked Freddie, as they reached the riverbank.

'Not really but I suppose I should,' said Clara, darting him a sidelong glance and wishing they could be like the other couples taking a stroll along the river. Some were with children and feeding the ducks and swans.

Freddie took her hand and clasped it firmly. 'How old did you think he was and what colour was his hair? How did he walk?'

Clara allowed herself a moment to enjoy the warmth and the strength of his hand before saying, 'He was middle-aged with greying ginger hair. I remember because he doffed his cap. As for his walk…he shuffled along.'

'Were his clothes new or shabby?'

'Workaday clothes, I'd say.'

Freddie nodded. 'You said he wished you good morning, so what was his voice like?'

'He had a Scottish accent.'

Freddie was quiet a few moments and then said, 'It might sound crazy but your description could fit Mrs Black's gardener.'

Clara looked at him doubtfully. 'You think so? I know I spoke to him when I visited Mrs Black. If it is him then that could explain why he seemed vaguely familiar. But what would he be doing here so early in the morning?'

'Are you sure it was the Bennetts' house he was looking at and not Kenny and Hanny's? If it is him then he might have had a message for me or Hanny from Joy.'

'If that was true then why did he go towards the footbridge?'

Freddie was silenced.

Clara tried to recall that encounter she'd had with Mrs Black's gardener. She had followed him along the footpath to the house, that was when he had turned and spoken to her. What had he said? She tried to remember. Something about what the old man in the village had said – and she felt almost sure he had mentioned her skin. That's right. Because she had told him that it was the colour it was because she worked in munitions. Then he had told her about working in a factory.

She glanced at Freddie. 'He'd been ill due to working in a factory.'

'What kind of factory?' he asked. 'Was it here in Chester?'

'I don't remember him saying, but whatever job he did, something happened to affect his brain.'

Freddie looked thoughtful. 'There's a lead factory near the Shropshire Union canal. I remember reading in the *Chester Chronicle* about a man suffering brain damage from working there.'

'I wonder who would know if Mrs Black's gardener had also worked there?' asked Clara.

Freddie shrugged. 'Mrs Black and possibly Joy. But neither are here. Of course, if Joy knew then she might have spoken to Hanny about him. Can you remember anything else he said to you?'

Clara closed her eyes and tried to picture that encounter with the man and gradually something else he had mentioned popped into her mind.

'Family! He had children and wanted to see them but Mrs Black wouldn't allow it.'

'How many children?' asked Freddie, gazing at her encouragingly.

Clara smiled. 'It was almost a year ago. I'm not super brain.'

He grinned. 'You're doing pretty well.'

They walked on in silence, both deep in thought.

Suddenly, Freddie said, 'I'm trying to remember

how old Joy was when Kenny, Alice and Tilly's father vanished from their lives.'

Clara's eyes widened. 'You mean...you think...wouldn't you recognise him?'

'I don't remember their father, so it must be fourteen or so years ago.'

'What about Joy? Surely she'd remember him?'

'Maybe she never saw much of him, and he's probably changed.'

'Where did the family live? Was it in your street?' asked Clara.

'No. I believe their yard was the other side of the entry to ours,' murmured Freddie, swinging her hand and looking thoughtful. 'You know, he could be Mal Moran. From the little I've heard about what went on in those days, he wouldn't have visited our house much. I know the mothers were friends from way back and that's probably why Alice and Hanny became close friends. But he didn't grow up in the area, he was from Scotland like my dah. And what with his working all day, us children wouldn't have seen much of him.'

'Then it probably is him,' said Clara excitedly. 'I told you he had a Scottish accent!'

Freddie let out a low whistle. 'You're right, you did. It's a tremendous coincidence if it isn't him.'

'So what do we do?' asked Clara. 'Tilly's bound to ask if I've remembered where I saw him when we get back.'

He nodded. 'You said that you believed he was harmless, do you still think that, knowing he used to beat his wife?'

Clara hesitated. 'I can't be absolutely sure, but I wouldn't have thought Mrs Black would employ him if she thought he was dangerous. Maybe he just wanted to have a look at his children and grandchildren.'

Freddie nodded. 'You're right. But knowing Alice doesn't want Tilly to meet her father, I think we have to keep quiet until Alice and Seb get back, and then we tell them what we think.'

Clara agreed.

'Now,' he said, his eyes warm as they met hers. 'Shall we talk of something else? Are you looking forward to the party? It's only a few days away.'

She was relieved to change the subject. 'Yes, although, if Alice isn't back by then, I'll have to look after Georgie.'

'There'll be others there with children,' he said firmly. 'I'm sure they won't mind watching him for a short while if there's any dancing at the party.'

'You think there will be dancing? Because if there is, I don't know what I'm going to wear. I know Alice said I can borrow something of hers but I can't say I feel right about nosing through her clothes.' A sigh escaped her.

'Then borrow something from Tilly. You are much of a size and she has some nice clothes.'

Clara agreed that the younger girl certainly did know how to dress, but she very much doubted she would be asking for a loan of an outfit for the christening. She decided to put it out of her mind for now and instead asked him how he had enjoyed his time at the repair yard.

After that they talked idly as they continued to amble alongside the river, content just to be in one another's company. Yet Clara felt each had moved a step closer to knowing the other better after the walk.

By the time they returned to the house it was dusk and she half-expected Freddie to say goodnight and go home, but he was to prove how solicitous he was of hers and Tilly's safety by making a search of the gardens before banging on the door and ordering Tilly to open up. He waited until she had done so before saying goodnight, and then waited until they were both inside and had closed the door before leaving.

Tilly shot the bolts and then, without a word, went into the drawing room. Clara guessed from her moody expression that if the younger girl was desperate for a heart to heart, she was expecting Clara to initiate it. She felt sorry for Tilly, but she accepted Freddie's decision that it would be best to wait until Alice returned before saying anything about their suspicions concerning the identity of the man she had seen across the way. As for Tilly's prowler, could he possibly have been a figment of her imagination?

As Clara climbed the stairs, she was aware of the sound of music. Pausing, she listened a moment and was impressed by Tilly's piano playing. Then she carried on up the stairs to bed.

CHAPTER TWENTY-TWO

It was Maundy Thursday and Clara was in the garden playing ball with Georgie when she heard someone at the front door. Telling Georgie to be a good boy, she hurried to the front of the house. A telegraph boy was just about to wheel his bicycle away when she called to him. He handed her an envelope. She opened it and read the brief message. *We will both be home this evening. Love Alice and Seb*.

Relief soared inside Clara and she fumbled for a penny in her pocket and was glad to find one. She handed it to the boy and watched as he went on down the path. She stood a moment gazing into space, hoping all was well with her cousin's arm. Then she began to think about food. She had already bought ingredients for that evening's meal. As she walked round the side of the house, she wondered what she could give Alice and Seb to eat.

Then she saw what Georgie was doing in the

garden and a roar escaped her as she began to run. He had found a trowel from somewhere and dug in the soil, dislocating a plant in the process. Not only were his clothes filthy but he was pulling leaves from the plant and stuffing them in his mouth.

'Oh, hell,' she wailed, praying that the plant was not poisonous. It would be terrible if Alice and Seb arrived home to find their youngest son had died due to her negligence. She prised open his mouth and tried to remove every scrap of greenery from its interior. He protested and bit her finger. It took all her willpower not to smack him.

'Naughty,' she said fiercely.

'What's the trouble?' asked a voice behind her.

Clara turned her head and saw a woman standing there with a pram. 'Can I help you?' she asked

'I'm Emma Davies, a friend of the family. I'm looking for Alice.'

'She's away. She and Seb will be back late this evening. Perhaps if you can come back tomorrow?'

Emma hesitated. 'Perhaps I should try Hanny again. I got no answer when I knocked earlier.'

'She's probably gone shopping and her mother mightn't have heard you,' said Clara, giving her attention to Georgie once more.

'What's he done?'

Clara said grimly, 'I left him playing ball while I answered the door. When I got back he'd found a trowel from somewhere and dug up this plant and has been eating it. I'm worried in case it's poisonous.'

Emma left the pram and inspected the plant in question. She plucked a leaf and squeezed it between her fingers and sniffed it. 'It's bergamot, if I'm not mistaken, and safe to eat.'

'That's a relief! My mam used to put potherbs in her stews but I've never come across this one before.' She smiled up at Emma.

'Neither had I until Mrs Black had me picking the leaves from her garden for her potions.'

'You know Mrs Black?' said Clara, her eyes bright with interest.

Emma nodded. 'I used to work for her. I keep thinking I must make the effort to visit her in Eastham but, what with the children and my mam not being too good since my brothers were killed, I've just not had the chance.' Her face was almost unbelievably sad.

Clara felt for her. 'I am so sorry. I lost my dad.'

Emma sighed. 'The twins were only twenty and my dad's a swine. As for Chris, who's...missing...' Her voice trailed off and there was a long silence. She changed the subject. 'So would I be right in thinking you're Clara?'

'My fame's gone before me, has it?' joked Clara.

Emma smiled. 'You have a look of Seb and all that Hanny said was good.'

Clara thanked her then gasped because she saw that Georgie was now stuffing soil down the front of his blouson. 'What are you doing?' she cried, realising she had neglected her duties yet again. She grabbed his hand and removed the trowel from his grasp before pulling him to his feet. 'You'll have to excuse me. I'm going to have to deal with him.'

Emma tried to conceal a smile. 'Would you like me to replant that bergamot? You don't want it to die.'

'Yes, please,' answered Clara, swinging Georgie up into her arms. Immediately he began to struggle to get down, but Clara wasn't having any nonsense and carried him, kicking and yelling towards the house. She was halfway up the garden when she thought of something and turned and shouted, 'Perhaps you'd like to come in and have a cup of tea. Hanny might be back by the time you've drunk it.'

'Thanks. I won't say no,' said Emma. 'It's a bit of a walk from Garden Lane.'

'Where's that?'

'The other side of Chester. You go in. I'll see you in a few minutes.'

By the time Emma entered the kitchen with her baby daughter, Georgie's hands and face were clean and he was rolling a piece of dough on a corner of the table. 'That's quietened him down,' said Emma, watching him. 'Do you look after kids for a living?'

Clara laughed. 'No! Although, I'm enjoying my

time here and I'll miss him when I go back home. My proper job is as a cashier in a cinema, but we had to close down due to the flu.'

'Terrible disease,' said Emma. 'You think all is well and your men are safe and then that happens.'

'But thousands have survived and are steadily getting demobbed. I saw this photo in this newspaper the potatoes were wrapped in.' Clara spread the sheet on the table. 'Don't they look relieved.'

Emma gazed at the picture of the soldiers and then the colour drained from her face. 'What is it?' asked Clara. 'You look like you've seen a ghost.'

Emma did not speak but fumbled for a chair. Clara hurried to help her because she was holding her child.

'It's the strangest thing…' said Emma.

'What is?'

Emma cleared her throat but no words came.

Clara felt quite concerned for her. 'Are you all right? Would you like me to go and see if Hanny is back yet?'

Emma gazed at her. 'Would you? I'll keep my eye on the kettle and Georgie. It's just that I'm still feeling a bit light-headed.'

Clara nodded and hurried out. But she only got as far as the gate when she saw Hanny coming from the direction of the bridge pushing the pram. Clara called her name.

Hanny came hurrying towards her. 'What is it? Is it news from Alice?'

'A telegram has come saying they'll be home this evening but that's not I want you for. I've a friend of yours here. An Emma Davies. She's taken a funny turn, so I offered to go and see if you were in.'

Hanny looked surprised. 'I wonder what's wrong.'

'Come and find out,' said Clara.

Hanny followed her to the back of the house and, leaving the sleeping twins outside in their pram, followed Clara into the kitchen.

Emma seemed to have recovered her composure but still looked worried. She flashed Hanny a relieved smile. 'I'm so glad to see you. I might be just imagining things but see if you can spot someone we know in this photo.' She placed a finger on the picture of the soldiers. 'This lot are about to be demobbed.'

Hanny rested both hands on the table and gazed down at the photograph. Her eyes scanned the faces of the men, most were looking straight ahead and smiling for the camera but there were those who looked impatient and one who presented only his profile. Her gaze fixed on him. 'Oh my God! It can't be. He's dead!' she cried.

'He doesn't look very dead there,' said Emma grimly.

Clara could contain her curiosity no longer. 'Who is it?'

'My brother Bert,' muttered Hanny, the muscles of her face taut. 'But there has to be a mistake. Are you sure this isn't a very old newspaper?'

'I'm not daft, Hanny. I checked the date. It's last month's,' said Emma, her fists clenching. 'How can this be right? He was supposed to have been killed in action and yet here he is, alive and kicking.'

'Which one are we looking at?' asked Clara, gazing over Hanny's shoulder.

Hanny pointed. 'You can't see his face properly but it's my brother all right. He's a handsome devil. I can't understand how he can be in this photo.'

'Does it give the name of the regiment the soldiers belong to?' Clara asked, glancing at the lines of print beneath the picture. 'Perhaps you could trace the soldiers that way.'

'Now there's an idea,' said Emma, giving Clara an approving stare. 'Trouble is, the men will most likely have dispersed by now. What we need is a detective.'

'Someone like Sherlock Holmes,' suggested Clara. 'Did you see that film with William Gillette playing Holmes?'

'I wish,' said Hanny, tapping her fingers on the newspaper.

'Unfortunately Holmes isn't available, so we need someone else to solve this mystery,' said Emma, folding the newspaper.

'If it's all right with you,' said Hanny, reaching

out a hand. 'I want that to show Kenny. Alice and Seb will need to see it, too. They have to be warned.' Her expression was stern. 'Bert might look like a Greek god but he'll be out to cause trouble.'

'But why?' asked Clara.

'Because he hates us,' said Hanny softly. 'He might be my brother but he's not the least bit like Freddie. Bert's a total swine.'

Emma said, 'I'd best go. The kids will be in for lunch, so I'll have to put my skates on or I won't make it home in time.'

'I'll have to get a move on, too,' said Hanny, tucking a strand of flaxen hair behind her ear. 'We'll see ourselves out, Clara. There's nothing you want?'

Clara shook her head. 'I need to get food for Alice and Seb but I'll go out later.'

Hanny nodded. 'Let us know when they arrive.'

A few minutes later, as Clara saw to Georgie's lunch, she turned over in her mind what she knew about Bert. She remembered Tilly telling her that this house was said to have been haunted by the ghost of the woman whose life he had destroyed. On such a lovely spring day, it was hard to believe that such violence could take place here. Yet it had, so it was no wonder Hanny and Emma insisted Seb and Alice must know that the man they believed to be dead was very much alive. She hoped the hours would not drag until they arrived home.

* * *

Clara watched as Alice kissed her children and Seb gave them a one-armed hug and a kiss. One might think they had been parted for a month instead of a week. She was reminded of her own parents and wished they were still alive. Freddie, who had come round, slipped out, unnoticed in all the excitement. When calm had been restored, the children were ushered to bed by Tilly with the promise that their parents would tell them a story later. Alice and Seb sat down to sausages, mashed potato and turnip.

'You are a gem, Clara,' said Seb, resting his splinted arm on the table and using just a fork to eat.

'Nice of you to say so.' Her cheeks were flushed and she was on pins, wondering not only when she should mention her suspicions about Mr Moran but also because she knew that, once Freddie arrived with Hanny and Kenny, Alice and Seb were in for another shock.

'Did you have a good journey?' she asked.

'It was OK,' said Seb.

Alice smiled. 'He means that it wasn't all right at all. It seemed to take ages. We had to change trains several times and nearly missed a connection. That would have meant waiting a couple more hours and we were impatient to get home to the children. They all look well, Clara.'

'That's more because of you than me,' she responded. 'You've only been away a few days. I haven't had time to undo all your care.'

Alice said mischievously, 'And do you feel that is enough time to put you off children for life?'

Clara sat down and told them about her day, including the episode about the plant being dug up and her fear that Georgie might have poisoned himself. They laughed several times and Seb said that eyes in the back of one's head as well as an extra pair of hands were needed where kids were involved.

It was at that point in the conversation that there was a knock on the back door and Hanny called, 'Can we come in?'

'Of course,' called Seb.

The door opened and Hanny entered, followed by Freddie. Greetings and hugs were exchanged between Hanny, Alice and Seb. A pot of tea was made and they joined the other adults at the table. Initially, the conversation involved Seb's operation and the physiotherapy he would need to undergo in Liverpool. It was not until all had been said on that matter and the meal was finished that the crumpled newspaper was produced and spread on the table by Hanny. Clara had cleared the dishes away and was now washing them, but she was able to hear clearly what was being said.

'What's this?' asked Seb, glancing at Hanny and Freddie.

Freddie's expression was grave but it was Hanny

who said, 'Have a look at this picture, Alice.' She pointed at the photograph.

'Who am I looking for?' asked Alice.

Hanny leant over. 'Look closely and see if you recognise anyone.'

Alice did as she was bid, wondering who it was she was supposed to be looking for – and then she saw him. 'What is this? How old is this paper?' she cried, looking at the top of the page.

'Several of us have done that,' said Freddie, resting his elbows on the table. 'This really is a week for surprises. Hanny had to point Bert out to me. I was only a kid when he went to prison but as soon as she showed me where to look, I recognised him.'

'I thought he was dead,' said Seb, rubbing his scarred cheek. 'Someone show him to me.'

Alice flattened the newspaper so that the picture was uppermost again. 'I'd almost forgotten you were never on the scene when he was around,' she said, 'although you saw him at his trial.'

'Briefly,' agreed Seb. 'But I was working so couldn't be there for the whole of it.' He looked at Freddie and Hanny. 'I'm tired. I can't think straight at the moment. How can he be alive?'

There was a silence. Then Freddie said, 'He must have switched identity with another soldier.'

'But would it be that easy?' asked Alice with a tremor in her voice. 'I can't believe this is happening just when everything seemed like it was about to start going right for us again.'

Seb reached out and took her hand. She clung to it. 'I doubt it was easy for him to do, but not as difficult as you might think with so many men being slaughtered. There were times when whole units were destroyed almost to the last man. Say Bert survived, and other surviving soldiers from here, there and everywhere ended up fighting as one unit and he was amongst them.'

'But how was it we were informed he was dead?' asked Hanny.

Seb sighed and his face screwed up with concentration. 'OK. Let's imagine that Bert saw one of his comrades have his head blown off.'

Alice drew in a sharp breath, as did Hanny and Clara, who had returned to the table.

'Sorry, ladies,' said Seb stiffly.

'Shall I carry on?' asked Freddie, his face alight. 'I can see where you're going with this. Bert removed the fallen soldier's identity tag and anything else that would say who he was and replaced them with his own. Then he scarpered. Could be that he laid low for a while, waiting for the worst of the fighting to be over. Men went missing and so it's possible that at first no one noticed his absence. Then, when he saw his opportunity, he joined up with soldiers from other units who had never met him or the fallen soldier before. They'd accept whatever he said and, somehow, the lucky sod survived to return to Blighty a free man.'

'Could be that he knew enough about the dead man to know that he had no family waiting for him back home,' said Seb, 'so no awkward questions to answer when he arrived in England.'

Silence.

'So where is he now?' asked Alice. 'You remember what he said when it all went wrong for him, don't you, Hanny?' She gazed at her friend with a fixed stark expression.

'That he'd get back at us,' she replied.

Clara glanced at Freddie and saw the anger in his face. 'There's no need for you to fear him now,' he said. 'Things have changed. I'm a man now, not a kid to be bullied by him.'

'Aye, they've changed in as much that you've grown up, but Kenny's still crippled and Seb's not exactly fighting fit,' cried Hanny. 'And what about Tilly? Remember how he lured her away from us once before and then let her go just to prove that he could do it? He's been that close...' she measured two inches with her fingers, 'to ruining our lives. We can't allow him to do it again. Tilly's so pretty and he likes them young.' Her voice broke.

'You're so right,' said Alice, barely above a whisper. 'Trouble is, Tilly wouldn't recognise him if she saw him. She was only a little girl when he went to prison.'

'She does know what he looks like,' interrupted Clara. 'I remember her telling me that she had seen his likeness.' She hesitated, before adding, 'She also mentioned seeing someone hiding in the front garden the other night.'

Alice paled. 'I'd almost forgotten about that – but surely it couldn't have been Bert?'

'How are we to know?' asked Seb grimly.

'She did say the person ran away,' said Clara. 'Would Bert have done so?'

The others stared at her.

'I wouldn't have thought he would,' murmured Hanny. 'But she's spoken of Bert to you – that surprises me.'

Clara nodded. 'It was in relation to something that happened in this house.'

Hanny exchanged glances with Alice but neither spoke. Instead, Freddie said, 'Anyhow, she's not a kid anymore, so Bert won't find it easy to lure her away this time with a promise of ice cream.'

'You remember that?' said Hanny.

Freddie nodded. 'It was your wedding day and you'd rigged me out in a kilt and velvet doublet. I felt a right cissy.'

'I'd have liked to have seen that,' said Clara softly.

Her remark somehow lightened the atmosphere. Freddie winked at her and the others smiled. 'Sorry. I shouldn't have interrupted,' she said, blushing.

Hanny's eyes were sombre. 'I'm angry with myself for allowing the thought of Bert to frighten me like this. If he's got any sense at all he'll stay away from us. After all, he's supposed to be dead and surely he won't want us knowing he's alive.'

'Even so, we should tell the police,' said Seb firmly. 'With his prison record he'd be in serious trouble if he tries anything on.'

'You're right,' said Freddie.

'But what if they don't believe us?' said Alice, leaning across the table towards her husband and remembering the way he had spoken about Bert on Christmas Eve last year.

'Why shouldn't they?' he asked. 'We've got the newspaper picture and they're bound to have a photograph of him in their records, either here or in Liverpool.'

'We know what a crafty so-and-so he is, though,' said Freddie, glowering. 'I'd like to get my hands on him.'

'Don't underestimate his strength,' warned Hanny. 'I'm just grateful that Emma saw the picture and recognised Bert. We know now to be on our guard. The question is, do we tell Tilly that Bert's alive, or leave her in ignorance?'

'I honestly don't like worrying her,' said Alice.

'You're overprotective, Alice,' said Freddie bluntly. 'You've kept quiet about her father all these years and that's served only to make her more curious about him. What if your father were to come looking for her? She wouldn't even recognise him.' He darted a look at Clara.

She tried to interpret that look. Did he expect her to tell Alice and the rest of them of her suspicions right now? But before she could decide, Alice said, 'Don't mention him,' in a faint voice. 'Haven't I got enough on my plate to cope with right now?'

Seb frowned Freddie down. 'Enough. We don't need anything more to worry about than we have already right now.'

'Sorry,' said Freddie. 'Perhaps Clara and I are best leaving you three alone if you want to discuss anything more about this in private.' He reached out a hand to her. 'Shall we go for a walk?'

She nodded, relieved to get away. Without a word, she fetched her coat and hat and went with him. As they walked down to the river she thought again about Mrs Black warning her about getting involved with her cousin's family and taking on their worries. She understood now what she had meant but it was too late for her to step back and have no more to do with them. She cared too much about what happened to them.

'It's Good Friday tomorrow,' said Freddie. 'Shall we have a day out together? Perhaps we could have a run to Moreton. Mother was left a house by an aunt and none of us have visited it for ages. We could check it out and then have a walk along the beach. Now Alice and Seb are back, surely you're free to do what you want.'

'I'd like to go with you. Although I'm wondering if Alice will want me to leave tomorrow,' said Clara, biting on her lip.

Freddie raised his eyebrows and said easily, 'It doesn't make sense your going home and then having to return on Sunday. But if you want to see how your grandmother and lodger are getting on without you, I can take you to Liverpool. Is that what you want?'

She thought about his suggestion for only a few seconds, knowing she would much prefer to go to Moreton and told him so. 'As long as Alice is prepared to put up with me for a few more nights.'

'I can't see her saying no,' said Freddie, 'so that's settled.'

Clara did not argue with him and could only hope he was right. After that she asked him to tell her more about his brother and what happened at Hanny's wedding.

'Bert was determined to ruin it and had threatened to abduct Tilly,' said Freddie, his eyes darkening.

'But why would he want to do that?' asked Clara, incredulous that a brother could behave in such a way towards a sister as nice as Hanny.

Freddie gave a twisted smile. 'I don't know all the reasons because I was simply too young to be aware of all that was going on at the time, but I know Hanny left home for what seemed ages to me and Joy told me Bert was to blame. Then while Hanny was missing there was an accident and my sister Grace was killed. Bert was held responsible, having gone against a warning Mother had given him. Hanny came home after that because Mother was in such a state. Alice came back into our lives and Bert made up to her and they were going to get married, then suddenly, the day before it was to take place, she called it off. He beat her up and...'

Clara gasped. 'So that's why Alice is scared of him?'

He nodded. 'Kenny was away but he returned and had a fight with Bert. I overheard Hanny telling Joy all about it.' Freddie's eyes gleamed. 'Bert left home after that but still managed to cause trouble in the years that followed. He wrote to Mother saying he was emigrating to Australia. It was a lie but it's stuck in her mind and now she firmly believes that he's living on the other side of the world. She had a breakdown and just couldn't face the truth about his going to prison.'

Clara slipped her hand into his and squeezed it. 'I suppose it's understandable that a mother doesn't want to believe her children can behave so badly.'

Freddie returned the pressure of her fingers. 'Bert was her blue-eye and could do no wrong. But I've two sisters who've more than compensated for

Mother's lack of affection towards me. And now I've met you...' His voice trailed off and there was an expression in his eyes that caused her pulse to race, but he said no more.

After that they walked in silence, but Clara felt as if they had moved another step closer. Of course, it was early days to be thinking of marriage, yet here she was doing so. Really, she must put the thought out of her mind for now. Freddie had to make his way in the world and she had her gran still to consider.

When they returned to the crescent, they parted at the Bennetts' gate, having arranged for Freddie to pick Clara up at nine o'clock the next morning.

On entering the house, Clara half expected everyone to have gone to bed but she found Alice sitting in the drawing room. There was no sign of anyone else. She wondered whether Tilly had been told about Bert or not. She did not like to appear as if she was prying so did not mention it, only asking whether she could stay on until after the christening party.

'Of course you can,' said Alice, smiling as she put down her sewing and dropped a newspaper on top of it. 'Hanny and I were thinking that would be the most sensible thing for you to do.'

Clara's eyes lit up. 'Thanks. Freddie's taking me to Moreton tomorrow for a day out, if that's all right with you?'

'Of course it's all right,' said Alice, smiling. 'How could I say no after your being so willing to help us? Make yourself some sandwiches for a picnic.'

Clara thanked her and wondered if now was the time to mention the man she had seen across the way but, recalling Seb's words about having enough on their plate, she thought better of it. Instead, she said good night and went up to bed, looking forward to her day out with Freddie tomorrow and hoping the weather would be fine.

Clara woke early and managed to use the bathroom before any one else was up. She made breakfast and some fish paste sandwiches, remembering once upon a time she would have attended a Stations of the Cross service during Holy Week. She had not done that for years, but she was looking forward to the christening service with the family on Easter Sunday. She slipped out without anyone being aware of it, glad in a way that she did not have to explain to Tilly where she was off to at that time of the morning.

Freddie was already waiting for her and she hurried to meet him. 'Don't you just love being up and out early at this time of year?' she said.

'We met a year ago this month,' he said. 'I remember shortly afterwards I had to get up early like this so I could say my goodbyes to Joy because I was going back to sea the next day. I didn't want to leave, not only because of the war and the family but because it was spring and the country was looking its best. I remember thinking how terrible it would be if I never saw it again.'

'But you're here. Thank goodness.' She sighed happily.

'Aye. Thank goodness.' He lowered his head and pressed his lips against hers for a brief moment before taking her bag from her. 'Sandwiches?' he asked, cocking a dark eyebrow.

Clara nodded, still feeling the pressure of his lips on hers and hoping he would kiss her again before the day was out. She was determined to put her worries behind her and just knew it was going to be a lovely day.

Freddie placed her sandwiches in his knapsack and she offered to carry it. 'Otherwise it's going to be in my face,' she said with a teasing smile.

'Of course. I wasn't thinking,' said Freddie, adjusting the straps and helping her on with it. His mind was set on giving Clara a great day out and he was not going to allow thoughts of his evil brother to spoil his enjoyment, but he wished he knew Bert's whereabouts.

CHAPTER TWENTY-THREE

Eastertide, 1919.

Bert stood outside a theatrical wigmakers shop on Mount Pleasant in Liverpool, perusing examples of the owner's handiwork. His blue eyes were calculating as he considered the wigs on show. Being tall and handsome, he had never found it a drawback having golden locks, but maybe it was possible there were those who might find him even more attractive if he was tall, *dark* and handsome. But that was not his main reason for being here. Altering his appearance was essential if he was to snatch Alice's daughter without being recognised. Besides, there were people, even in Liverpool, who might remember him, despite not having seen him for a while.

He turned and surveyed the boarding house on the other side of the road and his eyes were like chips of ice as he recalled the months he had spent there. For a bit of *how's yer father*, the landlady, Mrs O'Shaunnessy, had treated him very well, until he had dipped into the savings she had hidden under the mattress and then she had shopped him. In court, he had told the judge and jury that he had taken it for services rendered, that older women were so susceptible to a mouthful of flannel from a young man. The words had struck home and she had screeched abuse at him across the courtroom but he had felt that, in some small way, he had got his revenge on her. Her reputation had hit rock bottom and, according to the woman in the neighbouring house, Mrs O'Shaunnessy had ended up on the streets.

Yet his main concern was not her but those who'd betrayed him. It had come as a shock to him to discover that Hanny and Kenny now lived in that medium's house in Victoria Crescent, with twin babies and his mother and brother. He was going to make fools of them. Never in a thousand years would they imagine he was still alive.

Bert thought back to when he first became aware of Lenny Marks. A nervous talker who just wouldn't shut up, Bert had absorbed enough of his life story to prove useful. A single man, Lenny had grown up in an orphanage, so had no relatives waiting for his return. It had been easy to step into his shoes after he had been killed by an exploding bomb and exchange their identities. But not so easy staying alive as Lenny in the horrors of the fighting that followed.

Still, Bert had survived and Lenny's demob payout had proved useful, but it wouldn't last. After the lousy life he had led for the last nine years, he now envisaged a more comfortable lifestyle for the future. Having served his time as an apprentice engineer in a Chester company that specialised in hydraulic-powered hoists used for coaling steamships, he had done a similar job here in Liverpool in the last years of the old king's reign, and then had come prison. His eyes were bleak as he remembered those times. No wonder he had volunteered to fight. He shuddered inwardly at the memory.

Yet Bert felt intense pleasure knowing those responsible for having him locked up were going to suffer. Believing him dead, it would drive them mad trying to puzzle out who was behind what he had in mind. When the bombs were exploding on the field of battle, he had imagined each one of the men who had worked against him having their bodies torn apart. The women had haunted his dreams too, but he'd had something different in mind for the them. Yet now, having seen Alice's children, he had settled on something that would hurt her far more than anything else he could imagine.

He grinned, thinking of the man he had seen loitering in Victoria Crescent a couple of times. Bert had been careful not to be seen when he had gone there. He had recognised the middle-aged man as Mal Moran and his plan would punish not only Alice and her husband but the man whom Bert held responsible for causing his mother brain damage years ago. It had been a bit of a shock to see him there, and the same where his younger brother was concerned. It was years since Bert had seen Freddie and he had hoped that he might have been killed in the war. Although he bore no responsibility for Bert having been jailed, he'd been an annoying little sod as a kid and Hanny had often dared to tear a strip off Bert for chastising the pest. He wondered about the identity of the young woman he had seen with Freddie. Quite a good-looking girl; possibly there was something between her and his brother.

But he was allowing his mind to wonder and must concentrate on the matter in hand. While in prison, he had listened to some of the old lags talking and picked up enough information to know what not to do to get caught if he took to a life of crime. First and foremost was not to be known by the local bobbies. Second was not to let your victims get a look at your face. Third, don't steal stuff you'll need a fence to get rid of and who'll take a fair whack of your ill-gotten gains. Leave jewellery and stuff to someone else and go for the money.

He stared in the window again at wigs of varying

styles and colour. There was a rusty coloured one that would be just the job to convince Alice and the rest of them that it was Mal Moran who had abducted her daughter. Still, perhaps he should consider having several wigs for his life of crime. It would cause confusion when a bobby took out his notebook and asked for a description of the thief from a witness. Bert felt for the gun in his pocket, a war souvenir, and chuckled to himself before opening the door of the wig shop and stepping inside.

'You'll never believe this!' said Tilly, glancing up from the *Liverpool Echo* that evening. 'A gunman walked into a wigmakers' shop yesterday and stole several wigs and emptied the till.'

'Was he bald?' asked Alice, kicking off her shoes and wriggling her toes. She had been up early sewing and then on her feet most of the afternoon baking for the christening party in the morning.

'The owner said he wore a trilby and didn't even try on any of the wigs,' murmured Tilly.

'So it was a snatch and grab,' said Seb, glancing at Clara as she entered the drawing room with Georgie. 'Did you get them?' he asked.

She nodded with a smile and handed him the brown paper shopping bag by its strings containing Easter eggs for the children. 'What's this about a snatch and grab?' she asked

Tilly said, 'You can read it yourself,' and gave Clara the newspaper.

She read the piece and then looked up. 'What's the world coming to when robbers are using guns? And what strange things to steal – wigs!'

'I agree. It's scary,' said Alice.

Clara and Tilly exchanged glances and giggled.

'What's so funny?' asked Alice, looking surprised.

'It being scary stealing wigs,' said Tilly, her eyes dancing with mischief.

'You know perfectly well what I meant,' said Alice, enjoying the joke.

'Oh look,' said Clara, who was reading a short article just beneath that item. 'They're starting battlefield tours. A party of British women are visiting France next week.' She looked up. 'I suppose there'll be lots of women wanting to see where their menfolk died and to visit their graves.'

'Would you want to visit your dad's grave?' asked Tilly.

Clara's brow knitted as she gave that some thought. 'I'm sure if Mam was still alive she would want to go. Maybe one day I'll go if I can afford it. There's times when it still feels unbelievable that he is dead. It's different with Mam, because I was there when she died and I know where she's buried.' The others gazed at her in silence. 'Sorry, not a cheerful subject, is it?' She pulled a face.

'Don't apologise,' said Seb roughly. 'Why shouldn't you talk about how you feel about your father's death? I hope you can go there one day. Maybe I could go with you. I might never have known your father in life but I'd like to pay my respects at his graveside.'

Clara was touched. 'I'd like that,' she said sincerely.

'I suppose they'll have a reporter writing up the first tours,' mused Tilly, swinging her foot. 'I wish I could grow up faster. If only I was older I could have gone out there.'

'Stop wishing your life away,' said Alice. She smiled up at Clara. 'Can I have a look at the paper?'

Clara passed it to her and then sat down next to Tilly, who asked, 'So what are you wearing tomorrow for the christening?'

Clara parried the question with one of her own. 'What are you?'

'Depends on the weather,' said Tilly. 'If it's nice then I'll wear a yellow and green frock. It's not new but I've taken up the hem and I have a matching bolero to go with it.'

Alice looked up from the newspaper. 'That sounds like the outfit I made for you last year. I notice here in the newspaper that TJ Hughes are advertising dress gingham for one shilling and nine pence halfpenny a yard. I wouldn't mind some of that to make Flora a new frock. Too late for an

Easter christening but it would be nice for Whit.'
She glanced at Clara. 'Which reminds me...if you've
a minute, I've something I want to show you. It's
upstairs.'

'OK,' said Clara, wondering what it could be as
she rose to her feet.

Alice and Seb exchanged a smile and then she led
the way upstairs and into their bedroom.

'It's just a little something I made for you,' said
Alice, going over to her dressing table and lifting
a hat from it. She held it out to Clara. 'Try it on.
If it doesn't fit I still have time to alter it. I
thought you might like a new Easter bonnet to
wear to church,' she added, her green eyes
sparkling.

Clara could not conceal her delight. The hat was
made of deep pink buckram with paler pink flowers
sewn onto the crown. It had a stylish narrow brim
and a white ribbon tied into a bow at the side. She
put on the hat with great care and was delighted
when it fitted perfectly. 'How did you know my
size?' she asked, admiring her reflection in the
mirror on the dressing table.

'Experience.'

'I should get my hair cut short,' murmured Clara.

'I've been thinking the same thing recently about
mine and Flora's,' said Alice. 'Long hair takes such
ages to dry. Short hair wouldn't have looked right
with the big hats before the war, but I think you

could get away wearing that hat with either long or short hair.'

'Thanks for making it for me,' said Clara, giving her an impulsive hug.

'I enjoyed doing it and your reaction even more. It does my heart good.' She hesitated. 'I do have a pink costume that might fit you and will go perfectly with the hat. I last wore it before I started with Georgie and I've put on some weight since then. If you'd like to try it on I'll get it out. There's plenty of wear in it.' She smiled ruefully. 'I should have had more sense than to buy that colour material with my hair, but you can have it if you want.'

'I'd love to try it on,' said Clara, her brown eyes shining.

Alice looked pleased and went over to the wardrobe and produced the costume almost immediately. Clara undressed and tried on the skirt, blouse and jacket and could not believe the vision that gazed back at her was really her.

'I don't know what to say,' she said. 'I've never had anything this good.'

'It's almost a perfect fit,' said Alice, gazing at her measuringly. 'Just a few inches off the hem.'

'Whatever you say,' said Clara, thinking that she could not wait for Freddie to see her in her new outfit.

It was twenty-four hours since she had last seen

him and most likely she would not see him again until tomorrow as he was helping out with a job at the yard. Her thoughts returned to their day out. It had been almost perfect. The only downside was when they had arrived at his mother's house and discovered that a window had been broken. There had been no damage inside but it was obvious that someone had slept there and used some of the stores left in the larder. They both agreed that most likely it had been a tramp. Freddie had found a piece of wood in the small lean-to and nailed it inside so that it covered the broken pane. After that, he had left his motorbike round the back and they had walked across the flat coastal expanse with its scattering of trees bent double with the strength of the winter winds from the sea, the Leasowe lighthouse visible in the distance. They had ended up running hand in hand towards the sand dunes and the sea beyond but they did not have the seascape to themselves – some cocklers and fishermen had arrived there before them. They picnicked on the beach and splashed in the sea and talked about their childhood. Freddie had kissed her once again, but that was only when they had returned for the motorbike before heading back to Chester.

'Well, what do you think?' asked Alice, rousing Clara from her happy thoughts.

She focused once more on her reflection and

smiled at herself, thinking what did it matter if her shoes didn't match when the rest of her did. 'I think it's perfect. Thanks very much.'

'You're welcome,' said Alice, smiling. 'Roll on tomorrow.'

Surprisingly, when Easter Sunday morning dawned, Clara woke feeling a little depressed. She put that down to the thought that, after the party, her break in Chester would be over and she would have to return home. Which meant she would see less of Freddie. How could she possibly expect him to make the journey daily to see her? She was so unsure of herself that it occurred to her that maybe he might just have been flirting with her and they would see little of each other in the future. Determinedly, she put a damper on such thoughts and remembered her new Easter bonnet and the costume that Alice had given to her. She had to make the most of this day.

The christening service that followed at St Mary-without-the-Walls might not have gone off without a hitch but Clara found it fascinating. She had never been to a Catholic baptism before, never mind a Protestant one, and the liturgy being in English instead of Latin proved of great interest to her. Seb and Alice, Freddie and Joy were standing as the twins' godparents, so Clara and Tilly had charge of the other children.

Baby Allan cried when the holy water was sprinkled on his forehead and, from behind, Clara heard a man's voice say *sotto voce*, 'That's the devil coming out of him.' She was tempted to look behind her but at that moment Georgie pulled a prayer book off the ledge and dropped it.

It was only as they were making their way out of church that Tilly, who was looking extremely pretty in the yellow and green frock with matching bolero, whispered, 'Did you hear what that man said about the devil?'

Clara turned quickly to face her. 'I wasn't sure you heard.'

Tilly nodded and said thoughtfully, 'I don't really believe in children being born in sin. I suppose you do, being a Catholic?'

'It's not something I spend my time thinking about,' replied Clara, recalling her grandmother's words about not getting involved in a religious debate.

'That man obviously did. I wonder who he was. I didn't recognise his voice and I've been to this church with Kenny and Hanny several times.' Tilly gazed about her as if looking for the man.

'He's probably someone who only comes on high days and holidays,' suggested Clara.

'You could be right,' agreed Tilly, still looking about her. 'Oh, there's Freddie talking to Seb. I must have a quick word with him. Will you keep your eye on the kids until Alice comes for them? She's talking to Emma at the moment.' She hurried off.

Clara frowned as she watched the younger girl seize Freddie's sleeve and whisper in his ear. She experienced a stab of envy and realised that she was still having difficulty coming to terms with the closeness between them. She wondered again if Freddie was just flirting with her and whether there was any future for them together. Then James and Flora ran off before she could prevent them in the direction of Emma's children, so that Clara was left with just Georgie to keep in hand. The party had began to move off so she followed them. They did not have far to go to Hanny and Kenny's apartment. Joy suddenly turned and looked at Clara. Her expression was serious as she beckoned her to catch up. She swung Georgie up into her arms and hurried towards Joy.

'So how have you enjoyed your time at Alice's?' asked Joy.

'Very much. But I'll be going home this evening.'

'Freddie seemed to think you'd be going in the morning,' said Joy surprised.

'I had thought of it, but I actually start work tomorrow, so don't want to be rushed,' said Clara. 'He doesn't have to take me, I can catch a train.'

'That's up to you,' said Joy, slowing her pace, 'but I think he's planning on taking you home. By the way, he mentioned what your gran said about wanting a visit from Mrs Black. She'll be home in a couple of days, so I'll broach the subject once she's settled in.'

'Gran's got a cheek asking,' she said indignantly, 'but do you think Mrs Black will come?' Clara stopped a few feet away from the front gate to Hanny and Kenny's home.

'It wouldn't surprise me, but you might have to wait for it to happen. There's a lot of dates written in her appointment book.' Joy frowned as she watched the rest of the party go up the path. 'Looks like we're here,' she said. 'I just hope Mother behaves herself and doesn't go on about Bert again.' Joy's attractive plump features were baffled as she led the way through the gate. Clara followed, with Georgie in her arms, up the path and through the front entrance. She closed the door firmly behind her.

An hour later Clara was finding the noise and the crush in the drawing room a bit too much, so made her way out through the french windows onto the balcony outside. She'd had little time to speak to Freddie as he was helping serve drinks while Tilly was taking plates of food around to the guests.

Clara rested her arms on the wrought-iron ledge of the balcony and gazed down over the garden. She could see Georgie's dark head and Flora's auburn one, as well as Emma's elder daughter's soft brown hair. Then her searching eyes wandered to the Dee and the footbridge. There were plenty of day trippers on the river as, although, the weather was cloudy, it was not threatening rain. Then she saw someone who appeared familiar. He was shuffling along the bridge and was wearing a cloth cap over rusty hair that stuck out from beneath it. She watched him, convinced more than ever that he was the man she had followed that day she had visited Mrs Black.

She was about to turn away and go in search of Freddie when a child's scream drew her attention to the garden below. She could scarcely believe her eyes when she saw a man tucking a struggling Flora beneath his arm. Then, as she watched, he hit the little girl across the head and she fell silent. 'Oh my God,' whispered Clara, scarcely aware of Georgie, with his fingers in his mouth, staring after the man heading for the path that led round the side of the house. As for Emma's daughter, she had started to whimper and look about her for her mother.

Clara delayed no longer but hurried into the drawing room. She knew that if she stopped to explain the man would get away. She forced her way through the throng and out onto the landing, where, to her relief, she almost collided with Freddie. 'There's a man!' she cried, seizing hold of his arm, almost causing him to drop the tray he carried.

Freddie gazed down into her distressed face and

instantly placed the tray on a convenient chair. 'What man?'

'I'll tell you on the way,' she said, 'Outside.' She hung on to Freddie's arm as he moved towards the stairs. 'He's taking Flora away. He looked like Mr Moran but I'm sure it's not him because I've only just seem him crossing the bridge.'

Freddie didn't wait to hear any more but hurried downstairs. They were just in time to catch sight of the back of the man and Flora's dangling legs as he went through the gate.

'Hoy, you!' roared Freddie, running down the path.

Clara followed him and then almost ran into the back of him because he stopped abruptly. She realised why when she saw two men, similarly dressed and with the same rusty hair and caps, a couple of yards away. The kidnapper still had Flora wedged beneath his left arm but in his right hand, he held a revolver. He was standing with his back against a garden fence so that he faced both Freddie and the man Clara presumed was Mr Moran.

'Let the little lass go,' he growled, 'or it'll be the worse for ye, laddie.'

'Get out of my way,' snarled Flora's captor. 'I'd shoot you as soon as look at you.'

'Yer asked for it,' said Mr Moran and he went for him.

The sound of the gun going off so shocked Clara

that, for a moment, she could not move. Then she stared in dismay at Mr Moran as he buckled at the knees and fell to the ground. Blood seeped through the fingers clutching his shirt just beneath his shoulder.

Freddie was not so immobilised and he launched himself at the gunman. A smack on the jaw with the butt of the gun sent Freddie crashing to the ground. Terrified that the man might yet shoot again, Clara darted forward and seized hold of Flora. 'Let her go!' she cried.

'You bloody let go,' said her captor, struggling to hold the girl.

Clara was aware of the smell of peppermints and eau-de-cologne as she gazed into the snarling face. She saw what she was later to think of as pure evil in the vivid blue eyes. Her heart was pounding with fear but still she refused to let go of Flora. The girl had began to stir and struggle and Clara had trouble holding her. Then the sound of the gun going off so close to her ear almost deafened her. She felt the wind of the bullet as it narrowly missed her cheek. Then, suddenly, she and Flora were tumbling backwards.

Clara landed on her back on the pavement, still holding the girl. She lay there, gasping for air, half expecting to hear the gun go off again. Instead, there was the sound of running feet and she managed to lift her head and realised that the gunman had escaped. Hastily, she looked in Freddie's direction and saw that his eyes were open. He smiled lopsidedly at Clara and got to his feet.

People began to appear as if from nowhere. 'He's got away,' said one of the neighbours. 'What's the world coming to when one hears guns going off outside your own front door on an Easter Sunday?'

Freddie did not answer but went over to Clara. 'Are you OK?' he asked, taking Flora from her. The child clung to him.

'Just a bit shaken,' replied Clara, noticing that his jaw was bruised and swollen.

He looked relieved. 'Thank God for that. Blast! I should have been of more help, but Hanny was right, if it was Bert – and who else could it be? – he was bloody strong.'

'He smelt of peppermints and eau-de-cologne.'

Freddie stared at her. 'It is our Bert. I remember he used to be forever sucking mints. Damn. I wish he hadn't got away.'

'Never mind him now. What do we do about him?' asked Clara, gazing down at Mr Moran, who still lay on the ground, bleeding from the shoulder.

The woman who had spoken before, said, 'I have a telephone. I'll call the local exchange and ask them to get in touch with the police and the hospital.'

Freddie thanked her. A man standing nearby was complaining that such hooligans should be hanged and offered to go in search of the bobby on the beat.

Suddenly, there was a commotion from the direction of Hanny and Kenny's home. Joy, Tilly, Alice, Seb and James came into view. Alice looked frightened and immediately went up to Freddie and took Flora from him. Her daughter put her arms round her neck and said, 'Mummy, Mummy, the nasty man hit me!'

'I know, sweetheart. Emma's daughter said a man carried you away.' Alice hugged Flora to her. 'Is this him on the ground?' she asked in a shaking voice as she turned and looked down at the prone figure.

But before Flora could speak, Clara said, 'It wasn't your father.' She watched the colour drain from Alice's face as she recognised the man. 'He stood up to him and got shot for his bravery.'

Tilly looked down at the injured man. 'Isn't he the one we saw the other day, Clara?' Her voice trailed off and she took a deep breath before adding, 'You did say "your father" to Alice, didn't you?'

'Yes,' said Clara, looking at Alice. 'Bert had a gun.' She turned to Freddie. 'At least, we presume that's who it was, don't we?'

Freddie's eyes were stormy. 'I don't think it was a coincidence that the man who attempted to abduct Flora was dressed just like this poor fella. I'm sure it was Bert. I just didn't think he'd have a go at us so soon. I should have gone after him. In fact, I think I will try and find him.'

Clara grabbed his sleeve. 'He's had a running start on you and, with it being Easter, he'll have lost himself in the crowds by now.'

'Our Hanny babbled something about Bert being alive to me earlier. I told her I didn't believe it. Are you saying now that it's true?' asked Joy in a shaky voice.

'It's true all right,' said Alice, hugging her daughter tightly. 'He would have kidnapped Flora if it hadn't been for Freddie and Clara.'

'No. Clara said it was your father...*my father*...who was shot trying to stop him,' said Tilly in wonder, bending down over Mal Moran. 'We must take him to the hospital.'

'A neighbour's phoning for an ambulance,' said Clara. 'We need to stem the blood, though.'

'Here, use this,' said Freddie, handing his handkerchief to Tilly.

Alice gazed down at the figure on the ground and, for several moments, did not speak or move. Then she said, tight-lipped, 'Are you sure he wasn't in league with Bert?'

Joy gazed down at the wounded man and said in an odd tone, 'This is Mrs Black's gardener. I couldn't remember where I'd seen him before. She called him Malcolm but it never occurred to me that he could be Mr Moran. He couldn't possibly be in league with Bert. My brother hated him for what he did to Mother.'

'Mrs Black! I should have known she'd be involved with him somehow,' said Alice with loathing in her voice. 'All this time I've wondered where he was and he's been with her.'

'Not with her,' said Joy hastily. 'He lives in the gatehouse. I knew he was from the asylum and I just presumed he was one of her lame dogs. If I'd known his true identity, I'm not sure what I'd have done, because he works hard and has never hurt anyone while he's been there.'

'If he intended no one any harm, then what's he doing here?' asked Alice, her green eyes as hard as glass.

'I can answer that, lassie,' muttered her father, wincing and shifting uncomfortably on the ground and glancing away from Tilly's pretty face, so close to his as she attempted to stem the blood. 'I know ye have reason to hate me, but I've never stopped caring for yer, Alice. I've longed to beg for yer forgiveness, little as I deserve it. But Eudora insisted that I kept ma distance from ma children. But I grew desperate and wanted to see ye and Matilda.'

'I don't want to hear this.' Alice's voice was strained. 'You were forever asking Mam to forgive you but you still beat her.'

A spasm of pain crossed his face. 'I was mad, lass,' he groaned. 'Yer must have realised that. She knew something was up with me when I was getting pains in ma head. She forgave me time and time again because she lived her faith. If I could change things I would, but it's too late now for that.' He closed his eyes.

Tilly let out a cry and held up the blood-soaked handkerchief. 'This isn't the right time for recriminations. He's hurt and, whatever he's done wrong, if it weren't for him we wouldn't have Flora with us now. You heard what Clara said.' She dropped the handkerchief and, placing her hands beneath her skirts, tugged down her petticoat, while Clara became the focus of several pairs of eyes.

'Yes, Clara, why didn't you tell us that you'd seen this man loitering outside our house? You knew that Tilly saw a man in the garden the night before,' said Alice angrily. 'Is it because you're friendly with Mrs Black, too?'

Clara tilted her chin. 'He couldn't have been the prowler. He's not sprightly enough. Besides, Freddie and I didn't know for certain he was your father.'

'That's true,' said Freddie. 'We were going to tell you when you and Seb came home, but then we discovered that Bert was alive.'

'And Seb said you had enough on your plate to cope with,' added Clara.

'OK, I can accept that,' said Seb, speaking up for the first time.

Clara looked at him gratefully.

Tilly was now stemming the blood with her petticoat. 'He's my father and I don't want him to die.'

'You never had to live with him and see our mother suffer,' said Alice coldly. 'She was far too good for him.'

'But you heard his explanation,' said Tilly in a desperate voice. 'I remember asking you if we had a lunatic in the family because you mentioned his madness, but you still wouldn't talk about him to me. Instead you clammed up as usual.'

'Calm down, kid,' said Freddie. 'An ambulance will soon be here.'

'I'm just scared because of all this blood.'

'Shouldn't we try and keep him warm?' asked Clara. 'He could be in shock.'

'I'm going inside,' said Alice, glancing at Seb. 'Are you coming? I think Kenny should know about Dad.'

'You know what's happening here, Alice,' said Joy abruptly. 'You're forgetting about the gunman in all this. If it was our Bert with a gun, he's far more dangerous than your father and a real worry to us.'

Alice muttered, 'I wouldn't argue. I'm leaving now to speak to Kenny.' She walked away.

For a moment Seb lingered, gazing down at the man whom Alice had expressed fear of for years but who now had helped save his daughter from a fate he did not want to contemplate. He pitied not only his wife but his father-in-law, too, but could not speak his thoughts aloud. Instead, he followed Alice indoors.

Clara went and fetched a blanket and returned as quickly as she could. She was trying not to allow her emotions to get the better of her but there were several moments when she had wanted to scream herself. One, when Freddie had fallen to the ground and she feared Bert might shoot him, and secondly, when he had handed the handkerchief to Tilly and not her. It was natural, of course, as it was Tilly's father and she was kneeling beside him, and yet it had felt to her as if it was another sign of their closeness, and it made her feel unsure of him. Still, she had to hide her feelings.

She covered most of Mal with the blanket. A few minutes later Kenny arrived on the scene. 'You shouldn't be here, Tilly,' he said. 'Alice is really upset about all this and wants you to have nothing to do with him.'

'I don't know what Alice told you,' said Freddie, getting up from his haunches. 'But your father acted bravely.'

'I'm not asking you for a character assessment for him, Freddie,' said Kenny sharply, facing him. 'I know what he's done. Why don't you, Tilly and Clara go indoors and get yourselves a drink? I'll stay with Dad.'

Tilly's lovely face was drawn. 'No. I'm not a child. I'd rather wait and see him into an ambulance.'

Kenny's face was suddenly overshadowed by anger and sadness. 'Someone else can do that. You know nothing about our father. Believe me, he's no hero, so you'll do as I say.'

Tilly's mouth set in a determined line. 'I know you and Alice want me to hate him but I can't. If it's true that he's sick, then he needs caring for. He didn't sound mad when he spoke to me. I think the past should be forgotten.'

Clara had been listening and could not remain silent any longer. 'He told me that factories were dangerous places and that lead had damaged his brain.'

Kenny stared at her. 'I know the doctor's opinion but there was more than one reason for his behaviour when Alice and I were children. Believe me, I've tried to forgive him for what he did, but there's still memories that hurt. It's worse for Alice. Now, if you don't mind leaving with Tilly, Clara?' he asked in a restrained voice.

Clara decided she had had enough and looked at Freddie. 'I'd like to go home, please. Could you give me a lift to the railway station?'

Before he could answer there was a clanging of a bell and an ambulance arrived on the scene. Within minutes, the wounded Mal was safely loaded into the ambulance.

There were tears in Tilly's eyes. 'I want to go with him,' she said.

'No, Tilly.' It was Joy who spoke. 'Mrs Black will have my life if I don't keep my eye on him and see he's cared for. I'll need to report back to her about what's happened here when she returns.' She beckoned her brother over. 'A word, Freddie.'

He drew close to her and she said in his ear, 'I find it worrying, all this talk about Bert. He could return here, in disguise, and watch all our comings and goings. I'm going to be in the house on my own without Mr Moran around to keep a watch out until Mrs Black gets back from Scotland. I wonder if you'd like to come and stay at the house until she does?'

Freddie understood his sister's fear. 'OK. I'll take Clara home first. I want to see her safely to her door.'

'Perhaps she's realising now what she's let herself in for, getting involved with us,' said Joy, in earshot of Clara.

He looked at Clara who stared at him blankly. Frowning, he turned back to his sister. 'Will I pick you up at the hospital and take you to Eastham or will you come back here and wait for me?'

'I'll stay at Chester Infirmary until you turn up,' said Joy. 'I'm not going to be wandering the streets if Bert's on the prowl. But you do realise if the police get involved in this, they're going to want to speak to you and Clara?'

'Then the quicker we're on our way the better,' he said.

The words were hardly out of his mouth when a bobby arrived. Kenny took Tilly indoors but Clara and Freddie stayed outside, giving the policeman an account of what had happened. Freddie told him of their suspicions about the identity of the gunman. After the police had gone, Freddie instantly said that he would take her home. 'Do you want to go inside and say your goodbyes?' he asked.

She shook her head. 'I'll just fetch my things and then slip away.'

Freddie thought he understood how she felt. 'I'll get the bike.'

It took them just over an hour to reach Liverpool. As Clara got off the bike and smoothed the skirt of her pink costume and accepted her bag from him, she was thinking that perhaps today signalled a parting of the ways, not only from Freddie but Seb and the rest of the family, too.

'You'll thank Hanny and Kenny for inviting me to the christening, won't you?' she said, not looking Freddie in the eye and biting down hard on her lip to stop it trembling. 'And Seb and Alice, thank them, too, for allowing me to stay at their house.'

Freddie leant towards her and kissed her lightly on the lips. 'I've enjoyed our time together. This isn't goodbye.'

She wanted to believe him but there was such a

serious expression on his face that she had her doubts about them ever seeing each other again. She watched him roar off down the street towards West Derby Road and then, brushing the tears from her eyes, she went indoors.

CHAPTER TWENTY-FOUR

'Nice to see you back,' said Mary, coming out of the parlour as Clara walked up the lobby.

'Is Gran OK? I hope she hasn't been a nuisance.' Clara had a struggle to show real interest.

Mary smiled. 'I'm used to difficult patients but, to be honest, I haven't had to do much for her. She managed to drag herself to the lavatory and to the front door. I put out a chair for her and she sat there, watching the children playing in the street and talking to the neighbours.'

'Goodness, that's a first,' said Clara, truly surprised. 'Where is she now?'

'She's gone upstairs for a nap. I think she's tired herself out.'

'I'll go up and see her in a minute,' said Clara, rubbing her forehead, where she had the beginning of a headache. Also, her bottom was hurting from where she had landed on the ground after tugging Flora out of Bert's grasp. 'Any news from the Palladium or any post?'

'Both as it happens,' said Mary, gazing at her with concern. 'Are you all right?'

'I'm fine,' lied Clara. 'So what news of the Palladium?'

'A Mr Bennett popped round and asked if you'd heard from your aunt recently.'

Clara was taken aback. 'Did Gran speak to him?'

'No. It was evening and I met him on the front step. I told him you were away for a few days and that we expected you back in time for work on Monday. He said he would see you then.'

'Right,' said Clara, wondering why he should be asking her about her aunt. 'Did he say how Mrs Walsh was?'

'I didn't think to ask. He did say to let you know that there's going to be continuous performances from now on. Apparently Liverpool's Medical Officer believes the flu epidemic is just about over and so life can get back to what passes for normal these days.'

'That must be a relief to you,' said Clara, pushing open the kitchen door.

Mary agreed and followed her into the room. 'We've been aware at the hospital that the cases of flu were petering out.'

'People definitely aren't as scared to go in company as they were a while ago. There were plenty of trippers down at the Pierhead and on the ferries,' said Clara, removing her hat.

Mary suddenly seemed to notice it. 'Now, that's lovely,' she said, her eyes warm with admiration. 'Can I have a look at it?'

'Of course,' said Clara, smiling as she handed it to her. 'Try it on if you like. My cousin's wife, Alice, made it for me as a thank you for looking after her son. She also gave me this outfit.'

'They really go well together,' said Mary. 'One gets so fed up of seeing black all the time. May I really try it on?' she said, going over to the mirror above the fireplace in the kitchen.

'I said so, didn't I?' Clara followed her over. It was then that she noticed the picture postcard on the mantelshelf. She picked it up and saw that it was from New Orleans. Her heart seemed to flip over as she read the words in big bold black letters on the reverse side. They were brief and to the point.

Dear Clara,
Your letter made me sad. I remember your father,
Denny, as a little boy. Perhaps we can meet when I
return.
Yours, Gabrielle Waters.

'Has Gran seen this?' asked Clara.

Mary nodded, gazing at her reflection and turning her head this way and that. 'This really is a pretty hat. Do you think she'd make me one? I'd pay her, of course.'

'I can't say,' Clara murmured, not wanting to make any promises. 'She used to be a milliner but she doesn't work now. When did the postcard come?'

'Yesterday. Your gran got herself into a stew over it. I think if there had been a fire in the grate she would have burnt it, but I told her that it was addressed to you and she shouldn't even think of destroying it.'

Clara tapped the card against the palm of her hand. 'My aunt doesn't mention her at all, that's what's such a blow to her.'

'I thought it might be something like that,' said Mary. 'This hat. Will you ask your cousin's wife? I don't expect it to be exactly the same and yellow is more my colour.'

'Perhaps. I suppose I could write and ask her,' said Clara, having no intention of doing so at the moment.

'Thanks,' said Mary, removing the hat and placing it on the sideboard.

Clara brushed a strand of dark hair from out of her left eye and wondered why she had such a strong feeling that none of the family would get in touch with her again. For the last few days, the main reason for her contacting them had slipped her mind because she had been so engrossed in the affairs of the rest of the family instead of just her aunt. Now she knew what a big problem they had in the gun-wielding Bert. It was possible that they might decide that they did not want her involved.

She sighed and tried to put all that had happened today out of her mind for now. It wasn't as if she didn't have a life apart from them. She had her job and her gran to care for, and she even had the company of a lodger now, so it wasn't as if she was going to be lonely. She glanced down at the postcard and wondered if Gabrielle really meant what she said about them meeting when she returned to England. She supposed it was going to be a matter of just wait and see.

Mary excused herself and left Clara alone. She put on the kettle, thinking to take up a cup of tea to Bernie and have a chat. She was bound to want to know how her visit to Seb's and Alice's had gone. Clara wondered if she could even begin to talk about Alice's obvious difficulty in forgiving her father and of the others in the family who were not about to absolve Bert of his wrong deeds. She was beginning to realise that forgiveness did not come cheap. It came at a cost and sometimes the price was too high. She thought of the war and the millions who had died, including her dad. Her initial anger and pain had faded, but who had she blamed for his death when it happened? The Germans, the British generals, or the Government for being prepared to sacrifice so many men's lives? Britain certainly hadn't forgiven Germany, and those involved in settling terms for peace were still wrangling over the price that country would have to pay to absolve itself from what the Government obviously saw as the crime of war.

Clara shook herself. She was getting gloomy. Today was Easter Sunday, when Christians were supposed to celebrate Jesus rising from the dead after dying for the sins of mankind. *Father, forgive them for they know not what they do.* That was what he had said on the cross. Perhaps she was mistaken, believing that her family across the Mersey were going to cut her off. Only time would tell. With a feeling that was almost relief, she heard the kettle boiling and made a pot of tea.

She carried a tray upstairs and found her grandmother propped up against a couple of pillows and with the curtains closed.

'Who's that there?' wheezed Bernie. 'Go away all of you. I won't have it.'

A startled Clara said, 'It's me, Gran.'

'Thank God for that,' said Bernie, hoisting herself further up in the bed. 'I've been seeing ghosts. Put the gaslight on, girl.'

'It's still daylight, Gran. I'll open the curtains. I've brought you a cup of tea.' Clara placed the cup and saucer on a chair by the bed before going over and pulling back the curtains.

Bernie blinked in the evening light. 'You're a good girl. Has the lad gone?'

'What lad?'

'That one from the séance. I thought I heard his motorbike. I thought he might have been bringing Mrs Black to see me.'

Clara had forgotten about Bernie wanting to see Mrs Black. 'There's nothing wrong with your ears, Gran. Freddie did drop me off but couldn't stay. Mrs Black's away at the moment but he's going to stay at her house with his sister until she returns. She'll get your message.'

'I'm glad to hear it. At least he's doing more for me than me own daughter.' Bernie sniffed. 'Did yer read that postcard of hers?'

Clara sat on the bed. 'You can't write much on one of them,' she said diplomatically.

Bernie slurped her tea. 'I don't know why yer take her side. She's done nuthin' for yer.'

Clara protested, 'I'm not doing anything of the sort. I'm just speaking the truth.'

'But is Gertie?' asked Bernie, her rheumy eyes sad. 'She might write about meeting yer, but will she really come?'

Clara decided to be positive. 'Why say it if she doesn't mean it? Anyway, it's not about to happen overnight. Let's think of something else... Now the weather's improving, perhaps you should get out and about again, Gran. With the Palladium opening up once more you could watch films for free. Matinée or evening! Why don't you come?'

'Free, yer say?' muttered Bernie.

Clara nodded.

'Perhaps in a few days, when I'm feeling more meself,' said Bernie. 'Now, tell me how yer got on caring for that great-grandson of mine. And what was the baptism like?'

Clara made herself more comfortable on the bed and told her about her time there. Of course, she did not tell Bernie everything. No mention was made of kidnap and guns and her almost getting shot. Now she was home, Clara felt almost as if the incident had happened in a dream or a film. Thinking of films reminded her of what Mary had said about Mr Bennett visiting and asking about her aunt. At least when she saw him tomorrow, she would be able to tell him about the postcard and the possibility of her aunt getting in touch with her.

Clara gazed up at the long stone-faced frontage of the Palladium and the ground-level windows that showed two posters advertising coming films. She sighed with pleasure as she noticed that Mary Pickford in *Johanna Enlists* would be showing at the end of the week. The following Monday, Charlie Chaplin would be starring.

Posters for today's film were displayed above the steeply roofed metal veranda and round the other side of the main entrance. It was *The Cook*, with Fatty Arbuckle and Buster Keaton, which was also showing on Tuesday and Wednesday. The main doors were closed and so she entered the building by a side door. No sooner was she inside than the sound of music filled her ears and she almost skipped towards one of the doors that led into the auditorium.

She gazed at the rows and rows of empty seats and imagined them full of people enjoying the music and the film. Then she noticed two of the usherettes and Mr and Mrs Walsh in a huddle near the front stalls. They were talking but she could not hear what they were saying because of the music. She looked for Mr Bennett and spotted him playing his clarinet, but knew she would have to wait a while before she could speak to him. Then she realised that Mrs Walsh had seen her and was signalling for her to come and join them. Clara did so, expecting to be asked how she was feeling and to be given her orders for the day.

Several hours later, Clara was sitting in the pay box, taking money and issuing tickets. There was quite a queue despite it being a bank holiday and the weather fair. She guessed there were always those who would rather sit and be entertained than be active outdoors and was glad of it because it was really the audience that paid her wages. The day passed pleasantly and she had a chance to watch part of the film but, due to the performances being continuous, she had little opportunity to speak to Mr Bennett. She had to wait until after the last performance, when he appeared just as she was about to leave.

'Hello, Clara,' he said in his rather deep, pleasant voice. 'Sorry I haven't had time to speak to you until now.' He looked genuinely contrite.

'Can't be helped,' she said. 'I've been busy, too. But I have to leave now or Gran might start worrying about me.'

He placed a homburg hat on his silver hair and said, 'I'll walk along with you, if I may?'

'Of course.'

They left the picture house, saying goodnight to the doorman on the way. The main road was still busy at that hour, so he took her elbow as they crossed to the other side. As they passed St Michael's church he asked, with old-fashioned courtesy, if she minded if he smoked. She shook her head and he lit a cigarette. She waited patiently for him to get to the point and he did, eventually, as they rounded the corner into Boundary Lane.

'I had a letter from a musician friend of mine in New York. He told me that your aunt is searching for me. Do you have any idea why?' he asked without preamble.

Clara stared at him in surprise. 'I don't see why you should think I would know. I've never met

Aunt Gabrielle. I wrote to her a few months ago because Gran wants to see her before she dies. I didn't even realise there was a connection between the two of you until I went in search of her. I was told by a person close to her that she'd once been married to a musician called Bennett, who left her penniless in America.'

Mr Bennett almost dropped his cigarette and looked dismayed. 'That's not true. I had the chance of work along with a couple of other musicians but she wasn't included in the deal because they didn't need a female singer. My accepting the job meant my leaving her for a short while, but I gave her money and told her to stay where she was and I'd come back for her. Trouble was, when I did, she wasn't there…had disappeared without a trace.'

Clara thought he sounded like he was telling the truth, but was he? 'Perhaps she believed you had deserted her, so she had to do something herself to survive,' she suggested.

He frowned. 'Gertie wasn't penniless, but she was ambitious. I'd known her since she was a kid. My dad heard her singing in a pub. He and Mother were music teachers and he said that, with a bit of training, she could make good. Trouble was, Gertie was impatient and thought she could get to the top without any hard work.'

Clara found this all very interesting but had to ask, 'Are you worried about her looking for you? If it's because you think you're still married to her you can forget it. She divorced you for desertion a few years back, so she could marry someone else.'

He did not appear shocked but did not answer her immediately, instead he drew smoke deep into his lungs before blowing out a smoke ring. 'I'm surprised at your mention of her divorcing me. She used to go on about not feeling properly married because we tied the knot aboard ship. Gertie, being Catholic, would have liked a church do but we were young and wanted to be together.'

Clara could understand their feelings but was curious as to why her aunt should be searching for him after all these years. 'I received a postcard from her. It was from New Orleans. Did your musician friend not tell her that you'd returned to Liverpool?'

He shook his head and looked thoughtful. 'When you're in a band like I was in America, performing at nightclubs and music halls, you get hangers-on who can be a nuisance. He thought she might be one of them because I was doing very well over there at one time. So he told her that I'd moved on years ago and suggested she try a place in New Orleans.'

'So she doesn't know you're here?'

'Nope.' His eyes glinted in the light of a lamp. 'But I'd still like to know why she's looking for me. I did wonder whether there was a kid.'

'She does have a son who happens to have your surname but I was told he wasn't yours.'

Mr Bennett looked disappointed. 'Shame. I was always too busy working or moving on to marry again. What's Gertie's boy like?'

Clara told him a little about Seb and his war injuries and found Mr Bennett sympathetic. 'It's a darn shame.' They had reached her front door and he held out his hand. 'It's been interesting talking to you, Clara. I'll see you tomorrow.'

She smiled. 'I've enjoyed talking to you, too. I wonder, if Aunt Gertie does get in touch with me, would you want me to let her know where you are?'

He said easily, 'Let me think about it. A lot of water has passed under the bridge since Gertie and I last saw each other. Goodnight.'

'Goodnight,' she echoed and went inside.

As Clara undressed and climbed into bed, she thought about the two young lovers who had been Gertie and Robbie. What would their lives have been like if they had stayed together? Seb wouldn't be here, that was for sure, and so perhaps it was meant for them to part. She sighed, thinking now of Freddie. Would she see him again? At least if he was staying at Mrs Black's then he would be seeing little of Tilly. Would he or Joy remember to give her gran's message to Mrs Black? If they did, would she respond by coming to visit her?

* * *

It had been a long train journey from Scotland and then another from Liverpool, but Eudora Black was finally home. She gazed at the gatehouse as the taxi approached the gateposts. Despite it being a damp, cold evening at the end of April, there was no smoke coming from the chimney. She wondered if Malcolm was working in the garden, although it was surely rather late in the day for him to be doing so.

The vehicle motored up the drive and came to a halt in front of her house. She waited for the driver to get out and open the door for her. He carried her luggage to the porch and then she paid him and bid him a good evening. For a moment she stood there, gazing at the sweep of lawns and flowerbeds of wallflowers and tulips, and felt a sense of peace descend upon her. So different from the place she had visited up north.

The door opened and she heard Joy's voice. 'You're later than I thought you would be. Was it a bad journey?'

Eudora turned and smiled into her housekeeper's welcoming face. 'Hello, Joy dear. The journey was foul and it's a relief to be home. I hope you've something tasty in for supper and we're not out of sherry.'

'I'll soon whip something up for you. I made a simnel cake because although you weren't here for Easter, I know how partial you are to marzipan.'

'Good for you,' said Eudora, wiping her feet on the coconut mat. 'How have things been here?'

'A lot's been happening.' Joy hesitated. 'Mr Moran's in hospital.'

Eudora's mouth fell open and she watched silently as Joy carried in her suitcase. She was even more surprised when Freddie appeared from the direction of the kitchen. 'Will I carry your suitcase up to your room for you?' he asked.

Eudora closed her mouth and began to ease off a pale lilac kid glove. 'What are you doing here, Freddie? And why is Malcolm in hospital?'

'I'll pour you a sherry, shall I?' said Joy. 'You'll need it.'

'Then I'll have it in the drawing room.'

Her high heels clicked on the parquet floor as she headed in that direction, removing her mauve feather-bedecked lilac felt hat while on the move. Once inside the drawing room, she flung her purple jacket on the back of the sofa and sat down, hoping that anything she had done in Scotland was not to blame for Malcolm being in hospital.

She waited until Joy had produced a plate with a slice of simnel cake and Freddie had handed her a glass of sherry before saying, 'So why is Malcolm in hospital?'

'He was shot,' said Freddie, his expression sympathetic.

Eudora's cheeks blanched. 'Shot? Was there an

attempted break-in here while I was away? Is that why you're here?'

'No! It happened in Chester and we think it was our brother, Bert, who was responsible,' said Freddie.

Eudora blinked. 'I don't understand! Joy told me he was killed in France.'

'That's what we believed, but Emma saw a picture of demobbed soldiers in a newspaper and he was one of them. We reckon he switched identity with a dead soldier,' said Freddie.

Eudora gulped down the sherry and asked for a refill. 'My dears, what a terrible shock for you. Sit down, both of you.' She waved them to the sofa. 'Tell me the whole story and how Malcolm was involved. Is his life in danger?'

Joy shook her head. 'He lost a lot of blood, so he's weak. I went with him in the ambulance. The doctor managed to dig the bullet out from his shoulder. They reckon it was from a revolver issued to soldiers during the war. The police are investigating.'

'When did this happen?'

'The day of the twins' christening,' said Freddie. 'I'd best tell you the whole story, as I was there.'

'Yes. You do, while Joy whips me up something savoury.' Eudora smiled at her. 'An omelette will do, dear, with some smoked salmon and cheese, if we have any.'

'I made sure I had some in ready,' said Joy, as she left the room.

Freddie proceeded to tell Eudora about the attempted kidnap. After finishing his tale, he sat back and watched the differing expressions flitter across her face, wondering what she made of it all.

'So Malcolm went against my advice,' she said crossly. 'I suppose that shouldn't surprise me. He has shown great interest in Tilly and his grandchildren over the years. I must go and see him. He's in Chester Infirmary?'

Freddie nodded. 'You weren't thinking of going this evening? Visiting hours are over and I doubt they'd let you in.'

'No, it would be foolish. I'll wait until tomorrow as his life is not in danger. How did you get here?'

'By motorbike.' He hesitated, 'If you were thinking of my giving you a lift to the station tomorrow...' He stared at the smartly dressed middle-aged woman sitting opposite him.

She threw back her head and laughed. 'You think I'm game for that? No, Freddie dear, I've reached that age when I like my comfort. I have a better idea. You can return to Chester and hire an automobile for me as you've done in the past. It could be that I'll be going backwards and forwards to Chester several times during the coming week and I can't be bothered with train travel after the journey I've had today.'

Freddie was delighted and felt rash enough to say, 'That's good news for the company. It needs the money. Are you sure you wouldn't prefer buying a motor, Mrs Black? You are a bit out of the way here and one would prove handy.'

Eudora's smile deepened. 'I can see you might make a decent businessman one day, Freddie. I'll let you persuade me. My investments have produced some very good dividends during the war but now it's over, I need to consider something new to invest my money in. There's obviously a future for the automobile, would you say?'

'Hell, yes,' said Freddie, leaning forward with enthusiasm written clearly on his young face.

She nodded, liking what she knew of him and trusting his word. 'I'll need a chauffeur,' she said. 'Do you think you can fill that role? Just until I'm ready to learn to drive myself, perhaps? You could also do some gardening and odd jobs now Malcolm's indisposed.'

Freddie grinned. 'It's fine by me. I'll bring you some information about the latest models soon to be in production.'

'Yes. And in the meantime, sound out Kenny as to whether he would be interested in an investment from me. Although, I'm not sure if Sebastian will be in favour if Alice has any say in the matter.' Eudora's expression was mischievous.

'Seb's no fool. He knows the business needs

investment. If he's any sense, he'll not mention to Alice where it's coming from.'

Just then Joy entered the room, carrying a tray. 'I hope you'll find this satisfactory, madam?' she said with a smile and placed the tray on an occasional table.

Eudora gazed at the fluffy omelette with the orange strips of smoked salmon and picked up her knife and fork. 'It looks perfect. Now, is there anything else I need to know.'

'Clara,' said Freddie.

'What about her?' said Eudora.

'She said that her grandmother would like a visit from you.'

'Would she, indeed?' murmured Eudora, then was silent for several minutes. 'On her last legs, is she?'

'Her condition is unchanged, as far as I know,' said Freddie. 'They now have a lodger, thanks to you.'

Eudora looked thoughtful. 'I've several clients to see over the next few weeks and then there's that conference on Spirituality in Chester soon, isn't there, Joy?'

'Yes. The third week in May.'

'Then Bernie O'Toole will have to wait until after that,' said Eudora. 'Freddie can drive me there. Perhaps we'll make a weekend of it. We can go on the Friday and stay at the Adelphi Hotel, and on the

Saturday I'll enjoy doing some shopping in the morning and we'll take in a matinée at the theatre in the afternoon. We will visit Bernie O'Toole in the evening. Of course, Clara will be working, no doubt, but you can take her for a short drive on Sunday morning while I visit the Spiritualist church off London Road. Joy, you will write and make the arrangements for the last weekend in May.' She beamed at them both. 'Is that clear?'

Joy and Freddie could only nod and wonder at the super organisational powers of their employer.

The following evening, Freddie dropped Eudora outside Chester Infirmary. He made himself comfortable and opened the *Liverpool Echo* and turned the pages over desultorily, thinking of Clara and wondering what she would make of him turning up with Mrs Black at the end of May. So far he had resisted writing to her, still uneasy about involving her in their troubles. He knew Bert of old and guessed that, if he were true to form, he would want to get back at him and Clara for spoiling his attempt to kidnap Flora.

Suddenly, a headline caught Freddie's eye and he read the article beneath. It concerned an outbreak of robberies with violence in Liverpool. It appeared that at first the police had been baffled by the number of robberies involving a lone robber, especially when the description of him given by witnesses differed. Yet all had described the words and actions he used as similar. Now apparently it had occurred to the police that it might be the same man and they had connected him with a robbery on a wigmaker's shop in Mount Pleasant, who had threatened the owner with a gun.

Once upon a time it would not have occurred to Freddie to relate guns and armed robbery to his brother. But he was convinced that the gunman on Easter Sunday had been Bert and that he had disguised himself with a wig made of hair similar to that of Mr Moran. So did this mean that his brother was living in Liverpool and had taken to a life of crime? He thought of Clara dwelling in the same city and felt a stab of anxiety. He told himself that he was being stupid. Liverpool was a big city, much larger than Chester, so what were the odds of Bert meeting Clara? And anyway, Freddie doubted that he would have got a decent enough look at Clara to remember her face, and as long as Bert could not connect her with the Kirks, Morans or Bennetts, she should be safe.

He frowned, wondering if it was worth mentioning the article to Mrs Black. He knew she had business connections in Liverpool and he had a vague memory from years ago of hearing Hanny talking about the medium once hiring a detective to trace Mr Moran. Perhaps he would speak of it when she left the hospital and they were on their way back to Eastham. He wondered how she and Mr Moran were getting on with each other and how long she would keep him waiting.

Eudora had been directed to the ward where Malcolm lay resting in bed. She had been told by a nurse not only that he already had a visitor, but that she must not excite him because he had been causing something of a disturbance. She wondered about the visitor as she made her way down the ward between the long line of beds. Then she spotted him talking to a pretty adolescent girl in a yellow and green frock with red-gold hair. It was a while since Eudora had set eyes on Tilly Moran, but she was pleased to do so now. It meant the girl had enough spirit to stand up to her sister.

'My dears, how lovely to see you talking together,' said Eudora, as she approached. 'I confess I was wrong when I thought it was best if you never met.'

Tilly gazed at her with interest as she rose to her feet and held out a hand. 'You're Mrs Black. Dad said that you would come. Apparently he told the nurses the same but he called you *his angel of mercy* and one of them apparently knew of your reputation and said that he was a stupid old man.'

Eudora liked the girl's frankness and shook her hand. 'You're not like your sister.'

'No. Alice and I are very different.'

'Does Alice know you're here?'

Tilly smiled. 'It would only upset her if I told her. Please, have my chair and talk to Dad. It's time I was going. He wants to go home, by the way.'

'Then I'll see that he does as soon as possible.'

Tilly hesitated before saying, 'Can I visit him there?'

'If that's what you wish.'

Tilly nodded and bent over her father and kissed his cheek. 'I'll see you soon,' she said.

Eudora and Mal watched as she walked away with a bounce in her stride up the long ward. When she reached the entrance she turned and waved to them. Then she disappeared through the doors.

'She has ma colour hair and eyes but her mother's pretty face and nature,' said Mal huskily. 'I don't deserve that she should care for me.'

'Why not, haven't you suffered enough?' said Eudora briskly, determined to keep her emotions firmly under control.

'I need to be punished.'

'That's your mother speaking,' she said sternly. 'Banish all thought of her and allow Tilly's unjudgmental spirit to lighten the remains of the darkness that still exists in your mind.' She paused. 'I discovered something very interesting when I was up in Scotland. You have a cousin up there who remembers Clara O'Toole's mother's family. She said your mother knew them, too. Amazing, isn't it, how the spirit works?'

Mal rested his head against the pillows and gazed at her with warmth in his eyes. 'I'm glad yer back. I mightn't be able to make sense of half what yer say but it's gud to see ye. Can yer get me out of here?'

She nodded, having decided that she would hire a nurse to take care of Malcolm once he was home. It would be much better for his daughter to visit him there. No doubt right now Tilly was having a word with Freddie outside. She would leave it to his good sense whether he drove the girl home or not.

'Freddie! I presume you brought Mrs Black here?' asked Tilly, walking over to the black shiny automobile and stroking its bonnet.

'Of course. You were in the office when I spoke to Kenny about it.' He looked her up and down. 'You're looking nice and summery. I presume neither Alice, Seb or Kenny know you're here?'

'Heavens, no.' She glanced over her shoulder and then laughed. 'I am feeling a little on edge, though.'

'Would you like me to give you a lift home?'

She gave him a teasing look. 'What would Clara think? Or Mrs Black for that matter, if I took you away from your duties?'

'I think they'd both understand,' he said soberly.

She gave him a startled look. 'What do you mean

by that? Surely you can't think Bert might still be hanging around, wanting to get back at the family? It's daylight, there's plenty of people around and I'm not a child anymore.'

Freddie got out of the car and opened the passenger door. 'If you've spoken to Mrs Black, I'm sure she'll expect me to see you safely to your front door.'

'But aren't you supposed to wait for her?'

Freddie sighed. 'Just get in. I don't want to waste time arguing. Besides, I've something to tell you and I want you to pass it on to Seb and Alice.' He handed the *Liverpool Echo* over to her. 'You can read the article on page four while I drive.'

'What am I supposed to be looking for?'

'It's about an armed robber.'

Tilly's eyes widened as she read the article while he drove through the ancient streets towards the Dee. 'You think there's a connection with Bert, don't you?'

He nodded.

'OK. I'll give it to Seb. Is there anything else you want me to tell him?'

'Clara.'

She gave him a sidelong glance. 'You really are nice looking,' she murmured.

'I'm not for you,' he said firmly. 'So save the flattery. We grew up almost like brother and sister. I really like you but that's all it is, Tilly. That's why you must tell Seb not to get in touch with Clara. We have to keep our distance, so she doesn't join those Bert wants to destroy.'

Tilly shivered. 'You're cruel and you're getting to sound as bad as the others. Do you really believe he wants to destroy us?'

Freddie nodded.

After that she had no more to say but sighed heavily several times on the way home. He dropped her off outside the house and waited until she was inside before he drove off.

CHAPTER TWENTY-FIVE

'Have you seen this?' Alice's voice sounded odd as she tossed a postcard onto Seb's lap. 'It was behind the clock.'

He looked up from the brochure he was reading. 'I know. I put it there.'

She was surprised. 'Then you've read it?'

'Of course I've read it. It's addressed to me.'

'But it must be from your mother. Why didn't you tell me it had arrived?'

Seb groaned. 'Alice, I put it behind the clock while I thought what I should do about it.'

'But why didn't you mention it to me?' She switched on a lamp before sitting beside him and picking up the postcard.

'Because I knew what you'd say – that she must be mad.'

'I haven't read it, so what's she done that would make me say that?'

Before Seb could answer there was the sound of

the front door opening and Tilly calling, 'I'm home.'

'Where've you been, young lady?' called Alice.

Tilly did not answer, and when she entered the room, she immediately went over to Seb and dropped the *Liverpool Echo* on his lap. 'There's an article on page four that Freddie wants you to read. He also wants you not to get in touch with Clara.'

It was Alice's turn to groan. 'I knew it was a big mistake for him and Clara to get involved with each other. She's going to be hurt.'

'It's possible he could be in love with her,' said Tilly, plucking the postcard from her sister's fingers and gazing at the picture. 'This is from New Orleans. Is it from Seb's ma?'

'Who else?' said Alice, reaching up a hand. 'Give it back to me. I haven't read it yet.'

'Hell's bells! She's heading for Chicago in search of her first husband, Mr Robbie Bennett,' said Tilly, emphasising the Bennett. 'I thought she'd divorced him to marry Seb's uncle and no longer had anything to do with him.'

Alice frowned. 'Is that what it says?'

'She actually does ask after Seb's arm and the children, as well,' said Tilly, holding the postcard just out of her sister's reach. 'She finishes by saying, *Next stop: Chicago. If you need to get in touch with me I'll be staying at the Morrison Hotel on the corner of Madison Street.*'

Alice said, 'Unless there are two musicians called Robbie Bennett, she's not going to find him there.'

'Why not?' said Tilly, sitting down and picking up the *Red Letter* magazine from the arm of the sofa. 'Have you seen what they're offering in this? *A Magic Fortune Card*.'

'Will you two shut up a minute,' muttered Seb, glancing at them. 'Have you read this, Tilly?'

'Yes. I think Freddie believes the armed robber is Bert,' she said with a grimace. 'He was talking about Bert just beforehand. He said that Bert deliberately disguised himself as my father, probably hoping to lay the blame for Flora's kidnap on him.'

'Which means Bert must have been skulking in the crescent while your father was here,' said Seb, tapping his fingers on the arm of the sofa.

'Can I see the article?' asked Alice, stretching out a hand.

'The first robbery took place at a wigmaker's shop,' Tilly continued. 'Even the police seem to think the robber is using different wigs to disguise himself.'

Alice read the article and then folded the newspaper carefully. 'I can only say I'm glad it's happening in Liverpool and not here. Bert's probably realised we'll have reported the incident to the police and is steering clear of us for now.'

Tilly seized on her words. 'You believe he will try and harm us?'

Alice's throat moved convulsively and then she nodded. 'It's the way he works. He likes to play cat and mouse. He'll draw away and then, when we think we're safe, he'll pounce.'

Tilly felt cold all over. 'Do you think he knows we know he's alive?' she asked.

'I have no idea,' said Alice in a low voice. 'We just have to be on our guard and hope the police will catch him.' She dropped the newspaper on the floor and held up her hand for the postcard. 'You asked why I think Gabrielle is wasting her time looking for her first husband. It's because Clara told me that there's a musician called Robbie Bennett in the Palladium Orchestra who spent time in America. He's come home to support his widowed sister and her children.'

Seb and Tilly stared at her. 'It has to be the same man,' said Seb.

'I agree,' said Alice, her green eyes sparkling with amusement. 'Your ma's on a wild goose chase. I wonder, when she lands up in Chicago and doesn't find him there, where will she go next?'

Tilly thought of Donald Pierce and the atlas she had borrowed from the library so she could pinpoint where he lived in the United States. 'Chicago is a long way from New Orleans,' she said. 'It'll take her a couple of days or more to get there.'

Seb nodded. 'You're right.' He took the postcard from Alice and left the room.

'Oh dear,' sighed Alice. 'I should have kept my mouth shut. Unless his mother leaves that hotel before Seb's letter can reach her, the next thing we know she'll be turning up on our doorstep.'

'Or Clara's,' said Tilly, tapping her fingers together. 'At least it's one way of reuniting Seb's mother and his granny and keeping Clara in touch with us.' She decided that perhaps it was time she put pen to paper and let Clara know what might transpire in the coming weeks where her aunt was concerned. Maybe she should also mention the article in the newspaper and about Freddie's concern for her.

Clara flicked over a page of *The Picture Show* magazine. It was an advance copy and had cost her tuppence. To anyone interested in filmmaking it was compulsive reading, having articles such as 'Husbands and Wives on Film', 'My Screen Debut' and 'Flickers in Film Land'. It was a fine May day but a strong breeze was keeping the temperature down, so she felt happier indoors until she had to go to work.

'There's a couple of letters here,' said Bernie, shuffling into the kitchen. 'And for a change they're not both for you.'

'Oh!' Clara shot her a glance. 'Where's mine then?'

Bernie threw it over to her and then settled

herself in her chair with the one addressed to her on her lap. She peered through her spectacles at the writing as she tore open the envelope. 'Bloody hell, it's joined-up writing and there's a helluva lot of words here,' she complained.

'D'you want me to read it to you after I've read mine?' asked Clara, putting her magazine aside. 'Yours could be from Mrs Black.'

Bernie turned the page over and looked at the signature. 'Yeah. It says *Warm-est re-gar-ds, Eudora Black*.'

Clara smiled. 'I told you so.'

'All right, clever clogs, tell me if she's coming or not?'

'In a minute.' Clara did not recognise the writing on the envelope and her heart increased its beat as she wondered if it could be from Freddie. It settled down again when she turned over the sheet of paper and saw that, to her surprise, it was signed *Tilly*. She wondered what the girl was writing to her for and went back to the beginning and began to read.

Dear Clara,

I thought you might like to know about a few things that have happened over here since you went home. First, my father is improving and Mrs Black will soon be taking him home to her house. She has told me that I can go and see him there, so I will take the opportunity of doing so whenever I can.

Recently, I saw Freddie, who is now working for Mrs Black as her chauffeur, gardener and general odd job man, and I have to say I believe he likes you lots. We all do here, but don't want you to get tangled up in our troubles, so don't take it amiss if you don't see us for a while. We believe that Bert is waiting ready to pounce just like a cat waiting outside a mouse hole. Always a thorn in the family's side, we suspect he is wanted by the police in Liverpool because there was a report in the newspaper. He's an armed robber who disguises himself with different wigs, which he also stole. The other thing I have to tell you is about your aunt, Seb's mother. He had a postcard from her and apparently she's searching for her first husband and was on her way to Chicago. Anyway, Alice remembered you telling her about a musician called Robbie Bennett and she's told Seb that he's over here. His mother gave the name of a hotel in Chicago, so he's written to tell her that she's on a wild goose chase and to come home. So it's possible you might see her soon. Hopefully before your grandmother passes away.

Best wishes, Tilly.

Clara took a deep breath because she felt as if she had read the letter at breakneck speed. Maybe that was due to Tilly's lack of paragraphs, probably done to save paper. Still, she appreciated the girl writing to her in such an informative way and would write and tell her so. What she had said about Freddie made Clara want to question how Tilly knew this about him. Had they discussed her? She supposed she was going to have to wait to find that out. The news about her aunt was, of course, not surprising, but the bit about Seb telling his mother to come home would certainly be of interest to Mr Bennett and her gran. But perhaps she should keep mum about that until her aunt actually made an appearance. As for what Tilly had said about Bert being an armed robber, that was terrifying. Yet it would be foolish of her to get worked up about it. As Tilly had said, he was wanted by the police, so no doubt they could be looked upon as cats ready to pounce on a rat.

'Haven't you finished reading that letter yet?' demanded Bernie.

'Yes.' Clara pocketed the sheet of paper and reached out for Mrs Black's letter and began to read aloud.

'Dear Mrs O'Toole,

'I do so hope you are keeping reasonably well and your chest is not giving you too much trouble. I also pray that Clara is feeling herself once more after her bout of flu. Such a horrible disease. Anyway, I will get to the point of this letter.

'Young Freddie Kirk informed me that you

wished me to visit you. I am very busy the next few weeks but, if it is convenient to yourself and Clara, I will call the evening of Saturday May 31st. There is no need to answer this unless it is not convenient. I plan to stay in Liverpool for the weekend and Freddie will be driving me...' Clara paused when she read those last words and had to clear her throat before continuing, *'I plan to visit the Spiritualist church on Sunday morning and have suggested to Freddie that he might like to take Clara out for some fresh air during that time. Until then,*

   'Warmest regards,

   'Eudora Black.'

'She does write nice, doesn't she?' said Bernie with a smirk. 'She's a bit of a matchmaker, too.'

Clara's response was, 'Does that evening suit you, Gran?' but her head was in a whirl at the thought of seeing Freddie in a few weeks' time.

A laugh rumbled deep in Bernie's bosom. 'Where else have I got to go, duck? I'm already looking forward to it.'

'A pity I won't be here that evening.'

'Your day will come, duck,' said Bernie, leaning forward and patting her hand.

'I hope so. At least in your case, Gran, you haven't long to wait.'

CHAPTER TWENTY-SIX

'Buy a flag, buy a flag for the sailors,' urged the woman, standing outside Vines public house in Lime Street.

'Give her some money, Freddie dear, and then we must be on our way,' said Eudora, handing him a florin before settling herself in the passenger seat of the car. 'Really, it's time the poor woman went home, she must have been there all day.'

He pushed the coin through the slot in the tin and took the two tiny flags with *King George's Day for Sailors* printed on them along with the two pins offered to him, then climbed back into the car.

Eudora took them from him and pinned his flag onto his lapel. 'We must be seen to support the sailors. We would have starved without their bravery during the war.'

'You can say that again, missus,' said the woman.

Eudora gave her a keen look, thinking there was something odd about the voice. She shook her head and told Freddie to drive off. Soon they were bowling along London Road and up Brunswick Road into West Derby Road, past the Palladium Picture Palace where Clara worked and within a few minutes, they were turning into the street of red brick houses where the O'Tooles lived. Being careful to avoid the children who were still playing out with ropes and balls, Freddie parked the vehicle neatly outside Clara's home. Discovering the front door had been left on the latch, he called up the lobby to announce their arrival.

'Come in, lad,' called a faint voice. 'I'm in the parlour.'

Freddie returned to the car to assist Eudora before reaching for the hamper she had ordered from Cooper's store on Church Street late yesterday afternoon. Eudora smoothed down her skirts and, after a moment surveying the house, told him to lead the way.

Freddie entered the parlour and found Bernie sitting in an armchair, dressed in her best pink blouse and a navy blue serge skirt that brushed the floor. 'Nice to see yer, lad,' she wheezed.

'And you, Mrs O'Toole. I hope you're well.'

'Fair to middlin',' she replied, eyeing the hamper. 'What's that yer've got there?'

It was Eudora who answered, 'Just a few treats, dear. I hope they'll meet with your approval. Freddie, place it on the floor and you'd best find some plates, glasses and cutlery before unpacking it. Of course, we must save some food for dear Clara,' she said, removing her gloves.

Bernie opened her mouth enough to tell him the best dishes were in the sideboard and gaped as Freddie took out a bottle of port, slices of chicken breast and boiled ham, bread rolls and a box of petit fours.

Then she found her voice, 'Bleedin' hell! What it is to be rich!'

Eudora's eyes sparkled. 'I admit that having money does have its advantages, Mrs O'Toole. One of them is giving pleasure to other people.'

'Listen to you,' gasped Bernie. 'I can hardly believe yer little Edie from the old street.'

'Yer'd rather I talked like this, girl?' she said, reverting to the speech of her childhood. 'I can, like, if yer really want me to.'

'Na, No. Yer might start me laughin' and that'll kill me,' spluttered Bernie.

'And we don't want that just yet, do we?' said Eudora seriously.

The smile died in Bernie's eyes. 'Did yer really speak to my Denny?'

'Do you believe I did?'

'I dunno. But I don't want any jiggery-pokery here.'

Eudora's expression was a mixture of horror and amusement. 'I don't indulge in jiggery-pokery, but I think you're wise not risking getting in touch with him again. Even the Bible owns to there being evil spirits and that a war is being waged in the spiritual realm.'

'So yer really do believe there's life after death?'

'Yes, dear. Otherwise, I'd be utterly unconvincing at what I do.' She raised a hand and wiggled it in Freddie's direction. 'Open the port, dear, and have a glass yourself.'

Freddie did as instructed, and when the glasses were charged, Eudora lifted her glass. 'Shall we have a toast? To the young people. May life be better for them than it was for us.'

'Humph!' muttered Bernie, downing her port in one go. She held the glass out to Freddie and, at a nod from Eudora, he filled it again. 'It looks to me like life's done you a lot of favours, Edie. Why didn't Gertie do as well as you?'

Eudora placed her fox fur on the back of the chair and her expression was thoughtful as she sipped her port. 'Gertie could have had the same good fortune as me if she hadn't been so impatient and reckless.'

'She married, though, had me a grandson,' said Bernie with a hint of pride.

A shadow crossed Eudora's face and her tone was sharp when she spoke, 'That's true, but she didn't marry the father because he was already married. After his wife died, he still didn't marry her because he considered her beneath him.'

Bernie spluttered port wine into her glass. 'Are you saying that my grandson's a bastard?'

'Yes. But I'll say no more on that matter. I suspect life will improve for Sebastian in the not too distant future.'

'What about my Gertie?' croaked Bernie, putting down her glass. 'What is she doing in America? Surely she isn't hoping to go on the stage again?'

'Perhaps she's hoping to relive her youth. I remember she was badly smitten by Robbie Bennett in those far off days.'

Bernie hit the arm of her chair. 'Never mind all this. Can you see her coming to see me in yer crystal ball?'

Eudora frowned and her right hand curled into a fist. 'I'm not a fortune teller, Mrs O'Toole, but my feeling is that she will. So tell me, what is it you want from me?'

'I'd like a new heart and liver but I don't suppose yer have any of them,' said Bernie.

Eudora's lips twitched. 'I wish it was in my power to say yes but I'm afraid new organs are beyond my abilities.' Eudora drained her glass. 'Be honest, you didn't really expect me to cure you, but maybe I can make you feel a little better.'

Bernie shook with laugher and broke into a coughing fit. It was a couple of minutes before she was able to say, 'Well, it was worth seeing yer, just to ask if yer had a bottle of your special tonic.'

Eudora winked at Freddie. 'Yes, I did think on to bring a bottle of my special tonic for you.'

Bernie watched as Eudora produced a bottle from her capacious handbag and handed it to her. The old woman poured some into her glass. 'Now, tell me more about this feeling of yours to do with Gertie?'

Eudora leant back in the chair and closed her eyes. There was silence and Bernie took a sup of the tonic as she waited. 'My feeling is that she will be sailing into your life very soon.'

Freddie raised his eyes to the ceiling and thought about what Tilly had told him about the telegram Seb had received yesterday. He wouldn't be at all surprised if Seb's mother was already in Liverpool.

It was several hours earlier in the day that Gabrielle Waters had stood on the deck of the liner, gazing down at Liverpool's dockland as the tugs that had guided the ship to berth chugged away. Her time in America had been one of enjoyment, frustration, boredom and eventual disbelief. She had visited clubs, music halls and theatres in New York, New Orleans and Chicago, where folk knew the name of Robbie Bennett. It had come as an almighty shock to receive a letter from her son informing her that Robbie had left for England several years ago.

Apparently, he was now earning a living playing in an orchestra in the picture house where her niece

Clara worked in Liverpool. Something of a coincidence, but these things happened. Unfortunately, Seb had not named the picture house. So she had two choices: either she called at her mother's house or she toured Liverpool's picture palaces in search of Robbie. Her fingers curled into fists for, although she was willing to meet her niece, she still had no desire to see her mother.

She pursed her lips, wondering if she had made the right move by wiring ahead to her son, thanking him for his letter and also informing him that she would be staying in Liverpool at the Stork Hotel for the next few days. She desired a few days settling back into the country on her own. Besides, the hotel had memories for her. Situated in Queen Square in the centre of the city, not far from Lime Street, it was where she had often stayed with Seb's father. She had found it a romantic place as a young woman. Once the home of a rich eighteenth-century merchant, William Roe, it had class.

A tinny voice informing passengers that it was time to disembark roused her from these thoughts. She was tired and not looking forward to the bother of going through customs and all the rigmarole involved before she could get to the hotel. Still, once she had a wash and brush up she would be as right as rain. Then she would start her search for Robbie that evening at the Scala picture house on Lime Street.

* * *

As it was still a fine evening when Eudora and Freddie left Bernie, she suggested that Freddie leave down the car hood. So it was that, as he drove along Lime Street in the direction of the Adelphi Hotel, she spotted Gertie. Although Eudora knew from Tilly that her erstwhile childhood friend was heading home, she had not expected to see her so soon standing on the steps of the Scala picture house, pulling on a black hat with an enormous red ostrich feather. The colours were duplicated in the black dress and jacket she wore, which had red braiding around the collar and sleeves.

'Stop here, Freddie,' urged Eudora, tapping him on the arm.

'I can't stop, Mrs Black,' he responded without taking his eyes from the road. 'There's a carriage just behind me. I'll pull over once I'm past this cyclist.' He wondered what was so urgent as they were only yards from the Adelphi hotel. At last he drew up by the kerb opposite Vines public house, where earlier the flag seller had stood.

Eudora twisted in her seat and gazed behind her. 'Get out, Freddie. You'll have to run after her.'

'Who?' he asked, screwing up his face as he climbed out of the car.

'Gertie, of course. That woman in black,' she cried, pointing.

From where he was standing, Freddie could see

several women dressed in mourning clothes. 'I need more clues than that,' he muttered.

'She's crossing the road now and is wearing a black hat with a red ostrich feather.'

'Right,' said Freddie, spotting his quarry. 'What d'you want me to do when I catch her?'

'Bring her here, of course. It must have been meant that I was to see her. Tell her that I've been to visit her mother.'

Freddie grinned, thinking there might be high jinks when his employer and Clara's aunt met. But she was already out of sight because a tram was rattling towards him. He skirted round it and ran, and then caught sight of her in Elliot Street, just outside St John's Market.

He touched her shoulder. 'Excuse me, but my employer wishes to speak to you.'

Gabrielle spun round and stared at him in the fading light. 'I assure you, young man, that if this is some trick to rob me, I have a rock in my handbag and I won't hesitate to use it.'

Instantly, Freddie could trace the likeness to Seb and Clara in her features and thought how pleased Clara would be to see her. 'My employer is Mrs Eudora Black.'

Gabrielle blinked and then her mouth tightened. 'I don't wish to speak to her.'

'She's been to visit your mother.'

'What! How dare she?' said Gabrielle in a

seething voice and her hands tightened on her handbag. 'Where is she?'

'We're parked on Lime Street.' She gave a sharp nod and fell into step beside him. 'I'm Freddie Kirk, by the way.'

She stared at him and shook her head as if in disbelief. 'What is it about *that woman* that she's got you working for her now?'

'I'm only working for Mrs Black temporarily, chauffeuring her about and doing odd jobs while Alice's father is recovering. He works for her.'

'Alice's father! I always suspected there was something between the two of them. You can't trust that woman. I remember when she moved to the crescent, the men were going in and out of her door like nobody's business.'

'They worked for her, collected rents and saw that repairs were done to her property over here.'

She glared at him. 'I can see you're the kind that has an answer to everything. Say no more, just lead me to her. I'll not have her saying things to Mam without me putting my side.'

An amused Freddie did as she said. Suddenly, it seemed possible that Seb's mother would visit her ailing mother that evening and he wanted to be there to see Clara's expression when her aunt made her appearance. Surely she would have finished at the Palladium by now.

On reaching the car he stated the obvious, 'Here's Mrs Waters, Mrs Black.'

The two women eyed each other up.

'Where did you get that hat?' asked Eudora, who was wearing a cream linen suit and fox fur wrap with a russet coloured hat with a tangerine rose attached to its brim.

'Where did you buy that dead animal?' retorted Gabrielle.

'At a furrier's shop that you couldn't possibly afford to frequent,' said Eudora in honeyed tones. 'I did not say I didn't like your hat, so shall we agree that we both pass muster as women of means. Climb in and we can talk.'

'I'll need to light the lamps if you're going to talk in the car, Mrs Black,' said Freddie.

'Then do so, dear,' she said.

'We should also move on. It's Saturday night and you'll soon have drunks staggering out of this pub.'

Eudora sighed heavily. 'I take your point. You light the lamps while I have a quick word.'

'Help me into the car, young man,' commanded Gabrielle.

He did so and went to light the lamps.

Gabrielle adjusted her skirts and then looked at Eudora. 'Well, what were you doing visiting the old cow?'

Eudora tutted. 'Really, Gertie, have you still not forgiven her?'

'Don't call me Gertie. You haven't answered my question.'

'She asked me to visit her. I think she sees me as a link to you and she doesn't have long to live. If your religion means anything to you, you should give her peace of mind before she passes over.'

Gabrielle was silent, wondering about the forces that had brought her here to Lime Street at the same time as her old rival. Did God have a hand in it, or was it the devil? She came to a decision. 'If I'm going to see her then it has to be now. Tomorrow I might change my mind.'

'But I've just come back from there!' exclaimed Eudora. 'Do you know what time it is?'

'You don't have to come with me. Just lend me your car,' said Gabrielle.

Freddie, who had been listening to their conversation, lifted his head. 'Make a decision, ladies, I can't stay here much longer.'

Eudora sighed. 'Take us back to the O'Tooles' house, Freddie dear.'

To his delight it was Clara who answered the door. For a moment she just stared at him as if she could eat him. Then he said, 'Hello, love. Can we come in? I've got your aunt here with me.'

She reached out and clutched him and gazed at the shadowy shapes of the two women adjusting their hats. 'You're serious?' she whispered.

'Too right I am. Aren't you pleased?'

'Of course! I can't wait to see Gran's face.' Her voice trailed off as the taller of the women approached.

Clara could not see her face clearly but when she spoke, her words were beautifully articulated. 'So you're Dennis's daughter. I'm so pleased to meet you.' Gabrielle surprised her by engulfing her in a scented embrace. 'I think you deserve a medal.'

'Fo-for what?' stammered Clara, staring over her aunt's shoulder at Freddie.

'Coping with Mam, of course.' Gabrielle kissed her niece on both cheeks before releasing her.

Clara pushed a lock of hair that had come loose behind her ear. 'You'd best come in. Gran's in the kitchen. I only hope…' She did not finish what she was thinking.

'Right!' Gabrielle squared her shoulders, adjusted her hat once more and tilted her chin. 'You lead the way, luv.'

Her aunt's use of the word *luv* took Clara by surprise, but her step did not falter as she walked up the lobby.

Clara could scarcely contain her emotions. 'Gran, I've a surprise for you,' she managed in a croaky voice, wondering whether daughter and mother would recognise each other after all these years.

'The prodigal has returned, Ma,' said Gabrielle. There was no break in Bernie's laboured breathing – she had dozed off and was unaware of her eldest daughter's presence. 'Holy Mary, mother of God, what does she look like?' muttered Gabrielle, scowling. 'I know. She reminds me of the old sow on the farm.'

'That's a lovely thing to say about your mother,' said Eudora, who had slipped into the kitchen after her.

Gabrielle shrugged and placed her handbag on the table. 'When I imagined seeing her again, it was never like this.'

'Strange, isn't it?' said Eudora, walking over to the old woman and gently shaking her shoulder. 'Mrs O'Toole, wake up. You'll never guess who's come to visit you,' she cooed.

Bernie's breathing seemed to catch in her throat and for a moment it seemed as it might stop altogether and then her heart continued its laboured beat. She opened her eyes and blinked sleepily at those gathered there. Her gaze fixed on Freddie and then Eudora. 'Yer've done it,' she wheezed. 'Yer've brought my Denny back to me.'

'Don't be so daft, Mam. Even Edie's not that bloody brilliant. She can't perform miracles,' said Gabrielle.

'Sadly, that's true,' sighed Eudora.

Bernie's face sagged with disappointment and then her eyes lifted and she gazed at the tall, black-clad figure a couple of feet away.

'Better late than never, hey, Mam?' said Gabrielle.

'Yer came!' Bernie's face looked almost luminous.

Not so her eldest daughter's. 'I thought I'd like to hear you beg for my forgiveness after all these years,' she said harshly. 'You really were a lousy mother.'

Bernie flinched and her chest heaved as she struggled with her breathing. 'I've bloody changed me mind,' she gasped. 'I think...yer've a lot to be grateful to me for. Yer...yer... wouldn't be dressed to the nines...if it weren't for me. Yer could have ended up like yer sisters: three dead from consumption, another from septicaemia and another in childbirth from a stupid, careless midwife coming from laying out the dead and not washing her hands. So yous be grateful, girl, that I drove yer away.'

'Holy Mary, you still can't do it, can you?' shouted Gabrielle, bending over her. 'You couldn't then and you can't now. It sticks in your throat, saying sorry for all the times you beat me.'

Bernie's face quivered as if it was about to collapse.

'Stop it!' cried Clara, shoving her aside and placing an arm about her grandmother's shoulders.

Bernie reached up and clung to her granddaughter's hand. 'Yer wrong,' she whispered.

'I am sorry. Will that do yer, girl?'

'It'll have to, won't it,' said Gabrielle, her voice trembling now. 'I hope your conscience is clear and you're ready to meet St Peter at the pearly gates.' She took a deep breath. 'As for me, I've got a man to find.' She glanced at Freddie. 'You! Get me back to my hotel. I've finished here.'

Clara stared at her with tears in her eyes. 'I wish I'd never written to you. Where is your conscience? Where is your forgiveness?'

The blood rushed to Gabrielle's cheeks. 'Don't talk to me like that, girl. No doubt she pampered you, the daughter of her only son. You didn't have my life with her. I'm out of here.' Without another word she walked out of the kitchen.

Freddie placed a hand on Clara's shoulder and squeezed it gently. 'You did what your gran wanted, love. You've nothing to berate yourself about. I'll see you in the morning.'

Eudora looked at them and said quietly, 'Come, Freddie. Time we were going. Give your grandmother a dose of my tonic, Clara. It'll calm her down. Forgive me if I have done anything to bring you pain.'

Clara nodded, too upset to speak.

For several minutes she did not move, and then she fetched the tonic, poured some in a glass and placed it in Bernie's hand. She seemed so weak that Clara helped to raise it to her lips. She drank and then rested her head against the back of her chair and closed her eyes.

Clara left her a moment to wash the glass and put the bottle away. She felt all knotted up inside, furious with her aunt for being so unforgiving. Then it struck her that the kitchen was extremely quiet. She hurried over to Bernie and bent over her. She fumbled for her grandmother's pulse, only to find that she had gone.

CHAPTER TWENTY-SEVEN

'I wonder if he was there,' said Clara, crunching into a slice of toast.

'Who? Where?' asked Mary absently.

'Dad, when Gran passed over.'

'Oh, don't start talking like that, Clara.' Mary stood up and said briskly, 'With your gran dead you'll have a bedroom to spare. I know someone if you'd like to take in another lodger. You're free to do what you want now.'

Clara stared at her and said coolly, 'It's early days to be thinking like that. I've a funeral to arrange and people I need to get in touch with.' It was with a sense of relief that she thought of Freddie, who should arrive at the house sometime soon. The doctor had been and written out the death note and Clara had been to early mass and spoken to the priest. It would be tomorrow before she could visit the undertaker's. Thank God it was Sunday and she didn't have to go to work.

Mary left her alone and Clara decided to stew the rabbit she had bought for their Sunday lunch. Gran would hate for it to be wasted and Freddie might eat her share. She sighed, thinking of the old woman laid out upstairs on her bed. It had been a struggle getting her body up there but, between them, she and Mary had managed. Clara found it strange that she should still be listening out for Bernie's laboured breathing. It was going to take some time getting used to her not being around but, as Mary had said, Clara was now free to do what she wanted. At the moment, all she wanted was to see Freddie.

Clara did not have long to wait. Three-quarters of an hour after Mary had left the house there was a knock on the front door. She hurried to answer it and was so relieved to see Freddie's smiling face that she flung herself at him.

'Hey, that's a nice welcome,' he said, swinging her up in the air.

'I'm just so glad to see you. Wait till I tell you what's happened!'

He set her down on her feet and gazed into her eyes. 'Your gran…'

'Dead. Almost straight after you went.'

'Let's go inside.'

Once in the kitchen, he sat on the sofa and pulled her down onto his knee and held her close. 'I won't say sorry. She'd lived to a good age and…'

'I know what you mean. I just wish Aunt Gertie could have forgiven her. You'll tell Mrs Black?'

'Sure.'

'I don't know when the funeral will be yet but you'll come, won't you?'

He nodded. 'Mrs Black is bound to want to come, too. I don't know about your aunt. We dropped her off in Lime Street.'

Clara's face hardened. 'You didn't tell her where I worked, did you?'

'No.' He kissed the side of her face. 'She asked but one look from Mrs Black was enough for me to keep my mouth shut. You could have cut the atmosphere with a knife. She only said two things to your aunt.'

'What were they?'

'That you had to travel to get there and that one day she would seek forgiveness and remember this day.' He grimaced. 'I tell you, it sounded really ominous.'

'What did my aunt say?'

'Nothing.'

Clara looked into his eyes. 'I suppose you couldn't see her expression?' He shook his dark head and kissed her lightly on the lips. 'Well, I hope she's regretting her hardheartedness.'

'I wouldn't bank on it,' he said. 'Now, before I kiss you properly, do you want me to get word to Seb about what's happened?'

'Please. I'll let you know when the funeral is tomorrow. You'll still be at Mrs Black's in the next week or so?'

'As far as I know.' He drew her close and kissed her several times. She was aware of a rising passion between them but he went no further than canoodling. She nestled in his arms, aware that a long courtship might prove too much for their self control. One thing was for sure, her grandmother's death signalled change in the coming months.

A couple of days before the funeral, on the 3rd of June, Liverpool welcomed the King's Regulars home. They had fought at Mons and Ypres, and Clara stood in the crowd as the soldiers made their way to the town hall for a reception and wept for her father and all the young men who had died as she had not done for her gran.

On the day of the funeral she was dry-eyed. She had sent word to Freddie and Mrs Black concerning its date and not heard back from them but she trusted in their coming.

There were few people in church because Bernie O'Toole had not been a popular woman. Mary was working but the people who mattered where there. She was delighted to see Freddie, Seb, Mrs Black and, surprisingly, Robbie Bennett. She smiled at them as she followed the coffin, a lone slender figure in black. But when she sat in a front pew, she was soon joined by Freddie and Seb. She felt strangely detached from the proceedings, yet wanted it to be over as soon as possible. She was extremely conscious of Freddie sitting on one side of her and Seb on the other. Even so, it was a relief when the service was over and they came out to discover that the clouds had rolled away and the sun was shining. There was still the burial to face but she did not expect them to go with her, so she offered her hand to Seb and thanked him for coming.

He took her hand in both of his and said seriously, 'I felt I had to come. After all, you're family.'

His words touched her. 'It means a lot to me.' Her voice was husky as she gazed into his battle scarred face; he was wearing his silver eye patch. 'How is your arm?'

'I've been seeing a physiotherapist in Rodney Street and I'll be visiting him this afternoon.' He smiled and flexed his arm gingerly. 'I've still some way to go but it's improving. I've told James I'll take him fishing soon.'

'I'm so glad. How are Alice and the children?'

'You'll have to come and see for yourself soon.' He hesitated. 'I never thanked you for your part in saving Flora. I thank you now.'

Clara smiled. 'She's family.' She hesitated to ask about his mother but he seemed to read her mind.

'Ma's not here, I see. I did telephone the Stork Hotel, where she was staying, and left a message.'

'It doesn't matter. Gran said what she needed to say to her. It's just a little sad that your mother couldn't find it in her heart to forgive. I feel angry with her, but I hope it'll pass.' She hesitated. 'There's someone I'd like you to meet. You probably noticed the handsome, white-haired gentleman who was in church. He's talking to Mrs Black now.'

Seb nodded. 'Who is he?'

'Robbie Bennett.'

Seb's face lit up with interest. Clara linked her arm through his and hurried him over to Robbie and Mrs Black. 'Excuse me, you two, but I'd like to introduce my cousin, Sebastian Bennett, to you Mr Bennett,' she said with a twinkle in her eye.

Robbie's face brightened. He held out a hand to Seb. 'I'm delighted to meet you.'

'Likewise,' said Seb, smiling. 'You won't know it but for years I believed you were my father.'

'I wish I was,' said Robbie sincerely. 'I'd have liked a son but I never remarried.'

Clara winked at Mrs Black and was about to draw her to one side and thank her for coming when someone tapped Clara on the arm. 'Time for us to go, Miss O'Toole.' It was the undertaker.

Seb, Eudora and Robbie all kissed her. 'I'll leave you, Freddie, dear,' said Mrs Black.

'But how will you get into town?' asked Clara.

The older woman's eyes sparkled. 'Robbie and I are old friends and he can drive an automobile, so he's running me there. Freddie can join me later.'

Clara thanked the three of them for coming, wondering what Gabrielle would think if she knew that the man she was seeking had been at her mother's funeral. When she and Freddie were seated side by side in the carriage, he asked her why she was smiling, Clara told him.

'The joke's rather on her, isn't it?' said Freddie, slipping his arm round her. 'It would be even more so if she knew that he and Mrs Black had gone off together.'

'But it's not what I wanted for my aunt. I felt sorry for the young Gertie who ran away from home. I admired her for her courage and talent for going on the stage. I wanted us to have a proper aunt-niece relationship. Part of me still wants that for both of us. After all, who has she got to love her if she cuts herself off from the family and Mr Bennett decides that he wants to have nothing to do with her?' asked Clara sadly.

Freddie had no answer but thought his Clara was perhaps too soft-hearted for her own good. Yet he would not have her any different. He remembered her views on forgiveness and his face hardened as he thought of his brother. He was another who had cut himself off from his family and Freddie hoped he would stay away. But he would not be able to relax and think of a future with Clara until his brother was behind bars once more.

CHAPTER TWENTY-EIGHT

It was the following Saturday evening and Clara was busy taking money and issuing tickets for the first evening showing. Her wrists were aching but there weren't many left in the queue now and soon she would be able to relax. Tomorrow she would be seeing Freddie, who was coming over to take her out.

'One in the front stalls,' said the woman the other side of the pay box window, shoving a florin through the opening at the bottom.

'Sorry, madam, there's no more seats in the front stalls. We've a couple in the rear stalls,' said Clara.

The woman clicked her tongue in exasperation. 'I suppose that will have to do. I am right in thinking that the Palladium Orchestra will be playing a medley of popular music tonight, as well?'

There was something about the woman's voice that caused Clara to look at her more closely and her heart did a peculiar little jump. She might have only seen her aunt once but she recognised her and her black hat with the red ostrich feather. Hell! What was she going to do? The last thing she wanted was a scene between Gabrielle and Robbie Bennett, who had expressed disgust at his former wife's behaviour towards her mother.

'Hmmm! I'm sorry. My mistake, there are no seats left in the stalls, madam,' she said.

Gabrielle frowned and then brought her face closer to the glass. 'I know you. It is you, isn't it?'

'If you mean, am I your niece? Then yes, I am,' replied Clara, her eyes smouldering. 'Not that I'm proud of it. Gran died after you left, you know.'

Gabrielle said sharply, 'She's no loss. Is that why you've decided not to let me in, because you blame me? You've got no right. This is a public place and you can't stop me coming inside.'

Clara tilted her chin. 'I've no intention of preventing you from seeing the film, but if you're going to make a scene I can call the doorman. There are a few seats left in the balcony. You can have one of them if you wish. It'll cost you sixpence, madam.'

'It's not what I wanted. Isn't there a box?'

'No, madam.'

'Will you hurry up and make up your bloody mind, missus,' said a man's voice behind Gabrielle. 'We're going to miss the music.'

She turned and glared at him. 'Keep your hair on!

Where's your manners?' She faced Clara once again, 'A ticket in the balcony, please.'

Clara issued her a ticket and gave her change.

'Many at the funeral?' asked Gabrielle as she pocketed the money.

'No. But those who mattered were there,' said Clara, feeling a desire to annoy her aunt even further. 'Your son came, and Mr Bennett and Mrs Black.'

Consternation glinted in Gertie's eyes. 'Damn! I suppose they spoke to each other?'

'Yes. Will you move on, please, madam? You're holding up the queue.'

Gabrielle moved away.

Clara turned to the next customer and automatically dealt with him whilst thinking about her aunt, wondering whether she had done the right thing in selling her a ticket in the balcony. She would probably get a better view of the orchestra pit from above and was bound to spot Robbie Bennett. But then it was more than thirty years since they had last seen each other, so maybe she might not recognise him.

Gabrielle was not at all pleased when the usherette directed her to a seat between two large people. Somehow she managed to pull down the tip-up seat and sit down, and immediately became aware of their body odour. Her annoyance grew when a man behind asked her to remove her hat. She would have refused but decided to be reasonable, thinking she must be mad to be doing what she was doing. She had visited at least fourteen cinemas since arriving in Liverpool, taking in matinée and evening performances. She had seen some good films and heard some excellent music, but her money was dwindling. She had left the Stork Hotel and was staying in a boarding house. Soon she would have to speak to her solicitor about taking an income from the farm. Still, she was here now and the orchestra had just launched into a cheerful toe-tapping tune that was very different from so many popular songs that could bring a lump to the throat, such as Ivor Novello's 'Keep the Home Fires Burning' or 'Roses are Blooming in Picardy'. This one was 'Has Anybody Seen My Gal?' and she remembered hearing it sung in New York. There were a lot of *cootchie coos* in the lyrics and the tune just seemed to bounce along. Her gaze searched the bent heads of the men playing; violinists, percussionists, wind and brass. It really was an excellent orchestra, playing with a youthful vigour which belied their years. If only she could see their faces properly.

They next played 'Alexander's Ragtime Band' and Gertie's toes started to tap and she longed to get up and dance, imagining being held by the man who had haunted her dreams for the last few months. He would sweep her off her feet and make her feel loved all over again. Then the music came to an end, the glass shaded electric lights suspended on chains from the ceiling were dimmed and the velvet curtains swung back to reveal the screen. She heard the whirr of the projectors in the box to the rear of the balcony and the orchestra began to play. She took from her handbag a bag of icing sugar coated toffee bon-bons as the title *Daddy Long Legs* flickered onto the screen. She remembered seeing it in America just before she had left there. A romantic comedy starring Mary Pickford. The film did not completely hold her attention this time and her mind began to drift to that exchange with her niece outside in the foyer. Obviously Clara did not approve of her at all and blamed her for Bernie's death. She wondered if her mother had managed to get absolution from a priest before she died. She thought of herself joking about her mother standing at the pearly gates and wondered where she was buried. Perhaps she should visit her grave with some flowers. It was June and the right month for roses; yes, that would salve her conscience, although why she should think it needed salving she didn't know. What had her mother said about Gabrielle owing her? Something to do with forcing her to run away and enjoy some success on the stage and marriage. Her thoughts returned to those days and she felt a mixture of pleasure, sadness and guilt, which she quickly brushed aside. Guilt got you nowhere. Her mother had been an old bitch.

The lights went up and the screen went blank. It was the interval. Soon the orchestra would perform again and the film recommence. Gabrielle blinked and looked down at the orchestra. The musicians were stretching, moving, exchanging words. Probably they were in need of refreshment as were some of the audience by the look of it. She decided that she rather liked being up here in the gods, gazing down on mere mortals. It was then, as she watched the musicians disperse, that her eyes rested on a clarinet player and she experienced a sense of déjà vu that made her feel quite strange. Could that be Robbie? She remembered that he'd had a good head of hair and although this man's luxuriant hair was white, he also had a distinctive nose. She determined to speak to him. Fortunately, the large man on her right had left his seat, so Gabrielle was able to leave the row of seats reasonably swiftly. She hurried into the foyer where she saw the silver-haired musician smoking a cigarette and talking to Clara.

A mixture of confused emotions exploded inside Gabrielle and she spoke in a voice that seemed to vibrate and fill the foyer. 'Am I right in thinking that you're Robbie Bennett?'

'Oh no,' muttered Clara.

Robbie removed his cigarette. 'Bloody hell! Clara

was just warning me that you were here, Gertie.'

Warned him! The words echoed in her head and she felt hurt by him all over again. 'I call myself Gabrielle these days. I never expected to see *you* again!' she said, her eyes blazing. 'You swine!'

'Hey, language, Gertie. We're in company. I know I shouldn't have left you the way I did but I came back for you once I'd made some money, but you'd gone.'

'You expect me to believe that? I was only eighteen and in a foreign country. I believed in you and you let me down. Take that!' She flung her bag of bon-bons at him.

Clara gasped as icing sugar cascaded onto the shoulders of his dinner jacket and down the lapels. 'Look what you've done! I've got to appear out front in this,' said Robbie. 'Where's your sense of dignity, woman? Ouch!' He dropped his cigarette, which had burnt down and scorched his fingers. 'Now see what you've done.'

'I'll go and get a cloth,' said Clara, hurrying off.

Gabrielle let out an outraged screech. 'It's only what you deserve. We were in love.'

'Maybe, for a short while,' said Robbie, dropping his voice. 'Now, if you don't mind, Gertie, I'd prefer it if you stopped making a show of yourself and me. I've got to go out front and play.'

Before she could respond, Clara appeared with a

damp cloth. He wiped himself down quickly and made a swift exit from the foyer. Clara turned to her aunt. 'Satisfied?'

There were tears in Gabrielle's brown eyes, so like Clara's. 'I'm going to fetch my hat and then I'm leaving. If you had any sense you'd stay clear of men. None of them can be trusted.' She walked away, making for the stairs up to the circle.

Clara returned to the pay box, unlocked the door and let herself in. The foyer was now deserted, even the doorman seemed to have vanished. She finished counting the takings. A task that had been interrupted. She entered the amount in the ledger and then bagged the money before unlocking the door. She had barely stepped over the threshold when a voice said, 'Give that to me!'

Clara clutched one of the heavy bags against her chest and shook her head. The man had bright red hair beneath a cap but sported a fair moustache. He was dressed all in black. 'Come any closer and I'll scream,' she said.

A laugh escaped him and he produced a gun. 'One peep out of you and you'll be sorry.'

Her heart thudded as she stared at the weapon. 'You'd shoot me just for a few pounds?'

'More than a few pounds, I should think, ducky.' He took several steps towards her. She shrank back against the door of the pay box, clutching the bag of money to her chest like a shield. He grabbed her by the shoulder and dragged her towards him. With part of her mind she was aware of the smell of peppermint and eau-de-cologne and was reminded of Easter Sunday and grappling with Bert. She let the bag of money slide downwards. She knew when it landed on his foot because he swore and hit her with the gun. 'Pick that up,' he ordered, thrusting her to the floor.

Suddenly there was the pad, pad, pad of footsteps on the stairs and then a voice said, 'What the bloody hell is going on here? Leave that girl alone.'

'Keep out of it, old woman,' he said menacingly.

'Old woman!' cried Gabrielle, outraged, and she flung her handbag at him. It struck him on the arm and the gun went off. Despite her throbbing head, Clara managed to grab the money bag and crawl towards the pay box.

The door of Mr Walsh's office opened. 'What's going on here?' he asked. A bullet whistled past his head and embedded itself in the door jamb. Hastily, he retreated into his office and locked the door behind him.

Gabrielle and the gunman faced each other. She had a really bad stinging pain in her left armpit and could feel blood trickling down her side and she felt quite faint. Only now did it occur to her that she had behaved stupidly, risking her life for her niece. A girl who didn't give a bugger about her. 'You don't really want to kill me,' she said, trying to sound convincing.

'You shouldn't have bloody interfered.' He fired again but in that instant, she swooned and slid to the floor. The bullet splattered the plaster work on the wall behind her and when he would have fired again the trigger clicked harmlessly.

The lavatory door opened and the doorman came out. His face was the colour of putty but when he saw the woman lying on the floor and the gunman pocketing a gun, he said, 'Hey, what have you done?'

The would-be-robber ignored him, stooping to pick up something and then stalking out. The doorman went after him but by the time he reached the pavement, there was no sign of the man.

He went back inside and called, 'Clara, luv, where are yer, girl?'

She stood up and saw her aunt lying on the floor. There was no doubt in Clara's mind that her aunt had risked her life for her. She shoved the money bag inside the pay box and ran to her aunt's side. The sight of the blood soaking through Gabrielle's clothing again reminded her of the day of the kidnapping when Mr Moran had been shot.

'Go and tell Mr Walsh to phone for an ambulance,' she said.

'Will do,' said the doorman.

As Clara stemmed the blood with the cloth

Robbie Bennett had used to wipe his jacket, she wondered if this was what war did to some men. Turning them to violence if they couldn't get what they wanted.

Mr Walsh appeared at her side. 'What happened, Clara? Did he get away with the takings?'

She shook her head and then wished she hadn't. The sudden movement sent pain shooting inside her skull and she bit down hard on her lower lip to prevent a cry. 'I wouldn't give it to him, he threatened me with a gun and when I still held on to it he hit me. He might have killed me if my aunt here hadn't thrown her handbag at him. The takings are in the pay box.'

He looked relieved. 'He was probably that wig thief. There's a reward out for him. Pity we weren't able to catch him. Even so, you deserve something for stopping him getting away with the money. I'll speak to Mr Ellis about this. I've sent for my own doctor and the police. Both should be here soon.'

Gabrielle began to stir. Her eyelids fluttered open and she looked up into Clara's bruised face. 'What happened?' she muttered.

'You fainted. Not surprising considering you were shot.'

Her aunt laughed weakly. 'I remember now. What a bloody fool I am.'

Clara smiled. 'You're a heroine, Aunt Gertie. You saved my life.'

'Gabrielle,' she corrected with a touch of asperity. 'I'll not answer to that name. Did he get away?'

'Yes.'

At that moment the doorman reappeared with a policeman. 'He's going to be wanting to question you but I'll tell him he'll have to wait until a doctor's seen to you both and you're at home.'

'Home where?' Gabrielle winced. 'I can't see my landlady wanting me turning up there with a policeman in tow, and as for the farm, I can't go back there. Too many unhappy memories.'

'Then you'll have to come to our house for now.'

Gabrielle laughed weakly. 'You are joking?'

Clara did not answer because the policeman was approaching, followed by another man carrying a black bag. He appeared to take in the scene immediately and approached them. 'Let's be having a look at you,' he said.

Clara moved out of the way and spoke to the policeman. He looked to be in his forties and told her that he was Sergeant Peter Jones. 'If you can tell me what happened, miss? It'll save me bothering you later.'

They sat down and she told him what had happened. He noted down her description of the would-be-robber, raising his eyebrows at her mention of bright red hair and a fair moustache. 'It sounds like the wig thief all right. Pity the doorman didn't prevent him escaping.'

'There was a strong smell of peppermints about the man and that makes me even more certain that he was Bert Kirk, who is a very violent man,' said Clara.

He gave her a sharp look. 'You sound like you know this man.'

Clara told him everything she knew about Bert and suggested that he look for the bullet that had missed her aunt. 'I think it hit the wall. If it matches the one taken from Mr Moran's shoulder it will prove they came from the same gun, won't it?'

'You been reading Sherlock Holmes, miss?' he said with a touch of humour.

She smiled, liking the man. So many men of his age would have talked down to her but he took her seriously and went to look for the bullet.

It had made a hole in the plaster and so he found it easily. He put it in an envelope and said that he would make a report to his superiors and most likely they would get in touch with their counterparts in Chester and ask them to inform Mr Sebastian Bennett about the injury to his mother and what had taken place here. 'An eye needs to be kept out in both cities for such a dangerous and wily criminal,' he added.

The doctor declared Gabrielle's injury only a flesh wound and said that she could go home but must rest. He gave her some pills to help her sleep. The sergeant said that he would see them to their front door. An offer Clara accepted without consulting her aunt, who was looking haggard. She thought it was time Gabrielle had someone to look after her and planned, in the morning, to seek Freddie's opinion about how best this could be done.

'I suppose that was Mam's bed I slept in last night,' said Gabrielle, easing herself down onto a chair at the table.

'Who else's?' said Clara, smiling at her aunt. She was still wearing her niece's spare nightie and, although her silver streaked black hair was mussed up, she was looking less drained this morning. 'The lodger has Mam and Dad's old room, but Gran didn't die in her own bed, if that's what's worrying you.'

'I took a couple of those pills the doctor gave me and went out like a light, so I didn't even think of it last night. Otherwise I might have expected her to haunt me.' A wry smile twisted Gabrielle's handsome features and she smoothed back her hair with a hand that shook. 'Holy Mary, mother of God, Clara, you look like you've been in the wars, too! The side of your face is black and blue.'

'Don't remind me,' said Clara, placing a plate of salt fish and buttered bread on the table in front of her aunt. 'I took one look at myself in the mirror this morning and nearly died of fright.'

Gabrielle laughed and then gazed down at the breakfast and said, 'This takes me back. It was a favourite of me dad's when he was home from sea.' She picked up a fork in her right hand and began to break up the fish. 'This won't do, you know, Clara. I can't have you spoiling me. One, I don't deserve it and two, I'm used to looking after myself. Anyhow, I'm definitely not staying here a second night.'

'That's up to you,' said Clara with a shrug. 'Are you planning on going back to your hotel?'

'Moved out of there and into a boarding house on Mount Pleasant, but I can't stay there much longer. My money's running out, so I need to see my solicitor.' She lifted her head and glanced across the table at her niece. 'You wouldn't mind making me a cup of tea, would you? I'm a bit parched.'

Clara said, 'I've already made a pot. I was just letting it draw.' She got up and poured the tea and placed a cup in front of her aunt. 'You're going to need help to pack. If you leave it until this evening, I'll be able to help you. Besides, Sergeant Jones wants to have a word with you, so he'll probably turn up here later.'

'Holy Mary, that means I'm going to have to get dressed and tidy meself up.' She grimaced. 'You haven't a blouse I could borrow, have you? The blood's ruined mine and it was one I bought in New York. I loved the colour and it's a really nice crêpe de Chine.'

'I'll see what I can find, but don't expect anything posh,' warned Clara, remembering what Joy had told her about Gabrielle thinking herself a cut above others, but so far this morning, she hadn't seemed a bit snobby.

'I'm grateful for anything,' said Gabrielle. 'As soon as I've finished this and drunk my tea, I'm going to have to start getting myself ready. As much as I hate to ask for it, I will need your help for that. Under my arm's painful and I do feel a bit stiff.' She added, 'By the way, do you know where my handbag is?'

Clara shook her head. 'You threw it at the gunman.'

'Then it must still be at the picture house.' She scowled.

'Mr Walsh has probably picked it up. We could see about it later.'

Gabrielle nodded.

Clara thought that the sooner they were both dressed and ready for company, the happier she would feel. Freddie would be here soon and she was hardly going to look her best as it was when he arrived.

But Sergeant Jones was the first to turn up and did so around about one o'clock. Clara had expected Freddie at twelve and hoped nothing had happened to him. She invited the policeman in and offered him a cup of tea. He thanked her and sat down, looking at Gabrielle. 'And how are you feeling today?'

'Fair to middling,' she replied chirpily. 'How are you, Sergeant?

He washed his craggy face and moustache with his hands. 'I was awake half the night, thinking about this case. Do you definitely believe, like Miss O'Toole, that he was wearing a wig?'

'Hair that red?' She smiled. 'I was on the stage for several years, Sergeant, I'd swear to it. You can get some that are made of real human hair but sometimes they're made of horse hair and dyed. I'd say the one he was wearing was probably for a character in a pantomime.' She was about to mention the robber's fair moustache when there was a knock at the door.

Clara excused herself, hoping it was Freddie.

It was but he was not alone. 'Hello, Freddie. Hello, Seb,' she said in surprise. 'What are you doing here?'

'Look at your face!' exclaimed Freddie, taking hold of her chin gently and tilting her face up to the sun. 'I'll bloody kill the swine when I get my hands on him.'

'You know about what happened last evening?' she asked, gazing into his blazing eyes.

'Yes, we both know,' said Seb grimly. 'A policeman called at our house early this morning so I caught a train to Eastham. Tilly told me that

Freddie was aiming to see you today and I thought we might as well come over here together, so here we are. Neither of us is happy about you and Ma being alone here without a man to protect you while Bert's on the loose. The police are desperate to catch him.'

'You'd best come in,' said Clara, removing Freddie's hand from her chin and holding it firmly. 'Although, at the moment we're not without protection. Police Sergeant Jones is here now, interviewing your Ma, Seb.'

The three of them went inside and Clara introduced Freddie and Seb to the sergeant. Seb shook his hand before turning to his mother. 'You should have come straight home instead of chasing after...' He stopped abruptly and took a deep breath. 'Well, never mind that now. I'm taking you back today and I'm not having any arguments.'

Gabrielle's lips trembled and her fingers plucked at her skirt. 'Easy for you to say that with Alice not here. I know what she'll think if I walk into your house with you.'

'Alice is as shocked as everyone else by what happened last night,' said Seb, his eye glinting. 'Anyway, she'll go along with my decision, no matter how she feels towards you.'

Clara spoke up, 'I bet none of you were told that your mother probably saved my life at risk to her own.'

Seb turned his head and looked at her in amazement. 'No. He just told us you'd both been hurt and that you suspected the gunman was Bert.'

'What concerns me,' said Freddie, frowning and drawing Clara down onto the sofa with him, 'is that Bert might try to rob the Palladium again. He's vengeful and, although he probably didn't recognise Clara as being the woman outside Hanny's house on Easter Sunday, he might want to get back at the cashier and woman who foiled his plans.'

Sergeant Jones murmured, 'Now you've said that about this man, I wonder…there's a possibility he could have removed his disguise and followed us back here. I can get a policeman to watch this house and the Palladium.'

'But the police couldn't do that for weeks and months on end, could they, Sergeant?' asked Freddie, his expression serious. 'Bert is a man who is prepared to wait to get his revenge. He's cunning. I say that Clara can't stay here or return to her job until Bert is found.'

'So where are you suggesting Miss O'Toole hides out, Mr Kirk?' asked the sergeant.

'My employer, Mrs Black, has offered for her to stay at her house in Eastham. Bert doesn't know the place, so she'll be safe there.' Freddie glanced at Clara and smiled. 'Besides, I'll be there to keep an eye on her.'

'Humph! I don't know why you think so well of

Edie,' said Gabrielle, wincing as she hunched her shoulders. 'I could tell you things about her.'

'We don't want to know,' said Clara hastily. 'If Freddie's right, then I'll be happy to stay at her house. I'm sure Mr Walsh will understand, in the circumstances. Besides, with the way my face looks right now, I don't think I'd be a particularly good advertisement for the Palladium!'

The sergeant said, 'I'll be seeing Mr Walsh soon, so I'll explain to him.'

'When you do, Sergeant Jones, ask him about my handbag, if you would,' said Gabrielle. 'I threw it at that swine and I didn't bring it here with me, so it must still be at the Palladium.'

'I'll need an address to see that it gets to you,' he said, his pencil poised above his notepad.

'Better make it my son's, then,' she murmured, glancing at Seb.

The sergeant wrote the address down and then put away his notebook and pencil. 'I'll be leaving you now then and I hope you both will soon recover from this terrible experience.'

Clara and Gabrielle smiled at him. 'Thank you, Sergeant,' they both said.

Seb saw him out and then came back to the sunlit kitchen. 'So what next?' he asked, gazing at his mother. 'Are you ready to go now or is there anything you need to fetch?'

'My luggage is at a small guest house in Lord

Nelson Street, so we'll have to go there.' She stretched out a hand to him. 'Help me up, please. I'm not feeling quite myself today.'

Seb placed an arm round her and hoisted her to her feet. 'We'll get my doctor to look at your wound.'

'I hope you've some money on you. I owe a pound to the landlady.' Gabrielle looked up into her son's face and touched his scarred cheek. 'It doesn't look as bad as it did when I first saw it.'

'Time heals,' he said.

They both smiled and he escorted her out of the house.

Clara and Freddie exchanged looks and he leant forward and kissed her gently. 'You'll need to pack some clothes,' he said.

She nodded. 'That won't take long, and I'll need to leave a note for Mary. She's out seeing a friend today.'

'Want any help?' he asked, lifting her to her feet.

She shook her head. 'You can wait outside in the car if you want. I won't be long.'

After Clara had packed a few things in a holdall and written a note, she glanced about the silent kitchen and could almost see her grandmother sitting in her old chair. She hoped she would have approved of the burgeoning relationship between her daughter and granddaughter. With mixed feelings, Clara picked up the holdall and left, uncertain whether she would ever live in this house again.

CHAPTER TWENTY-NINE

Bert lay on the bed with the crocodile skin handbag by his side. He stroked the powder puff from the container of face powder down his cheek, feeling a frisson of pleasure as he did so. Its delicate perfume brought back memories of several women he'd slept with, but then, suddenly another darker recollection came to him and he broke out into a sweat as he relived the shock of a woman dying on him. He thought he had managed to rid himself of that terrible memory, but every now and again the remembrance would come to him so unexpectedly that it never failed to scare the life out of him.

He threw the powder puff on the chair at the bedside and sat up. No more wasting time. He took the money from the handbag and pocketed it. Not much, but he had quite a few pounds tucked away now and, once he had settled several old scores, he was going to take a well earned holiday somewhere far away from England and enjoy himself.

He emptied the rest of the contents of the handbag onto the bed and had a closer look at them. He took up the passport and opened it, and read the name Mrs Gertrude Bernadette Waters. The address was a farm in Delamere, Cheshire. Waters! That was a name he knew only too well!

A shiver ran through him, as once again, he saw in his mind the limp body of Victoria Waters, the woman he had raped. She was haunting him! He tossed the passport on the bed and went over to the window, gazing out across the cobbled road of Mount Pleasant, where he saw a couple of nuns hurrying to the convent further up. Inexplicably, the nuns reminded him of his mother. He experienced a familiar pain when he thought of her, remembering how he had longed for her to visit him in prison.

He had waited in vain and for a while he had blamed his dah, but then he had learnt that his mother was in the lunatic asylum, a fact his father failed to mention. His blue eyes darkened. It was the women's fault; Hanny and Joy, Alice and her friend Emma, and that interfering Mrs Black. They were responsible not only for his degradation but the loss of his mother's support. The girl who had snatched Alice's daughter from him had joined their ranks, and now another woman, Mrs Gertrude Bernadette Waters, was there alongside them.

Pity he hadn't been able to hurt Mrs Black when he had seen her with Freddie in that motor in Lime

Street. His body began to shake with laughter. He had fooled them all right. Good disguise dressing up as a woman. It was the wig that had given him the idea. Good wheeze, as well, for getting money off the public. He had thought the medium had penetrated his disguise and she'd had him sweating for a second, but then they had driven off. But it was a good disguise and he was seriously considering using it again sometime in the future.

From his pocket he took a packet of strong mints and popped one into his mouth. Then he returned to the bed and rifled through the rest of the items on the bed and came across a solicitor's business card; the address was in Chester. That decided it, a visit to the city of his birth was meant to be. He would book himself in at the premier hotel in the city, the Grosvenor. No one was going to think of looking for him there. Perhaps he should take the name he had used years ago, before the war, when he had needed to go to ground; Albert Church. He would shave off his moustache and wear the dark curly-haired wig. It was time to make a move on his enemies, once and for all.

Alice had finished preparing the spare room for her mother-in-law, having placed a vase of pink roses on the dressing table. She had worked out some of her bad mood by beating the bedside rug out on the line and then banging pillows. She had told herself that she had to try and be a good Christian and make Gabrielle welcome. Of course, that was if she agreed to come, but Alice was convinced she would. Her heart sank. A short while ago she had begun to believe that life was going to get better but not only had Bert come back from the dead, but her dad was weaning Tilly away from them and now Seb's mother was about to appear on the scene again. When Seb had gone missing it had been an extremely testing time, and now she felt that God was testing her faith again and she knew that she must not be found wanting. She had to rise to the challenge that was Gabrielle. If Seb could forgive her for the pain she had caused him, then she must do so, too. After all, Gabrielle was not getting any younger and it was no fun at anytime having a gun pointed at you, never mind being shot. She thought of her dad bleeding as he had lain on the ground outside Hanny's. He had done wrong but her mother had forgiven him time and again, so couldn't she try and imitate her and close the rift that was growing between herself and Tilly?

She heard the sound of a car engine and then it stopped outside. Hurrying over to the window, she rested her hands on the sill and gazed down on the crescent. Seb was climbing out of the car and there was his mother and Clara; Freddie was in the driving seat. Would they all be coming in, needing something to eat and a drink? The joint might not stretch that far. Was Clara expecting to stay? She whipped off her apron and hurried downstairs.

Tilly must have heard the car, as well, because she already had the front door open and was welcoming Gabrielle and Clara into the house.

'I won't be staying long,' said Clara to Tilly. 'I'm going with Freddie to Mrs Black's. She's invited me to stay with her.'

'But you and Freddie will have a cup of tea, won't you?' called Alice from the stairs.

Clara looked up and smiled. 'A cup of tea would be very nice.'

'Your face!' cried Alice, holding out both hands to her.

'She's a brave girl,' said Gabrielle, gazing at them both.

'No braver than you,' said Clara, returning her gaze.

Gabrielle shook her head. 'I was just plain stupid. He got my dander up and I let fly.'

'Just as you did to Mr Robbie Bennett,' teased Clara.

'What's this about Mr Robbie Bennett?' asked Alice, squeezing Clara's hands before freeing them. 'Seb told me about his meeting with him.'

Gabrielle groaned and put a hand to her head. 'Don't tell her, Clara. I've been all kinds of a fool but from now on I'm going to leave him where he belongs...in the past.'

'That's a good start for your new life,' said Seb, thinking that it was a pity because he had rather taken to Robbie. He put down one of his mother's suitcases and flexed his fingers. Freddie was just behind him with the other one.

The hall suddenly seemed crowded. 'You can take them upstairs,' said Alice, wondering what Seb meant by *your new life*. Was she going to live here with them from now on? She sent up a quick prayer. 'I've put you in old Mrs Waters' bedroom, mother-in-law,' she said. 'It has been done up.'

Gabrielle looked at her, remembering all the letters Alice had sent to her without any real words of reproach. 'Call me Gabrielle,' she said. 'I'll go up straightaway, if you don't mind? I'm a bit tired and would like to lie down for an hour.'

'Of course,' said Alice, trying not to sound relieved. 'Do you want a cup of tea brought up?'

'No. I'll make myself one later, if you don't mind me in your kitchen?'

Alice remembered when the kitchen had been Gabrielle's kingdom and magnanimously said, 'Make yourself at home. Seb's told the children about your macaroons. Perhaps, when you have a chance, you can make them some.'

Gabrielle flushed with pleasure and felt a tightness in her throat so that she could only nod before going upstairs.

'That went off better than I thought it would,'

whispered Seb against his wife's ear. Then he went upstairs in his mother's wake.

Tilly turned to Clara. 'So, are you going to tell us all what happened?'

'Once I've had my cup of tea,' she replied.

It took a good half hour telling the whole story and when Clara had finished, Tilly said, 'Can I have an exclusive on this? It just might be the piece that gets me published in the newspapers.'

Clara said, 'If that's what you want to do.'

'But keep her name and whereabouts a secret,' said Freddie.

'As if I needed telling that Bert might read newspapers,' responded Tilly, sticking her tongue out at him.

Freddie took Clara's hand and drew her to her feet. 'It's time we were going.'

They said their goodbyes and left. Soon they were bowling along the country lanes that led to Eastham. Clara had her eyes closed and could smell the sweet scent of dog roses. She was thinking about Mrs Black and wondered if she dared ask her how she and Robbie Bennett had found each other's company when they met at her grandmother's funeral.

'I suppose you didn't sleep too well last night?' asked Freddie, rousing Clara from her reverie.

'No. My face was painful and my mind kept going over what had happened. Do you really believe Bert will have another go at stealing the takings from the Palladium?'

'If he does, the police are going to be ready for him. But then perhaps that'll occur to Bert, so he'll do something entirely different. At least at Mrs Black's you can relax.'

'I'm not used to relaxing.' Clara smothered a yawn.

'Then learn,' said Freddie, glancing at her with a tender expression. 'Being tense all the time isn't good for anyone. I know that from being at sea, never knowing when a U-boat would torpedo us.'

'Thank God the war's over,' said Clara, opening her eyes and meeting his gaze and feeling warmed by it.

'Amen,' he said. 'So, you learn from me and relax for the next few days...although, no doubt it won't be long before Mrs Black or Joy finds you something to do.'

Eudora rose from the rustic seat and enveloped Clara in a hug. 'My dear, how are you? What a thing to happen! You could so easily have been seriously injured or killed.'

Clara felt slightly awkward being embraced by a woman whom she felt was generally very much in control of her feelings. 'I'm fine, just a bit tired.'

'Then you must rest. Later I'll give you some witch hazel for the bruising.' Eudora released her and turned to where Joy was sitting in a deckchair doing some sewing. 'Joy, dear, sherry and some of those little biscuits you've baked, please? And Freddie, if you could fetch a couple more deckchairs from the old stable. I want to hear from Clara all that has happened, though I'm sure you already know most of it.'

'I never tire of hearing Clara's voice,' said Freddie, winking at her before moving away to fetch the deckchairs. Joy touched Clara's shoulder as she passed on her way to the house. 'Glad you're safe,' she murmured.

Eudora waved Clara to the deckchair vacated by Joy. 'Now, dear, tell me all.'

So Clara told her tale yet again, aware that Eudora was listening closely. She was also aware of Mr Moran not far away, tying up a rambling rose, and thought that no doubt he was listening, too. By the time she had finished, the sherry and biscuits had arrived and Joy heard the end of the story.

'I never thought Bert would come to this,' said Joy, handing first Eudora a glass of sherry and then Clara. 'When we were young, he was so religious, used to win prizes at Bible Class and charmed the old ladies in our street. Mother, of course, thought the sun shone out of him.'

Eudora glanced at Mal. 'Some mothers have a lot to answer for. When I first studied Bert's character more than fifteen years ago, I realised that he was a crafty, unstable, arrogant, cruel bully. Despite being a churchgoer and knowing his Bible, he had somehow managed to confuse what it says about what is right and wrong. He also did not seem to realise what was acceptable in those times is not so today. Clara and Joy, you must not go to Liverpool or Chester unaccompanied until he is caught.' Eudora's dark eyes were thoughtful as she sipped her sherry. 'Bert must realise by now that he is a hunted man in Liverpool. He must go undisguised some of the time, so if the police accept for certain that he's their thief and they have a photograph of him, then they will publish it in the Liverpool newspapers.'

They were silent for several minutes and then Joy said, 'He'll come back to Chester.'

'But in a different disguise,' muttered Freddie, tapping his fingers against his teeth.

Clara said, 'He could be close by and we might not recognise him. Say he has a knife, as well as a gun. We could be walking along a street...'

'You don't go amongst crowds and Freddie will drive you,' said Eudora.

'We're going to have to warn the others about this. He could be in the crescent, anywhere, and none of us would know it,' said Freddie heavily.

'I'm sure they're all on their guard, my dear,' said Eudora. 'But you can write and let them know our thoughts if you wish.'

A fortnight passed with no sign of Bert. Freddie and Clara visited Liverpool during that time. She spoke to Mary and agreed to her friend renting her grandmother's room. Then she visited the Palladium and spoke to Mr Walsh, asking whether her aunt's handbag had been found.

He frowned. 'No, it wasn't. Anyway, about your job here, Clara. You're to take all the time you need to recover from your nasty experience. My wife is filling in for you at the moment...with the police keeping an eye on us, of course.' His brow cleared. 'But if you're worrying about money, you don't have to. I was hoping you'd drop by because I've an envelope in the safe for you. A little reward from the company for saving the takings.'

Clara was delighted to accept the envelope and then asked, 'Have you seen any more of Sergeant Jones?'

'You're thinking of the other reward for information leading to the capture of the gunman, no doubt,' he said, gazing thoughtfully at them both. 'He has dropped by here a couple of times and he might again. I'll tell him you called and of our conversation. He has your address across the water?'

'No. But he has my cousin's address in Chester and can get in touch with me through him.'

He nodded and then shook both their hands.

Clara did not open the envelope until they were

outside and was pleased to find a five pound note. 'Your bravery is worth more than that,' said Freddie, putting his arm round her.

She smiled. 'More would have been nice but every bit helps. I bet the reward for the capture of the wig robber is a lot more, but at least I'll be able to give Mrs Black something for my keep.'

'I doubt she'll take it from you,' he said. 'I think she enjoys having young people around and you do help Joy. Anyway, will you be writing to your aunt about her handbag?'

'Yes. But she might already know. The sergeant did say he'd get in touch with her.'

Gabrielle had heard from the sergeant that her handbag had not been found and she was really annoyed that someone must have waltzed off with it. They should have handed it in at the pay box. Money and cosmetics could be replaced fairly easily but not her passport and other things. She was starting to get used to living with a family again but life could not be said to be normal. Seb and Alice were trying to behave as if all was well so as not to frighten the children, but the idea of Bert lurking about nearby was affecting their routine.

Seb and Kenny worked from home as much as possible so that the women were not left alone too much. Mrs Black had invested in the company and ordered an automobile, a second-hand roadster that was like a mini charabanc. It needed some repairs but their mechanic was looking forward to getting to work on it.

On a day in July when the newspapers were full of the Victory Parade in Paris – the war had finally been declared officially over after the Germans had been landed with a ten billion pound bill – Seb received the news that the bullet that had hit Alice's father had matched one fired at his mother in the Palladium. Better late than never, he thought, when he read the letter that evening. At least it confirmed what they had believed. He decided he must let Kenny know. Besides, he had forgotten to discuss with him something earlier in the day. It was Tilly's sixteenth birthday that month and the start of the school holidays. He popped his head through the half-opened door of the drawing room, where his mother and Alice were listening to Tilly playing the piano and said, 'I'm just going up to see Kenny for a mo'.'

'You be careful,' warned Alice. 'I know there's been no sign of Bert so far and he's probably not out to get you but...'

Seb tapped his pocket significantly and smiled reassuringly at his wife. 'I am armed. Bolt the door after me and I'll bang like a billio to be let in when I come back.'

'A password! We need a password,' said Tilly seriously. 'What if he was to disguise his voice?'

'Good idea,' said Gabrielle, turning over the pages of sheet music. 'I must admit I'm getting a bit fed up of all this and feel like going somewhere far away…but with no passport…'

'Think about that while I'm out,' said Seb.

'No. Let's think of one now. How about macaroons?' said his mother.

Seb grinned. 'I meant about going away. But macaroons as a password isn't bad.' He shook his finger at her. 'You still haven't made any yet, Ma, and the kids are desperate to taste them.'

'She still isn't herself yet,' said Alice, thinking of Gabrielle's healing underarm. 'But I have to admit, I've been thinking of your mocha coffee,' she added, remembering the time her mother-in-law had taken pity on her when she had worked for the Waters and been feeling down. She rose and followed her husband out of the room.

As they reached the front door, Seb said, 'You know, I won't be happy until Bert's dead. If I could get my hands on him…'

Alice wanted to warn him that Bert was a strong and ruthless person, but Seb knew that. Besides, if she had said it he might believe she considered him no match for Bert. The movement in Seb's arm was much improved but he would always have a weakness there. She prayed that, if Bert did arrive on the scene, she would have a chance to get her children to safety and run for the police. She bolted the door after him.

It was dusk as Seb walked soft-footedly down the path towards the front gate. His hand was in his pocket, fingering the wrench that he was prepared to use on Bert if the opportunity arose. He was alert for any sound of rustling beneath the trees or in the undergrowth. He could smell the heady scent of roses mingling with that of night scented stock and, for a moment, he recalled the day he had first seen Alice. He had been in this very garden, helping the old gardener. Gosh, they'd had lots of happy times, and how dare that swine Bert threaten their happiness now?

A neighbour called across to him, asking how he was, and for a few minutes they had a conversation before the man went inside his house. Seb strode the short distance to the Morans' front door and pulled the bell rope. His mind was turning over his mother's idea of getting away. Several moments passed and still he stood waiting on the step.

He rang again and stepped back to gaze up at the first floor window. He caught the faint sound of an infant crying and was about to pull the bell rope again when he felt a blow on the back of his head. The force of it caused him to lose his balance temporarily. He staggered but managed to remain upright, fumbling for the wrench in his pocket as he

did so. He turned to face his assailant and saw the
next blow coming. He was able to parry it with the
wrench but the shock of the crash of weapons sent
an agonising pain up his arm. The wrench fell from
his tingling fingers. He was dizzy with the pain but
fought back, bringing his knee up sharply between
the man's legs. His assailant squealed and, clutching
himself, doubling over and groaning, he turned and
wobbled in a knock-kneed fashion down the path
to the gate.

Seb would have followed him but hot and cold
waves of pain were sweeping over him and he
crashed back against the front door. It opened and
he landed in the hall at the feet of two elderly
women.

'This is the last straw,' said the first one.

'We're moving out,' said the other.

'I'm not drunk,' he gasped, staring blearily up
at the music teachers who occupied the ground
floor.

'We didn't say you were, Mr Bennett,' stated the
first. 'But we've been thinking of moving to Rhyl
ever since the twins were born. We're too old to
cope with little ones once they start running about.'

'What's going on?' asked Hanny.

Neither of them had heard her coming
downstairs.

'A visitor for you, Mrs Moran, and we're letting
you know now that in the near future we'll be

moving out,' chorused both women before leaving her to attend to Seb.

'I've been expecting them to say that for ages,' said Hanny, gazing anxiously at Seb. 'What are you doing down there?'

'I was attacked. Give us a hand up, if you would? I've jarred my arm.'

She helped him to his feet. 'Bert, d'you think?'

'I only got a brief glimpse of him but who else would attack me? At least I managed to hurt him, but he got away. Shut the door and bolt it. Then let's go upstairs.' Seb pressed his lips tightly together as he pushed himself away from the wall. He swayed and Hanny had to put an arm round him to stop him falling. 'You'd best lean on me and maybe we should get the doctor out to you.'

'I'll be fine,' he said fiercely.

She did not argue with him.

They found Kenny standing in the doorway of the drawing room, nursing one of the twins. 'I thought I heard your voice, Seb. You look grim. What's happened?'

'He was attacked on *our* doorstep,' said Hanny, her eyes smouldering.

Kenny's face hardened. 'So it's started. What about Alice and the children? Will they be all right with you here?'

'Alice knows not to open the door to anyone,'

said Seb. 'We've even come up with a password this evening.'

They went into the drawing room and the first thing he noticed was Mrs Kirk dozing on the sofa, so he made for one of the armchairs and sat down. Only now did he feel the back of his head, but thankfully there wasn't much of a lump. 'Is that where he hit you?' asked Hanny, taking a look.

'Yes. Fortunately, I've taken to carrying a weapon, although what good it would do against a gun...' Seb explored his right arm with gentle fingers. The pain had subsided and he could not feel any change in the shape of the limb. 'I think it's all right,' he said with relief.

'You need a drink,' said Kenny, handing the baby to Hanny. 'I'll pour you a medicinal brandy. Bert must be off his head.'

'My Bert's in Australia.'

The three of them jumped at the sound of Mrs Kirk's voice.

'So he is, Mother,' said Hanny swiftly. 'Are you ready for bed?'

The old woman smiled up at her. 'I am a bit tired. Would you like me to put the baby to bed? I'll be passing their nursery.'

'Why not?' Hanny placed her daughter in her mother's arms and saw her out onto the landing.

Kenny handed Seb his brandy. 'Best thing for her that she believes Bert's in Australia. Imagine how she might react if she knew the truth,' he said.

'If he hadn't hit my arm, I might have stopped him from getting away,' growled Seb, annoyed with himself.

Hanny said, 'I bet he'll lie low for a while before having another go at one of us. He'll probably think we'll get in touch with the police and they might set a watch.'

'They can't do that forever. We have to work out a strategy to protect ourselves and catch him,' said Seb, draining his glass and rising to his feet. 'Anyway, Ma said something earlier that made me think. She mentioned needing to get away. I think it's a good idea, especially with the school holidays coming up. Also, we need to think about what we're going to do to celebrate Tilly's sixteenth birthday.'

They both agreed and said, 'We'll give it some thought.'

Seb was extra careful going home but there was no sign of his attacker. He banged on the door and said the password and was soon inside his own house. Once in the drawing room he told the others what had happened.

'We need to get away from here,' said Alice fiercely, after inspecting the lump on Seb's head. 'I'm not risking the children's lives by staying here for the whole of the school holidays, but where can we go that isn't expensive?'

Seb said, 'You and Ma could take the children to the farm. I'll have to stay here because of the business.'

Alice protested.

Gabrielle spoke up. 'I've just had a thought. It might have been *him* who picked up my missing handbag, and if he did, he has my passport with my name and the address of the farm.'

Seb swore beneath his breath and went over to the drinks cabinet. 'So what do we do?' asked Alice, following him over.

'We need to bring him out into the open and deal with him,' said Seb firmly.

'But he has a gun!' cried Alice.

'I'm not going to let him frighten me away from my own home,' said Seb, his eye glinting. 'Hanny believes he'll lie low for a while again, and it's true he did that after the abduction attempt, but he mightn't this time. You and the children have to get away.'

'And what do we use for money for this *long* holiday?' asked Alice, hating the thought of leaving Seb behind. A few months ago they had said they'd never be parted again.

'It doesn't have to be an expensive holiday and you don't have to go far,' said Seb, looking pensive. 'I could hire a tent for you at Moreton-by-the-sea and I could drive you there.'

'I'm not going,' said Tilly, 'I've writing to do. I

sold the last article to the *Chronicle*. Perhaps I could stay at the yard if you and Kenny decide to visit Moreton and stay overnight. There's still my old bedroom there.'

Alice opened her mouth to protest at the idea of camping. It was something she had never done in her life, but Gabrielle looked at her and chuckled. 'I'm game if you are, girl. And just think, the children will see it as a big adventure.' Alice said no more but wondered what Hanny would think of such a plan.

She was soon to find out as she called on Hanny the next morning. When she heard about Seb's idea for a holiday, she was all in favour of it. 'I wouldn't mind going to Moreton, but camping with the twins and Mother wouldn't be easy.'

'Cockles,' said Mrs Kirk, who was changing one of the twins' nappies.

Hanny stared at her, and then she remembered how her mother used to visit her Great-aunt Joan, who had been a cockle picker at Moreton. Suddenly she remembered her great-aunt's house, which had been left to her mother. Hopefully Bert, if he thought about the place at all, would think they had sold it after Great-aunt Joan died. She recalled that Freddie had been the last to visit the place. Did he still have the keys or did Joy? She, herself, couldn't remember where they were. She told Alice about the house.

'I'll get in touch with Freddie and Joy and ask about the keys. Mother and I could stay there with the twins while you camp. You could always come and eat with us if you have trouble cooking over a campfire,' she added with a twinkle.

When Hanny told Kenny about it, he also thought it was a brilliant idea. 'Although if Tilly's not going to Moreton, we'll have to think again about having a party on her actual birthday.'

Hanny agreed, so they wired Freddie and Joy and also mentioned his picking Hanny, her mother and the twins up and driving them there. Freddie wired back almost immediately, saying that he knew where the keys were and he would be happy to take them there on his day off. He did not say so in the wire, but he had decided to take Clara with him so that she could have a few days at the house with Hanny and the children. He was of the opinion that some sea air would be good for her.

CHAPTER THIRTY

'A motor. We're going to have to get ourselves a motor,' muttered Bert to his reflection in the glass. He removed the wig and scratched his head. 'How the hell did Freddie manage to get his hands on such a motor? He's only a bloody kid, twenty at the most. What kind of money is he on?'

His day hadn't gone at all well, despite his having such high hopes of tricking not only the two families in Victoria Crescent but the police, as well, if they were around. He had planned trailing the first person out of either house and sliding a knife between their ribs from behind if it was Kenny or Alice's husband. But his scheme for Hanny, Alice, Tilly or one of the children was very different.

Unfortunately, by the time he had breakfasted at the Grosvenor and changed into his disguise, it was past ten o'clock. The first two out of Hanny's house were two old ladies, and he wasn't bothered with them. They had looked his way but there had been nothing suspicious in their gazes and that was because his disguise was brilliant. No one took much notice of an old woman tap-tap-tapping with her stick along the pavement.

But it had not done him a bit of good. First Freddie had zoomed off with the girl who had snatched Alice's daughter from him, accompanied by Hanny, his mother, the twins and their baggage. Then from the Waters old residence, Alice had emerged with her kids, husband, and the middle-aged woman he recognised from the passport. They had climbed into another motor laden with baggage and driven off. Annoyingly, he had no means to follow them and had no idea where they were going.

Still, Kenny and Tilly appeared to have stayed behind, not that the girl had ever done him any harm. In fact, she had liked him. He wished Alice's husband had remained behind. Bert's blue eyes were icy cold as he thought about what he would like to do to him. A stab in the back or shooting him out of hand was too humane. He shuddered at the remembrance of the pain the man had inflicted on him. Something slow and painful had more appeal – castration, that would ruin Alice's marriage.

That thought cheered him up and Bert hummed to himself as he stripped off and washed himself in the sink. It was not going to be easy catching Alice's husband off-guard and he obviously knew how to handle himself, but if he was patient, sooner or later the swine would relax and then he would have him. His body shook with laughter thinking about it. In the meantime, he intended carrying on enjoying himself here in Chester by pretending to be a tourist.

He put on a clean shirt and collar and then a bow tie, flannels and a blazer. Replacing the black wig, he combed it neatly before pocketing his wallet and picking up his cane. The walking stick had been an inspiration. If people believed you had been injured in the war they were inclined to treat you with respectful sympathy. He had been practising his limp, so had no trouble adopting it when he left his room and went downstairs to the dining room. He was looking forward to afternoon tea, and then he intended to stroll down to the river and along the Groves to ogle all the pretty girls. During the next few days he would resume his watch on the two houses in Victoria Crescent in a variety of disguises. So far he had only seen a policeman on the beat. But who was to say that there were not a couple more around in plain clothes?

It was a few days after the departure of the women and children that Sergeant Peter Jones knocked on the door of the house on Victoria Crescent. He had come with an excuse handy for his visit but really his reasons were mixed. He was genuinely concerned about Mrs Waters and would like to see for himself how she was getting along, but also he was interested in what she had said about having performed on the stage after hearing from a musician at the Palladium that she was a singer. He did not have long to wait before hearing footsteps approaching.

'Who is it?' asked a male voice.

'It's Sergeant Jones from Liverpool.'

Seb could think of no way that Bert could know the name of the policeman who had interviewed his mother and Clara, so he opened the door and looked keenly at the tall, upright figure with a pleasant craggy face and luxurious moustache, dressed in a grey suit and wearing a trilby. He instantly recognised him. 'How do you do, Sergeant? Nice to see you again. Please come in.'

Sergeant Jones thanked him and wiped his feet on the mat. Seb closed the door and automatically bolted it. 'What can I do for you?' he asked.

'I've come to see how Mrs Waters is and to tell you, if you didn't know already, that the bullet from the gun that was fired at her matched that taken from Mr Moran, who was shot over here. So young Mr Kirk and Miss O'Toole were right about the gunman's identity.'

Seb smiled. 'It was good of you to come all this way but I'm afraid you've had a wasted journey. We have already been informed about the bullets. I'm sorry, too, if you wished to see Ma. She's not here –

she's gone on holiday with my wife and children.' The sergeant's face expressed such disappointment that Seb's interest was stirred. 'Was there something else you wished to speak to her about?'

The sergeant cleared his throat. 'A musician at the Palladium mentioned that Mrs Waters used to be a singer, so I thought she might be interested in coming to hear our Glee Club perform. The concert is next week and it's to raise money for the poor children of Liverpool.'

Seb could see no reason why his mother might not wish to go to a concert. And if it was in company with the sergeant she should be safe. 'If you want to talk to Ma, I can tell you where to find her. I'm sure she'll be glad to see you.'

Immediately, the sergeant's face brightened. 'Thank you. As long as it's not too far away, I'll be delighted to seek her out.'

So Seb told him about the family camping out at Moreton. He made him a cup of tea and they discussed the robbery and the fact that there had been no sign of the wig robber since the last sighting of him at the Palladium. He then saw him out, intending to catch up on some paperwork.

Bert was enjoying his role playing and had seriously begun to believe that he had missed his calling in life and should have gone on the stage. Today he was pretending to be a street sweeper, and in that guise he had watched a tall, middle-aged man, neatly dressed and of an upright bearing, enter Alice's home. Bert had had enough to do with the bobbies to know one when he saw one and waited with interest to see him leave. After half an hour he did so, talking for a moment on the step to Alice's husband, who had returned from wherever he had taken his family. A snatch of conversation reached his ears. 'Thank you for the information, Sergeant.'

'Thank you, Mr Bennett. I do hope you're right and she'll be glad to see me.'

Bert stiffened. *She?* Which of the women was he referring to? Did it matter? This sergeant had been told where to find one of them. All he had to do was follow him. Hallelujah, the bobby was on foot. Bert continued to pretend to sweep the street but this time he worked faster in order to catch up with the man striding towards the footbridge over the Dee. Once out of the crescent, he abandoned his brush and hurried after the sergeant.

Fortunately, a neighbour had been watching the road sweeper from an upper window and now the woman hurried downstairs and across to the Bennetts' house and knocked on the door. She had been the person who had telephoned for an ambulance when Mr Moran had been shot. Such goings-on were frightening and she wanted the person responsible caught.

'Who is it?' called Seb.

'It's Mrs Taylor from across the road, Mr Bennett. I have something important to tell you.'

Seb opened the door. 'What is it, Mrs Taylor?'

'The road sweeper who was here before. He didn't have a shovel or a little rubbish cart to put the sweepings in. As soon as the man came out of your house, he went after him.'

Seb's expression was instantly alert. 'Thanks, Mrs Taylor. I can't say I took much notice of him. Can you give me a description?'

She described a scruffy-looking fellow with spiky red hair sticking out from beneath a cloth cap. He sounds familiar, thought Seb. 'I presume he went towards the footbridge?' he asked.

She nodded.

Seb wasted no time in grabbing his jacket, keys and wallet and leaving the house. Knowing the sergeant's destination, Seb was not too worried about not being able to catch up with the two men after their head-start, but he was angry with himself for giving Bert the opportunity to hurt his family. Unfortunately, the automobile he had used to take the family to Moreton was at the yard having a small repair done. He would have to take the train. When he reached the ticket box, it was to be told that the earliest connection to the train for Moreton had just pulled out and there would not be another one for half an hour.

With a half-an-hour head-start, Seb knew Bert

could easily reach Moreton ahead of him. What if
he was armed? How well would the sergeant be
able to protect his family if he was taken by
surprise? Seb really needed a motor. Perhaps the
repair had been done. This time Seb ran across the
road from the station and headed for Canal Side.
Kenny was in the office talking to Tilly. Seb told
them briefly what had happened and was assured
that the repair had been done and there was petrol
in the tank.

'Perhaps I should come with you,' said Tilly, her
eyes brimming with excitement. 'What a story if
you were to catch him!'

'Haven't I enough people to worry about?'
snapped Seb, starting the engine.

She blinked. 'Sorry. It's just that...'

Kenny's expression was strained. 'I wish I could
come with you but with this foot of mine, I'd be
more of a hindrance.'

'Damn! I wish we had a telephone. Modern
businesses should all have one. I could have got in
touch with Freddie at Mrs Black's because he's
nearer to Moreton. He could get there quicker.
He'd want to be in on this anyway because Clara's
at the house with Hanny and the children.'

'I could telephone Eastham post office from our
post office,' said Tilly swiftly. 'I could say it's a
matter of life and death and they could take a
message to him.'

'You do that,' said Seb, flashing her a grateful smile.

He did not linger any longer but drove out of the yard. Fortunately, it was situated on the edge of the city and soon he was zooming along the Chester–Birkenhead road. He tried to stop his mind from wandering and to keep his thoughts on the road. No point in fearing the worst, surely Bert wouldn't be mad enough to shoot his whole family? The thought made him break out in a sweat. If he'd had a gun, surely he would have used it when Seb, himself, had stood in the doorway talking to the sergeant. A knife. Perhaps he had a knife and not all of them would get killed. Who might he intend as his first victim…?

He must stop thinking like that. The women were strong and Bert wouldn't find them easy to cope with if they banded together. Of course, it might not have been Bert who was the street sweeper. It could have been a plain-clothes policeman watching out for him. All might be well. He might have panicked himself and Kenny needlessly.

A horn blasted him into awareness and he realised that he had veered across to the other side of the road. His heart pounded with fright. What good would he be if the sweeper was Bert and he got himself killed? He must stay calm and drive sensibly and pray, if there was a God up there, that he would get there in time to save his family.

* * *

Clara was singing softly to herself as she arrived back at the cottage with milk, bread, butter and eggs. She had wheeled the twins in their pram so Hanny could do some washing while Mrs Kirk did some tidying up. The old woman had livened up since they had come to Moreton and was more talkative. The place seemed to have triggered her memory. She parked the pram beneath the window overlooking the heath. The front door and windows were open and all was quiet. Stepping inside, she found Mrs Kirk in the front room, polishing the furniture.

'Hello, I'm back,' said Clara, smiling at the dumpy figure.

Susannah Kirk gave her a faint smile. 'You're Clara. You've been to the shops.'

'That's right. Where's Hanny?'

'Hanging out the washing. This is Auntie Joan's house and I used to bring the children here. We'd go down to the shore and pick cockles.' She smiled happily at the memory.

Clara had heard this before and she, herself, always said the same thing. 'They were happy days?'

Susannah nodded. 'Bert would look after the girls. Such a handsome boy and good, as well. But Hanny was naughty and would go in too far. She would have drowned if he hadn't saved her.'

'That's not true. He tried to drown me,' said

Hanny, looking through the window at her mother. 'I don't know how many times I have to tell you.'

Her mother pouted. 'He loved you.'

'Strange kind of love,' said Hanny.

'He's in Australia.'

Hanny and Clara exchanged looks but Hanny only said, 'If I could get someone to stay here with Mother during the summer months I'd do so. She's happy here and I've loads to do at home now the music teachers have moved out of the house. Kenny and I decided to write to Mrs Black and ask her if we can rent the whole house in Victoria Crescent. It'll be much better for him with his foot if we're on the ground floor and we could sublet a couple of rooms upstairs to help pay the higher rent.'

'It sounds like a good idea,' said Clara.

Hanny smiled. 'I don't think our Freddie will stay with Mrs Black much longer.' She changed the subject. 'You must be hot after the walk to the shops. Fancy a glass of ginger beer?'

Clara thanked her and was about to sit down when she heard the sound of a car engine. It was one she recognised and so she hurried to the front door.

'Freddie, what a nice surprise.' She smiled with pleasure at the sight of his beloved face. Then she realised he was not returning her smile. 'What is it?'

He seized her by the arms and pushed her inside the house. 'He's not arrived yet then?'

'Who?' she asked, bewildered.

'Bert. You all have to leave here.'

A chill ran through her. 'How did he find out we're here?'

'Never mind that now.' He looked around the room and saw his mother. 'Where's Hanny and the twins? Alice and the children aren't around, are they?'

'No! They're at the camping site.'

Hanny came out of the kitchen. 'Freddie, what are you doing here?' she asked.

'You've got to get out of here,' said Freddie urgently, going over to her. 'Seb is pretty certain Bert's on his way.'

A muscle clenched in Hanny's cheek and she placed the glasses of ginger beer carefully on a table. 'How did he find out?'

'I'm not going to waste time telling you,' he said. 'You and Clara take Mother and the twins and get in the car. With a bit of luck I can get you to safety before he arrives.'

'Too late for that,' sneered a voice from the doorway.

Oh my God, thought Clara, staring at the scruffy figure wearing a bright red wig. It's him!

Freddie whirled round and found himself looking down the barrel of a revolver.

Hanny clenched a fist. 'Is that really you, Bert?'

His laugh was chilling. 'Good disguise, isn't it? I

realise now I've been wasting my talent. I should have gone on the stage...or no, the flickers. I'd make a handsome gentleman detective, don't you think?'

'So you've cast yourself as the hero?' said Freddie harshly. 'Are there any bullets in that gun?'

Bert turned cold eyes on him. 'Like to call my bluff, little brother? Do you really think I'd carry round an empty gun? What good would that be to a handsome, gentleman *thief* like me? Now I have some business to take care of.' He switched his attention to Hanny. 'Perhaps I'll start with you. It's all your fault I ended up in jail. If you hadn't told Dah and then Alice about my loving you, then everything would have turned out fine.'

Her jaw clenched and she hissed, 'Give it its proper name, Bert, and I wasn't the only one you tried to ruin, was I?'

He snarled, 'I loved you. I loved all my sisters.'

'Stop this right now. Stop playing with that gun.' Susannah Kirk's quavering voice took them all by surprise.

The gun swivelled round and now it pointed at her. 'Be quiet, Mother. You let your Bert down, too. You never came to visit him while he was in prison, when he really needed you. You were weak.'

Two spots of colour appeared high on her cheeks. 'I don't know you. My Bert never went to prison. He's in Australia.'

Bert threw back his head and laughed. 'I could always fool you, Mother.'

Freddie lunged at Bert, not knowing if the weapon was loaded or not. There was a short explosion as the brothers struggled for possession of the gun and then it went spinning out of Bert's hand. Clara screamed, terrified that Freddie's reckless act might have resulted in his death. Then she realised that he was still grappling with his brother with such a determined expression on his face that she was convinced he was intent on killing him. She wished there was something she could do but Hanny had gripped her arm and pulled her out of the way as furniture was knocked over and the glasses of ginger beer smashed on the floor. Clara wished she could see the gun. Bert was strong and it was definitely a no-holds-barred fight, dirty and savage. Clara had not thought Freddie had it in him to fight in such a way. Then in the struggle Bert's wig was wrenched from his head and fell to the floor. She watched as Susannah bent and picked up, not only the wig, but her searching hand found the gun, as well.

'Stop this at once or I will shoot,' she said.

The brothers took no notice at first, but then she fired the gun. Both Hanny and Clara screamed this time. The bullet narrowly missed both of them and the bang was enough for the brothers to stagger apart.

Bert held out his hand. 'Give me the gun, Mother.' He touched his fair hair. 'I'm your Bert. Can't you see?'

She shook her grey head, her round, almost wrinkle-free face stern. 'No. My Bert's in Australia.'

Bert tried to wipe the blood from his face. 'No. I'm your Bert.'

She glared at him. 'My Bert wouldn't have a gun. My Bert's a good boy. He's in Australia.'

A profanity burst from Bert's mouth and he reached out for the gun. There was a bang and he staggered back, clutching his chest. His knees buckled and he fell to the floor.

No one moved.

Then Hanny stirred and went over to her mother. She put an arm round her shoulders and took the gun from her hand. 'He wasn't my Bert,' whispered Susannah.

'No, Mother. He never was,' said Hanny gently.

Clara turned to Freddie and put her arms round him. His face was bloodied and she felt that, if she had not held him, he just might have fallen. She was still too shocked by what had happened to speak.

By evening Bert's body had been removed, and the police had interviewed those who had witnessed the shooting. They had also tried to question his mother but it was soon obvious to the police that she was a confused old woman, not responsible for her actions. They also spoke to Sergeant Jones, who was shocked to learn that Bert had followed him to Moreton. Seb was also interviewed, and it was he who broached the matter of a reward with the police.

Hanny decided it would be best if she and her mother and the twins returned to Chester that night. So Freddie and Clara helped her to pack and went with them. Alice, Seb and Gabrielle were not there to wave them off because they, too, made up their minds to take the children home after promising to return to the seaside in a week or so. They were too emotionally wrought to discuss what had happened, but Gabrielle was touched when Seb told her about the sergeant wishing to invite her to a concert in aid of the poor children of Liverpool. 'I might just go,' she said.

It was pitch black by the time Freddie and Clara reached Mrs Black's. Yet the lights were on in the drawing room and as soon as the car drew up outside the house, the front door opened and Eudora and Joy appeared in the doorway.

'Is everyone safe?' called Joy.

'Yes,' said Clara.

'What about Bert?'

Neither Clara nor Freddie answered immediately because they were climbing out of the car. She placed her arm through his and together they walked towards the two women waiting for them. As the light in the hall fell on their faces, Eudora said, 'My dears, you look exhausted...and Freddie, you've definitely been in a fight.'

'He's dead,' said Freddie.

Joy's soft brown eyes widened. 'You killed him?'

He shook his head. 'I wanted to but... You're never going to believe this...'

'If it's going to be a long story, Freddie dear, then let's have you both inside,' said Eudora. 'I have a bottle of champagne I've been saving for a special day and I think today is that day.' She patted him on the shoulder and kissed Clara.

'I think I'd rather a bottle of beer, if you don't mind?' said Freddie with a twinkle in his eye. 'I'm hellishly thirsty. I don't mind a half glass of champagne for a toast.'

'You've got a nerve,' said Joy, shaking her head at him and then she hugged them both. 'I think I can find you a bottle of beer.'

An hour later Clara and Freddie had told their tale. He perched on the arm of the sofa with his hand resting on her shoulder. The grazes on his face and knuckles had been cleansed and anointed with iodine by Clara earlier.

'Well, it's nice to know that Bert's not going to come back from the dead this time,' said Joy. 'Pity that he turned out the way he did. He had so many opportunities for good.'

Freddie's face hardened. 'Don't start feeling sorry for him. He was evil.'

Clara shuddered as she thought of that fight in the cottage. Freddie's arm slipped around her. 'What is it, sweetheart?'

'I was just thinking how close we came to losing each other today.'

'I know,' he said soberly. 'Can't risk that again. We'll have to get married so we can look after each other.'

Joy gasped. Clara blushed and smiled. 'If that's a proposal, I accept.'

He kissed her.

Eudora rose to her feet. 'Enough kissing for now. Save it for when you're alone. Let's have a toast. To Clara and Freddie, may the sun shine on your path from now on.'

They drank to that wish. Then Joy refilled their glasses and they drank several more toasts. Eudora said, 'I'll even drink to your aunt, Clara. I must admit, I'm still trying to come to terms with the idea of Gertie having a policeman follower.'

'Hardly that at her age, surely?' said Joy, topping up their glasses.

'Oh, I don't know, dear. Love can strike at any age and in different ways.' There was a dreamy expression on her face that startled them all.

'I bet Tilly will call tomorrow with pencil sharpened and notebook at the ready,' said Clara.

'She'll be in hot pursuit of a story from us.'

Freddie hugged her against him. 'You're right. But after today, I think she's going to have to start looking for her own.'

EPILOGUE

'I think we should pull out all the stops for Tilly, seeing as how we actually forgot her birthday in all the excitement,' said Hanny, accepting a glass of sherry and a macaroon from Seb.

Alice said, 'You're right. I feel bad about that – and when I think she didn't even remind us.' She kicked off her shoes and curled her legs beneath her on the sofa. It was two days later and the four of them were alone.

'We've so much to be thankful for and it should be a double celebration,' said Seb firmly. 'No more Bert – not ever – thanks to Mrs Kirk.'

'Praise God,' said Alice, sipping her sherry and glancing across at her dearest friend. 'Hanny, do you think your mother really didn't have any idea it was Bert confronting her?'

Hanny did not hesitate. 'Yes. Her feelings for him have never altered. He's still her blue-eye and living in Australia.' She sighed. 'I wish I could understand how her mind works but I never will. Still, if she's happy...'

'The main thing is he's dead,' said Kenny, smiling. 'I won't be crying crocodile tears for him at his funeral.'

His wife and half-sister looked at him from startled eyes. 'I haven't even given a thought to his funeral,' said Hanny.

Seb grinned. 'I should think not. Besides, I wouldn't be surprised if he's still officially dead according to army records.'

'So the family won't be getting his money then,' said Hanny, with a twinkle in her eyes. No doubt the police will confiscate any money he has tucked away...but there's always the reward for his capture, dead or alive.'

'I think that should go to Freddy,' said Seb. 'After all, it was he who risked his life.'

'Yet again,' murmured Kenny.

'It wouldn't surprise me if we were to hear some good news from Freddie and Clara any day now,' said Hanny.

'Tilly won't be pleased about that,' sighed Alice. 'I wonder if she'll ever get married.'

'There's always Don,' murmured Seb. 'Pity he couldn't be here for her birthday, although she's far too young to get married yet.'

'Besides, she wants a writing career,' said Kenny positively. 'What if we club together and buy her the tools of her trade. Pencils, pens, pads – and a typewriter.'

Alice stared at him. 'You really are pushing the boat out. You know how much they cost!'

Kenny and Seb exchanged glances. 'Well, I reckon business is really going to start picking up now,' said Kenny.

'I guess I know what she wants more than anything,' said Seb abruptly.

The other three looked at him but it was Alice who murmured, 'Don't say it.'

'I have to,' said Seb, grimacing. 'Your father, invite him to the party. I believe he helped save Flora's life.'

There was a silence.

Kenny and Alice exchanged glances and both sighed. 'Perhaps just this once,' he said heavily.

Alice did not speak. The others waited and a minute ticked by before she eventually muttered, 'OK! Just this once, mind, because I know it'll make Tilly's day. There's no way, though, I'm inviting Mrs Black.' Seb and Kenny darted a glance at each other. 'I saw that,' she snapped, 'but if you think I'm going to invite her the answer is...no, no, no!'

a&b

If you liked this, you'll love the other books by
the enthralling pen of June Francis.

Turn the page to find out more...

JUNE FRANCIS

'A beautiful compelling love story'
Woman's Realm

'All the atmosphere and colour that
romance fans have come to expect...another
surefire success'
Liverpool Echo

'An evocative tale...full of pain, passion,
nostalgia and deep dark secrets'
Crosby Herald

'A slice of life in the early 1900s...reading it
is like sitting up with the gods, spying on
people below... Real people. Real emotions.
Another excellent book from one of our
best saga writers'
Historical Novels Review

Step by Step

978-0-7490-8329-8 • £6.99 • Paperback

Growing up in the back streets of historic Chester at the beginning of the 1900s, childhood friends Hannah Kirk and Alice Moran are used to supporting each other when life gets tough. But when Alice's mother dies in childbirth and her violent father attacks Hannah's mother, the two girls are torn apart. Will they ever be free of the weight of the past, or will the years of guilt and pain that now separate their lives become too much of an obstacle to overcome?

A Place to Call Home

978-0-7490-8324-3 • £6.99 • Paperback

With the Second World War looming on the horizon and the deaths of her mother and siblings in recent memory, life has taken a dark turn for young Greta Peters. But the sudden appearance of a young man in her home marks the start of a fresh beginning in her life. As a tentative friendship develops between Greta and the youth, Alexander Armstrong, she learns the real reason for his break-in and determines to help him in his search. But at the end of their quest, will they find true love in each other's arms?

A Dream to Share

978-0-7490-8249-9 • £6.99 • Paperback

As the Edwardian era comes to an end, a young maid, Emma, strives to keep her family from poverty whilst attempting to discover the identity of the man she blames for her sister's death. A chance meeting with another struggling servant, Alice, introduces her to the affluent Waters household and the spirited suffragette Victoria. But as she learns more of Alice's past, Emma becomes convinced they have more in common than their jobs. And just as Emma finds a love of her own, she is drawn into danger as she realises someone is seeking revenge…

Look for the Silver Lining

978-0-7490-8109-6 • £6.99 • Paperback

Cut off from her family, pregnant and desperately missing her soldier husband, Nellie Lachlan faces the horrors of the Blitz alone. But when her mother is killed by a bomb blast, Nellie seizes the chance to be reunited with her two sisters. Together, the three women get through the difficult days of the war as best they can. But when tragedy strikes, only the love and support of her family pull Nellie through. The end of the war brings unexpected challenges, as does the reappearance of a man Nellie thought she would never see again.

OTHER TITLES AVAILABLE FROM
ALLISON & BUSBY
BY JUNE FRANCIS

• Step by Step	978-0-7490-8329-8	£6.99
• A Place to Call Home	978-0-7490-8324-3	£6.99
• A Dream to Share	978-0-7490-8249-9	£6.99
• Look for the Silver Lining	978-0-7490-8109-6	£6.99

All Allison & Busby titles can be ordered from our
website, *www.allisonandbusby.com*,
or from your local bookshop and are also available
by post from:

Bookpost, PO Box 29, Douglas, Isle of Man, IM99 1BQ
Credit cards accepted. For details:
Telephone: +44(0)1624 677237
Fax: +44(0)1624 670923
Email: bookshop@enterprise.net
www.bookpost.co.uk

Free postage and packing in the United Kingdom.

Prices shown above were correct at the time
of going to press. Allison & Busby reserves the right to
show new retail prices on covers which may differ from
those previously advertised in the text or elsewhere.